FORBIDDEN
THE SWEET

He put his arms round me and held me
close to him. I could feel his heart beating
against mine. I was in love with him and
this was different from loving Jean-Louis
or anyone I had loved before.

This was something I had never experienced, had never understood, had been
vaguely aware existed . . . in romances of
the past. Tristan and Isolde, Abelard and
Heloise . . . the sort of overwhelming passion for the sake of which people sacrificed
everything . . . even that which they held
most dear.

"Zipporah." He was saying my name as
I never heard it said before. I seemed
to be floating along in his arms. We had
left the world and all its little conventions
a long way beyond. We were together
. . . we belonged together . . . and there was
no holding back the tide of passion which
was enveloping us . . .

The Adulteress

PHILIPPA CARR

FAWCETT CREST • NEW YORK

A Fawcett Crest Book
Published by Ballantine Books
Copyright © 1982 by Philippa Carr

Library of Congress Catalog Card Number: 81-15874

ISBN 0-449-20143-0

This edition published by arrangement with G. P. Putnam's Sons

Manufactured in the United States of America

First Ballantine Books Edition: August 1983

Contents

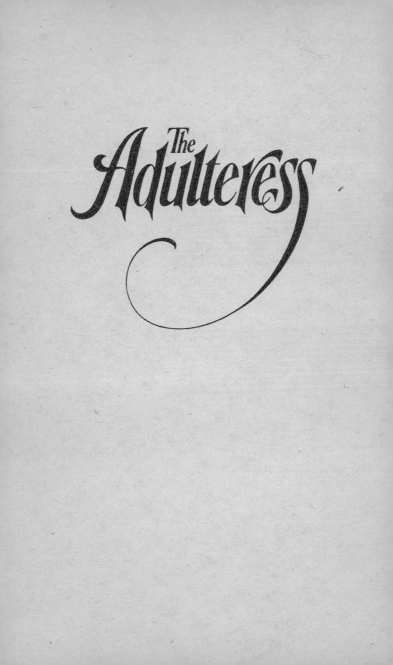

The Adulteress

THE FAMILY TREE

William Farland m Dulce
|
Damask m Bruno
|
Catharine m Felipe Gonzáles (1)
|
Roberto

m Jake Pennlyon (2)
|
Linnet — Damask
m
Colum Casvellyn
|
Connell

Tamsyn m Fennimore Landor
|
Fennimore — The Twins

Bersaba
m
(1) Luke Longridge
|
Lucas

Angelet
m
Richard Tolworthy
|
Richard

(2) Richard Tolworthy
|
Arabella — Richard — Angelique — Fennimore
m
(1) Edwin Eversleigh
|
Edwin m Jane
|
Carl

(2) Carleton Eversleigh
|
Priscilla — Carl
m
Leigh Main
|
Carlotta (by Jocelyn) — Damaris
| |
Clarissa (by John Field)   m Jeremy Granthorn
m |
Lance Clavering   Sabrina m Richard Frenshaw
| |
Zipporah   Richard (Dickon)

A Cry for Help

*I*t *has always surprised me that people who have lived con-*
ventionally, observing all the rules laid down by society,
will suddenly appear to change their entire personality and act
in a manner alien to everything they have been before. That I
should be one of them was as great a shock to me as it would
have been to those who knew me well—if they ever discovered
it; that was why it was absolutely necessary to keep it secret;
there were, of course, other, more practical, reasons for doing
so.

I have often tried to understand how it could have happened
to me. I have tried to make excuses. Is it possible for people
to be *possessed*? Some of the mystics of the past declared they
were. Was it some inner force? Was it the spirit of one long
departed which had entered my body and made me throw aside
the principles of a lifetime and act as I did? What is the use
of trying to placate my conscience? The rational explanation
can only be that I did not know myself until I came face to
face with temptation.

It really began on that spring day which was just like any other day in my ten-year marriage to Jean-Louis Ransome. Life had flowed smoothly and pleasantly for us. Jean-Louis and I agreed on most things; we had known each other since childhood and had been brought up in the same nursery, for my mother had taken charge of him just before I was born when he was about four years old. His own French mother had left him in my mother's charge when he had shown so determinedly that he did not want to go away with her and her new husband.

Ours had been one of those predicted marriages which pleased everybody. Perhaps it had been too easy, and because everything had fallen so neatly into place we had become the ordinary conventional people we were.

So there was I in the flower room, I remember, arranging the daffodils I had picked a short while before from our garden which merged into the woods and which we agreed we would keep a little wild because we both liked it that way. At this time of year the daffodils seemed to spring up everywhere. I loved their subtle scent, their bright yellowness the color of sunshine and the way they proudly held up their trumpets as though proclaiming the coming of summer. I always filled the house with them. I was the sort of person who quickly formed habits and went on with them mainly because I had for so many years.

There was a sink in the flower room and I had filled my containers with water and was enjoying the arrangements in an epergne of pale green glass which set off the yellow flowers perfectly when I heard the sound of horses' hooves on the gravel and then . . . voices.

I looked up a little ruefully. I enjoyed visitors but I wished they had waited until I had finished with the flowers.

Sabrina and Dickon were coming toward the house so I reached for a cloth and dried my hands, and went out to meet them.

Sabrina was my mother's cousin—a rather strikingly beautiful woman to whom dramatic things had happened a long time ago. She was about ten years my senior, which meant she must be forty years old at this time. She didn't look it, though there was often a haunted expression in her eyes and sometimes one caught her staring into space as though she were looking back over the years. Then she would look really sad. She had always been a member of our household, and my mother had been a mother to her. Dickon was Sabrina's son, on whom she doted rather more than was good for him, I fancied. He had been born after the death of her husband.

"Zipporah!" cried Sabrina. I had often wondered why I had been given such a name. There were no other Zipporahs in the family. When I asked my mother why she had chosen it, she said: "I just wanted something unusual. I liked it, and your father, of course, made no objections." I discovered that it came from the Bible and was disappointed that the life of my biblical namesake had been no more exciting than my own. All she appeared to have done was married Moses and borne a lot of children. She had been as insignificant as I was, except of course that in the whole of my marriage—to my sorrow and that of Jean-Louis—we had not been blessed with offspring.

"Zipporah," continued Sabrina, "your mother wants you to come over to supper. Could you and Jean-Louis manage this evening? There's something she wants to talk about."

"I should think so," I said, embracing her. "Hello, Dickon."

He acknowledged my greeting coolly. My mother and Sabrina had made him the very center of their lives. I sometimes wondered what Dickon would grow up like. He was only ten years old now, so perhaps he would change when he went away to school.

"Do come in," I said, and we went past the open door of the flower room.

"Oh, you were doing the daffodils," said Sabrina with a smile. "I might have known."

Was I so predictable? I supposed so.

"I hope I didn't interrupt the ritual," she added.

"No . . . no. Of course not. It's lovely to see you. Are you out for a ride?"

"Yes and called in . . . only for a moment."

3

"You'll have a glass of wine and some of cook's biscuits."

Sabrina said: "I don't think we'll stop for that."

But Dickon interrupted her: "Yes, please," he said. "*I* should like some biscuits."

Sabrina smiled fondly. "Dickon is very partial to those wine biscuits of yours. We must get the recipe, Dickon."

"Cook is very jealous of her recipes," I said.

"You could order her to give it to our cook," retorted Dickon.

"Oh, I wouldn't dare," I said lightly.

"So, Dickon, you will have to wait until you visit Zipporah for your wine biscuits."

The refreshment came. Dickon hastily finished all the biscuits, which would please cook anyway. She was very susceptible about her food and lapped up compliments. A good one could put her in a very pleasant mood for a whole day; while the faintest hint of criticism could, as one of the maids said, make life in the kitchen a hell on earth.

"It sounds as though something important has happened," I said.

"Well, it could be. It's a letter from old Carl . . . you know, Lord Eversleigh."

"Oh . . . yes of course. What does he want?"

"He's worried about the Eversleigh estate. Because he has no son to inherit."

"I suppose it would have gone to the general, if he hadn't died."

"Strange really to think there is no one in the direct line . . . no male, that is. Everybody seemed to have girls. A pity old Carl didn't have a boy."

"Didn't he have one who died at birth?"

"Oh yes . . . long ago . . . and the child's mother died with him. That was a terrible blow. He never got over it, they said. He never married again, although I believe he had . . . friends. However, that's past history and the old man is now a bit anxious and his thoughts have settled on you."

"On me! But what about you? You're older than I."

"Your grandmother Carlotta was older than my mother,

4

Damaris, so I supposed you'd come first. Moreover, I wouldn't be considered. I've heard that he talked about my marrying that 'damned Jacobite.'"

"I think Jacobites were brave," put in Dickon. "I'll be a Jacobite if I want to."

"Thank heaven all that nonsense seems to be over now," I said. "The 'Forty-five finished it."

Then I was sorry I had said that because Sabrina had lost her husband at Culloden.

"We hope so," she said quietly. "Well, the fact is old Carl wants to see you, doubtless with a view to making you his heiress. He wrote to your mother, who would come before you, of course, but she is the daughter of that arch Jacobite, Hessenfield."

"How they seem to clutter our family," murmured Dickon.

"That leaves you," went on Sabrina. "Your father was a man Uncle Carl highly approved of, so the Jacobite strain is far removed and possibly wiped out, particularly as your father once fought for King George. So you are redeemed. The point is your mother wants you to come over so that we can discuss it all and decide what should be done."

"Jean-Louis couldn't leave the estate just now."

"It would only be for a short visit. Anyway, think about it and come over today."

"I'd like to go to Eversleigh," said Dickon.

His mother smiled at him fondly. "Dickon wants everything that's available, don't you, Dickon? Eversleigh is not for you, my son."

"You never know," said Dickon slyly.

"Talk about it with Jean-Louis," said Sabrina to me, "and we'll go into it thoroughly. Your mother will show you the letter. That will put you in picture."

I saw them off and went back to the daffodils.

Jean-Louis and I walked to Clavering Hall from the agent's house which had been our home since we had married. I had told Jean-Louis of old Carl's desire to see me and he had been a little disturbed, I think. He was very happy managing the Clavering estate, which was not large and where he had everything working peacefully and in perfect order. Jean-Louis was a man who did not change.

We walked arm in arm. Jean-Louis was saying that it would be difficult for us to leave Clavering just at this time. He thought we might go later when there was less to do on the estate.

I agreed with him. We rarely disagreed on anything. Ours was a very happy marriage. That was what made my actions all the more incomprehensible.

The only real cloud on our happiness was what appeared to be an inability to have children. My mother had spoken to me about it for she knew it grieved me. "It is sad," she admitted. "You would have made such good parents. Perhaps in time, though . . . perhaps a little patience . . ."

But time went on and still we had no child. I had seen Jean-Louis look at Dickon sometimes, with that rather wistful look in his eyes. He, too, was inclined to spoil the boy. It might have been because he was the only child in the family.

I did not take to Dickon in the same way and I never tried to analyze my feelings until afterward, when I started to become introspective—looking for reasons and finding only excuses. Could I have been jealous of him? My mother, whom I had loved only slightly less than my glamorous father, cared greatly for Dickon . . . more, I suspected, than she did for me, her own child. It was something to do with that long-ago romance with Dickon's father, but it was Sabrina who had had his child.

Our moods and emotions—Jean-Louis's and mine—were woven together in an intricate web and at this time I was not concerned with them. I was still the old Zipporah—quiet, unassuming, above all predictable.

When we reached the house my mother was waiting for us. She embraced me warmly; she was always tender toward me, but I think because she was so sure I would always do what was expected, and she would have no need to worry about me, she could dismiss me from her thoughts.

"It was lovely of you to come, Zipporah dear. And you too,

Jean-Louis," she said.

Jean-Louis took her hand and kissed it. He was always very grateful to my mother and had never stopped showing it.

That was because she had kept him when he was a very young boy and had been terrified of being taken away to go off with his own mother, who could not have been a very pleasant person because she had been involved in some murder mystery. But that was years ago.

"I want to show you Lord Eversleigh's letter," she said. "I don't know what you'll think about it. It will be strange if he should leave Eversleigh to you, Zipporah."

"I can't think he will. There must be someone else."

"We seem to have lost touch since your great-grandparents died. Yet Eversleigh used to be the very heart of the family. It's strange how things change."

It was indeed strange. Things had certainly changed when my father had disappeared suddenly from my life. Although my life had been so uneventful, there had been a time when I had lived on the fringe of great events. I should never forget my father; after all, I had been ten years old when he had gone. That was twenty years ago, but a man like him could never be forgotten. I had loved him more than anyone. He never cosseted me as my mother had done. He had laughed a great deal, had smelt of sandalwood and had always been exquisitely dressed, being what was known as a dandy. I had thought he was the most handsome person in the world. It was unfair—I knew even then—but I would have bartered all the loving care and attention of my mother for five minutes with him. He had never asked how I was getting on with lessons; it had never occurred to him that I might catch cold. He used to talk to me of his gambling feats. He had constantly gambled and he had made me feel the excitement which gripped him. He had treated me as though I were one of his cronies instead of his little daughter. He used to take me riding. We would race together and we had made little bets. He would bet I could not throw a conker a certain distance; he would wager things carelessly—the pin in his cravat, one of his rings, even a coin... anything that was to hand. My mother had hated it. I heard her say more than once: "You will teach the child to be a gambler like yourself."

I had hoped he would. There was nothing I wanted so much as to be exactly like him. He had gaiety and great charm which came from a certain carelessness toward life. Nothing had ever appeared to perturb him; he had shrugged his shoulders at life and later he had had the same attitude toward death. I did not know how he went to his death on that early morning—but I could guess.

That event devastated our household, though there had been rumblings of disaster before it happened. I couldn't help overhearing certain things. I knew that he had died—as the servants said—defending my mother's honor. This was because a man had died and in his bedroom had been found something belonging to my mother that indicated she had been with him at the time of his death.

It had been the end of a way of life—deeply upsetting to a girl of ten. We had gone to the country—not that that was new to me. We had always spent some part of the summer at Clavering Hall because it was part of my father's country estate.

Terrible days they had been, and made more so because I knew only half the story. Sabrina was involved in it. I heard her once say to my mother: "Oh, Clarissa, I am to blame for all this." And I knew that she had been the one in the dead man's bedroom, though everyone had thought it was my mother, and my father had died for that reason.

It had been bewildering, and when I asked questions I was told by Nanny Curlew—whom I had inherited from Sabrina—that little children should be seen and not heard. I was careful, for Nanny Curlew could relate gruesome stories of what happened to naughty children. If they listened to what was not intended for them, their ears grew long so that everyone knew what they had done; and those who grimaced or scowled or put out their tongues—unless told to by nurse or doctor—were often "struck all of a heap" and stayed like that for the rest of their lives. Being a logical little girl I did say that I had never

seen anyone with enormous ears and a tongue hanging out.
"You wait," she had said darkly, and looked at me so suspiciously that I hastily went to a looking glass to make sure that
my ears had not grown and that my tongue was still mobile.

Somebody said that time is the great healer, and that is
certainly true, for if it does not always heal, it dims the memory
and softens the pain; and after a while I became accustomed
to my father's absence; I settled into the country life at Clavering. After all, I had my mother, Sabrina and Jean-Louis as
well as the redoubtable and omnipotent Nanny Curlew. I accepted life. I did what was expected of me; I rarely questioned
why. I once heard Sabrina say to my mother: "At least Zipporah
has never given you a moment's anxiety, and I'll be ready to
swear never will." At first I was delighted to hear this but later
it made me ponder.

Then I was of age and there were dances and at one of
these Jean-Louis showed himself capable of jealousy because
he thought I was too interested in one of the sons of a
neighboring squire. Then we decided we would marry, but
Jean-Louis didn't want to do it while he was still under my
mother's roof. He was proud and independent. He was working on the estate and doing well. Tom Staples said he didn't
know how he'd manage without him; then Tom Staples suddenly had a heart attack and died. The estate manager's job
and house became vacant, so Jean-Louis stepped into his
shoes. He managed the estate and took over the house which
went with the post, and there was no reason then why we
shouldn't be married right away.

That had happened more than ten years ago in the fatal year
of '45. Drama touched us then in the return of the love of my
mother's youth who had been transported to Virginia thirty
years before for his part in the '15 rebellion. I was so immersed
in my own marriage at the time that I only vaguely realized
what was happening and that the returning Dickon was the
young lover of whom my mother had dreamed all through her
life—even when she was married to that most desirable of
men, my father. Alas, for her, the lover of her youth fell in

love with Sabrina, married her, and young Dickon was the result.

My poor mother! I realize her sufferings far more now than I did then. Sabrina came back to my mother after Culloden. Then Dickon was born—that was ten years ago—and Sabrina and my mother lived together in Clavering Hall, and I know now—understanding people's emotions so much more than I did before my own adventure—that they saw in him the Dickon they had both lost. Perhaps that brought them some consolation. But I was beginning to believe that it was having an adverse effect on Dickon's character.

So Jean-Louis and I were married, and he was a good husband to me; ours was the typical country existence; we went on, untroubled by outside events; there might be wars in Europe in which the country was involved but they affected us very little. We went from season to season, from Good Friday gloom to Easter rejoicing, to summer church fêtes on the lawn if the weather was good and in our vaulted hall if it were bad, to harvest festivals when everyone vied to produce the finest fruits and vegetables for display, to Christmas and all its rejoicing. That was our life.

Until this day when we had the message from Eversleigh Court.

My mother was pleased to see us as she always was.

"I'm so glad you could come today," she said. "I do want to talk to you about poor old Carl. Sabrina has given you an inkling, hasn't she? I am so sorry for him. He sounds so pathetic in his letter."

She slipped one arm through mine and the other through that of Jean-Louis.

"I thought just a family party so that we could really talk. Just Sabrina, myself and the two of you. Jean-Louis, dear, I do hope you will be able to manage to go with Zipporah."

Jean-Louis then began to launch into a description of the problems of the estate. He loved talking about them because they were of such paramount importance to him. He glowed with enthusiasm and I knew it would be a great sacrifice for him to spare time from it.

We went into the hall—which was very fine and, as usual in such buildings, the central feature of the house. It was a large house—meant for a big family. My mother would have liked Sabrina to marry again and live there with her children; I am sure she would have liked Jean-Louis and me to come there and have a family. That was what she wanted to be, the center of a big family; and all we had was Dickon.

It seemed now that Sabrina would never marry again. My mother might have done so too because she had been quite young when my father was killed. But they had both set up an image which they worshiped: Dickon—the hero of my mother's youth, whom she had adored through her life and who must have clouded her relationship with my father. It was ironic that she should still go on worshiping him even when he had proved faithless and turned to Sabrina. If he had not died a soldier's death at Culloden would he have remained on his pedestal? Those were the questions I began to ask myself afterwards. . . . Looking back it seemed to me that I saw life with the unpleasantness discreetly covered; I saw all that people wanted me to see, and I never attempted to lift the cloth of conventionality and look beneath.

Young Dickon had come as a salvation to those two bereaved women, and this boy—Dickon's son—had, so they believed, given them a reason for living. Planning for him, they had subdued their grief; they had found a new object for worship.

The house was as much home to me as the house which I had shared with Jean-Louis for the last ten years. Here I had grown up among the elegant furniture and tasteful decorations—the result of my father's love of beautiful things.

I stood in the hall and looked at the two elegant staircases winding upward—one to the east wing, one to the west wing. Such a large house for so few people! My mother often thought that, I knew, and she was grateful that she had Sabrina to share it with her. I had said to Jean-Louis that if ever Sabrina should marry and go away we should have to go to the hall to live. Jean-Louis agreed, but I knew he so cherished his independence and he loved our house because it was a symbol of that. He never forgot that he had been left to my mother rather as a changeling child. There was something very noble about Jean-Louis in a quiet way which makes my conduct all the more reprehensible ... but I must get on with my explanations as to how it came about.

There we were at supper in the dining room. The house had been left as my father had made it, and my mother would never willingly have it altered. Even the card room—the most important in the house—was left as it had been in his day, although there were no gaming parties nowadays, only a quiet game of whist occasionally when neighbors came in to join my mother and Sabrina—and of course there was no play for money. My mother was very much against that—puritanically, so some said, but of course we understood why.

Now we sat on the carved japanned chairs with their gilt decoration, which had been in the family for the last hundred years and of which my father had been rather proud, at the oak table with the apron of carved features imitating a fringed hanging which I remember my father's telling me had been made in France for someone at the court of Louis XV. He would often throw out information like that in the midst of light bantering chatter, which, I think, was perhaps why I had always found him so fascinating.

The butler was at the sideboard ladling out the soup which one of the maids was serving when the door was opened and Dickon came in.

"Dickon," said my mother and Sabrina simultaneously in those voices I knew so well, a little shocked, remonstrating and at the same time indulgently admiring his audacity. It seemed to say, This is wrong but what will the darling child do next, bless him!

"I want to have supper," he said.

"Dearest," said my mother, "you had your supper an hour ago. Shouldn't you be in bed?"

"No," he said.

"Why not?" said Sabrina. "It's bedtime."

"Because," said Dickon patiently, "I want to be here."

12

The butler was looking into the tureen as though it held the utmost interest for him; the maid was standing still holding a plate of soup in her hand, uncertain where to put it.

I had expected Sabrina to send him back to bed. Instead she looked helplessly at my mother, who lifted her shoulders. Dickon slid into a chair. He knew he had won. In fact, he had no doubt that victory would be his. I was fully aware that I was seeing a repetition of a recurring scene.

"Well, perhaps this once, eh, Sabrina?" said my mother almost cajolingly.

"You really shouldn't, darling," added Sabrina.

Dickon smiled winningly at her. "Just this once," he said.

My mother said: "Carry on serving, Thomas."

"Yes, my lady," said Thomas.

Dickon threw me a look which held triumph in it. He knew that I did not approve of what had happened and took a delight not only in getting his own way but in showing me what power he had over these doting women.

"Well," said my mother, "I must show you Carl's letter. I think then"—she smiled at Jean-Louis—"you will make a special effort to go . . . soon."

"It's a pity it is rather an awkward time of year." Jean-Louis frowned a little. He hated disappointing my mother and it was quite clear that she was very eager for us to go to Eversleigh quickly.

"Well, young Weston is quite good, isn't he?" said Sabrina.

Young Weston was a manager we had. He was certainly showing signs of promise but Jean-Louis cared so much about the estate that he was never very happy when he was not at the head of affairs. His desire never to leave Clavering had worked out well because we none of us wanted to go to London as my father used to. He had generally come to the country rather reluctantly and then only because of the card parties he gave; he had much preferred town life and had left everything in the care of Tom Staples and men like him. We had had several agents since Tom Staples's death but Jean-Louis was never entirely satisfied with them.

"He's hardly ready yet," said Jean-Louis.

My mother reached over and pressed my husband's hand.

"I know you'll manage something," she said. And of course he would. Jean-Louis was always eager to please everyone, that was why... But I must stop reproaching myself in this way.

Now that she knew that Jean-Louis most certainly would take me to Eversleigh my mother went on to reminisce about the old place.

"So long since I have seen it. I wonder if it still looks the same."

Sabrina said: "I daresay Enderby hasn't changed much. What a strange house that was! Haunted, they said. Things did seem to happen there."

I knew vaguely something of Enderby. It was nearby Eversleigh Court and the two houses had been connected because my grandmother Carlotta had inherited the place. There had been a tragedy before that. They weren't our family, but someone had committed suicide there.

Sabrina shivered and went on: "I don't think I ever want to go to Enderby again."

"Are there really ghosts there?" asked Dickon.

"Common sense," I replied.

"I like ghosts," he said, dismissing me and my common sense as he was prepared to dismiss anyone who interfered with his pleasure. "I *want* there to be ghosts."

"We must arrange it then," said Jean-Louis.

"I was happy in Enderby," said my mother. "I can still remember coming home from France and how wonderful it was to be in the heart of a loving family... something I shall never forget... and it was my home for a number of years... with Aunt Damaris and Uncle Jeremy."

I knew she was thinking of those terrible early days in France when her parents had died suddenly—through poison, it was said—and she had been left in the care of a French maid who sold flowers in the streets when the house was disbanded.

My mother had spoken of it often. She remembered her

mother, Carlotta, the great beauty of the family, wild Carlotta, with whom I was later to become obsessed but who was at that time just a dazzling ancestress to me.

"You will be interested to see it all, Zipporah," she said.

"It won't be necessary to stay more than a few weeks, will it?" asked Jean-Louis.

"No, I shouldn't think so. I think the old man is very lonely. He will be so delighted."

Dickon listened avidly. "I'll go instead," he said.

"No, darling," replied Sabrina. "You're not invited."

"But he's your relation too, and if he's yours he's mine."

"Well, it is Zipporah he is inviting."

"I could go to be her companion . . . instead of Jean-Louis."

"No," said Jean-Louis "I have to be there to take care of Zipporah."

"She doesn't want taking care of. She's old."

"All ladies need taking care of when they make journeys," said my mother.

Dickon was too busy consuming cold venison to answer that.

Jean-Louis said that he thought the best time would be in three weeks. He could then make the necessary arrangements, providing we did not stay for more than two weeks.

My mother smiled at him. "I knew you'd make it possible. Thanks, Jean-Louis. I will write immediately. Perhaps you could send a note at the same time, Zipporah."

I said I would and we finished dinner.

Dickon was yawning. It was long past his bedtime, and when Sabrina suggested he might like to go to bed he did not protest.

I went with my mother to write the note, leaving Sabrina and Jean-Louis together making desultory conversation. There was a bureau in the old card room and I said I would do it there.

"Wouldn't you like to come to the library?" my mother asked. "It's more comfortable there."

"No, I always like to be in the card room."

I went in and sat at the bureau. She stood beside me and touched my hair. "You were so fond of your father, weren't you?"

I nodded. "You look rather like him," she said. "Fair hair . . . almost golden, those blue eyes . . . startlingly blue; and you're tall too, as he was. Poor Lance! What a wasted life."

"He died nobly," I said.

"He would . . . He squandered his life as he did a fortune. . . . It was all so unnecessary and it could have been so different."

"It is so long now."

"Memories linger on for you, and you were only a child when he died. Only ten years old."

"Old enough to know him and to love him," I said.

"I know. And you feel close to him here."

"I remember him here. . . . He was happier here in this room than anywhere else in the house."

"Here he had his gaming parties. They were the only thing that made the country tolerable to him." She frowned, and I turned to the letter. It was brief. I thanked my kinsman for the invitation and told him that I with my husband would be visiting him in about three weeks. We would let him know the date of arrival later.

My mother read what I had written and nodded her approval.

Shortly afterward Jean-Louis and I left for home.

We had fixed the date of arrival for the first of June. We should go on horseback with two grooms for company and another to look after the saddlebags.

"Carriages," said my mother, "are far more dangerous, with so many highwaymen about. It is so much easier to attack a cumbersome coach; and with the grooms and Jean-Louis you'll be well protected."

There was another letter from Lord Eversleigh. He was almost pathetically pleased. When Sabrina read it she said: "One could almost think he was calling for help . . . or something like that."

16

Calling for help! What an odd thing to say. I read the letter again and could not see that there was anything in it except that an old man who had been separated too long from his relatives was eager to see them.

Sabrina shrugged her shoulders and said: "Well, he's delighted you're going."

I felt rather glad. Poor old man, he was clearly lonely.

It was a week before we were due to leave. I was sitting in the garden working on a square of tapestry for a fire screen when I heard the sound of voices. I recognized Dickon's imperious tones, and on impulse, putting down my tapestry, I went to the edge of the shrubbery and saw him. He was with another boy, Jake Carter, son of one of the gardeners, a boy who worked in the gardens with his father now and then. He was about Dickon's age and Dickon was often with him. I believe he bullied the boy shamefully and was not at all sure that Jake wanted to be with him. He had probably received threats if he did not comply, and indeed so besotted were my mother and Sabrina with Dickon that they might have listened to any complaint he made about a servant if the boy showed his displeasure if they refused to.

The boys were now some little distance off, but I could see they were carrying something which looked like a pail, and Jake was holding a paper which seemed to be crammed full of something.

I watched them disappear in the direction of Hassocks' farm which bordered on our grounds. The Hassocks were good farmers of whom Jean-Louis heartily approved. They kept their barns and hedges in good order, and Farmer Hassock was constantly in discussion with Jean-Louis about methods of improving the yield of the land.

I returned to my tapestry and after a while went indoors and up to my still room, where I set about preparing the containers for the strawberries, which I wanted to have picked and preserved before I went away.

It must have been an hour later when one of the servants came running up to me.

"Oh, mistress," she cried, "there's fire over at Hassocks'. The master has just ridden over. I thought you should know."

I ran out and saw immediately that one of the barns was blazing. Several of the servants had come hurrying out to join me and we all went together across the gardens into the Hassocks' field and toward the barn.

There was a lot of commotion. People were running about and shouting to each other; but I saw that they were getting the blaze under control.

One of the maids gave a little cry and then I saw Jean-Louis. He was lying on the ground and some of the men were trying to lift him onto a piece of wood which looked like a shutter.

I dashed over and knelt beside him. He was pale but conscious. He smiled at me wanly.

One of the men said: "Master have broken his leg, we think. We'll get him to the house . . . and perhaps you'd send for the doctor."

I was bewildered. The barn was smouldering black and scarred, with now and then a flame jutting out. The acrid smell of burning made us cough.

"Yes . . . quickly . . ." I said. "Get him to the house. One of you go for the doctor . . . at once."

One of the men servants dashed off and I turned my attention to Jean-Louis.

"Bit of mischief . . . looks like," said one of Farmer Hassock's laborers. "Looks like someone started a fire in the barn. Master were first in. The roof fell on him and got his leg. . . . A mercy we was working close by and got him from under."

"Let's get him into the house quickly," I said. "Is he all right on that shutter?"

"Best for him, mistress. Doctor'll soon put it to rights."

I noticed that Jean-Louis's leg was in a strange position and guessed there was a fracture. I was the sort of woman who could be calm in a crisis, suppressing my emotions and fears and putting all my efforts into doing what was necessary.

I knew that we had to set that fracture in some way before

moving him and I determined to make an effort to do so, although I was inexperienced of such cases. I sent the maids running into the house for the tallest, straightest walking stick they could find and something we could use for bandages.

They had placed Jean-Louis very carefully in his improvised stretcher and I took his hand. I guessed he was in pain but it was typical of him that he should be as concerned about my anxiety as his own suffering.

"I'm all right," he whispered. "Nothing . . . much . . ."

Then the walking stick, which I could use as a splint, and the torn-up sheets arrived. Carefully my helpers held his leg in place while I very gently bandaged the limb to the stick. Then Jean-Louis was carried into his bed, by which time the doctor had arrived.

It was a broken leg—nothing more—said the doctor. He complimented me on my prompt and right action in setting the bone at once—so saving a simple fracture from becoming a compound one.

I sat by his bed until he slept. Then I remembered those agonizing seconds when I had thought he might be dead and the terrible desolation which had swept over me. Dear Jean-Louis, what should I have done without him? I should be thankful for all the happiness we had together; I must not feel a slight resentment against a fate which had made me barren.

Jean-Louis had scarcely fallen into his sleep when my mother with Sabrina and Dickon arrived.

The two women were very shocked. They wanted to hear all about it.

"To think that Jean-Louis might have hurt himself seriously . . . and all for Hassock's barn!"

"Seeing a fire, he just naturally attempted to put it out."

"He should have called for help," said Sabrina.

"You may be sure," I said, "that Jean-Louis did whatever was best."

"But he might have been killed!"

"He wouldn't think of that," said my mother. "He would just go in and try to put the fire out. And if he hadn't, it could have spread into the fields and Hassock could have lost his corn."

"Better Hassock's corn than Jean-Louis," said Sabrina.

"Is there any idea how it started?" asked my mother.

"They'll find out," I said.

She looked at me steadily. "This will put an end to your plans for Eversleigh."

"Oh . . . yes. With all this happening I'd forgotten that."

"Poor old Carl. He'll be so disappointed."

"Perhaps you could go in my place, Sabrina," I said. "Take Dickon."

"Oh yes," cried Dickon. "I want to go to Eversleigh."

"Certainly not," replied Sabrina. "We shouldn't be welcome there. Remember, I'm the wife and you're the son of that damned Jacobite."

"Well, we shall have to see," said my mother. "What we have to do now is get Jean-Louis's leg mended."

"It will take the usual time," I pointed out.

"And if this fire was started wantonly . . . ?"

"Who would?" I asked.

"Someone for mischief, perhaps," said Sabrina.

While we were talking, two of Farmer Hassock's laborers came in. They were carrying what looked like the remains of a tin pail and there were some pieces of charred beef in it.

"We know how it started, mistress," he said. "Someone— who didn't know much about such things—was trying to cook some meat by making a fire in this old pail; there's some grid here . . . that were cooking it on . . . over the pail, seems like as not."

"Good heavens!" I cried. "Surely not a tramp?"

"Oh no, mistress. Tramps 'ud have more sense. One who did this 'adn't much. But that's how it started. They must have made a fire in the pail and it got out of hand. They got frightened and run for it."

"What about the pail? Where did it come from? Do you know?"

"No, mistress, but we'm going to find out if us can."

I had an uneasy night. I slept on the narrow couch in the dressing room adjoining our bedroom with the door open so that I could hear Jean-Louis if he awoke. He lay in our big bed with his leg in splints and I should have been relieved because there was nothing wrong except a broken leg which would heal in due course.

I was rather surprised to feel an acute sense of disappointment because I should have to cancel my visit to Eversleigh... for quite a long time, it seemed, for even when the bone set I doubted whether Jean-Louis would be fit for some time after to make the long and rather exhausting journey.

I had allowed myself to think a great deal about Eversleigh Court and I longed to take a look at Enderby, that house which had played such a big part in our family story. I had not realized how very much I had been looking forward to the adventure; and now it was postponed... for a very long time, I should imagine.

I dozed fitfully and in the middle of the night I woke up. I wondered what had wakened me. I listened. All was quiet in the bedroom. Then I knew. It was a startling idea. Why should I not go alone?

The more I pondered it, the more feasible it seemed. There would be a great shaking of heads. Young women did not travel alone. I was not such a young woman. I didn't propose to go quite alone, of course; I could take the two grooms and another for the packhorse just the same. The only difference would be that Jean-Louis would not be with me.

I was too excited to sleep after that, but lay in bed making plans for going to Eversleigh even though Jean-Louis would not be able to accompany me.

There was a great deal of excitement the next morning because the pail was traced to our garden. A pail was missing from one of the sheds, and in spite of its buckled and scarred appearance the one found in the barn was undoubtedly that one which was missing.

21

That dispensed with the tramp idea. It was one of our people who had caused the fire.

Farmer Hassock had declared that he'd beat the daylights out of the culprit when he found him, for this bit of mischief would cost a pretty penny.

Having discovered the identity of the pail the search for the culprit was a simple one. In the early afternoon Ned Carter came to see me — as Jean-Louis's deputy — dragging with him his son, Jake.

Jake's face was white and frightened and there were tear stains on his cheeks.

"This is the young imp of mischief, mistress," said Ned Carter. "I got it out of him. It was him what took the pail . . . to cook some meat, he said. And where does he get the meat? I ask. That's something I can't beat out of him. Though I will. When he has another taste of my belt! I'll find out. Well, it was him, see. It was him that had this wicked notion to steal the pail and take it in the barn where he tries to cook the meat what he got from who knows where. I tell him it'll be transportation for him or a gibbet fore long."

I felt sorry for Jake Carter. He was only a boy — a nervous child overcome with terror.

Memory stirred in me. I remembered the last time I had seen him and he had not been alone. Of course! It was an hour or so before the fire had started.

I knew then that the idea of taking the pail and the meat would not have been Jake's. He would have been ordered to do so and join in the expedition.

I said: "Jake, was somebody with you when you went to the barn?"

Jake looked more frightened than ever.

"No, mistress, 'twas by myself, I was. I didn't mean to do no harm. . . . There was this bit of meat like . . ."

"Where did you get the meat?"

He was silent. Of course I knew. I could picture how it happened.

"Answer mistress," said Ned, giving the boy a blow at the

side of his head which sent him staggering across to the wall, which saved him from falling.

"Just a minute, Ned," I said. "Don't be hasty. Please don't hit the boy until I have made some inquiries."

"But he's done it, mistress. Good as said so."

"Just a minute. I want to go over to the Hall."

Jake looked as if he were preparing to run and I was more convinced than ever.

"Come," I said, "we're going now."

My mother was surprised to see me marching in with Ned Carter and his terrified son.

"What's the trouble?" she cried.

"Is Dickon here?" I asked.

"He's out riding with Sabrina, I think. Why?"

"I want to see him rather urgently." It was fortunate, for at that moment they came in flushed from the ride. It couldn't have been more convenient.

Dickon betrayed himself in the first seconds, so taken off his guard was he to see the Carters there.

He turned to the door.

"I've forgotten my . . ."

He paused, for I was barring his way.

"Just a minute," I said. "Jake has been accused of starting the fire at Farmer Hassock's barn. But I don't think he was alone."

"I reckon he was," said Dickon.

"No," I said, "I reckon he had a companion, and that it was you."

"No," he cried. He strode over to the cowering Jake. "You been telling tales."

"He has not mentioned you," I said.

"Oh, Zipporah dear," said my mother. "Why bother with all this? How is poor Jean-Louis?"

"What is bothering me," I said with unaccustomed firmness, which the thought of any injustice could arouse in me, bringing me out of my mildness in a way which once or twice in my life had astonished people, "is that Jake Carter is being blamed

23

for something which he only did because he was forced to by someone else."

"No . . . no . . ." said Jake. "I done it. It was me that lighted the fire in the pail."

"I'm going out to Vesta," said Dickon. "I reckon her pups are just ready to be born. She might have them by now."

"You can wait a little while before you go to see them," I said. "For instance, after you have told us who took the meat from the pantry and who made Jake take the pail and accompany him to the barn where the fire was made and got out of hand, and then ran away with Jake."

"Why do you ask me?" he said insolently.

"Because I happen to know the answer and that you were this culprit."

"It's a lie," he said.

I took him by the arm. His glare was venomous. It shocked me to see such a look in one so young.

"I saw you," I said. "It's no use denying it. I saw you with the pail. You were carrying it . . . Jake had a bundle of something. I saw you making for the Hassock farm."

There was a deep silence.

Then Dickon said: "It's all silly. It was only a game. We didn't mean to set fire to the old barn."

"But you did," I said. "And you made Jake go with you. And then you left him to take the blame."

"Oh, we'll pay for the damage that was done to the barn," said Sabrina.

"Of course," I replied, "but that doesn't settle the matter."

"It does," said Dickon.

"Oh, no. You have to tell Ned Carter that his boy was not to blame."

"Oh, what a silly lot of trouble about nothing," he said.

I looked at him steadily. "I don't think it is nothing," I said. I went on: "Ned, you can go now. It was not Jake's fault, remember that. He was led into this. I am sure my husband will be very upset if he hears that you have punished the boy. He only did what he was ordered to do. You can go now."

There was a silence in the Hall after they had gone.

24

Sabrina and my mother were very upset. Dickon came over to me and looked at me through narrowed eyes.

He said in a very low voice: "I won't forget this."

"No," I answered, "nor shall I."

He ran out saying he was going to the stable to look for Vesta.

Sabrina said: "Of course boys do get up to these pranks."

"Yes," I admitted. "They do. But when they are caught good boys do not stand aside and let someone else take the blame, particularly someone who is not in a position to defend himself."

They were shocked into silence. They could not bear criticism of their beloved child.

Then I said quite suddenly so that I surprised myself:

"I've decided to go to Eversleigh as we arranged."

They were startled. "Jean-Louis . . ." began my mother.

"Cannot go, of course. He is well looked after here. I shall wait a week or so, of course, and when I consider I can leave him I shall go as arranged. I am sure Lord Eversleigh would be very upset if I didn't go and I shall only be away for a short while."

It was as though my other self was preparing to take possession.

There was a great deal of opposition to my proposal to go to Eversleigh without Jean-Louis. My mother said she would not have a moment's peace until she had heard that I had arrived safely, and after that there would be the journey home again to be undertaken. Sabrina added her voice to my mother's. There had rarely been so much highway robbery as there was at this time, she informed me, and those dreadful villains stopped at nothing.

Dickon added: "They shoot you dead, you know, if you won't hand over your money."

I felt he would be quite amused if such a mishap overtook me, for our relationship had not improved since the discovery of the cause of the fire in Farmer Hassock's barn.

Jean-Louis's reaction was as I expected it to be. One of resignation and determination that my desire to go should not be thwarted. He was hobbling round the house and was able to go round the estate in a kind of go-cart, which was a great relief to him for the frustration of being cut off from his work would have been hard to bear.

"You see," I explained to him, "I have a feeling that I must go. That second letter from the old man . . . there was something about it. Sabrina said it was like a cry for help. That's rather fanciful, I suppose, but on the other hand, there did seem to be something in it . . . in a strange sort of way."

"What worries me most is the journey," said Jean-Louis. "If I could feel that you would be safe . . ."

"Oh, Jean-Louis," I cried, "people are making journeys every day. We don't hear of the thousands who arrive safely. There is always such a lot of talk when there is a mishap."

"Some parts of the road are very dangerous . . . notorious haunts of highwaymen."

"We shall avoid those and I shall have protection."

"Your mother is very much against it."

"I know. She was in an accident when she was a child and has never forgotten it. I'll be all right, Jean-Louis."

He looked at me earnestly. "You very much want to go, don't you?"

"Yes," I said. "I have a strong feeling that I should."

"I understand." He did understand. He was a quiet and thoughtful man and often understood my thoughts before I had expressed them. I believe now that he was thinking that life was beginning to pall; that I was looking for excitement. He did not want me to grow vaguely dissatisfied, which perhaps I was doing without realizing it. However, being Jean-Louis he was constructive rather than destructive; instead of deciding that the journey was impossibly dangerous, he set about planning how to make it as safe as possible.

"I think you should have six grooms," he said. "They can return as soon as you are safely delivered; and then come back for you when you return. Those and one more for the saddle horse and you will be a considerable party."

I kissed him. I felt brimming over with love.

"Well?" he said.

"I think I have the best husband in the world," I told him.

It was typical of him that he should hide his apprehension from me; he seemed to grow quite excited about the preparations as I discussed with him what I should take and the route we should travel.

It was on a lovely morning when we set out—a typical June day with the sun newly risen to give us a pleasant early morning warmth and the promise of a fine day. We made good progress and the feeling of expectation was growing. Everything seemed to be more vivid than usual. Butterflies the purest white against the purple buddleia, the hum of the bees at work on vivid blue borage and clover, moon daisies in the fields with the buttercups and cowslips and the glimpse of the scarlet pimpernel on the edges of the cornfields—these miracles of nature, which I had taken for granted all my life, seemed especially wonderful.

We should have two stops on our journey and the arrangements at the inn had been most carefully made so, as expected, there was no difficulty about accommodation when we made our first stop in good time.

I did not sleep very well. I was too excited, and the next day, as soon as the first streaks of dawn were in the sky, I was getting ready to pursue our journey.

The morning passed swiftly and equally without untoward incident and then we were soon on the last lap of our journey.

We planned to reach Eversleigh by about four o'clock in the afternoon, but unfortunately, when we stopped at an inn for refreshment just before midday, we discovered one of the grooms' horses had cast a shoe. This would delay us a little, and we wondered whether we should leave the groom to wait for his horse and go on without him or all remain until his horse was fit for the road.

I was uncertain, but my mother had made me promise that I would not ride without all the grooms in attendance, and after some deliberation I decided that we should wait for the horse to be shod and then all go together, which should not delay us very long.

It did, however, take longer than I had at first thought it would, for the blacksmith was not in his forge; he had had an urgent call to go over to a nearby mansion where the squire had some commission for him. We were assured that he would return within a very short time. The short time grew into a long time, and I began to wonder whether it would have been wiser to go on without the groom. After all, we should only be one man short.

It was then four o'clock and we had planned to leave just after midday, and as I was deciding that we should go on, for we had no reservation at an inn for the night and did not know where we should find one, the blacksmith returned.

He would get the work done right away, he said, and the horse would be fit for the road before we could say "God bless the king."

It wasn't quite as speedy as that but eventually we were on the road. Thus it was that by the time we reached Eversleigh Court it was growing dark.

Jessie

*L*ong ago *I had been to Eversleigh Court and vaguely re-* membered it. I must have spent many Christmases there when I was a child because it had always been the center of the family. When the old people died and my mother went to live permanently in the country after the death of my father, we had not visited the old house. General Eversleigh, who had been fond of my mother, and who had in fact introduced my father into the family in the first place, had taken over the management of the estate for a while, but that other Carl— Lord Eversleigh's son—was the real heir to the estate as well as to the title, and when the general had died Carl Lord Eversleigh must have felt in duty bound to come back—I was not sure from where—and settle at Eversleigh.

My excitement was intense. I had during the journey been trying to look back and remember what I had heard about the family who had inhabited the great house during its heyday. I recalled there was a lot of talk about Enderby, that house of gloom which was wrapped in a kind of supernatural mystery.

I had decided I would take a look at it at the first opportunity, but in the meantime here was Eversleigh Court.

A high wall loomed up in front of us. The gates were open; I thought this must be to welcome us. We rode through. It was too dark to see the house clearly, but memories of long ago came flooding back and the vague feeling of familiarity was comforting.

There was no sound from the house. Then I caught sight of flickering light in one of the upper windows. There was a dark shadow there. Someone must have been standing there holding a candle and looking out—perhaps awaiting our arrival.

I was rather surprised that the great door remained closed, as we must have been expected, and the sound of the horses must have been heard on the gravel of the drive.

We waited a few moments for the grooms to come and take the horses, but no one came and the house remained in darkness.

I said: "As we're so late they must have thought we wouldn't arrive tonight. Ring the bell. That will let them know we're here."

One of the grooms dismounted and did as I bid. I remembered the bell from long ago. It had always fascinated me and I used to enjoy pulling the rope and listening to the clamor it made throughout the house.

I sat on my horse, looking at the door, waiting for the moment when it would be flung open and someone would appear to welcome us.

There was silence when the bell ceased to clang. I began to feel a little uneasy. This was not the welcome I had expected from Lord Eversleigh's letters.

At last the door opened. A young woman stood there. I could not see her very clearly but she struck me immediately as being something of a slattern.

"What you be wanting?" she demanded.

I said: "I am Mistress Zipporah Ransome. Lord Eversleigh is expecting me."

The woman looked amazed. I thought she was half-witted.

I tried to peer behind her but the hall was not lighted and there was only the dim glow from the one candle which she had set down when she unbolted the door.

One of my grooms held my horse while I dismounted and approached the door.

"Lord Eversleigh is expecting me," I said. "Take me to him. Who is in charge of the household?"

"That would be Mistress Jessie," she said.

"Then will you please call Mistress Jessie? In the meantime I will come in. Where are the stables? My grooms are tired and hungry. Is there someone who can help with the horses?"

"There's Jethro. I'll get Mistress Jessie."

"Please do so... quickly," I answered, "because we have had a long journey."

She was about to shut the door but I held it open and, as she scuttled away, stepped into the hall.

She had left her candle on the long oak table and it threw a rather eerie light about the place.

It occurred to me that there was something very strange going on here. I kept thinking of what Sabrina had said: "Calling for help!" It did not seem so very incongruous now.

I was startled by what appeared to be an apparition, for at the head of the stairs a figure had appeared. It was a woman, and in her hand was a candelabrum which she held high, striking a pose like a figure in some stage drama. In the flickering candlelight she looked amazingly handsome. She was tall, plump, but shapely and about her neck glittered what could be diamonds. They also glistened at her wrists and on her fingers—so many of them that I could see them even as she stood there in only the light from the candles.

She moved down the staircase in a stately fashion.

She wore a wig of luxuriant curls, very fair—golden, in fact—with one curl hanging over her left shoulder. Her hooped skirt stood out round her like a bell and it was of plum-colored velvet, cut away in the front to show the very ornate petticoat of bluish mauve with white flowers embroidered on it. She was clearly a very grand lady and I could not imagine what her

31

position in the house could be. As she came nearer I saw that the dazzling complexion had been applied rather too heavily to be natural and she wore a small black patch just beneath her large, rather protruding, blue eyes and another one beside her heavily rouged mouth.

I said: "I am Zipporah Ransome. Lord Eversleigh was eager that I should come to see him. He knew I was to arrive today. We are a little late, I know. One of the horses had to be shod."

The woman's eyes narrowed; she looked puzzled and I went on hastily: "Surely I am expected."

"I knew nothing of this," said the woman. Her accent was overgenteel and but for her clothes I would have thought she must be a housekeeper.

"I don't think I've heard who you are," I said. "Could you . . . ?"

"I am Mistress Stirling. They call me Mistress Jessie. I have been looking after Lord Eversleigh for the past two years."

"Looking after him . . . ?"

She smiled almost deprecatingly. "You might call me a sort of housekeeper."

"Oh, I see. And did he not tell you that he had invited me to come?"

"I never knew it." Her voice had lost a little of its assumed refinement. She was clearly annoyed at the omission and perhaps a little suspicious too.

"Well," I said, "this must be rather awkward. Perhaps I could see him."

She was thinking quickly. "You say you are Mistress Ransome?"

"Yes, I gather I am his nearest of kin . . . or at least my mother is. Lord Eversleigh is the son of my great-great-grandmother. I think that's right. It goes back rather a long way."

"And you say he wrote to you?"

"Yes . . . several letters. He asked me to come and see him. He was so insistent. So I promised and I was expected today. Could you take me to him?"

She said: "I've settled him down for the night. He is a very old man, you know."

"Yes, I do know that. But as he is expecting me he will be wondering why I am not here."

She shook her head. "You must be prepared. He has probably forgotten he invited you, as he told me nothing of it. He is not always very clear in his head, do you understand me?"

"Well, I did know that he was very old. Oh dear . . . perhaps I should not have come."

She laid her hand on my arm, familiarly, almost as a friend might do—certainly not as a housekeeper would; but it was beginning to dawn on me that she was implying she was no ordinary housekeeper.

"Now don't say that," she said almost archly. "I'll tell you what. I'll get a bed aired for you and I daresay you would like something to eat."

"Yes," I said. "I would indeed. And so would the grooms. There are six of them, no, seven including one with the saddlebags."

"My word. Quite a retinue, eh?"

She had relaxed. She gave the impression of one who has come face to face with a difficult situation and has decided how to deal with it.

"Well, I'll give orders, eh? . . . and we'll get you settled and in the morning you can see his lordship."

"But shouldn't he be told that I have arrived?"

"I reckon he's sleeping like a baby now. I'll tell you what. I'll go and see . . . I'll peep in, shall I? . . . and if he's awake I'll tell him. If he's sleeping, you wouldn't want me to wake him, I'm sure. He takes a bit of time to get off sometimes."

Her manner had completely changed; shocked surprise had been replaced by a familiar air which was almost patronizing. She was behaving as though she were mistress of the house but at the same time as no well-bred mistress would dream of behaving. I was aware of a slight sound, and turning sharply, thought I saw something move at the top of the staircase. It was not easy to see, for the candles gave only the dimmest of lights. We were being watched. I wondered by whom. Since I had stepped into this house I was prepared for anything.

"Now first of all it's food, eh," said the woman. "They'll be clearing away in the kitchens. You should have been here when supper was served. We could have treated you proud then. Well, they'll find something and I'll have them get a room ready for you. Now you come in here and give me just a minute or two and I'll have you and them grooms of yours all fed and bedded down in next to no time. How's that?"

I said: "Thank you. I'll go out and tell the grooms to go to the stables, shall I?"

"No, you'd better stay here. I'll see to it." She started to shout: "Jenny! Moll! Where are you? Come here at once, you lazy young sluts."

She smiled at me. "I have to keep my eyes on 'em," she explained. "There'd be nothing done if I don't. Place would be going to rack and ruin like it was when I come here."

She was speaking easily, naturally, now, in the manner, I expected, to which she was accustomed.

Two girls came running in.

"Now, you two," she said, ". . . I want a room got ready for this lady here. She's come visiting his lordship . . . who didn't see fit to tell us . . . doubtless he forgot it, poor old pet. Now, Moll, out to the stables. . . . Call Jethro . . . tell him to take in the horses and arrange for the men to be given somewhere to sleep and a bite to eat. We can sort all this out in the morning. Now, Mistress . . . what did you say your name was?"

"Mistress Ransome," I said.

"Now, Mistress Ransome, if you'll step into this winter parlor I'll have something sent in for you to eat while they get your room ready. Dear, dear, what a to-do, and all he had to do was tell me."

I was taken into a room which I remembered we used for meals when there were a few of us. Yes, they had called it the winter parlor.

I sat down uneasily. It was all so different from what I had expected.

Of course, I told myself, it would all have been so different if that horse had not cast a shoe and we had arrived at a reasonable time. Then Lord Eversleigh would not have gone to bed. He would have given me the welcome I was expecting. After all, it had been his idea that I should come. Delays on the road were frequent—any little mishap could mean delay. I guessed he had thought we would arrive tomorrow. It was odd, though, that he had had no preparations made for our stay.

I sat down and one of the maids came in to light the candelabrum.

I said to her: "Have you been here long?"

"About two years, my lady."

"The same as Mistress . . . Stirling."

"Yes, soon after her. We were most of us new then."

She looked at me apologetically and hurried out. All new when Mistress Stirling came. This was becoming a rather strange situation.

A maid, accompanied by Mistress Stirling, came in bringing a tray on which were cold venison and a piece of pie.

Mistress Stirling, whom I had begun to think of as Jessie, laid the tray on the table; I was very hungry but ever more curious. When the maid had gone Jessie sat opposite me and, leaning her arms on the table, stared at me while I ate.

"When did his lordship write to you?" she asked.

"Some weeks ago. It was to my mother that he wrote, as a matter of fact."

"To your mother . . . asking for you to visit." She gave rather a nervous giggle. "Did he say what for?"

"Oh well . . . we are of the same family. I suppose he felt it was a pity we did not meet more often."

A man put his head round the door.

"You'm wanting me, Mistress Jessie."

"Oh, Jethro," she said. "This lady's come a visiting his lordship. One of his relations, she says."

"I am one of his closest living relations," I said. "My name is Zipporah Ransome . . . Clavering, that was."

35

"Why, bless me," said the old man, "if it's not Miss Zipporah. I remember you well when you used to come to Eversleigh. Christmas, wasn't it? . . . and sometime there be summer holidays and winter ones too. I can remember you, miss, as a little 'un. Good little thing you was."

I was more relieved. The situation was becoming more natural. I remembered him now. He was Jethro, who had been in charge of the horses—head groom, I suppose one would call him. He had always been a favorite of mine because I had loved horses.

"Why, Jethro," I cried, standing up, and we clasped hands.

"Ah, 'tis good to see you here, Miss Zipporah. It must be years . . . And you a married lady now. Well, time do fly . . . and no mistake. And you've come to see his lordship?"

"Jethro," said Jessie. "I think you should go and make sure those grooms are settled. Have you given them something to eat?"

"Well, there's naught but bread and cheese and ale at this time of night. But they'm having some of that in the kitchen."

"And you can find somewhere for them to sleep."

Jethro nodded.

"I'll see 'ee tomorrow, perhaps, Mistress Zipporah."

He was looking at me earnestly and I, because of the strangeness of my reception, had the notion that he wanted to tell me something.

He went out.

"Gives himself airs because he's been here so long," said Jessie. "Some of them old codgers do. They fancy you can't do without them. Well, his lordship for some reason thinks a powerful lot of Jethro."

"We all did . . . I remember. So much is coming back to me now I'm here."

"Well, get a good night's rest, eh. I popped in to see his lordship but he's sleeping like a baby. Once he wakes he'd never get to sleep again and then we'd have a fidgety old man the next day, I can promise you."

"Is he . . . very much of an . . . invalid?"

36

"Lord bless you, no. Just feeble. Needs someone always at his elbow. That's where I come in. Is that pie good? It should be eaten straight from the oven, you know."

I said it was very good.

"I always like my victuals," confided Jessie. "And when you've finished . . . I'll have some hot water sent up and you can snuggle down, eh. You must be just about worn out."

I admitted that I should be pleased to have a night's rest.

"So you shall." She was smiling at me benignly and somehow such benignity sat ill on her features, for there was a sharp glint in her eyes which I found rather disconcerting. I should be glad when morning came, for I thought then I should be able to throw some light on the meaning of this strange reception.

Jessie herself took me up to my room. Memories of the house came back to me. I could vaguely remember the days of its grandeur. I had a feeling that it was rather different now.

Jessie threw open a door.

"Oh, here we are. They've made up the bed." She went to it and drew back the coverlet. "The warming pan's in. I have to watch them girls. My goodness me, they'd lead us a nice dance if I didn't. I've got an eye like a hawk. His lordship says to me: 'I don't know what we'd do without you, Jess.' I will say he's not a man to take things for granted. He knows what I do and he wants me to know he does . . . if you get my meaning." She was growing more and more familiar and was developing a habit of putting out a hand and giving me a gentle little push as she spoke. I found it repulsive and wanted to tell her to get out, while on the other hand I wanted to keep her there for more unusual revelations which I felt sure were to come.

The room was well furnished with a four-poster bed, court cupboard, a dressing table on which was a looking glass.

"There's the hot water. No need to send it down when you've finished. They'll take it in the morning."

"Thank you."

"Right you are. See you in the morning. Sleep well."

"Thank you."

She gave me another of those gentle little pushes and was gone.

Alone in the room, the strangeness of everything occupied my thoughts. I went to the door at once and the fact that there was no key in the lock dismayed me. I wondered how I should sleep in this strange atmosphere. I had come to the conclusion that I must be prepared for anything, however unusual.

Why did Lord Eversleigh employ such a woman as Jessie? Moreover, she seemed to have such power. The manner in which she behaved suggested that she might be the mistress of the house. And surely he should have given instructions that I was to arrive.

I was physically exhausted but my mind was so ill at ease that I knew I should find it difficult to sleep.

I went to the window. I could see nothing. It was so dark outside. I longed for sunrise. Whatever was happening would surely seem more reasonable then.

I saw that my bags had been brought up, and I hoped the grooms were feeling more comfortable than I was.

I unpacked one of the bags and took out my night things. What I must do was get to bed and to sleep, for there was nothing more I could do till morning.

I washed and undressed. I removed the warming pan and got into bed. I sunk into the luxury of feathers and felt almost drowsy in spite of everything, but just as I was dozing I would wake startled and sit up in bed listening. I realized that I was going to have a bad night. Well, I was prepared for that.

It must have been about an hour later when I heard a light footstep outside my room. I turned my eyes toward the door. I was sure someone was standing outside. It was a little lighter in the room now. The clouds had cleared and my eyes had accustomed to the darkness and as they turned to the door I saw the handle slowly turning.

"Come in," I called.

The handle no longer moved. There was silence. I sat up in bed, my heart beating so fast that I could hear it. Then I thought I detected the sound of retreating footsteps. I opened the door and looked out but I could see nothing.

The incident was certainly not conducive to sleep. I lay there listening.

It must have been half an hour or so later when I heard footsteps again. This time I slipped out of bed and stood behind the door, waiting.

Yes, they had paused at my door and the handle was slowly turned. This time I did not speak. I stood pressed against the wall, waiting, while the door opened slowly.

I had been expecting the stately figure of Jessie, but to my amazement it was a young girl who could not have been more than twelve years old who entered. She went straight to the bed and gasped to see it empty. By this time I had shut the door and, leaning against it, said: "Hello. What do you want?"

She spun round and stared at me, her eyes wide and bright. I think if I had not been barring her way she would have rushed out of the room.

My fears had ebbed away. I saw at once that instead of a rather sinister presence all I had to deal with was a curious little girl.

"Well," I said, "why have you come to pay me a visit at such an hour? It's very late, you know."

Still she said nothing. She stared down at her bare feet showing beneath her nightgown.

I went toward her. She looked at me in panic and I could see that she was preparing to make a dash for the door.

"Now you are here," I said, "and I must say in a rather unceremonious fashion, I think you owe me an explanation."

"I . . . I only wanted to see you."

"Who are you?"

"Evalina."

"And what are you doing here in this house . . . who are your parents?"

"We live here. This is my mama's house really. . . ."

I knew then. There was a faint resemblance. I said: "You must be Jessie's daughter?"

She nodded.

"I see, and you live here in your mother's house?"

"It's Lordy's really. . . ."

"Whose?"

"The old man. Lord Eversleigh's his real name. But we always call him Lordy."

"We . . . ?"

"It's my mama's name for him."

"I see. And he is a very great friend of yours, I suppose, since he lets you live in his house and call him Lordy."

"He couldn't do without us."

"Does he say so?"

She nodded.

"Why did you creep into my bedroom?"

"I saw you when you came."

"I saw you. You were at the top of the staircase."

"You didn't see me."

"I did. You should be a little more careful. You do seem to get caught. Look at you now."

"Are you going to tell on me?"

"I don't know. I'll see when I have finished the interrogation."

"The what?" She looked frightened, as though she feared some terrible ordeal.

"I'm going to ask you some questions. A lot will depend on how you answer."

"My mother would be angry. She gets angry sometimes. She'd say I was careless not to make sure you were asleep before I came in."

"So it would have been quite acceptable if you had not been caught."

She looked at me in wonderment. "Of course."

"A strange philosophy," I said.

"You do talk funny. Why have you come here? Is it to make trouble with Lordy?"

"I came because Lordy—as you call him—invited me."

"My mother is cross with him about that. She can't under-

stand how he could ask you without telling her. She's asking
a lot of questions... who took the message, and all that. I
reckon there'll be a terrible row."

"Why shouldn't Lord Eversleigh invite whom he wishes to
his house?"

"Well, he should ask mama first, shouldn't he?"

"Is your mother the housekeeper here?"

"Well, it's all different, you know."

"In what way?"

She giggled. Her face, which had seemed innocent at one
stage, had become rather sly. She might be young but she was
knowledgeable in some matters and she managed to convey a
meaning to the relationship between her mother and Lord Eversleigh which had come to me as a possibility and now seemed
a certainty.

This child was not the innocent I had been imagining. She
was a girl who listened, who spied and whose curiosity was
so intense that it brought her from her bed at night to take a
look at the new arrival who had brought such consternation to
her mother.

I did not pursue that line of conversation. The child's sala-
cious giggle had in a way answered it and certainly I did not
want to discuss this dubious relationship with her.

She said: "I'll go now. Good night. You ought to have been
asleep."

"It would certainly have suited your convenience. Tell me,
did you intend to examine my baggage?"

"I only wanted to have a quick look."

"Now you're here you will go at my pleasure. You will now
answer a few questions for me. How long have you been here?"

"It's about two years."

"You are happy here?"

"It's lovely. Different from..."

"From where you were before. Where were you?"

"In London."

"You and your mother. Where is your father?"

She shrugged her shoulders.

"Never had one . . . proper. . . . There were uncles. . . . They never stayed long, though."

I felt disgusted. The child was building up a picture of what I had suspected.

Jessie was a loose woman who had somehow managed to dupe Lord Eversleigh. How had she done it? I couldn't imagine any of the ancestors I remembered being taken in by such a woman. They would not have had her under their roofs for an hour.

"How did you get here?"

She was puzzled. I guessed she really did not know. All she could say was that they had lived near Covent Garden and her mother had had lodgers. . . . "People from the theater," she said. "My mama went on the stage once."

She looked a little wistful and I said: "You enjoyed that life then . . . better than this."

She hesitated. "There's good things to eat here . . . and mama's better . . . and Lordy couldn't do without us."

"Does he say so?"

"He's always telling mama so. She's always asking him."

"Where is your bedroom?"

She pointed vaguely upward.

"And your mother?"

"With Lordy, of course."

I felt sick with horror. It was just as I had suspected. I wondered with apprehension what the next day would bring.

"I'm getting cold," she said.

I was too and I felt I had discovered a great deal from Evalina.

"You'd better go back to your room up there now," I said.

She moved toward the door with alacrity.

"If I am going to stay here for a short while I want a key to my door."

"I'll bring it back."

"So you have it."

She smiled, nodded, hunching her shoulders. She looked mischievous and childish.

"Do you mean to say you took it so that you could creep in and look round my room when you wanted to?"

She cast down her eyes, still smiling.

"Is it in your room now?"

She nodded.

"Then go up and bring it down to me at once."

She hesitated. "If I do you won't say anything about this...."

I hesitated. There was a look of cupidity in her face. She was remarkably like her mother.

"All right," I said. "It's a bargain. Give me the key and your visit shall be a secret between us. Though I advise you not to do such a thing again."

She nodded and slipped away. In a short time she was back with the key.

She was smiling slyly at me.

Still wondering what revelations would come in the next days I locked the door and, feeling secure, went back to my bed, where after a while I slept deeply until morning.

I was awakened by the arrival of one of the maids bringing me hot water. The sun was streaming into the room showing me a shabbiness which I had not noticed in the darkness.

"Good morning," I said. "What is your name?"

"Moll," answered the girl, "Mistress Jessie says to come down when you're ready."

"Thank you," I said, and, giving me a curious look, she went out.

I got out of bed immediately while thoughts of last night came back to me. Today I should discover the true state of affairs and I was very much looking forward to seeing my kinsman. Lordy! I found myself smiling rather ruefully at the sobriquet. I was sure it had been bestowed by Jessie and it was really very revealing. So it was in a mood of expectancy that I descended to the dining room.

Jessie was already there. She was in a morning gown of cambric—lilac-colored and elaborately embroidered. She wore slightly less jewelry than last night but she was still overloaded with it. Her maquillage was more noticeable and the sun was more harsh than the gentle light of candles.

She greeted me effusively. "Oh, there you are! Had a good sleep, I hope. My goodness me, you must have been well nigh wore out last night." She had abandoned the attempt at refinement which she had adopted on our first meeting and I think I liked the present style better. It was certainly more natural. "Was the bed comfortable? Made up in a hurry, I'm afraid, and you know what these maids are like. It's one body's work looking after them."

I said that my bed was comfortable, but "it is always a little different in a strange bed."

"I'd agree on that one." Her laugh was high pitched and she was near enough to give me one of her playful pushes which I was too late to evade.

"Now what will you have to eat? Not expecting visitors, we wasn't, so you've caught us on the hop, so's to speak. But being as I'm one for the victuals, they don't do so bad in the kitchen."

It was true there was plenty to eat. There was fish and pies containing meat. I was not hungry and took a little fish, which was all I could manage. Jessie meanwhile sat opposite me as she had on the previous night.

"My! You eat like a little bird," she said. I guessed she had already breakfasted but she could not resist taking some of the pie and eating it in a way expressive of great enjoyment, smacking her lips and licking her fingers.

I said: "When shall I be able to see Lord Eversleigh?"

"Now, that's what I wanted to talk to you about. He's not so good in the mornings, poor pet. He needs time to pull himself together, you might say. Oh, he's no spring chicken, though he's good for his age." Her eyes sparkled rather reminiscently, I thought, and I was sure that had the table not separated us it would have been an occasion for one of her pushes.

"I am sure he will wish to see me when he knows that I am here."

"Oh yes, I expect you're right. Let's say give him an hour

or two, eh? I'll let you know when he's ready. Say about eleven o'clock."

I said I should look forward to eleven.

She stood up. "Well, I reckon you'll want to get those bags unpacked, eh? One or two things you may want to do. Take a walk in the gardens. They're very nice. Don't go too far away, though, and come in at eleven. I reckon he'll be ready then."

I went to my room, unpacked the little I had brought with me and then, taking her advice, went into the gardens. I noticed that they were not as well cared for as they might have been. The general atmosphere of the house pervaded the gardens.

At eleven o'clock I was back in the house and Jessie was waiting for me in the hall.

"His lordship is excited. He wants you to go up at once."

I followed her up the stairs. Memories from my childhood were coming back to me and parts of the house were already seeming familiar to me. I knew that we were going to the main bedroom. I remembered coming here with my mother to see my great-grandmother when she was ill.

Jessie unceremoniously opened the door and I followed her in.

There was the four-poster bed and sitting up in it an old man. His face was a whitish yellow and there was scarcely any flesh on his bones; he might have been a corpse but for his large lively brown eyes.

"Here she is, Lordy. Here's the little lady."

Those bright eyes were turned on me and a thin hand came out to grip mine.

"Zipporah!" he said. "So it's you, Clarissa's girl. You came."

I took his hand and held it firmly. His eyes glistened a little. Here at least was a welcome. I could tell that he was very glad I had come.

"She came because you asked her, pet," said Jessie. "And didn't let me know. Not very nice of you, was it, lovey? Arrived last night in the dark . . . and having no welcome ready. If you'd told me I'd have set the bells ringing for her."

He smiled at me almost deprecatingly. "Jessie takes good care of me," he said.

"I should think she does!" said Jessie. "Though sometimes you don't always deserve it, eh, naughty Lordy?"

He smiled at me. Was he trying to tell me something? If he was it was obvious that he wouldn't do so while Jessie was present.

"I am so pleased to see you," I said.

"And your husband?"

"He hasn't come with me. There was a fire in a barn nearby and he broke his leg attempting to put it out."

"So you came alone?"

"Accompanied by seven grooms."

He nodded. "Good of you. Good of you."

His dark eyes were expressive, luminous.

"Tell me," he went on. "Tell me, how is your mother? A dear girl . . . always. And your father . . . that was a tragedy. I knew him. One of the finest gentlemen that ever lived. And Sabrina . . . eh . . ."

"They are all well."

"Pity Sabrina married that damned Jacobite. We . . . we put paid to them, eh? Traitors all of them."

Jessie had sat by the bed. There was a bowl of sweetmeats on a nearby table. She took one and began sucking it. I guessed they had been put there for her benefit and the fact was borne home to me that she shared this bedchamber with that poor skeleton of a man in the bed. The idea of them together would have been comical if it hadn't seemed so tragic. She sat in a chair smiling at us benignly; yet behind that bland smile was the look of a watchdog. She was suspicious and angry that I had been sent for without her knowledge. I wondered how far he was under her control. Not completely, I suppose; but she was clearly a power in the house.

"Lordy can still get wild over the Jacobites," commented Jessie.

I raised my eyebrows a little and looked at him. Why didn't he send this insolent woman away?

46

He caught my expression and returned it with an almost apologetic smile and yet there was a message there. He wanted to talk to me in private I knew. Why did he not tell her to leave us!

Could it possibly be that he was *afraid* of her? A brazen forceful woman; a houseful of servants selected by her and an old man possessed of wealth, enfeebled, spending a great deal of time in his bed.

The situation was becoming clear, but I could not understand his docility.

I said: "I hear that Mistress Jessie is a good housekeeper."

She gave rather a raucous laugh. "More than that, eh, pet?"

He laughed with her and by the expression on his face I thought: He really cares for her. He *likes* her.

"Do you ever go out?" I asked.

"No, I haven't been out . . . for how long, Jessie? Months?" She nodded. "The trouble is I can't manage the stairs. A pity. I always liked the fresh air."

"He rests in the afternoon, don't you, pet? I tuck him up after dinner. That's round about one and then after a nice nap . . . he's rested."

Jessie had the sweetmeat bowl beside her. "There's no marzipan here," she commented. "I told them girls to keep it filled."

Her face was momentarily distorted with anger. Gone in that instant was the bland expression; but it was almost immediately replaced by the smile. If she could be like that over a sweetmeat, I thought, how would she be about something which affected her really deeply? That I had stumbled into a very strange and dangerous situation was becoming increasingly clear.

She went to the door and shouted "Moll." It gave us our opportunity. The thin old hand had seized mine urgently. "See Jethro," he whispered. "He will tell you what to do."

That was all. She had returned to the room. Only her desire for a sweetmeat had allowed her to leave us alone for a second.

"Them girls," she said. "I don't know what they're paid for."

I said quickly, as though continuing a conversation, "Yes, what shall I call you? Our relationship is rather a complicated one."

"Let's see," he said. "Now my parents were Edwin and Jane, and Edwin was the son of Arabella and Edwin. Then Arabella remarried my father's cousin Carleton—like me. It's a name that turns up in the family now and then. She had Priscilla and another Carl, who became a general. Priscilla had a daughter out of wedlock, Carlotta—wonderful Carlotta—and then she married and had Damaris. Carlotta had a daughter . . . again out of wedlock."

Jessie started to laugh. "Now we know where you get *your* naughtiness, Lordy."

He did not seem to hear her but went on: "And Carlotta's daughter was your mother, Clarissa. Now what does that make us? I think you'd better call me Uncle Carl, don't you? The poor general is no more, so there is no danger of my being mistaken for him."

"Yes," I said. "Uncle Carl then."

Very soon Moll came in with a bowl of sweetmeats. Jessie rose and seized on them eagerly. This gave us another opportunity and Uncle Carl seized it.

He did not speak but his lips framed the name: "Jethro."

We talked a little after that and I rose to go. Jessie was smirking. She did not know that I felt I had made some progress.

It was nearly midday when I left my kinsman, whom I now thought of as Uncle Carl. Dinner was served at quarter past twelve, Jessie told me, and she would see me then. It was a sumptuous meal. If I had learned anything it was that food meant a great deal to Jessie. It was due to her love of sweetmeats that I had a private word with Uncle Carl. I had to be grateful for that. My plans for the afternoon were already made. I was going to find Jethro.

The meal was served in the dining room. It consisted of several dishes, soup, fish, meats of three kinds and pies. Jessie

48

seemed to have a passion for pies. When I entered the dining room Jessie was already there with the girl I had met last night.

"My daughter, Evalina," she said.

Evalina curtsied. She looked slightly more demure than she had last night and I guessed the bold little girl was in great awe of her mother.

"She makes herself useful about the house, don't you, pet?"

Evalina looked at me half defiantly, half pleadingly. I guessed she was afraid I might mention our encounter of last night.

"You must be a great help to your mother," I said.

She relaxed visibly and gave me a half-grateful, half-conspiratorial smile. She had brought back the key of the room, she was reminding me, and I had made a bargain.

We sat down and I was rather glad that Jessie's desire for food made conversation spasmodic.

"I take Lordy's tray up," she said. "Always have to give him something as won't upset his stomach. It's a bit delicate, you know." I thought a bit of the hot roast beef would be just right for him. Her lips watered slightly at the mention of roast beef. "Lapped it up, he did. That's why we eat a little after midday; I like to see he's satisfied first. Then we tuck him down for his afternoon nap. He'll sleep right through till five of the clock. I like a bit of a nap myself in the afternoons. I hear it's a good habit. . . . Keeps you going till the early hours of morning. How about you, Mistress Ransome?"

"I don't take an afternoon nap but then I suppose I retire before the early hours of morning."

She laughed.

Evalina watched me furtively and paid little contribution to the conversation. I was glad when the meal was over. It was comforting to think that Jessie would be sleeping. . . . I wondered if she lay beside Uncle Carl on that big four-poster.

I went to my room.

When afternoon quiet had settled on the house, I lost no time. I went out and crossed the gardens to the stables. That was where I would be most likely to find Jethro. I looked around at the edge of a small field; there were two cottages and on the gate of one of these a young boy was swinging. He looked at me curiously and I said: "Hello." He continued to stare at me and I went on: "Do you know Jethro?" He nodded. "Where does he live?"

He pointed to the other cottage.

I thanked him and opened the gate of Jethro's home.

He must have been prepared, because as I went up the little path I heard a voice say: "Come in, Mistress Zipporah. I've been expecting you."

I stepped down into a dark room, rather cluttered with furniture and highly polished horse brasses around the fireplace. Over the door a horseshoe had been nailed.

"Lord Eversleigh wished me to see you," I said.

"That's right. I'm the only one he's got here, in a manner of speaking."

"How do you mean?"

"Well, she's in charge now. It's what Jessie wants that goes. That's how it is."

I said: "It's horrible. I had no idea I was going to find this. That woman . . ."

"Not such an unusual situation. A man like his lordship . . . begging your pardon, Miss Zipporah, but it's happened before and it'll happen again."

"Couldn't she be sent away? Surely she only has to be dismissed."

"His lordship would never agree. He dotes on her. She's his woman . . . if you'll forgive the expression, Mistress Zipporah."

"You mean she's got a hold on him."

"She's got him, mistress. He don't want her to go no more than she wants to go. He knows she's feathering her nest but he likes to provide the feathers."

I said: "It is the most extraordinary household."

"Well, you see, it's always been women with him and he can't be expected to change at his time of life."

"But there's something happening there. He whispered to me that he wanted you to tell me something."

"Ah yes, yes. . . . He wants me to tell you that he has got to see you on his own . . . without Jessie there. He wants that arranged."

"I could go to him and he could insist that we were alone. Why shouldn't we tell the housekeeper to leave us?"

"Jessie's not that sort of housekeeper. She'd never allow it and he would never upset her. No, mistress, what you have to do is get into his room when she's out of the house. Now she's a regular one in her habits. And she'll be out of the house say thirty minutes from now."

"How do you know?"

"Because she acts regular as clockwork."

"She said that Lord Eversleigh rested after dinner until five and that she did the same."

"Her resting! On a bed maybe—but not to rest . . . if you'll pardon the coarseness, Mistress Zipporah."

"I have come to the conclusion that coarseness is a part of this situation so I am prepared for it."

"After dinner," he said, "she tucks his lordship up and tells him to sleep. Then at half past one she's on her way to Amos Carew's house. She's very partial to him. Has been all the time. He got her here, you see. I reckon it was a put-up job between the two of them."

"Do you mean that Amos Carew is her lover? And who is he?"

Jethro nodded. "Who is he? He's the estate manager. His lordship couldn't do without him either. Amos brought Jessie down here as housekeeper and very soon after that she was in charge not only of the house but of his lordship. She's that sort of woman. She got rid of most of the servants except me . . . and one or two of them in the cottages. She couldn't very well turn us out of our homes. Then she brought in some of her own choosing. But I have to say this . . . both his lordship and Amos Carew seem very content. They think the world of her . . . both of 'em."

"It's horrible," I said.

"Shocking for a lady like you. But he does want to see you,

and he can see you while she's with Amos Carew. Just go into his room. He might be dozing but he'll be wide awake at the sight of you and then he'll tell you what he wants of you, why he's asked you here... but I don't think it's to get rid of Jessie... he just does not want to say what he's got to in front of her."

"I'll go back to the house and to his room."

"Bit too early yet, mistress. Wait till she's in Carew's house. You can see it from my top window. On a bit of hill, we are. And I can see Carew's clear from my top window. When she goes in it's two hours clear afore she's out and she's generally there before two. We should be on the watch. Will you step up?"

There was a short staircase in the room to Jethro's bedroom, which extended across the whole area of the cottage. There was a small window at either end of the room... one looking out over Jethro's vegetable patch, the other across fields to the house.

He had placed two chairs at this window. Now he said: "Look to the right of the house. See the manager's house. Always been the manager's house as long as I can remember, and my father and grandfather before me. Well, Amos Carew came here. He was a merry sort of fellow, people liked him. So did the girls. I reckon there's one or two of them who would have liked to set up house with him but he's not the marrying kind. And it wasn't long after he came that he brought Jessie here. She wheedled her way into the house and was a great favorite of his lordship. It got so he couldn't do without her. He gave her jewels and fine clothes and more or less the running of the house. Because he's an old man... well, she always kept on with Amos. So that is how it is."

"The more I hear the more sordid it becomes."

"That's because you're a lady bred and born but this sort of thing springs up now and then.... It's a pity, though, that it should be his lordship. There! Are you keeping your eyes open? It should be any minute now."

"As soon as we see her I shall hurry back to the house and go straight up to Lord Eversleigh's room."

"That's the idea, and when you find out what he wants if I can be of any help I'm here. She's late today."

"What is that house over there?"

"Why, that's Enderby."

"Oh yes . . . I remember Enderby."

"A queer sort of place that's always been."

"Who is there now?"

"It changed hands some time ago. It seems to do that. I think there's something strange about that house. Things have happened in it. People don't seem to stay. Don't mix much, these people. Have visitors from time to time. Foreigners, some of them."

"It's strange how a house gets a reputation."

"Haunted, they say. There's been tragedies there. Some say that part of the grounds are haunted too. There was rumor that someone was murdered and buried there."

"It always seemed rather gloomy as I remember."

"Ah yes, Enderby's not a place you'd forget. Look. There she is. You can just make her out. See, she keeps to the trees. . . . She'll have to come into the open before she can get to the house, though. 'Tis a mercy there is a good deal of her. She can't easy be missed." He chuckled. "I fancy she'll have a lot to tell Amos today."

I watched with a growing excitement. She walked into the house without knocking. She was evidently expected.

"I'll go back right away," I said. "And thank you, Jethro. I'll see you again soon."

"Right you are, mistress. Get in now. Go straight into his room. Never mind if he's dozing. Wake him up. That's what he wants."

I went quietly into the house and up the stairs. When I opened the door of Uncle Carl's room, he was propped up in bed, I think waiting for me.

Those wonderfully alive eyes lit up when they rested on me.

"You found Jethro," he said.

"Yes. He told me this was the time to find you alone."

"Jessie's sleeping. She likes her nap at this time of day."

There was a certain mischief in his eyes and it occurred to me then that he knew of her visits to the estate manager and the purpose of them. Perhaps I imagined that because I was becoming caught up in a situation which would have seemed impossible to me before I set foot in this house.

"My dear, it was good of you to come."

"I'm glad I did."

"And I'm rather glad that you came alone. Your husband might not have understood so readily."

"Oh . . . I am sure he would. . . . Tell me what it is I have to understand."

"Come and sit near the bed, so that I can see you. Ah, you have a look of Clarissa. A dear good girl . . . always. I think the women are the backbone of the family. . . . The men . . . they have their weaknesses but the women have been strong. But let us get down to business, shall we? We must make the most of what time we have. My dear, I want you to help me make my will."

"Oh."

"Yes, you see there are formalities. Things have to be signed and the lawyers have to come. It's rather difficult"—he smiled at me deprecatingly—"in the circumstances."

I decided to speak out boldly. I said: "You mean because of Jessie."

"Yes," he said. "Because of Jessie." He lifted a hand. "I know what you are going to say. Get rid of Jessie."

I nodded.

"This is something you won't understand. You have lived a conventional life, you had good parents, and now a good husband. We are not all so fortunate as you. Our lives don't run along such pleasant tracks. We ourselves are not always very pleasant people."

I said: "You are telling me that Jessie occupies a rather

special position in this household and because of that it is not easy to get rid of her."

"Well, she would have to go if I told her to. That could be arranged."

"And you want me to get your lawyers to do that."

"No. Oh dear me, no. I don't want to be rid of Jessie. I don't know what I'd do without her. . . . It is just for the will."

"And yet . . ."

"I told you it would be difficult for you to understand, didn't I? I am very fond of ladies. I always have been . . . from the age of about fourteen. I could not imaging my life without them. There were always ladies. I led a wild life. I had had a dozen mistresses by the time I was twenty. I am sorry. I am shocking you but you must understand. I don't want to upset Jessie. She means a great deal to me. My . . . comforts depend on her. But I don't want trouble and she can't have Eversleigh, can she? Can you imagine all those irate ancestors of our rising up against me? I'd be struck down before I could put pen to paper. Well, there is family pride in me too. No . . . Eversleigh for the Eversleighs. The long line must not be broken."

"I think I begin to understand, Uncle Carl."

"That is good. You may have heard about Felicity, my wife. . . . I was forty when we met. I loved her dearly. She was twenty two. Five years we were together. I was different then . . . the model husband . . . never wanted to stray from my own fireside. Then we were going to have a child. That seemed perfection. She died and the child with her. That was the lowest point of despair I have ever known."

"I'm sorry, uncle. I had heard of that."

"A common tragedy perhaps. Well, what did I do? I pulled myself out of my misery and went back to what I had been before Felicity came into my life. Women. . . . They had to be there, I couldn't do without them. There were always women. My namesake, that other uncle Carl of yours, the general, didn't approve of me at all. I should have been managing the estate after Leigh died and he had to do it because I wouldn't leave my life in London. He was an army man. . . . He hadn't the same feel for the place that had gone into it. And then when he died I changed again. I saw my duty. And suddenly I thought I'd come into my own . . . so I came back. I got quite fond of the place. You do, you know. All those ancestors hanging around in frames . . . they become part of you. I began to take a pride in old Eversleigh . . . and see what a fine thing it was for the old house to stand all those years in the same family . . . while we of frailer stuff than bricks and stone pass on. I had a good manager in Amos Carew. And then Jessie came along. I saw in Jessie that which had always attracted me in a woman . . . a sort of readiness . . . a sort of understanding that passes between you. You want the same thing and you're of one mind about it. You wouldn't understand that, dear child. You are so different. Jessie and I were like old friends from the start. She has given me a lot of pleasure."

"She runs the household."

"She is the housekeeper, you know."

"But . . . she seems to control everything."

"Myself, you mean."

"Well, I have to come when she is . . . sleeping."

"That's because I wouldn't want her upset. I don't want her to know about this will."

"She surely doesn't believe that she is going to inherit this house."

"She may think it could come to that. It couldn't possibly, of course, but I don't want her upset. So I want you to find some way of getting the lawyers here. If you could get into town and explain to them. I'll draw up what I want and you can take it in. Then they can come here with witnesses to do the signing . . . during an afternoon."

"I expect it could be managed."

"But Jessie mustn't know. It would make her really angry."

I was silent and he put his hand over mine. "Don't think hardly of Jessie. She's what she is and so am I . . . and so perhaps are we all. She brings me comfort in my old age. I couldn't do without her. I know a great deal about her . . . how she must seem to someone like you. But I want you to arrange this for me. I shall leave this house to you. I want you to have it because you're Carlotta's granddaughter. Carlotta was the loveliest creature I ever saw. Mind you, your mother was the daughter of that rogue Hessenfield, one of the greatest Jacobites of the times. But Carlotta was a wonderful creature. Beautiful . . . wild . . . passionate. I saw her only as a child but I recognized it all. I never forgot her. You remind me of her in a way. It's your eyes—that deep blue, almost violet. I remember hers were that color. She wanted to marry some rake who'd fascinated her. They used to meet at Enderby. . . . That was the story. Then he disappeared . . . very mysteriously. . . . There were a lot of rumors later on. Some said he was murdered and his body lies under the ground somewhere at Enderby. Oh, there were a great many stories about her. I often think about her . . . now I'm so much confined to my bed. She was so full of life . . . and so beautiful. And she died so young . . . she couldn't have been more than in her early twenties. . . . I often think about that. I'm old . . . ready to go, you might say. I've had my life. How do those feel who are cut off in the prime of youth and beauty . . . a whole life before them . . . and then . . . no more. I wonder someone like that doesn't try to come back . . . and finish her life. . . . You're thinking I'm a strange old man. Well, I am, I suppose. It's lying here . . . having time to think."

I said: "I'm glad I came."

"I can't tell you how glad I am. And you'll do this for me. You will . . . discreetly, I mean."

"I will do what I can. Will you draw up what you want to say and give it to me? I'll take it to the lawyer and they can prepare what they have to. And then there'll have to be the signatures. It'll have to be done here, I suppose. Is there anyone who could do it? Jethro . . ."

"No, not Jethro. I shall be leaving him something and I think therefore it's against the rules for anyone who is a beneficiary to sign. It has to be a disinterested party. You can find out from the lawyers."

"Well," I said, "the first thing for you to do is write the

instructions and then I will get them to the lawyer to be drawn up. After that we'll arrange about the signing."

"I can see you are a practical young woman."

"Can I find pen and paper somewhere?"

"In the desk."

I brought it to him and he started to write.

I took my seat by the window. I wondered whether Jessie might return early, for it was possible that she might be uneasy on account of my being in the house. Also there was Evalina. I was sure that child was a practiced spy.

I thought, what a strange situation I had walked into, and wondered what would have happened if Jean-Louis had been with me. I was sure he would have taken over the management of this matter with quiet efficiency.

Uncle Carl was writing steadily. All was quiet. I listened to the clock on the wall ticking the minutes away. There was a feeling of unreality in the air.

I looked back at the bed. Uncle Carl smiled at me.

"Here it is, my dear. If you take that in to Rosen, Stead and Rosen and tell them that's what I want we'll go on from there. Rosen, Stead and Rosen," he repeated. "They are in the town. You can't miss them. Number Eighty, The Street. There's only one street worthy of the name."

I took the paper.

"Come and sit by my bed," he said. "Tell me about your husband. He manages Clavering, I know."

"Yes, he has done so since the manager died. That was when we were married ten years ago."

"This is a very large estate. Carew's a good man, I believe. But it's always better when the landowner himself takes an active part. It makes it more of a family affair . . . if you know what I mean. These estates in England have always been run by the great families who regard their workpeople as a responsibility. The good ones have always taken an interest. I came to realize that . . . and when I did it was too late. I know the people regret the departure of my predecessors. The old ones talk a lot about them. I neglected my duty, Zipporah. I know it now."

"Well, you have this good manager and you are trying to put your affairs in order."

He nodded. "I've been an old reprobate . . . an old sinner. Sins come home to roost, Zipporah. At least I've had a long life . . . not like poor Carlotta."

I said I thought that Jessie would be stirring soon—a polite way of expressing what I meant. It only wanted a quarter to four.

I leaned over the bed and kissed his forehead. I did not want to be caught by Jessie with the papers in my hand. I tapped them significantly. "I will deal with these," I said, "and I'll see you later . . . alone."

He smiled at me and I went out.

The first thing to do was to hide the papers. I pondered for a while and finally decided to put them in the pocket of a rather voluminous skirt which was hanging in the cupboard. It would only be for a short while as I must get them to the lawyer at the earliest possible moment.

I sat by the window and saw Jessie return to the house, looking rather flushed and pleased, so the session must have been a good one. I imagined her telling her lover about my arrival and I wondered what they said about it. I was getting to get a clear picture. Jessie was obviously feathering her nest and, as Jethro said, Lordy was supplying the feathers. Jessie, devoted to the pleasures of the flesh, was determined to enjoy them—relying on Uncle Carl and Amos to supply her needs. I believed she was very shrewd and would have considered the possible impermanence of her position; no doubt she was endeavoring to prolong this very desirable way of life.

While I was ruminating there was a tap on my door and Jessie herself came in. She was elaborately dressed and must have spent the hour since her return on what I imagined must be a somewhat intricate operation.

She was smiling broadly and I did not think she could

possibly have an inkling of what had happened during her absence.

"Supper is about fifteen minutes past six," she said. "I see to Lordy at six and that gives me time to make sure he is all right before partaking myself. I shall be taking his up now . . . so can you be at the table shortly? There's suckling pig." Her mouth watered and her eyes glistened at the mention of the food. "It's best served piping hot."

I said I would be on time; and she gave me a little push.

"That's it," she said. "I can see you're one of the punctual ones. I never could abide them as kept good food getting cold just because they couldn't be at the table on time. Had a good afternoon? Manage to entertain yourself, did you?"

There was a shrewd glitter in her eyes and she was waiting as though for me to tell her. I felt a cold shiver run through me. This woman, I felt sure, was not quite what she seemed. I had to work hard to prevent my eyes straying to the cupboard.

I said coolly: "I had a very pleasant afternoon, thank you. Did you?"

"I did. There's nothing like a spell of bed in the afternoons."

I nodded and turned away.

"All right then," she said. "See you at supper."

And she was gone.

How could Uncle Carl endure such a woman? I wondered. But then people had strange tastes, and there was no accouting for them.

I went to the winter parlor precisely at a quarter past six. Jessie was there and with her Evalina.

"He's enjoying the suckling pig," said Jessie. "It's nice to see him take an interest in his food."

We sat down and fortunately Jessie was so intent on doing justice to the business of eating that she did not talk as much as usual.

Evalina said: "Do you like fairs, Mistress Ransome?"

"Fairs?" I said. "Oh yes, I do."

"We have one here twice a year. It's coming next week."

"Oh, that's interesting."

"The noise!" said Jessie. "And the mess they make! Farmer Brady will go on for weeks about the rubbish they leave behind. They have the common land close to some of Brady's fields. He don't like it much. People come from miles around."

"I like it," said Evalina. "There are fortune-tellers. Do you believe in fortune-tellers, Mistress Ransome?"

"I believe them when they tell me something good," I said, "but am inclined to disbelieve if it is bad."

"That's not very clever. If they tell you something bad you should be warned."

"But what's the good if it is written in the stars?" I said lightly.

Evalina regarded me with round eyes. "So you don't believe in being warned."

"I did not say that. But if a fortune-teller is telling the future and that is destined for you, how can I change it?"

Jessie paused in her chewing and said: "The servants will be there . . . the whole houseful of them. All through the day . . . you see."

"Will you be here for it, Mistress Ransome?" asked Evalina. "When is it?"

"The end of next week. They come on Thursday and stay there till Saturday night."

They were both watching me intently, I fancied.

"So much will depend," I said. "I can't stay very long. My husband would have been with me, you know, if he had not broken his leg. I shall have to get back. You understand."

"I understand perfectly, dearie," said Jessie. "You want to see your old uncle . . . and my goodness what a pleasure seeing you has given him . . . but at the same time you're worried about that husband of yours. I understand."

"I shall see. . . . I may have to go back."

Jessie was smiling at me intently.

"Whatever you say suits me, and I'm only too sorry that I didn't know you was coming and we gave you such a poor welcome. Whatever must you have thought of me!"

"It is my turn to understand," I said.

"Then we're all happy," said Jessie. "I'll have another slice of that pig... what about you?"

When the meal was over I rose and said I would take a stroll in the garden before going to bed.

"I reckon you're still tired from the journey," said Jessie soothingly.

I might be, but my mind was too full of strange impressions for me to be sleepy. I went up and sat for a while at my window while various images chased themselves round and round in my head. I felt as though I had been catapulted out of a sane world into one which was vaguely bizarre.

I thought of Sabrina's saying that she thought she detected a cry for help in Uncle Carl's letter. It *was* a cry for help in a way, though he was in no physical danger. On the other hand I had a feeling that Jessie could be capable of a great deal of deception and roguery to get her way, but unless Uncle Carl made a will in her favor—though even she must know that in view of the estates involved it would be unthinkable for him to do such a thing—it was better for her to keep him alive, for only as long as he lived could she enjoy this sybaritic existence. But that he should be obliged to go about the matter of making his will in this secretive manner was monstrous. He was afraid of a housekeeper—well, a little more than a housekeeper! It was amazing in what situations people's sexual desires could involve them.

I would try to complete this matter of the will as soon as I could. Then I would go home and consult with Jean-Louis. Perhaps I could get him to come to Eversleigh for a visit and see the state of affairs for himself. After all, if I were going to inherit our lives would be disrupted and it might mean that as Eversleigh would be of greater importance than Clavering we should have to come and live here. I believed that was what Uncle Carl would really want if he made me the heiress of the Eversleigh estates.

It would be a great upheaval in our lives and one I am sure which Jean-Louis would not want.

In the meantime I felt that my uncle should be rescued from this harpy. But how did one set about rescuing someone who so clearly did not want to be rescued?

Let well alone, perhaps, was the best thing. Go back home and hope that Uncle Carl lived on for many years.

I put on a cloak and went out of the house. The gardens were still beautiful though somewhat neglected. I looked back at the house and wondered if I were being watched from the windows. The thought made me shiver. Yes, I should be glad when I had completed the business and was on my way home. It was possible that when I moved out of the picture I would be able to see it more clearly. After all, what was it but an old man who had been something of a rake in his youth, and was still trying to be one, with a voluptuous housekeeper who was trying to get what she could while the state of affairs lasted and to satisfy her physical needs, which I imagined must be overwhelming, took a lover at the same time.

A sordid situation, perhaps, but not such an unusual one. Certainly not one to give a practical woman—as I prided myself I was—this feeling of menace.

I wanted to get away from those windows which seemed like so many prying eyes. I walked to the edge of the garden and through the shrubbery.

It was a pleasant evening. The sun was just beginning to set—a great red ball in the western sky. The clouds were tinged with pink merging into a fiery red.

I remembered an old rhyme.

> Sky's red,
> Billy's dead
> Fine day tomorrow

It was invariably right. Such a sky heralded a warm day to come. But who was Billy? I wondered, and why should they sing so happily about his death?

Death! Carlotta had died young. How uncle did brood on her! He must have been greatly impressed when he saw her.

She was a legend in the family. Someone admired for her beauty, and the hope was always there that none of the girls would take after her. None had, presumably. Carlotta had been unique. She had lived here, though she had died in Paris.

Strange . . . in these fields and lanes many years ago Carlotta had once walked when she was in her early teens. She used to go over to Enderby and there met her lover. They had carried on their passionate liaison there—and he was murdered in time . . . deservedly, and his body buried somewhere nearby.

I found my footsteps were leading me toward Enderby.

It was not very far. Ten minutes' walk—perhaps even less. I would walk to the house and then back. The air might make me sleepy, and I should be back just when it was beginning to get really dark.

I could see the house in the distance . . . a shadowy building in declining light, for the sun had now disappeared below the horizon and the clouds were fast losing their rosy glow.

I had come to that stretch of land close by the house which had once been a rose garden. Some of the bushes still remained. They were tall and overgrown but the flowers still bloomed on them. Few people had gone there in the old days. It had been said to be haunted. It was somewhere in that patch that the remains of Carlotta's murdered lover lay. It had been fenced in at one time when it had been a rose garden but the fence was now broken down in several places. I don't know what prompted me to step over the broken pales, but I did so.

There was a hushed feeling in the air—no wind at all, just a silence so deep that I was immediately aware of it. I took a few steps among the overgrown trees and then I saw what I took to be an apparition.

So startled was I that I gasped in dismay and felt myself turn cold as a shiver ran through me. A man was standing a few yards from me. It was as though he had risen from the ground.

He was splendid. I did not meet many elegant men in the country but my father had been noted for his attention to dress, and I recognized at once that this apparition must be attired in the height of fashion, although I had no idea what that was.

His coat was full, spreading round him; it was velvet in a shade of mulberry as far as I could see in the fading light; it had huge cuffs which turned back from the wrists almost to the elbows. Beneath the coat was a waistcoat heavily embroidered, fringed and laced, open to show a white cravat, a mass of frills. His wig was a profusion of white curls and on top of this he wore a cocked hat.

He took a few steps toward me. My impulse was to run but my limbs seemed numb and I was unable to move.

He spoke then. "Are you real?" he said. "Or one of the ghosts that are said to haunt this place?"

He took off his hat and bowed gracefully in a manner which was a little different from that to which I was accustomed. I noticed that he spoke with a faint accent which was not English.

I heard myself stammer: "I was thinking that of you. You seemed to rise out of the ground."

He laughed. "I was kneeling searching for a fob I had dropped. See . . . my eyeglass is attached to it." He waved the eyeglass before me. "It's a cursed nuisance to be without a fob and I doubt I can get a new one here. On my knees I was and then suddenly . . . I perceived an apparition."

"Oh," I said with a laugh. "I am so pleased that there is a logical explanation."

A faint odor of sandalwood wafted toward me. I could not explain what had happened but from the moment I met him I was possessed by an extraordinary excitement which was quite alien to me. It really was as though I had suddenly become some other than quiet, practical Zipporah.

"I'm afraid I shall have to give up the search for the time being," he said. He looked up at the sky.

"It will shortly be too dark to see anything," I agreed.

"A clear sky and there will be a crescent moon. But as you say, too dark to find anything in the grass."

There was a brief silence between us and I said: "Good

night. I must be getting home. Good luck with the fob. Perhaps in the morning . . ."

He had moved round me, almost as though he were barring my way.

"Home?" he asked. "Where is that?"

"I was referring to Eversleigh Court, where I am staying. Lord Eversleigh is a kinsman of mine. I am here on a visit."

"Visitors both. I am here . . . *en passant* too."

"Oh . . . where do you stay?"

He waved his hand. "Close by. The name of the house is Enderby."

"Oh . . . Enderby!"

"Oh yes, a haunted house, they say. My hosts snap their fingers at ghostly legends. Do you?"

"I have had very little concern with them."

"You have some way to go back."

"It's only a short walk."

"You are allowed out . . . so late."

I laughed, a little uneasily, for there was something about this encounter which was disturbing me a great deal. "I am not a young girl," I said. "I'm a married woman."

"And your husband allows . . . ?"

"My husband is at the moment a long way from here. I am just on a brief visit and shall return very soon, I imagine."

"Then I think," he said, "that you should allow me to escort you to Eversleigh Court."

"Thank you," I said.

He put out a hand to help me over the broken pales and gripped my arm tightly. "They could be dangerous in the dark," he said.

"Very few people come here in the dark. They wouldn't dare."

"We are brave, eh?"

"When I saw you rise up so suddenly I felt far from brave."

"And when I saw you I was overcome by excitement. At last a ghost, I said to myself. But I will tell you this: I am relieved that you are flesh and blood after all . . . which is so much more interesting, don't you agree? than the stuff that ghosts must be made of."

I agreed. "So you are visiting the owners of Enderby," I went on. "I don't know who they are. The place changes hands now and then, I believe."

"My friends are not at the house now. They have allowed me to stay there—with their staff of servants—while I have to be in England."

"It is only for a short time, you say?"

"A few weeks possibly. It is very convenient for me to have this house for my stay here."

"You are here on...business?"

"Yes...on business."

"Don't you find Enderby isolated...for business?"

"I find it very much to my taste."

"They say it's gloomy...ghostly...."

"Ah, but I have some very pleasant neighbors, I discover."

"Oh...who are they?"

He stopped and, laying his hand on my arm, smiled at me. I could see the gleam of very white teeth and felt again that faint embarrassment.

"A delightful lady whom I shall always think of as my very own specter."

"You mean me. Oh...well, we are scarcely neighbors. Birds of passage, shall we say?"

"That is a very interesting thing to be."

"So you don't know anyone at Eversleigh Court? Lord Eversleigh? The housekeeper...?"

"I know no one. I am a stranger here."

"How long have you been here?"

"A week."

"You have beaten me. I shall have been here a day and night."

"How fortunate that we met so soon."

That remark disturbed me so I decided not to pursue it.

I was faintly relieved and yet disappointed to see that we had come to the edge of the Eversleigh gardens.

"I am back now," I said. "Through the shrubbery and then across the lawns to the house. Thank you for escorting me . . . I do not know your name."

"It is Gerard d'Aubigné."

"Oh . . . you are . . . French?"

He bowed.

"You are thinking that perhaps in view of the relations between our countries I should not be here."

I shrugged my shoulders. "I know little of politics."

"I am glad. Could you tell me your name?"

"Zipporah Ransome."

"Zipporah! What a beautiful name."

"Its only distinction is that Moses' wife had it before me."

"Zipporah," he repeated.

"Good night."

"Oh, I must take you through the shrubbery."

"It's perfectly safe."

"I should feel happier."

I was silent as we walked through the trees, and then we were onto the lawn.

I turned rather determinedly and firmly said "Good night" again. I wondered what would be said if I were seen bringing him across the lawn to the house.

"Au revoir," he answered, taking my hand and kissing it.

I withdrew it quickly and ran across the lawn.

I was so disturbed that I had forgotten Uncle Carl's will and it was sometime after I had been in my room that I thought of the papers. I immediately went to the cupboard to reassure myself that they were still there. They were.

What a strange encounter that had been! I couldn't stop thinking of him. A Frenchman. Perhaps that accounted for the elegance and strangeness, yet the manner in which he had risen from nowhere was explained by the lost fob. But it had certainly given me a shock at the time and I supposed I hadn't recovered from that during the entire encounter.

I undressed thoughtfully; I was wide awake. My walk had done little to induce sleep. Everything about me was taking on an unreality. I could hardly believe that I had not been two nights in this place yet. I felt a sudden desire to be home where everything was quiet, and strange things did not happen.

I locked my door and went to the window to draw back the curtains as I liked to wake to the full light of day. He was standing there on the lawn looking up at the house. He saw me at once and bowed. I felt unable to move for some seconds and stood still, staring at him. He put his fingers to his lips and then threw his hand outward.

For a few seconds we stood still looking at each other. Then I turned abruptly and moved away from the window.

I was trembling, which was foolish; but he had a strange effect on me.

It was, I told myself, because I could not forget the way he had risen before my eyes. It had seemed so uncanny because I suppose it was on that haunted ground that a man was said to have been buried after he was murdered.

I blew out the candle and got into bed. But sleep evaded me. I kept going over the events of the day. I thought of Uncle Carl and his instructions and told myself I must get to the lawyer on the following day. But my nocturnal adventure imposed itself on those early impressions and I found myself going over it detail by detail.

Finally I rose and went to the window. I don't know if I was foolish enough to expect he would still be there. Of course he was not.

I went back to bed but it was nearly dawn before I finally slept.

Lovers' Meetings

When I awoke next morning I had made up my mind how I would act. I would see my uncle at eleven o'clock, for if I failed to do that Jessie's suspicions would be immediately aroused. So I had decided that I would choose the afternoon to go into the town and see Messrs. Rosen, Stead and Rosen. That would give me plenty of time, and when I saw Uncle Carl at eleven o'clock I could drop a hint to him as to when I should be going.

Jessie and Evalina had already breakfasted when I arrived downstairs, but that did not prevent Jessie's coming in to talk to me as I ate and to help herself to a few more tasty morsels.

"You'll be going along to see Lordy at eleven, I suppose," she said.

I told her I would.

"He'll be pleased, poor love. He's so excited you came to visit. I do what I can to amuse him. . . ." I almost steeled myself for the nudge which was fortunately impossible because once

71

more the table separated us, "but you know what it is. He's tired sometimes. . . . Sometimes wanders in his mind a bit."

I wasn't sure of that and had a notion she was safeguarding herself in some way.

However, at eleven I was sitting at Uncle Carl's bedside and I managed to let drop the information that I would explore the town that afternoon.

"It's a good half an hour's walk," said Jessie. "Would you like them to take you in the carriage?"

"No," I said quickly. I did not want any of the grooms reporting to her where I had been. "I would like to explore myself. It's a voyage of remembrance for me. It's like rediscovering my childhood."

"Well, we want you to do just as you like . . . don't we, Lordy?"

Uncle Carl pressed my hand understanding that that afternoon I should pay a call on the lawyers.

I felt I did not have to wait to see Jessie safely in the manager's house for her afternoon rendezvous, but set out soon after one o'clock to walk into the town.

The road passed close to Enderby and I don't think I was altogether surprised to come face to face with Gerard d'Aubigné. In fact I had an idea that he had been watching for me.

He was as elegant in daylight as in twilight and he looked very much the same as he had last night except that his coat was of brown velvet but still in the swinging, almost flaunting, style which gave an impression of a charming aggressiveness.

He bowed and said: "I'll confess I have waylaid you."

"Oh . . . why?"

"Overcome by an urgent desire to see my charming ghost by the light of day. I had a horrible feeling that I might have imagined the encounter."

"Even trespassing on our lawns?" I asked.

"What is a little trespass for a good cause? I had to see that you were safely home. Now where do you wish to go?"

"Actually I am on an errand for my uncle and am going into the town."

"It is quite a long way."

"Nothing much . . . half an hour's walk."

"I have an idea. My hosts have been so good to me. They have a most elegant little carriage . . . suitable for two or at most three including the driver. Two horses pull it along at a spanking pace. I suggest that I drive you into the town."

"That's kind of you but it really isn't necessary."

"Pleasant experiences do not have to be necessary. I should be desolate if you denied me this. I have used the carriage once or twice. It is an enchanting little vehicle. Come into the stables here and I will make it ready. We can be in town in less than half the time that it would take to walk and you will arrive fresh for your business."

I hesitated and he immediately placed his arm through mine and drew me toward the house.

The mystery of Enderby seemed to envelop me—or was it his presence? I had never felt quite like this before . . . this excitement, this feeling that something very unusual was going to happen to me.

Enderby looked gloomy even in afternoon sunshine. There was no one in the stables and I was amazed by the deftness with which he made the carriage ready.

The two bay mares pawed the ground as though impatient to be off. He patted first one and then the other.

"Yes, old girls," he said, "you know this is a special occasion, don't you?"

Then he turned to me and helped me into the carriage, himself taking the driver's seat.

Side by side we rattled along at a good speed. I sat back feeling as though I were in a dream, listening to the clop clop of the mares' hooves and putting a wary hand on the papers in my pocket to make sure that they were still there.

We pulled up at an inn and there we alighted. He asked me where I had to go and when I told him said he would take me there, leave me, and if I would come to the inn when I had finished my business he would drive me back to Eversleigh.

I agreed to this and, leaving the inn, walked along the main street until we came to the offices of Messrs. Rosen, Stead and Rosen.

An elderly clerk rose to greet me, and when I told him that I came on behalf of Lord Eversleigh and wished to see Mr. Rosen I immediately aroused his interest and was conducted into the reception room. He was sorry to say that Mr. Rosen senior was out of the office for a few days—away on urgent business, but he was sure either Mr. Stead or young Mr. Rosen would be able to help me.

Young Mr. Rosen—who seemed anything but young to me, being a man in his middle forties—came in to greet me and when I explained why I had come, he took me into his private office and glanced at the instructions Uncle Carl had given me. He nodded. "I understand," he said. "My father will be upset at not being here to meet you. He deals with all Lord Eversleigh's business; but this seems to be a straightforward matter of the will so it will present no problems. I will call on him myself," he went on. "I can bring one of the clerks with me to witness it. What is the best time?"

I felt embarrassed and said: "Oh . . . you cannot come to the house. That would not be a very good idea."

He looked puzzled and I hurried on. "Lord Eversleigh does not want . . . people at the house . . . to know that he has made this will. It is for this reason that he invited me to come to Eversleigh and . . . er . . . arrange it for him." I hurried on: "Are you aware of the state of affairs at Eversleigh Court?"

It was his turn to look faintly embarrassed. "I understand the estate is well managed and there is a housekeeper there."

I decided that it was no time for veiled hints and said: "Do you know of the relationship between Lord Eversleigh and the housekeeper?"

He coughed and said: "Well . . ."

"The fact is," I went on, "there is a very special friendship between them. I don't know whether she has pretensions as to

74

what will be left to her but Lord Eversleigh wishes the estate to remain in the family."

"But naturally. It would be unthinkable . . ."

"At the same time he does not wish to offend his house-keeper. Apparently he relies on her."

"I see . . . I see. So he does not wish it to be known that he is making this will."

"Exactly."

"And he is obviously not able to come into town to sign it."

"I'm afraid not. It will have to be done at the house. I have not really thought how that can be brought about. It must be done in the housekeeper's absence . . . that is Lord Eversleigh's wish."

"If you like to name a time . . ."

"I must think about it. Perhaps one afternoon. In the mean-time if you will draw up the will I can consult Lord Eversleigh and see what arrangements we can arrive at. I'm afraid you must find this rather an odd situation."

"My dear lady, in my profession we are constantly con-fronted by unusual situations."

He smiled at me and went on: "I should like my father to deal with this matter. He has always taken charge of Lord Eversleigh's affairs and knows more about what goes on at the Court than I do."

"He is not here, though."

"No, but I am expecting him back tomorrow. He will know the best way of dealing with the matter."

"Thank you."

"Perhaps you would look in again the day after tomorrow. I am sure the work will be done then and you will be able to see my father."

This I agreed to do.

As he said good-bye he asked me if I had ridden into the town. "It's quite a step from the Court," he added. I told him that a neighbor had driven me in and would take me back. That satisfied him, so I left the office and made my way to the inn.

Gerard d'Aubigné was waiting for me and he greeted me with the news that he had taken the opportunity of ordering a tankard of cider apiece. "They have some good cakes straight from the oven—the innkeeper's wife assures me—and I thought you would like a short rest before driving back."

"That's good of you." I said, and he led me into the inn parlor, where the hot cakes were already being put on a table with two tankards of cider.

"Was the business successful?" he asked.

"As successful as I could hope."

"You sound as though it was not entirely so."

"It's not completed, of course." The cider was cool, a little heady, I thought; but perhaps that was the company, and rather to my surprise I found myself telling him the story.

"It sounds so absurd . . . when one speaks of it in the light of day."

"Not at all absurd. Of course Lord Eversleigh cannot leave his estates to his Jessie; and of course he doesn't want her to know he's leaving them to someone else. It's perfectly understandable."

"But it seems so ridiculous. There is a peer of the realm, a man of substance . . . and he is afraid of his housekeeper!"

"Afraid of losing her. That is very different from being afraid of her. I'm afraid that you may disappear as suddenly as you came, but I'm certainly not afraid of you."

"Oh. I thought it was clear now that I'm an ordinary mortal."

"Far from ordinary," he said. "Now tell me about it . . . the life with the good husband whom you so regretted you must leave behind."

And I found myself telling him.

He listened very carefully as I, who was usually restrained told him of my wonderful father who had been killed in a duel, and how, ever since, we had lived quietly in the country and that I had married the companion of my childhood as everybody had expected and hoped I would.

"Do you always do what is expected of you?" he asked.

"Yes . . . I think perhaps I do."

"That must please them all very much . . . but the main thing is that you should be pleased, is it not?"

"It has all worked out very well and happily for me," I said.

He raised his eyebrows and smiled at me in a manner I did not understand and vaguely felt that it was better so.

"And you?" I said. "What of you?"

"Ah, like you I doubtless do what is expected of me. Alas, it is not always the good thing that is expected."

"And your home is in France. What part?"

"My home is in the country—a small place a few leagues from Paris—but I spend most of my time in Paris and am chiefly at court."

"You serve the king."

"We of the court of France do not so much serve the king as the king's mistress. The lady is the mistress of us all—by which I mean that we must obey her whims if we would remain in favor . . . not, of course, that we are the lady's lovers. The king is enough for her. She is by no means as lusty as your Jessie."

"Who is this lady?"

"Jeanne Antoinette Poisson . . . otherwise the Marquise de Pompadour." He spoke with a certain amount of bitterness, which I was quick to detect.

"I gather that you do not like the lady overmuch."

"One does not like the Pompadour . . . one merely does not offend her."

"I am surprised. You do not appear to me to be a meek man, to obey someone . . . someone of whom you obviously do not approve."

"I have a great desire to hold my place at court. I should not wish to be banished from a way of life which I find most interesting."

"The court, you mean."

"The affairs of the country," he said, smiling at me.

"So you are cautious."

"When there is need to be, yes. Mind you, I am of the nature to like to take a risk now and then."

77

"I hope you are not a gambler," I said, and suddenly I thought of my father's being carried into the house mortally wounded.

He put his hand over mind.

"You look really concerned," he said.

"No . . . of course not. It is no business of mine." I added: "Are you here on a diplomatic mission?"

"I am here," he said, "because it may be some time before I shall get an opportunity of being here again. If there is war between our countries . . ."

"War!"

"It's blowing up, you know. Then traffic is difficult."

"What war?"

"Perhaps it won't happen, but Frederick of Prussia is getting aggressive and Maria Theresa of Austria wants to get Silesia from him."

"Why should that concern us . . . your country and mine?"

"We the French have great friendship with Maria Theresa, and your King George is more German that English. You can be sure he will side with Frederick. Then we have a war and our countries will be enemies."

"I believe you are here on some secret mission," I said.

"Ah, I am arousing your interest at last."

"Are you . . . here on some secret matter?"

"I am going to say yes because then you will think how mysterious I am . . . how interesting."

"But if it is not so?"

"If it were you would not expect me to tell you, would you?" He changed the subject abruptly. "You may have to come back here the day after tomorrow. I am going to drive you."

"Oh . . . thank you."

Then he said: "We shall put our heads together and find out how we get the papers signed."

"Are you thinking that my business is almost as devious as yours?"

78

"Exactly that. You see why we are drawn together. Birds of a feather . . . is that what you say?"

So we talked until I realized that time was flying and I said I must go. I wished to be back before Jessie returned.

I sat up beside him as we drove back, and listening to the ringing of the horses' hooves on the road and sitting close to him so that his velvet jacket often touched my arm I realized that I was enjoying this with a different kind of emotion from any I had known before.

We arranged that on the day after tomorrow we should go into the town and collect the will. Then there would be the problem of getting it signed. I should have to think about that.

"Don't despair," he said. "I could slip into the house with my valet. It wouldn't be safe to ask any of the servants at Eversleigh. Who knows, they might be one of Jessie's spies?"

We laughed together. The whole affair seemed a tremendous joke. He talked about the conspiracy in a hollow voice, building up such a story of intrigue suggesting the most villainous motives for Jessie and the estate manager, whom he called her paramour, that we were quite hilarious, making the most wild suggestions in mock serious tones.

All too soon we arrived back at Eversleigh.

"The day after tomorrow then we escape into the town to collect the papers," whispered Gerard.

I agreed that we should.

"I shall see you then . . . unless you should stroll towards Enderby . . . or I should happen to be near Eversleigh way tomorrow."

I hesitated. "I have to see my uncle. Let us make it the day after tomorrow. We must be careful."

He put his fingers to his lips. "Take care," he whispered. "The enemy may be on our trail."

Then we were laughing again and I felt quite ridiculously happy in a way which I didn't remember feeling before.

I was behaving in a way very unlike my usual custom, and with a stranger. I should have been wary then, but I had not yet begun to know myself.

* * *

I did not see him next day. After we parted that strange mood of exultation left me and the matter of my uncle's will no longer seemed the joke it had as we drove back from the town. It was just a sordid matter of an old man being besotted about a younger woman and so dependent on her that he had to bribe her to stay with him.

I began to feel I had been rather indiscreet to have told so much to someone I hardly knew. But when I was with him I felt that I knew him very well. I felt a closeness . . . an intimacy.

Looking back I realize how unsophisticated I must have been not to realize what was happening.

However, perhaps I did feel faintly uneasy, for the next day I did not stroll down to Enderby, and if he came near Eversleigh I did not see him, for I did not go beyond the closed-in gardens.

I saw my uncle during the morning with Jessie present nibbling her sweetmeats and looking, I thought, even more pleased with herself than usual. During that morning session we had a caller. It was Amos Carew, and he came up to my uncle's bedroom while I was there so I had an opportunity to study him.

He had bright dark eyes and a very curly beard and lots of dark curly hair. A hairy man. That was how I would describe him to Gerard when we next met. I smiled inwardly at the prospect.

My uncle clearly thought highly of Amos Carew.

"Here you are, Amos. This is my . . . well, we haven't quite worked out the relationship, but her mother is, I think, my nearest relation and so we call each other niece and uncle. That is a title which fits a lot of relationships even when it is not entirely accurate."

"Well, I'm pleased to meet you, madam," said Amos Carew. He took my hand and squeezed it in a manner which was decidedly painful. I thought he was going to crack my bones.

"I have heard of you," I said, "so it is a pleasure to meet you."

He laughed. Amos Carew laughed a great deal, I soon noticed. He had a variety of laughs—overhearty, deprecating, just amused. It could be due to nervousness, but no. I didn't think he would ever be nervous. Cautious perhaps . . .

"His lordship likes me to pop in now and then to give him an account of things."

"Yes, of course," I said. "I am sure the estate is of great interest to him."

"Well, it's hard for his lordship." The little laugh followed the words. Sympathetic this time, I thought. "Cooped up, you might say," he went on. "And he was always a one for the outdoor life, wasn't that so, your lordship?"

"Ah yes, I liked being out. Walking . . . fishing . . ."

"What you would call an all-round sportsman, eh, pet?" Jessie looked at Amos and a significant glance passed between them. Amos laughed again. This time appreciation for a sportsman coupled with sympathy for his present plight.

"I would like you to show my . . . er . . . niece something of the estate sometimes, Amos."

"Gladly, my lord."

"Well, you must take her on the rounds. Would you like that, Zipporah?"

"Very much," I said.

"You'll get some notion of the size of it. I think you'll find it a good deal bigger than your Clavering." He turned to Amos. "My niece's husband should have come with her," he went on, "but was prevented by an unfortunate accident. Next time . . . he'll be with her."

"That will be right and proper, my lord."

"Yes."

I listened to them talking about the estate. Uncle Carl seemed intent on taking it all in and now and then would throw a glance at me. I also listened with interest because Jean-Louis often talked to me about the difficulties at Clavering so I understood what they were talking about.

When Amos Carew said he must go Jessie conducted him to the door. I was watching them in a mirror and I saw her whisper something to him.

There's some sort of conspiracy going on, I thought. Then I laughed at myself. Gerard with his mock seriousness and his jokes had made me see something in this situation which was nothing more than a besotted man and a grasping woman, who, while she played the role of my uncle's mistress, was in fact conducting a love affair with his manager.

At dinner I thought Jessie seemed particularly pleased with herself and went off rather earlier than usual for her rendezvous with Amos.

I made my way to my uncle's room, for I felt I had much to tell him.

He was eagerly awaiting me; he looked very much alive and his brown eyes sparkled almost with mischief, I thought.

He took my hand as I bent over to kiss him.

"Sit down, my dear, and tell me what you have done and then . . . I have something to tell *you*."

I immediately explained how I had gone into the town on the previous day and seen the younger Mr. Rosen, who was drawing up the will which I should collect tomorrow.

He nodded. "That is good. Then it must be signed and sent to Rosen. Ha, ha. Poor Jessie. She will get a shock, I fear. But it is the only way."

"But, uncle," I said, "she cannot expect to inherit a large family estate. I am sure she does not."

He laughed. "You don't know Jessie," he said fondly. "Jessie has large ideas. Poor Jess . . . but I've fooled her, I'm afraid. I . . . er . . . signed something . . . yesterday . . . I had to make her happy."

"You signed something!"

He gave me a grin and touched his lips. I thought then that it was just possible he was not quite in possession of his senses.

He said: "You're here now. You've seen Rosen. . . . Well, I thought it was safe to sign something . . . for Jessie."

"You mean . . . a will."

"Well, sort of. Not all drawn up, of course, but Jessie wouldn't know the difference. I've signed a paper dated yesterday that she should have everything . . . the house, the estate . . . all except one or two little legacies which I would think about later."

I was astonished. I really thought I had wandered into a madhouse.

"Uncle Carl!" I cried in dismay.

"Now don't scold. I like to see her happy. That letter will satisfy her and stop her getting at me, and it'll become null and void when I sign my will because that will cancel anything else I have signed previously. That's something to tell Rosen."

I sat back in my chair gazing at him in wonder.

He looked at me almost pathetically and said: "I always liked a peaceful life and I've found out that you can get it with a few promises . . . as long as you cover your tracks, you see. I've signed Jessie's paper. She's happy. I'm happy. We're all happy. She'll get a shock . . . but only when I'm not here to see it."

I was silent. It really was turning out to be a grotesque situation.

The next day Gerard d'Aubigné drove me into the town and I saw Mr. Rosen senior this time. He welcomed me warmly and tried to press a glass of wine on me but as I supposed I should be drinking cider at the inn later, I declined. He had drawn up the will, shaken his head gravely over what he called "the situation at the Court" and when I told him that Uncle Carl had already signed what he called "something" which was in favor of Jessie, he was horrified.

"We must get this will signed as soon as possible," he said. "Mind you, we should contest any letter that woman produced, but to get the will signed and sealed and put into security here is the safest way of dealing with the situation. In view of what you have told me I think I should return with you and my assistant can witness Lord Eversleigh's signature."

"I am sure he would be most distressed if you did. I know it sounds ridiculous, but if you came to the house the shock would be so great for him that I would fear the consequences. He is really deeply devoted to this woman and I am sure it is only some inborn sense of duty to his family which makes him refrain from leaving everything to her. He relies on her. It is incongruous and if I hadn't seen it for myself I should not have believed it. Lord Eversleigh trusts me to do this for him and I must do it in the way he wishes."

Mr. Rosen looked grave.

"How soon could you get him to sign the will and return it to me?"

"I was driven into town by a neighbor. If I could get him with one of his servants to Lord Eversleigh's room and the will was signed, then I could bring it back to you tomorrow."

"Could you do this?"

"I could try."

"Very well . . . though it is unorthodox. I don't like it at all. You say he has signed something for this woman. She must be quite unscrupulous. Lord Eversleigh could be in a dangerous situation."

"You mean that she . . ." I was looking at him in horror and he said gravely: "I do not say that she would shorten his life. But considering the circumstances . . . with someone of that kind . . . not of very high morals, we must admit . . . it could be dangerous." He looked at me quizzically. "It is a very strange case. I have from time to time heard rumors of what is going on at the Court. It was never so in the old days. Everything was in such perfect order. You as a member of the family know that. You understand that the will must be signed by two witnesses who are not beneficiaries. You are one, you know that. I am sure."

"Yes, Lord Eversleigh told me."

"As the daughter of Lady Clavering you are in the line of succession, as it were, and I understand it is Lord Eversleigh's desire that you should inherit the estate. That is natural . . . it is the only course. Your ancestors would rise in their graves if it should pass to that vulgar creature."

"It won't," I said. "I will get the will signed and returned to you tomorrow."

Mr. Rosen senior shook his head doubtfully. It was all very

unethical in his view and I believe he was contemplating even then returning with me and making sure that the will was effectively dealt with.

However, I did impress on him that in view of Uncle Carl's trust in me I must try to do it as he wished. I left him and went back to the inn. There I told Gerard what had happened and he agreed with me that we should return immediately without waiting for refreshment. He would get his valet or one of his trusted servants and we would get the will signed before Jessie's return.

There was just time to do it if we made haste and were lucky.

It was very exciting driving back at full speed and exhilarating too as Gerard talked all the time of how best we could get the will signed quickly and back to the solicitor. It was wonderful the way in which he had made my problem his.

I had thought he dramatized the situation in order to amuse me but he was beginning to convince me that it could be something far removed from a joke: an unscrupulous woman and her lover with a doting old man in their grasp, who, although he was not senile, was really a little unbalanced surely and ready to pay too dearly for peace and comfort in his last days.

Gerard took a watch from his pocket. He said: "We could be back at Enderby just before half past three. I could get my man and we'd go straight to the Court. We'll sneak upstairs and get the will signed and witnessed, and then if you would trust me I would take it back to the solicitors immediately."

"I could take it tomorrow."

"Well, so we could. But in view of the people in that house ...I mean the kind of people they are...the will should be in the solicitor's hands and I don't like the idea of your having it in that house."

"Do you think they would come and murder me to get possession of it?"

"Gad!" he said. "That would be monstrous. I couldn't let

that happen. I would never be happy again for the rest of my life."

I laughed. "You do make the most extravagant statements."

He was silent. Then he said: "Seriously, I am uneasy. Let's try it."

He whipped up the horses and we rattled along to Enderby.

It all happened quickly from then on. It seemed to me a breathtaking mad sort of adventure—different from anything that had ever happened to me before. Gerard took charge and I couldn't help admiring the speed and efficiency with which he arranged everything.

"You are making a diplomatic incident of it," I said.

"I am, after all, a diplomat. But I assure you . . . this is the best and safest way to get this matter settled."

It was still a quarter of an hour to four o'clock when I took the two men to my uncle's bedroom. He expressed little surprise when I introduced them and explained why they had come. I produced the will and the necessary signatures were affixed. Gerard rolled the paper up and put it under his arm.

Uncle Carl patted my hand and said: "Clever girl!"

"And now," said Gerard, "it is for us to get this into town."

"We must go," I said, "quickly."

"Yes," said Uncle Carl, "before Jessie wakes up." He was smiling and his eyes danced with excitement. There was a certain mischief in him and for a fleeting moment I wondered whether he had conjured up the whole thing out of a fairly ordinary situation. In the moment I couldn't believe that even Jessie would hope for an instant that she could inherit Eversleigh Court.

It seemed then that we were all playing a part in some sort of farce which the old man had contrived to make his dull life more exciting.

However, we must continue with it, so we took our leave and went silently down the stairs.

As we came into the hall there was a movement on the stairs. I turned sharply. Evalina was coming down.

"Oh?" she cried. "Have we visitors?"

"This is the housekeeper's daughter," I said to Gerard.

Evalina had run up to us and was smiling innocently at Gerard.

He bowed and turned away and I led them out of the house.

I saw them into the carriage and went back into the house. Evalina was still in the hall.

"I didn't know we had callers," she said. "I know who they are. They're from Enderby."

I went past her. She was looking at me curiously, as though she was waiting for an explanation. I was determined not to give her one. It was so impertinent for the housekeeper's daughter to interrogate me about callers.

I went to my room and to the window. I saw that Jessie was just returning to the house. Evalina would tell her about the callers. She might be suspicious because she was very shrewd. But by this time Gerard would be on his way to the solicitors.

At supper that night there was a faint atmosphere of suspicion which I detected immediately. Jessie ate with her usual gusto then she smiled at me ingratiatingly and said: "Evalina said them people from Enderby called today."

"Just being neighborly," I said.

"They never called before."

"Oh?"

"I reckon they heard you was here. They never called on Lordy before."

I lifted my shoulders.

Evalina said: "One of them was a fine-looking man."

"H'm," I murmured.

She was wary; she was watchful; I could see she was puzzled and did not like the idea of callers.

I escaped to my room immediately after the meal. I wondered whether Gerard had deposited the will with Messrs. Rosen, Stead and Rosen. If he had my mission was accomplished. It was a comfort to think that the documents would be safe at the solicitors' and my responsibility was over.

But I couldn't rest. I had an eerie feeling that there was

something rather sinister building up in this house, that Uncle Carl was aware of it in a way and that he encouraged it. Perhaps he found life dull, confined to his room as he was; perhaps he wanted dramatic things to happen.

I was getting fanciful, and I felt an irresistible desire to get out of the house. I put on my cloak and went out. My steps took me toward Enderby. I wanted to see Gerard, to make sure that he had deposited the will at the solicitors'. If I had his word for this I would sleep more easily.

I paused awhile at the haunted patch looking beyond the broken pales to that spot where he had seemed to rise up from the earth before I went on toward the house. There was definitely something eerie about it. It had such a repelling air that I almost turned and fled. The wind in the trees seemed to be moaning something. If I listened and let loose my imagination I could believe they were saying *Go away*. I had a feeling then that I should go away and I could go into town tomorrow morning and see Mr. Rosen. I could ascertain whether the will had been deposited with them and if it had been, plan to go home at once, my mission accomplished. Should I feel sorry for Uncle Carl in such a situation? I thought not. After all it was of his own making and he clearly wanted it as it was.

He could turn out both Jessie and Amos Carew if he wanted to. The agent could be replaced; and as for Jessie, well, I am sure it would not be difficult to find a good hardworking housekeeper who would run the house and servants as it used to be in the days of my great-grandparents.

While I was musing thus the door opened and a man came out.

He looked surprised to see me and I said quickly: "I wondered if Monsieur Gerard d'Aubigné was at home."

He said he would inquire and, taking me into the hall, went away.

Enderby certainly had what people called atmosphere. One was aware of it on taking the first step inside the place. The great hall with its vaulted ceiling and minstrels' gallery at one end and the screens to the kitchen at the other seemed full of shadows. I remembered that it had always looked like that. It was as though there were ghosts waiting to spring out. One was aware of an impending sense of doom in the house. Happiness never stayed there long, I had heard someone say. I knew my mother's childhood had not been an unhappy one; but that seemed to be the only period when people seemed to live normal lives within those walls.

While I brooded thus Gerard came down the stairs. He ran when he saw me and came toward me, his hands outstretched. He took mine and kissed first one then the other.

"I was expecting you," he said.

"Expecting me?"

"Yes, you wanted to make sure, didn't you? You were tormented with doubts. Should you have trusted me with such a mission? Oh . . . Zipporah, have I not shown you that I will serve you with my life if need be?"

"How you do love to make everything dramatic. Did you deliver the will?"

"To Mr. Rosen senior himself. He studied it, approved and has it in his safekeeping."

"Oh . . . thank you."

He smiled at me quizzically. "You can trust me, you know."

"I know it really. I am just a little anxious. I know we were laughing about it all . . . but I've suddenly felt that it is not such a laughing matter."

"You will have some refreshment?"

"No. I have just had supper. I must get back now."

"Oh, stay awhile." He had taken my hand and was drawing me toward him.

I felt the house beckoning me . . . almost as though it were waiting, drawing me in . . . and I was afraid. All I had ever heard about Enderby seemed to be warning me. Was it a premonition? Perhaps.

"No," I said firmly. "I just wanted to make sure nothing had gone wrong."

He looked disappointed but resigned. "I will walk back with you," he said.

We came out of the house together and I could not suppress a feeling of relief as we walked away from it.

It was growing dark now. It reminded me of the first time we had met. We passed the haunted patch and he pressed my arm.

"A wonderful moment," he said. "That first encounter of ours."

"I don't know how to thank you for what you have done for me."

"There is no need for thanks. I would willingly do anything you asked me."

"That is being a little rash. How do you know what I might ask?"

"The more difficult the request the more I should enjoy it."

"I suppose at the French court you are well versed in extravagant conversation."

"Perhaps, but what I say to you, I mean."

"Well, I am grateful. And I think that now my mission is accomplished I should go home."

"Please don't say that," he said.

"I must go."

"Not yet. I have a feeling that this matter is not yet completed."

"Do you think my uncle is . . . in danger?"

"It has occurred to me. Here is a rapacious woman . . . she thinks she will inherit a big estate. The only thing between her and it is that frail old man in his bed. Think of the temptation. Does Jessie seem the sort of woman who would resist it?"

"I don't know. She seemed rather fond of him."

"She has her lover. . . . Do you think they plan to share Eversleigh between them?"

"I have been thinking that I should be happier if Jessie knew about that will and that whatever she got him to sign will be useless. If she knew this she would certainly not wish to 'shorten his life,' as Mr. Rosen put it. She would keep him alive so that she could go on enjoying what comforts she has now and perhaps feathering her nest."

"That sounds reasonable to me. I think Lord Eversleigh is safe while you are there. She would attempt nothing which you might see. Therefore, you must stay. Your mission is not yet accomplished."

"Do you think I could tell Uncle Carl that he must let Jessie know there is a will with the solicitor?"

"I think so . . . in time. Not just yet. Let him get over all the excitement of today. Do you agree?"

"Perhaps you are right. I am sorry to have involved you in this."

"It has added spice to my visit. I do assure you."

We had come into the shrubbery.

"Good night," I said.

He took my hand and held it for a long time. He was smiling at me in a certain way and I had a great desire to stay there with him.

I should have been warned.

As I went into the house I saw Evalina. She ran past me and up the stairs. At the top she turned back and looked at me almost maliciously.

I thought: That girl is everywhere.

And I went to my room. I knew as soon as one instinctively does that certain things were not quite in the place in which one had left them. I hurriedly went to my cupboard. Now I was sure of it.

I turned the key in the lock of my door and thoughtfully prepared for bed.

Evalina had reported what she had seen and obviously suspicions had been aroused. I was more thankful than ever that Gerard had taken the will to Rosen. If I had kept it it would certainly have been discovered by whoever had searched my room.

That night I had a nightmare. I was in Enderby Hall and suddenly ghosts from the past rose up and came toward me. I put out my hands to hold them off but they came nearer and nearer. And among them was Gerard. . . . There was earth on his clothes and his face was deathly white. He was one of them . . . one of those ghosts from the past.

He had something in his hand. It was a scroll of paper. Uncle Carl's will!

And he began to laugh . . . evilly . . . and all the time his luminous eyes were fixed on me.

Then someone was calling to me. "Danger. . . . Get away while there is time."

I woke up with a terrible start. It had all seemed so real.

I lay staring into the darkness. Who was Gerard? I asked. What did I know of him? When I looked back over the last days my conduct seemed inexplicable. I had formed a friendship with this stranger whom I had known for a few hours when I told him the secrets of my family; I had entrusted him with the will.

I must be losing my senses. The old Zipporah looking accusingly at my new self who had taken on this task and had brought in a stranger to help. What could I have done? I could have written home, I could have told them of the situation here, asked advice. If Jean-Louis was not fit to come, Sabrina could.

That was what the old Zipporah would have done. The new one seemed to have come into being since I had strayed out on that night and Gerard d'Aubigné had risen like a ghost from the haunted ground.

I had made up my mind. Tomorrow I would call in at Rosen, Stead and Rosen and assure myself that the will had indeed been deposited.

This censorious mood directed against my new self persisted during the morning. I did not get a chance to convey anything to my uncle at the eleven o'clock session. Jessie was watching us intently the whole time, but in the afternoon I walked into the town.

Mr. Rosen greeted me with pleasure and I immediately asked him if Monsieur Gerard d'Aubigné had delivered the will yesterday afternoon.

"Indeed yes," he said. "A charming and most helpful gentleman. Now we need have no qualms. Everything is perfectly in order.

I felt ashamed of myself for distrusting Gerard.

I felt worse still when I passed the inn and saw the carriage there.

I was walking hurriedly along the road when I heard it clopping after me.

He pulled up and smiled at me rather roguishly.

"You could have trusted me," he said.

I decided that I would be perfectly frank with him and not pretend that I had gone into the town for some other purpose. "I had to make sure," I said.

"Of course."

He helped me into the carriage.

"And now," he said, "you are satisfied."

"I am, and I do thank you most sincerely for your help."

He smiled as we gamboled along.

It was the day of the fair. I had been seeing Gerard every day. I had felt I had to make some amends for my lack of trust in him and from then on our friendship seemed to grow. I think he must have known that I suffered some qualms of uneasiness, wondering whether it was right for a married woman to see so much of a man who was not her husband. He stressed that we were, as he put it, birds of passage, implying that our association was an interlude in our lives. Very soon we should have to go our separate ways but there was no reason why we should not take with us pleasant memories of our meetings.

I think this acted as a sort of palliative. I would remind myself of it on those occasions when quite suddenly the thought would come to me that my friendship with this man was becoming too deep, too involved and was different from anything that had ever happened to me before.

And so to the day of the fair.

I think the whole of the community must have gone. Jessie went off with Amos Carew. Uncle Carl insisted. He was tired, he said, and wanted to rest. Most of the servants had gone and after the midday meal all those who were not already at the fair left the house.

It was, Jessie had explained to me, the event of the year—or the half year, as it came twice—and everybody had to make the most of it. "You'll be looking in, I daresay," she said to me.

I said that I would.

I had arranged to meet Gerard. He had said nothing about the fair but I figured he would like to have a look at it.

He met me just beyond the shrubbery and our steps led up past Enderby.

He said: "I think everyone from the house has gone to the fair today. It seems so different without them. I'd like to show you the house. Have you ever gone through it?"

"No. I've heard about it but it was sold before I was born. My mother lived there as a girl but her aunt, who had brought her up, died and her husband was heartbroken. He was drowned and I don't think anyone was sure whether it was suicide or an accident. Neither my mother nor her cousin Sabrina, who lives with her, ever wants to talk about it very much."

"Come and take a look," he said.

"I thought you would want to go to the fair."

"I'd rather show you the house. You ought to see it and now that there is no one here there is an opportunity. Besides, it seems different when it's empty. It has a great deal of atmosphere."

He had taken my arm and was drawing me toward the house. I was reminded of my dream when I had fancied something had been warning me. I knew that when I had dreamed that I had imagined I was in that house, but I felt myself drawn on by an irresistible impulse and yet I was aware of another part of myself warning me not to enter that house of ill omen.

He had opened the door and we stood in the hall. It had a vaulted ceiling and fine paneling. I had seen many halls like it and yet there were shadows here. In the stillness I felt my heart start to beat so fast that I could almost hear it. He put an

arm around me. I drew back and he said: "You looked
. . . vulnerable . . . as though you need protection."

I laughed but it sounded hollow. "I am really quite well
able to look after myself."

"I know it." He was looking at me intently. "You would
never do what you did not want to."

My eyes had strayed to the minstrels' gallery.

"Yes," he said, "that's one of the haunted spots. There are
many of them. I've discovered that the servants won't go into
the gallery alone. Come, Zipporah, let us defy the ghosts."

He took my hand and we mounted the stairs.

There was a carved door. It creaked as he opened it.

"Come," he whispered and I stepped with him into the
gallery.

"It's colder up here."

"That's the spirit," he said. "The ghosts come from the
dead."

He took my chin in his hands and looked into my face.

"You're a tiny bit scared," he said. "Oh yes, you are, my
practical commonsensical Zipporah. Confess it, you are a little
affected by Enderby."

"Are you?" I asked.

"To tell you the truth," he said, "I like it. It's no ordinary
house, but who wants an ordinary house? When I am here I
say to myself: Is it true? Do the spirits of those long dead
sometimes return to haunt the scenes of their sins . . . or their
triumphs? Who can be sure? No one can. That's the exciting
thing about it. It's mystery . . . wrapped in mystery, and one is
never sure whether one is going to find the answer. Don't you
find that fascinating?"

"Yes, of course."

We stood at the rail looking down at the hall. "It's full of
shadows," he said. "Why?"

"Because of the trees and shrubs which grow too close and
too high. Cut them down and have lawns all about the house
and the light would be let in."

"Perhaps the ghosts wouldn't like it. Come on. Let me show you the rest of the house."

"Where are the people who live here?"

"They are away. It is lent to me in their absence."

"It was very convenient for you."

"Oh very. I couldn't have found a more pleasant spot."

"But it is so far away from London."

"Well, it has its little town wherein the good firm of Rosen, Stead and Rosen are housed."

"But for a man of affairs..."

"This suits my affairs very well. I am near the sea... That is good, but best of all I am close to Eversleigh Court and because of that I met you, Zipporah."

I sat quickly: "I think I should be returning home to Clavering soon. They will be missing me and I have done what I came to do."

"Don't talk of that now. Live in the present. It's good to live in the present. The past is usually full of regrets. Never feel regrets, Zipporah. They change nothing. As for the future, that is the unknown. It is the present that has to be lived and living is the whole meaning of existence."

"Too many generalizations are never quite true," I said.

I was already beginning to feel the spell of the house... or perhaps it was his presence. I felt like another person. Trying to make excuses later I told myself that from the moment I had entered the house I had been taken into the possession of someone else.

We reached the top of the stairs, our footsteps echoing on the bare wooden boards. He opened a door and we were in a corridor.

I said: "How silent it seems! A strange sort of alliance ... almost as though..."

"Perhaps the ghosts have come out today. I've got an idea they don't much care for those giggling servants. They like a silent house."

"*We* are here," I said.

"On a tour of exploration. I am sure they want the house to live up to its eerie reputation.

"This is not an exceptionally large house," he said. "There are five rooms on this landing. Above are the servants' quarters. How quiet it seems."

He opened a door. I was in a room in which was a large four-poster bed. The hangings were of brocade—white and gold. There was other furniture in the room but it was dominated by the large bed.

I had the uncanny feeling then that I had been there before. Or did I imagine that afterward. My emotions at this stage were so intense because I knew that I was being propelled toward some tremendous climax. I was trying to hold back yet urging myself forward.

"They prepared this room for me when I arrived," I heard him say. "I believe it was a sort of honor. It's the bridal suite."

"But you brought no bride," I said.

He had taken my hands and was looking steadily at me. I tried to withdraw them but I could not do so. I was not sure whether it was because he held them so firmly or because my own will would not allow me to relinquish the contact.

Somewhere in the recesses of my mind I remembered something I had heard about this room. Hadn't the bed curtains been blood red . . . rich, velvet at one time; and hadn't they been changed to white and gold. There was a reason.

The past seemed to be closing round me and I was a part of it. I wanted to escape from it. I wanted to be in the present . . . I wanted to live as I never had before.

Then he put his arms round me and held me close to him. I could feel his heart beating against mine. I was in love with him and this was different from loving Jean-Louis or anyone I had loved before. This was something I had never experienced, had never understood, had been vaguely aware existed . . . in romances of the past. Tristan and Isolde, Abelard and Héloïse . . . the sort of overwhelming passion for the sake of which people sacrificed everything . . . even that which they held most dear.

"Zipporah." He was saying my name as I had never heard it said before. I seemed to be floating along in his arms. We had left the world and all its little conventions a long way behind. We were together . . . we belonged together . . . and there was no holding back the tide of passion which was enveloping us.

I heard myself say: "No . . . no . . . I must go. . . ."

And I heard his gentle laughter as he loosened my dress. I was still protesting but without any real conviction, I knew, and he knew it too. I was desperately trying to remember so many things. I was Zipporah Ransome, wife of Jean-Louis; our marriage was a happy one . . . my family . . .

It was no use, I was not with them . . . I was here in this house with my lover.

Yes, he was my lover. I had been conscious of this tremendous attraction between us from the first. It had happened in that very moment he had risen from the ground and stood before me.

It was no use fighting, I must let this emotion sweep over me, submerge me . . . teach me what I had never known before—that I was a deeply sensuous woman who had never before been aware of this.

I made no attempt now to hold him off. I was his completely and he knew it. Perhaps being wise in the ways of women he had always known it.

Afterward we lay on the bed side by side. It was so still, and then away in the distance I could hear the shouting and laughter of the fair.

It occurred to me that I would remember that forever as the background to my ecstasy of passion and my shame.

I put my hand to my face. There were tears there. How had I shed them? What were they? Tears of happiness, the result of this tremendous excitement which had taken possession of me, tears of shame . . . for that was there too.

He put his arms about me and held me close to him. "I love you," he said.

"I love you," I answered.

"Dear Zipporah . . . be happy. . . ."

"I am . . . and then I'm not."

"It had to be."

"It should never have been."

"It has been."

"Oh God," I said, and I was praying aloud. I wanted to go back. I didn't want this to have happened. "Let me go back. . . . Let it be early this afternoon. Let me walk in the opposite direction . . . away from Enderby."

He stroked my face.

"Dearest," he said, "it had to be . . . right from the first it had to be. Whatever happens now we have had this. It is worth everything . . . all the anticipation that was, all the regretting to come. We met as we did. We went through our little adventure of the will, but that is not the point. There are people who are meant to love . . . to mate . . . they must. It is their destiny. Don't blame yourself because you were suddenly awakened. You have been dormant too long, my darling Zipporah."

"What have I done?" I said. "My husband . . ."

He held me fast against him. "Come away with me," he said. "You will never have to face him then."

"Leave my home . . . my husband . . . my family . . ."

"For me."

"I could never do that. That would be the ultimate betrayal."

"You were meant to love as we have loved. We would have a wonderful life together."

"No," I said. "I must go from here. We must not meet again. This must be forgotten. It must be as though it never was. I must go home to my husband . . . to my family. We must forget . . . forget. . . ."

"Do you think I am ever going to forget? Are you?"

"I shall live with this all the rest of my life. I shall never be at peace again. I feel now that I shall wake up and find that it never really happened."

"And the most exciting experience of your life was not real! You want that!"

"I don't know. But I must go. What if anyone came back

and found me here . . . like this . . . ?" I half rose but he had pulled me back. He held me firmly, and he was laughing, a hint of triumph in his voice.

Then he was making love to me again and my resolutions slipped away. I was drowned once more in that sea of passion. There was nothing else that mattered. I was powerless to resist.

As I lay exhausted by my emotion, listening to the sounds of the fair in the distance, I felt I was now irrevocably lost.

The curtains about the bed were half drawn and the sun glinting through the windows touched them with a shade of red. Through my half-closed eyes for a few moments they might have been red velvet. . . .

There is something strange here, I thought, something uncanny. I knew then that I had started to make my excuses.

I did not rise. I lay there beside him and I listened to his seductive voice telling me that we could go away together. We could leave for France by the end of the week. He would make me happy as I had not dreamed of happiness. He knew that he had opened a new world to me. He had shown me a side to my nature that I had never known existed. I had been happy with Jean-Louis; our life had been, as I thought, satisfactory in all ways. It could never be so again because I knew that with my husband I had never explored those realms of erotic excitement to which Gerard had introduced me. I would always crave for them . . . long for them. It was as though he had opened a door to a part of my nature which I had not known existed and the new experiences to which I had been introduced would make demands upon me. I should never be satisfied with my marriage after this.

How long did we lie there with the sounds of the fair going on and on in the background? I had no notion of time . . . it slipped away. There were moments when I forgot everything but our passion. I deliberately refused to think of anything else; not that I had to make a great effort. But I did know that time was passing and even he—reckless as I guessed him to be— was aware of that. The servants would be coming back. How could my presence in the house be explained?

So he agreed that we must go. I soberly dressed. I could not understand my mood, which was half defiant, half exultant. If I could go back, would I? No, I would not. I had lived this afternoon as I would never have believed was possible. I didn't want to change anything . . . not yet. Let me live in my magic cocoon a little longer.

He turned to me and held me in his arms, tenderly kissing my brow, stroking my hair, telling me he loved me.

"We must meet soon," he said. "I must talk to you. . . . We must make plans."

"I shall go back to my home. I must."

"I shall not allow it. When can we meet? Tonight? Come out by the shrubbery."

At last I said I would.

We went down the staircase past the haunted gallery. The house seemed different now . . . at peace, in a way, contented, almost laughing at us. I was very fanciful. It was all part of building up excuses, trying to plead extenuating circumstances, fate perhaps, for what I had done.

The sounds from the fair were louder out of doors.

We walked together back to Eversleigh. In the shrubbery he kissed me passionately.

"We belong together," he said. "Never forget it."

Then I tore myself away and ran into the house.

I made for my room and on the way I passed Uncle Carl's room. On impulse I looked in. He was sitting in his chair and he looked grotesque, I thought, out of bed with his long nose and pointed chin, his parchment skin and his very lively dark eyes.

"Oh," he said, "have you been to the fair, Carlotta?"

"Carlotta?" I said. "Carlotta's dead. It's Zipporah."

"Of course. Of course. You looked so like her . . . for the moment I'd forgotten."

I felt shaken. I thought: It shows. What have I done? It has branded me in some way. He knew. . . . That is why he called me Carlotta.

"Is Jessie in?" he asked.

"She may be still at the fair."

"She'll be in now, I'll swear. It's nearly supper time."

I left him. I could not bear those lively eyes looking at me. I was sure they saw something different about me.

I went to my room. I looked at myself in the mirror. "Carlotta," he had said. Yes . . . I looked different. There was something about me . . . a sparkle . . . a shine almost. My eyes, which had been a darkish blue, looked darker . . . almost a violet shade.

I had changed.

"I have become an adulteress," I murmured.

I had exhausted all the excuses. In fact there were none. For the next afternoon I was lying on the bed behind the brocade curtains with my love. I was crafty. I said to myself: I have already sinned against Jean-Louis, against my honor, my principles . . . nothing can change that. And to go again, to be with him . . . to experience that emotional turmoil . . . what does it matter? I am already an adulteress. I shall still be one however many times I give way to temptation.

So I went and the experience seemed even more alluring than before. Perhaps I had managed to quieten my conscience. I had stepped over the border of what seemed to me—in my role of the old Zipporah—as depravity. I was there, so what difference could one more step make?

I was in love with Gerard, which was different from loving Jean-Louis. Jean-Louis was kind, considerate, tender, all that I had wanted in a husband until I met Gerard. It might be that Gerard could not compare with Jean-Louis in tenderness and consideration . . . I did not know. That fact appalled me. I did not really know this man and yet the physical attraction between us was so overwhelming as to be irresistible.

So I went back to my white and gold brocade bed and I learned that I had never really known myself before. I was a deeply sensuous woman; having overcome my first terrors, subdued my intruding conscience, I could now give myself to passion and I gave myself completely and utterly.

And there we lay and once more the sounds of the fair were

our background and the house seemed to be applauding because it knew that I had betrayed my husband in a manner which I would never have thought possible.

I could think of nothing else but being alone with Gerard, of exciting and erotic lovemaking. I was a different person. I did not know this woman I had become and yet she was myself . . . and if I were honest I would admit that I would not have her otherwise.

I was vital. I was alive as I had not been before. Everything seemed to have changed. I had stepped out of a way of life where I had gone on at a slow steady trot for so many years. Now I was flying into realms hitherto unknown. Oh, I was fanciful. But this was such a wonderful thing that had happened to me.

During the days that followed we were meeting regularly. We could not go to the house now but there was a cottage belonging to Enderby and this was uninhabited because the gardener who had occupied it had died suddenly and it was being renovated before it was given to one of the other servants. There were ladders and wood shavings about the place. But there was some furniture and it was a place where we could meet. We could no longer go to the house, of course, for we should have been detected at once. Gerard had plans for taking me in, and for visiting me. He liked to discuss them but we both knew that they could not be satisfactorily carried out. So we met at the gardener's cottage after supper each evening. I was sometimes late coming back to Eversleigh.

It was dangerous, I knew; there must have been a change in me. Sometimes I could sense both Uncle Carl and Jessie watching me. They would both be experts on eroticism I was sure. Perhaps living as I had through such ecstatic moments, first at Enderby and then in the cottage, had had its effect on me and connoisseurs such as those two recognized this.

Uncle Carl called me Carlotta now and then, as though he saw some change in the Zipporah who had first come to the house. As for Jessie, she seemed to be secretly amused.

I wondered then if she discussed me with Uncle Carl or with Amos Carew.

The thought made me squirm but it did nothing to prevent my joyful appearance at those meetings with my lover.

I knew it couldn't last. I should have to go back. The time was short. I knew it. We both knew it; and the knowledge added to the intensity of our passion.

There were times when he drove me out in the carriage. We went for miles and sometimes we lay in faraway woods where we felt safe from those who knew us. We made love under trees and in the bracken... each time seemed more exciting than the last. I had long told myself that it was no use resisting temptation now. I was a sinful, erring wife and if I never sinned and erred again nothing could alter that. It was brief... it was passing... the thought gave a terrible poignancy to our relationship; I think it made us determined to extract the very last bit of joy from it. We were abandoned; our senses took control. Nothing else mattered to us in our wildly demanding love.

He urged me to go away with him. I knew then that as he belonged to the diplomatic circles at the French court he was in England on business for his country. I knew too that in view of the existing state of affairs between our countries he must be some sort of spy; I knew that he was at Enderby because it was remote and that he made secret journeys to the coast.

It seemed to me that I was not only an adulteress but was spending my time with an enemy of my country. I knew nothing of him, yet I had never so intimately known anyone before. All I knew was that there was some irresistible attraction between us; that if I could have my greatest wish granted it would be that I could wipe out everything that had happened before in my life and start afresh now with him.

And so I went on slipping deeper and deeper into this life of the senses.

We did discuss the matter of Uncle Carl's will. He said to me once: "Your uncle may be in acute danger. If that woman has a paper which she thinks will give her the estate, it is almost certain that she will find some means of getting her hands on it."

"I know, What shall I do?"

"She should know that there is a will—signed and sealed—with the solicitor."

"My uncle will never tell her."

"You must. I think he is safe for the time being because you are there. You are his safeguard, but if you should go away I wouldn't give much for his chances. She must know."

"She would badger him to sign another paper."

"She must be told that it would not be valid. That it would have to be signed by responsible people, that Rosen would have to draw it up."

"That's not exactly true, is it?"

"I don't think so. I don't know the laws of England. But it is what she should be told. I don't think your uncle should be left to her tender mercies."

That was all we said about it, but it stayed in my mind. I felt very uneasy. I had forgotten the half-comic half-sinister situation in this house, so absorbed had I been by my own affairs.

It was a week after the first day of the fair when messengers arrived from Clavering. They brought a letter from my mother.

> Dear Zipporah—[she wrote]
> I am glad that you have been able to help your uncle. He must have been very pleased to see you but now I have rather bad news for you. I think you should come home at once. We all miss you very much. Poor Jean-Louis is quite lost without you and the doctor is a little worried about him. Apparently it was not only his leg which was broken. They think he has done something to his spine. He can't walk as he did and is getting about with a stick. You know how active he has always been and this has depressed him rather and I really think you should be with him just now.

I let the letter drop from my hand. Some spinal injury. It was tragic. He was a man of action, used to an outdoor life.

He walks with a stick. How bad was he? I knew that it would be like my mother to break the news gently.

I must go back to him at once. I must devote my life to him. I must expiate this terrible wrong I had done him.

I picked up the letter.

You know what he thinks of you. You are everything to him. He misses you so dreadfully—we all do. But Jean-Louis needs you . . . particularly just now that this has happened. . . .

I would go back at once. A terrible depression enveloped me. Had I really been thinking that I could have slipped away from all my responsibilities and blithely gone to France with Gerard? I believe for a few moments I had entertained the thought. I was doubly ashamed of myself. My mother's letter had brought it all back so vividly . . . the kindness, the unending patience and love I had had from Jean-Louis, my lawful husband.

I was depraved. I was wanton. I was wicked.

Well, I was an adulteress.

I went over to Enderby where Gerard was waiting for me.

"I must make my plans to go home now . . . at once," I told him. "I've had a letter. Jean-Louis's accident was more than a broken leg. He has injured his spine. I wonder if he is going to be an invalid."

Gerard looked at me incredulously.

"Yes," I went on, "I have had a letter from my mother. I shall have to go soon. I can't delay. This is terrible."

He held me against him and I felt the desire rising within me potent as ever. I felt I could not bear to leave him. I leaned my head against him. I was looking blankly into a future which did not hold him. I saw the dreary years stretching ahead of me.

He said: "I too must go. . . ."

"It's the end then."

"It need not be," he said. "It is for you to decide."

"Jean-Louis has been hurt."

"What of me? What of us?"

"He is my husband," I said. "I have vowed to love him . . . in sickness . . . in health. If only I had never come here."

"Don't regret it. You have loved . . . you have lived."

"And I shall live on to regret . . . all my life."

He said abruptly: "When do you propose to go?"

"Before the week is out."

He bowed his head. Then he took my hand and kissed it. "Zipporah," he said, "if ever you should change your mind . . ."

"Do you mean, you will be waiting for me?"

He nodded. "But you have not yet gone. There is still a little time left to me . . . to us . . . time for me to persuade you. . . ."

I shook my head. "I know I have been weak . . . I have been wicked . . . but there are some things which even I could not do."

I don't think he believed me. After all, I had been so eager, so willing, that he thought that when the time came I would abandon everything for him.

I knew I never would. I knew that no matter what happened I had to go back to Jean-Louis.

I had made up my mind that I was going to warn Uncle Carl. I did not mention my imminent departure to Jessie as I intended to speak to him first and I chose the afternoon when I knew we should be safe from intrusion.

He looked pleased to see me and into his eyes there crept that mischievous look which I did not understand. Sometimes I wondered how far his mind wandered into the past because lately it had become increasingly clear that he confused me with my ancestress Carlotta, who had clearly made a great impression on him in his youth.

I realized that almost immediately after my arrival I had met Gerard and even from that first meeting I had been so obsessed with him that the full implication of what might be happening in this house had not struck me so forcibly as it did now that I was on the point of departure.

A cry for help, Sabrina had said. Well, it was, in a way. Not that he was asking for help—although I was sure he was aware of the dangers of his situation. He did not seem to care about danger. He was like an onlooker watching with amusement the strange antics of human beings—even though he himself was one of the main actors in the drama.

Sometimes I thought he was too old to care what happened and as long as Jessie was there to administer to his comforts he was quite prepared for anything she might do—in fact took a lively interest in waiting to see which turn her actions would take.

It was all very strange—as everything had been since my arrival.

Therefore I had made up my mind that I must speak plainly to him and point out the danger in which he could be.

I began by telling him about my mother's letter.

"My husband is not as well as we thought. At first it seemed that he suffered only from a broken leg and we thought that as soon as that mended he would be all right. There seems to be some complication, so I must go home."

He nodded. "So you will be leaving us. I shall be sorry."

"I will come again . . . perhaps with Jean-Louis or my mother or Sabrina."

"That would be good. I trust you have enjoyed your stay here."

"Oh yes . . . yes."

He was smiling, was it secretly? "It seems to agree with you, Carlotta."

I looked at him steadily and said: "I am Zipporah."

"Of course. My mind wanders. I'm back in the past years and years ago. It's not the first time, is it? I suppose it's because you have a look of her. I notice it more every day."

I said: "Uncle Carl, I want to say something to you which you might not like. You must understand I am only thinking of you."

I saw the faintly imperceptible twitch of his lips which I had come to know indicated amusement.

"My dear child," he said, "you are so good to me...so kind...so solicitous of my welfare. You have already gone to great trouble to do what I asked. I thought your French gentleman charming...quite charming...." His bright eyes were on my face. "And so do you, eh?"

I knew the color was rising to my cheeks, and I thought: He knows. How can he know? Has Jessie spied on me? Has she talked about me with him?

"It was good of him to get me quickly into the town and to help us with the will." I went on quickly: "It is that that I wanted to speak to you about, Uncle Carl."

"It's all sealed and settled now. I've done my duty. Eversleigh will be for you and your heirs. I feel the family ghosts are all nodding their heads in approval. Carl was an old reprobate, they are saying, but he has done his duty at last. Let's all turn over in our tombs and go to sleep. We'll give him a talking to when he comes to join us."

He was smiling at me in that mischievous way and I plunged on. "Uncle Carl, there's something I must say to you. You must not be persuaded to sign anything else...like that paper you did before."

He nodded.

I stumbled on. "You see, if people think they are going to inherit a great deal they could go to any lengths to get their hands on it."

He laughed. It was high pitched, almost falsetto. He looked shrewd and I wondered of how much he was aware and if his forgetfulness and the air of senility he sometimes assumed was all part of the role he was playing.

"You mean Jess...?" he said.

"It's a great temptation...particularly for people who have never had a great deal and perhaps are a little anxious about the future."

"Jess would always find a place for herself."

"I've no doubt, but she wouldn't have many opportunities like this. I'll be completely frank, Uncle Carl."

"Oh. It always frightens me when people are going to be completely frank. I wonder if anyone ever is . . . about everything. . . . A little frank, yes . . . but completely frank . . . ."

"I hope you won't be offended but I am anxious about you and I don't want to go away . . . leaving things as they are."

"All's well. Old Rosen has the will."

"Jessie doesn't know it."

"Poor Jess! What a shock for her."

"She thinks because of this piece of paper you've signed that all this goes to her. It wasn't very wise of you, Uncle Carl."

"No," he said, "my life is strewn with unwisdom."

"You see . . ."

He was looking at me encouragingly. "You must say exactly what you mean, my dear."

"Very well. I'm concerned about you. I couldn't go away peacefully thinking that you might be in some sort of . . ."

"Predicament?"

"Danger," I said boldly. "Uncle Carl, I think Jessie ought to know that you have signed that will and that . . ."

"And that she would gain little by my death." How sharp he was. He seemed to be able to look right into my mind. I thought. He is playing a part as well as everyone else here.

"Yes," I said boldly. "Yes."

He nodded. "You are a good girl," he said. "I'm glad this will be yours one day. You'll do the right thing by it . . . and your children will manage the estate in accordance with the wishes of the ancestors watching from on high or from below, where it seems likely the majority of us will be."

"You joke, Uncle Carl."

"Life is a bit of a joke, eh? It's like a play. We strut and fret our hour upon the stage, eh? That's what I've often thought. I loved the play. I would have liked to have been an actor. Who ever heard of an Eversleigh being an actor? Oh, those ancestors of ours. They wouldn't have liked that. The next best thing was sitting in the boxes looking on. . . . I've always liked it, Carlotta . . . bless you, Zipporah. I've done it when I could. I look on and see how people are going to act . . . what part they're going to play. . . ."

"You mean, Uncle Carl," I said, "that you are something of a manipulator. You create situations and watch how they work it out."

"No, no, not that. I let events take care of themselves and watch. . . . I will admit that sometimes I give a hand but that's only in the nature of things."

He laughed again. It was strange laughter and I thought: He sees life as a play; he is watching us act; he is sitting in his box waiting for what the actors on the stage will do next.

"Uncle Carl," I said, "I want Jessie to know that you have signed a will and that it is with the solicitors."

He nodded.

I said: "Then she will cherish you, for she can only enjoy the comforts of this house—which I am sure she fully appreciates—while you are here to provide them."

"You're clever," he said. "And you're good to me."

"Then have I your permission to tell her?"

"My dear child, I never tell people what they should do. That would spoil the action, wouldn't it? They have to act as the spirit moves them. I like to see what they will do."

He was strange . . . not mad, for at times his brain worked most efficiently; but he wanted to live life in his own way. I could imagine that some years before he must have been an extremely active man. He had lived to excess after his marriage, I was sure. And now that he was old and incapable of moving from this room he created his own shadow play.

He knew a great deal about us—that Jessie was here for all the advantage it could bring her; he was aware that Amos Carew was her lover; he might even have guessed at the relationship between Gerard and myself—and it was all of immense interest to him. We were the players on the stage who provided the interest which his own life had denied him now that he was old.

He would not prevent my telling Jessie about the will because that would interfere with the natural actions of human beings. He knew very well that his life could be in danger if she thought she would inherit Eversleigh on his death. But he was ready to risk that for the sake of the play.

After the orderly manner in which my life had been lived until I came on this visit it seemed incredible. I felt I had stepped into a world of fantasy and melodrama, a world of cynicism where what other people thought of as sin was simply the order of the day.

They were amoral, without that sense of duty and honor which, until I came here, had been the rule of life with me. And who was I to criticize? I had been caught up in this web of intrigue since I had come here.

However, I had made up my mind that I was going to let Jessie know that it was to her advantage to keep Uncle Carl alive, for with his death all the blessings which she now enjoyed would be cut off.

After breakfast the next morning, I asked if I could have a word with her, and, looking rather surprised, she led me into the winter parlor.

I said: "I have had a letter from my mother. My husband is not well. I shall be returning home at the end of the week."

"I'm sorry to hear that," she said. "You must be worried, poor dear."

"I must get back, you see."

"Have you told Lordy?"

"Yes, I have."

She nodded.

"There is something else I wanted to say to you."

"Say on, my dear."

"I want to assure myself—and my family will want this too—as to the state of Lord Eversleigh's health."

"Oh, he's in good health, dear."

"I want the doctor's opinion. You understand my family

will expect that, so I am going to ask him to call and give a thorough examination."

"Lordy won't like that."

"Well, I shall ask him to come in any case."

"For his age he'd take a lot of beating."

"It would be good to have that confirmed."

"Oh well, you must suit yourself."

"I shall. There is another matter. You must have guessed that Lord Eversleigh asked me here for a purpose."

"Why bless you, you're his relation. He just wanted to see you."

"Yes, but something else. He's made a will. It is now with Messrs. Rosen, Stead and Rosen . . . you know, the solicitors in the town."

I was watching her closely. She lowered her eyes and I knew that she was afraid for me to see any sign of anger or speculation.

"Well," I went on, "you're comfortable here, and there is no reason why this situation might not go on for many years . . . as long as we keep Lord Eversleigh healthy and strong. You see . . ."

She did see. Under the carmine of her cheeks she had flushed and I saw the color spread down her neck. I was telling her as clearly as I could without actually stating the fact that I considered her capable of . . . murder.

She recovered herself quickly. She was a good actress. I am sure she satisfied Uncle Carl in that respect as in many others: "Oh, I'll take care of him. You've nothing to fret about on that score. I'll keep him hale and hearty till he's a hundred."

"I am sure you will, and of course he is contented in his mind now that his will has been completed and is in safe hands. I had to get it properly executed. You can be sure that if this had not been so there could have been some difficulty. You know what solicitors are. . . . They spot loopholes. However, they have supervised this one and so we know that it is valid."

She hated me. How she hated me! I could feel it in her false smile. I was determined to get the doctor and have a verdict on my uncle's health. I knew that I had shaken her.

I was glad, concerning myself over this matter took my mind from my own desperate situation.

The time was passing. Soon I must be on my way home. Gerard was still waiting for a miracle. I really think he believed that I would abandon everything and go away with him.

The doctor came and spent an hour or so with Uncle Carl. His verdict was that my uncle's organs were in a sound condition. His inability to walk far was due to advanced rheumatism. With proper care he had years before him.

I conveyed this news to Jessie. She had recovered from the first shock of our encounter and was particularly ingratiating toward me.

She said: "Well, that's good news. You can rest assured, dearie, that every attention he needs he shall get. I'll make sure he's taken good care of."

She would, I believed, because if he were to die she would no longer have a comfortable home. I daresay the feathers for the nest might become more expensive. Well, that was Uncle Carl's affair.

Whether she upbraided him for making the will after signing that "something" in her favor, I did not know. But what I did know was that Jessie was on the alert and she knew that if anything untoward happened to Uncle Carl I would be there with strong supporters to discover the reason why.

I thought I had made quite a good job of my mission and but for my own deplorable conduct I could be proud of myself.

Everything about me had changed. I was bolder. The way I had tackled Jessie had shown that; I was tolerant. I accepted her situation at Eversleigh. Of course I did. How could I condemn my uncle's relationship with his housekeeper... I who stole out of the house to make love with a man whom I had only known for a few weeks.

But I was leaving. I was determined on that. It was only when I lay in Gerard's arms that I wavered; but even then I knew I could not face the ultimate betrayal. I would have to go back and try to forget; I saw before me a dreary lifetime of trying to expiate my sin. It would be there always to haunt me . . . there would be so much to remind me and I should never be truly happy again.

Gerard was getting frantic. The time was flying. I had two more days before I would set out for Clavering. The grooms who would accompany me had arrived at Eversleigh and were already preparing for our journey.

I was still meeting Gerard; we were still making frantic love; there was a desperation in our relationship and never had our encounters seemed so sweet as they did now that we knew that soon they would be over.

On the afternoon two days before my departure we arranged to meet at the cottage which we had made our rendezvous. I arrived first and as I did so a voice from above called: "Who's there?"

It was not Gerard.

A young woman was coming down the stairs.

"Oh," she said, "you're the lady from Eversleigh."

She curtsied and looked at me with respect.

I was astounded but I grasped the situation at once. This was the new tenant.

I said: "I saw the door open . . ."

"Well, 'tis good of you to take the interest, mistress. Ted and me is so pleased to get the place. Had our eyes on it since old Barnaby died. And they've done it up so beautiful."

"It's . . . it's very nice," I said.

"Lucky we be. Able to keep some of the bits and pieces too. Cramped we was in me mum's place. Now we'll be on our own. Like to see upstairs, mistress?"

She was proud, longing to show me. I said I would like to see it.

So I followed her up. There were curtains at the window . . . chintz, pretty.

She followed my gaze and said: "I put them up this morning. Surprising what a difference curtains make . . . and a bit of carpet. That bed was here. . . . Nice, ain't it? We had to use one of me mum's. We're glad to have that."

I looked at the bed on which I had known such hours of ecstasy.

There was a sound from below and I knew it was Gerard. I hurried to the stairs. I had to speak to him before he said something which might betray us.

I called out: "Who's there? I was just being shown the cottage."

He stood in the small room looking incongruous there as he must always have looked but I hadn't noticed until now.

I said: "Oh, it is Monsieur d'Aubigné from Enderby. You must have been attracted by the open door as I was. I've been talking to the new tenant."

He bowed to the pretty young woman, who flushed at such attention.

"I apologize for the trespass. I saw the door open and I believe it has been empty for some time."

"They been doing it up for us, sir."

"She and her husband are so happy to have their own place. Thank you for showing me."

She gave another curtsy and said: "Pleasure's mine, mistress."

Gerard bowed to me, said "Good day" and we walked away in opposite directions. I thought, how calm he is, how gracefully he dealt with the situation. I suppose I had done the same.

We were born deceivers, both of us. But the pretty little tenant had not thought it strange. She had been too happy in her own good fortune to pay much attention to us.

It was not long before Gerard, having turned in his tracks, was walking beside me.

"So," he said, "we have lost our meeting place. I had grown to love it."

"It was very reckless of us to go there. We might have been disturbed at any time."

He said: "Where shall we meet now? If you are really going to leave me on Friday . . ."

"I am, Gerard. I must."

"Tomorrow then will be our last day. How am I going to bear being without you?"

"I wonder how I shall bear being without you."

"There is the remedy."

"It just is not possible."

"Everything is possible."

"At too great a price."

"Surely . . ."

"No," I said. "Please, Gerard, understand. I have been your mistress . . . I have broken my marriage vows . . . I have behaved as I never thought it possible . . . but this is the end. All that I have done will not hurt Jean-Louis . . . if he never knows of it. I shall go back and try to be a good wife."

"You torture me," he said.

"I torture myself."

So we talked, and although I wavered a little, one fact remained clear. I could not leave Jean-Louis.

So we came to that last night. He wanted so much to be with me throughout. Perhaps if the cottage had been vacant I would have gone there and stayed with him and somehow made my way back to the house through the early hours of morning.

Although I knew Gerard was reckless and adventurous I was unprepared for what happened.

I was to leave early on the following day. The grooms had said that we should start just after dawn, which would enable us to get a fair distance on the first day when we would stop at the inn we had used on the journey to Eversleigh.

I said I would retire early. I had said good-bye to Uncle Carl for I did not want to disturb him in the morning; Jessie had said she would be up to see me off with Evalina.

My bags were packed. I was ready.

I had said good-bye to Gerard that afternoon. He had not tried to persuade me and seemed to have realized at last the futility of it.

I was about to get into bed when I heard a scratching at my window.

117

I went there and to my amazement and overwhelming joy there was Gerard. He had climbed up with the help of the creeper and was urging me to let him in.

I opened the window and in a few seconds I was in his arms.

"You didn't think I was not going to be with you, did you?" he demanded.

That night was one of bitter sweetness for me. The unexpected joy of being with him, the heartbreaking knowledge that it would be the last time, made it different from any of those times we had spent together.

There was a frenzy in our passion; it was the ultimate joy mingled with the abject sorrow. I felt that in every gesture he was begging me to abandon everything and go with him.

We lay side by side listening to the gentle breeze rustling the leaves of the trees; the light of a half moon shone into the room. I wanted to preserve every moment as I used to press rose petals in my Bible at home and look at them afterward and recall the day I had picked them.

"You can't let me go alone," he said.

But I only shook my head in sorrow.

At dawn I must rise. I must prepare myself to start on my journey . . . away from ecstasy to the long dreary years ahead, remembering, almost regretting, living with my terrible guilt. I wondered how well I would do that; whether I should be able to keep my guilty secret from them. Would Jean-Louis guess something tremendous had happened to me? I would be different, I was sure. My mother and Sabrina . . . No. When I came to think of it they had put me aside as some cherished object that was in safekeeping. Their anxieties and plans were all for Dickon.

"Don't go away from me," whispered Gerard. He knew me so well that he read my thoughts and he knew they had strayed from him to the people I should have to face at Clavering.

Then he kissed me and held me and we were as one.

We lay together, hands clasped, talking in whispers.

He said: "When you go back . . . if you go back . . . you will realize how desolate you are without me. . . . You will see that we *must* be together. . . ."

"I shall be desolate. I shall so desperately want to be with you . . . but I know I must be with my husband."

"You cannot look into the future. You don't know what will happen. I am going to give you the address of my château in France. I have written it for you. You will always be able to find me there."

I felt a certain lifting of my gloom. When I rode out tomorrow I should not have entirely lost him.

"Always there will be the hope," he said. "Every day I shall to myself say perhaps today there will be news of her. . . ."

I answered: "I must stay with my husband while he needs me . . . but if it should come to pass . . ."

And as we talked I thought I heard a movement. The creak of a board, the sudden rather uncanny awareness that someone is close by. I sat up in bed, listening.

"What is it?" said Gerard.

I put my fingers to my lips and went to the door. Fortunately I had locked it. I knew that someone was on the other side of that door . . . listening. I thought I heard a quick intake of breath.

Then I knew. I heard the creaking of a board once more. Someone was stealthily making her . . . or his . . . way along the corridor.

Gerard was looking at me questioningly.

As I went back to bed I said: "Someone was out there. Whoever it was would have heard our talking."

"We spoke in whispers."

"Nevertheless, someone in this house knows that there is someone in my room."

"The amorous housekeeper? She can't talk."

"I don't know."

But the experience had made me uneasy.

Dawn came all too quickly. I had to be up and away. Gerard held me fast, made one last entreaty. I felt better now that I had his address.

Most reluctantly he left me, coming back to me several

times and holding me fast again and again as though he refused to let me go.

And at length, because the minutes were racing by, he went out by the window. I watched him lower himself to the ground with the help of the jutting window decorations and the creeper.

He stood there looking at me and I could not take my eyes from him. I wanted that last sight of him to be etched forever in my mind.

Dawn was in the sky and I was ready. The grooms were waiting. I had said good-bye to my uncle the previous night so, I had remarked, I could slip away without disturbing him.

But Jessie and Evalina were there to see me go.

They both watched me . . . slyly, I thought, and I detected a certain speculation in their eyes and I guessed that it was one of them who had listened outside my door last night. One of them knew that I had had a lover in my room.

The journey back was uneventful. I scarcely noticed the places through which we passed. My thoughts were back with Gerard. My heart was heavy; I believed that I could never again know any happiness. I saw before me a life of dreary acceptance.

A great welcome was awaiting me, and when Jean-Louis came toward me — walking with a stick — my conscience smote me so fiercely that I was almost in tears. He thought my emotion was due to our reunion and I could see that he was happily gratified.

"It's seemed so long," he cried. "Oh, I'm so happy that you are back."

"And how are you, Jean-Louis?" I said. "I was so distressed. What is this about your spine?"

"Nothing much. I think they're making a fuss. I just get a sort of crick in my back if I walk too fast."

I looked into his dear face and I knew that he was making light of his ailment. His first thought would be that he didn't want to worry me. I felt mean, besmirched . . . wicked.

My mother with Sabrina and Dickon were waiting for me.

They embraced me lovingly. Dickon was dancing round. "What was it like?" he cried. "Tell us about Eversleigh. When are you going to have it?"

"Not for years and years, I hope," I said. "Uncle Carl . . . I call him uncle because we couldn't quite work out the relationship . . . is going to live for a long time."

"How do you know?" asked Dickon, narrowing his eyes.

"Because, Dickon, I called in the doctor and he gave a good report."

"A doctor?" said Sabrina "Is he ill then?"

"No . . . no, but I thought in the circumstances it was a good thing."

My mother was laughing. "You've clearly had an interesting time," she said.

"Yes . . . yes, very."

"You must tell us *all* about it."

Oh, not all, not all! I thought.

So I was back. It was like stepping into a world of reality after having visited some fantastic planet.

I listened to their account of all that had happened while I was away. It seemed very tame and expected.

"It was like years," Jean-Louis told me.

My mother came to my room when I was alone there. Clearly she wanted confidences.

"Jean Louis?" I asked anxiously.

"Oh, it was sad that you weren't here when we discovered this thing. Some damage to his spine. They don't know what. Poor Jean-Louis, he is so brave . . . pretends it is nothing much, but I am sure there is some pain. Don't look so sad, dear. It'll be better now you're home. He missed you so much. I think he was terribly worried. He got it into his head that something might happen and he'd lose you. All these tales about high-waymen. I think they're rather exaggerated."

"Of course they are. We don't hear about the thousands of people who make safe journeys . . . only those who come to grief."

"That's what I told him. But he seemed to get it into his

121

mind that something might go wrong. I expect he was feeling low about all this. Now you're back, darling, everything will be all right."

How could I ever have deserted them! I had always known in my heart that I never could.

So I resumed my quiet life. I discovered that Jean-Louis's trouble was more than he would have us believe. I was sure that often he felt pain although he did not mention it. He was so pleased that I was home and nothing could have been more apparent.

There must have been a change in my attitude. I was more tender, more thoughtful than I had been before. He noticed it and thought it was due to his disability; he must have no suspicion, I told myself, of the terrible remorse from which I felt I would never escape.

Sometimes during the night I thought of Gerard, dreamed of him. Poor Jean-Louis, with whom I had never quite attained the heights of passion, had been a tender lover, thoughtful always—and still was, but my mind was filled with erotic imaginings of my experiences with my lost lover.

I suppose it was inevitable. I was, it appeared, able to bear children, the fault—if that was what it could be called—lay with Jean-Louis; and after my careless abandon, the frequency of our lovemaking, it would have been strange if—my partner being a normal potent man—I did not conceive.

And this, of course, was exactly what had happened.

A few weeks after my return I knew for sure that I was pregnant and I was equally sure who was the father of my child.

Here was a dilemma. It had not occurred to me that this would happen because I had always thought of myself as a barren woman. Why is it that when a couple are not fruitful it is always assumed that the deficiency is with the woman?

It was clearly not so in my case.

There was only one course open to me for our sanity, for our happiness. Jean-Louis must believe that the child was his. This would be a perfectly reasonable assumption, particularly as he and my mother—the entire family—would never believe that I would break my marriage vows.

Then it should not be difficult. I had been away from home for three weeks. What if I had conceived a short time before I had left, which was possible? No one could question the time of the child's arrival.

The first suspicion had shocked me a little and then I began to glory in the knowledge. I was to have a child. I had longed to be a mother. The fact that I was to become one would lift me out of that terrible depression which parting with Gerard had given me. I knew that if Jean-Louis was aware that he was to become a father he would be so excited that he too would benefit from the news. As for my mother and Sabrina, they would be overjoyed. In their opinion the one flaw in my marriage had been that it was childless.

I should be the only one who would see this as a result of my sin. I had been brazen, shameless . . . and now there was to be a result—a child of that illicit union to keep the memory of it green throughout the years.

I had fallen deeper into deceit, and although this news would bring great joy to all my family, I should be constantly reminded of those three ecstatic weeks when I had stepped aside from morality, virtue and all the principles which I had been brought up to revere.

Suppose I confessed what I had done? Suppose I told them who was the father of my child? I would only create unhappiness. No, I must go on living with my deceit for ever and the child would be a living reminder of it.

When I told Jean-Louis he was overcome with emotion.

I said: "I know it is what you have always wanted . . . what we have always wanted."

"You are wonderful," he said. "I think always my happiness has depended on you . . . and now this. . . ."

I felt the knife turning in the wound which was my conscience.

My mother and Sabrina were delighted. There was nothing that could please them more than a child in the family.

Dickon shrugged his shoulders and feigned indifference. "Babies can be a terrible nuisance," he declared. "They cry and have to be watched."

"Oh, Dickon, darling," cried Sabrina, "you were a baby once."

"Well, I grew out of it."

"So do we all," Sabrina reminded him.

"Sometimes they get stillborn," he said, "which means they die being born. Some people used to put them out on the hillside to toughen them up. I think it was the Romans or the Stoics or somebody like that. It was good for them. The weak ones died and those that were really strong lived."

"My baby will not be put on the hillside," I said. "He . . . or she . . . will toughen up very satisfactorily in the nursery."

Dickon glowered. He had never forgiven me for my discovery about the burned barn. That, I remembered, had been the cause of Jean-Louis's trouble. No one had ever mentioned it in that connection. It was the sort of thing Sabrina and my mother would be very anxious to keep from stressing.

The preparations for the baby helped me considerably. I was saved from brooding as I was sure I should have done if I had not had this great event to look forward to.

Often I thought of Gerard, of course. I went over and over our meeting—the strangeness of finding him in the haunted patch and the manner in which he had risen from the ground. Almost uncanny. . . . It was as though he had been sent for the purpose of . . . what, destroying me? No, never that. Giving me a glimpse of the ecstasy two people could find in each other . . . giving me my child.

Then I would think of Uncle Carl sitting there watching me shrewdly, calling me Carlotta. Had he really been wandering in his mind? Did he really see that long-dead girl in me?

Sometimes my fancy wandered on. I let myself believe that I had been possessed. Uncle Carl had said: "She was cut off when she was young . . . she never lived out her life . . . and she was so full of life." What a fantasy! Suppose she had come back and entered my body . . . and suppose Gerard was a reincarnation of that lover whom she had met at Enderby!

It was excuses, really. I was trying to say Yes. I met him, I loved him, I gave way abandonedly. I did so. . . . But it was not really sensible Zipporah, it was long-dead passionate Carlotta.

Such feeble reasoning must be dismissed as the worthless excuse it was. I had reveled in my lover. It had been no other than myself, a passionate, sensuous woman who had been awakened to what she really was. I knew myself now. I knew I had been vaguely dissatisfied without knowing it. I now realized that I had wanted the sort of love which Gerard had given me.

Be sensible, I admonished myself. Don't shirk the facts. This is you . . . wanton adulteress, about to bear the child of a guilty union and pass that child off as your husband's.

It was not the first time such a situation had arisen. But that it should be you. . . .

It showed how strange life was, how one could never be sure of people and how easy it was to be ignorant of oneself until such circumstances arose to throw a light on that subject.

My baby was a little girl. She was strong and healthy and on impulse I wanted to call her Charlotte.

Charlotte, I thought. It's not quite Carlotta . . . but near it. Living evidence of that time when I seemed to become another person, when I behaved as my long-dead ancestress might have done.

So my daughter was born, and Charlotte, being, as my mother said, a somewhat severe name, we began to call this adorable creature Lottie.

Revelation in a Barn

Two years had passed since the birth of Lottie. I adored her. She was more than a long-wished-for child. She it was who had made bearable those months after I had said goodbye to Gerard. Preparing for her had occupied my time; I had found then that I could shut out almost everything in contemplating the joy her arrival would bring me.

Of course I had moments of deepest depression when I felt weighed down by my guilt; but Jean-Louis's joy in the prospect of the child soothed me considerably. I could say to myself: But for what I have done this could not be happening now. But that could not make me forget the great deceit, and my conscience, after lying dormant for a few days, would rise up to torment me.

I had not paid another visit to Eversleigh but I was constantly saying that I must do so. I received letters from Uncle Carl and I gathered from them that everything was as it had been when I left. "Jessie takes good care of me," he wrote, and I could hear him chuckle as he wrote that. He would remember that it was I who had insisted that she be told about the will for his own safety. I believed I had at least done what was best for him.

Jean-Louis was rather concerned about the state of affairs on the Continent, and I paid more attention to the talk about this than I ever had before because of what I believed to be Gerard's involvement. There was a great deal of speculation about Madame de Pompadour, who was the power behind the French throne. Jean-Louis had engaged a young man, James Fenton, as agent and this was a sign that he could not do as much as he had done previously. James Fenton was a good agent; he had been for a spell in the army and seemed very knowledgeable about the military position. He interested Jean-Louis in it, saying that wars affected us all. We were indifferent in England because the war was not fought on our soil. We had had experience of how devastating that could be during our own civil war, but we felt remote from what was happening on the Continent; all the same, we should remember that England was involved in it.

I wondered often about Gerard. I guessed that the purpose of his visit to England had had something to do with the political situation. No doubt he had been discovering how England would react to events on the Continent and perhaps even assessing the effectiveness of our defenses along the coast and sending messages back across the sea. I would listen avidly to James Fenton, who noticed my interest and was delighted by it. He directed his remarks to me as often as he did to Jean-Louis; and the three of us would become involved in discussions of the rights and wrongs and the possible effects of the conflict.

"The Pompadour rules France," said James, "not so much because of the hold she has on Louis but because he is too lazy to do so himself. He loves to leave affairs in her hands . . . which are capable enough . . . but perhaps not so good for France. She is a clever woman. She holds her sway over the king by seeing to his needs . . . in every direction. She procures little girls to amuse him in his bedchamber. It is said he has a penchant for young girls. The Parc aux Cerfs proves that."

As I had never heard of the Parc aux Cerfs James explained that it was the Deer Park—an establishment where young girls from all walks of life whose only qualifications need to be beauty and a certain sensuality were trained to pander to the king's pleasure.

Jean-Louis looked uneasy as though he did not like such matters to be discussed in my company.

"I'm sorry to speak of something so distasteful," said James to me, "but to understand the situation you must know Louis and the Pompadour, and why she has this hold over him."

I lowered my eyes. They could not guess that I myself was far from ignorant of the delights of sensual love.

There was a treaty which was called the Alliance des Trois Cotillons—the alliance of "three petticoats," which referred to the agreement between Madame de Pompadour, Maria Theresa of Austria and Empress Elizabeth of Russia. It was important to us because no sooner had it been signed than England declared war on France.

Gerard's country and mine were enemies—they had always been that, of course, but now they were engaged in a war . . . fighting on opposing sides. I wondered whether this would bring him back to England . . . secretly. . . . For a time I used to look out for him, telling myself that he would suddenly appear. Nothing of this sort happened and then I asked myself whether love affairs like that which there had been between us were commonplace with him. Could it be that he loved violently, dramatically . . . and then passed on to the next?

That was something I could not bear to contemplate. I had been shameful but at least for me it was for no *petite passion*, no passing whim of the moment.

And so the time began to slip by.

I had acquired an excellent nanny for Lottie. She was a great-niece of Nanny Curlew who had long since retired. But, said my mother, it was always wise to keep nannies in the family and we could be sure that a relative of Nanny Curlew's would have been brought up to serve nobly in the honorable tradition.

And so it proved. From the moment she was installed in the household we knew we had a treasure in Nanny Derring. Dickon had scornfully rejected nannies some time ago, and because they could deny him nothing, the guardian of his nursery had been found another post and Dickon now went to the vicarage for lessons, which he shared with the vicar's son, Tom, and which were taught by the resident curate. In due course he would go away to school.

Lottie grew more beautiful every day. She was very pretty with magnificent eyes—dark blue, fringed with incredibly long almost black lashes. "Her eyes are darker than yours were at her age," said my mother. "Hers are violet. They always said that my mother, Carlotta, had violet eyes."

Remarks like that always unnerved me temporarily. I wondered whether my mother noticed it.

Lottie also had a good deal of dark hair. It was almost black.

"She looks like a little French doll," said Sabrina.

"French!" I cried.

"Well, Jean-Louis had a hand in it, didn't he?" said Sabrina. "Sometimes I get the impression that you think you are wholly responsible for her."

I must be careful. It could be over some small thing that I would betray myself. There was every reason why Lottie should look French. After all, the man who was supposed to be her father was of the same race as her actual one.

Jean-Louis adored her and she was fond of him. I was deeply moved to see him carry her round on his shoulder. I knew it was painful for him because to do so he abandoned his stick, but she loved it and was always trying to clamber up. She was now beginning to talk and was enchanting, murmuring to herself usually about Lottie—which was the word she used more than any other. Everything belonged to Lottie, she seemed to think; she was demanding, showed a lively interest in all around her, loved us to sing or tell her nursery rhymes and she had an endearing habit of watching our mouths as we talked or sang, trying to imitate us. She was the center of our life. Jean-Louis said to me as he watched: "I still cannot believe that we really have a child. Sometimes I dream that it was all fancy and wake up in such gloom . . . until I remember or she comes in [which she was beginning to do now] at an early hour in the morning to be with us."

She did more than anything else to ease my conscience, but sometimes I would have a fearful sense of foreboding and when I looked back at all I had done and how I had brazenly carried off my deceit I was still amazed at myself.

People talked about the war but not with any great seriousness. There had always been wars and as long as they remained outside our country we were not greatly concerned. When there were triumphs for us we heard a great deal about them; when there were disasters they were briefly glossed over. We did hear about the execution of Admiral Byng, though. He had lost Minorca to the French and was accused of treachery and cowardice. People were shocked by the case and for a time talked of little else. Prime Minister Pitt had tried to persuade the king to pardon him but to no avail, and he was shot on the quarterdeck of his ship in Portsmouth Harbor.

Jean-Louis was indignant. "It's harsh and unjust," he said. "Byng might have failed through bad tactics but that does not merit execution."

James Fenton said that such executions were performed for reasons other than justice. The French were evidently very interested in the outcome. The writer Voltaire said he was slain "pour encourager les autres" and solely for that reason. Someone else said that Byng was afraid of too much responsibility and was shot to let those about him know that in war those who could not take quick decisions were no use to their country.

In any case the interest in the case seemed to bring the fact that we were at war home to a good many people.

"How will it affect the war?" I asked James.

"Oh, the capture of Minorca is a feather in the French cap."

Such talk always set me wondering about Gerard. It seemed so strange that we who had been so close, should now be so far apart that we had no idea what the other was doing. I wondered what he would think if he knew there had been a child.

It was when Lottie was two years old that I had the irresistible urge to return to Eversleigh.

I talked it over with my mother and Sabrina. "I think a great deal about Uncle Carl and that strange ménage of his. I said I would visit again. Do you think I should?"

"Lottie is a little young to travel," she said.

"I had thought of leaving her here. Nanny is well able to look after her. Jean-Louis is not really fit for a long journey . . . no, I thought of . . ."

"Not going alone!" cried my mother.

"Well . . . I went before."

Dickon happened to have come in while we were talking. He was now getting on for thirteen—very tall for his age, full of self-importance, arrogant, ruthless, I judged him to be. He did not improve as he grew up.

"I'll go with you," he said.

"I'll be perfectly all right . . . with the grooms. I'll go as I went before."

But Dickon was set on going, and as my mother and Sabrina always went out of their way to satisfy his demands they came up with the idea that Sabrina and he might go with me. And no sooner had it been suggested than Dickon was so taken with the idea that he would not have it otherwise than that we should go together.

I wrote to Uncle Carl and had an enthusiastic reply. He would be delighted to see us, and asked us to come as soon as possible.

It was spring—the best time for traveling; the days remained light for longer and the weather was more to be relied on.

Both Dickon and Sabrina were in high spirits. It was true that Dickon wanted us to move faster, which the grooms pointed out to him was not possible if the saddle horse was to keep up with us. "Let him come on after," said Dickon.

I said: "You know we must all keep together. You must have heard that often enough."

"Highwaymen. Everybody's scared of highwaymen. I'm not."

"No, for the reason that you have never encountered one."

"I'd soon frighten him off."

Sabrina said: "Dickon!" half reproving, half admiring; and I merely ignored him.

The journey passed without mishap and on this occasion we arrived at Eversleigh in the early afternoon.

Sabrina remembered the place well and grew reflective, excited but a little sad. I guessed so many memories—some not very pleasant—were stirring in her mind. She had spent the early part of her childhood at Enderby and in the days before Eversleigh Court had passed into Uncle Carl's hands it had been a very orderly, rather conventionally run estate.

Jessie came out to meet us. I noticed that she displayed a little more discretion in her appearance than she had on that first occasion. She wore a blue muslin dress with a frilly white fischu and cuffs. There was only the smallest patch beside her left eye.

Evalina was there with her mother, almost a young woman now. I guessed she must be about fifteen years of age.

"His lordship is excited about your visit," Jessie told us. "He has ordered that you are to be taken to him the minute you arrived."

Oh yes, she was creating a different image. Now it seemed that his lordship gave the orders in the house; on the previous occasion it had clearly been Jessie who did this.

Evalina and Dickon eyed each other with interest, but Dickon's main attention was for the house. He was rather quiet—which was unusual for him—gazing about him. I could see that he was impressed.

"Your rooms are all ready for you," said Jessie. "And I was wondering if you would like a light snack, say . . . or wait for supper."

I looked at Sabrina, who hesitated, I knew, because she thought Dickon would certainly be hungry. However, for once he did not seem interested in food. He was indeed taken with his surroundings.

I said I was prepared to wait. Sabrina said the same.

"Well then, would you like to come straight to his lordship?" She looked at me. "It was his orders," she said.

So while our baggage was brought in we went to Uncle Carl's room. He was seated in a chair by the window. He looked exactly the same as I remembered him—parchment-wrinkled skin and those strikingly lively dark eyes.

He turned to us and gave an exclamation of delight.

"Ah . . . you're here. Come in. Come in. Oh, this is a pleasure. Now . . . you're Sabrina. Ah yes, of course . . . Damaris's girl. Good girl Damaris, and of course my dear Zipporah." He gripped my hand and held it firmly. "And this . . ."

"He's Richard, we call him Dickon . . . my son," said Sabrina.

"Yes, yes . . . indeed. Welcome . . . welcome . . . Now, Jessie, have you given them something to eat?"

"Why bless you, they've only just come and it was your orders that they was to be brought straight to you. They say they'll wait till supper."

"Well . . . well. Bring chairs for them, Jessie."

She did so, smiling at us, the stones in her ears twinkling.

"Now is there anything else you want before I leave you for a little family chat? When you're ready pull the bell rope. I'll have hot water sent to your rooms. I expect you want to wash and change. You must be tired after your journey." She turned to Uncle Carl and lifted a finger. "Don't forget they've had a long journey."

"No. I don't forget. It was good of you to come to see me. Would you want to go straight to your rooms?"

"In a little while," I said. "But it is wonderful to see you looked after so well."

His bright eyes looked straight into mine. "Jessie takes good care of me . . . thank *you*." I was not sure whether or not he winked at me.

We talked awhile; mostly he was recalling the past. Sabrina

was more conversant with that, being older than I and having been part of the earlier scene. Dickon got up and walked round the room examining the paneling and the wonderful old fireplace which was intricately carved with scenes from the Wars of the Roses.

I had never known him so quiet.

Uncle Carl asked solicitously after Jean-Louis and thanked me for the letters I had sent since we had last been together. It was all very conventional conversation and I began to think that it all seemed very normal and quite different from on that previous visit. After a while Dickon pulled the bell rope and it was Jessie who came up to take us to our rooms. She behaved with decorum and only occasionally stepped out of her role as housekeeper to assume that of mistress of the house.

I had the same room as I had had before, and I felt poignant memories flooding over me. I went to the window through which Gerard had climbed. Behind me was the bed on which we had spent that last ecstatic and melancholy night.

I wished I had not come. The memories were all bitter now.

Sabrina came in. She sat on my bed and smiled at me.

"I wasn't expecting it to be so . . . normal. . . ."

"No," I said. "Nor I. What did you think of Jessie?"

"Too flamboyant. Too much carmine and white lead."

"She's very subdued compared with what she was. Do you think she gives herself an air?"

"In a way. I expect it's because she is so useful. She runs the household, that's obvious . . . and from what I've seen does it rather well."

"Yes," I said. "It's different. . . ."

"Oh, I expect she was just trying to show how important she was to the household. Perhaps now that's obvious and she feels she doesn't have to assert herself. She's blowsy. Probably on the stage at one time and now feels this is a good safe place to settle in."

"But you know she got Uncle Carl to sign a paper. . . ."

"I remember your telling us. Well, that was long ago, wasn't it? She seems to have settled down. Not the ideal housekeeper,

I suppose . . . but we'll watch her while we're here. Dickon, by the way, is completely fascinated by the place. He thinks it so interesting. He's going to explore tomorrow, he says."

"I noticed how interested he was."

"He is so enthusiastic about old places. It's wonderful to see him so excited. He can be very serious at times. I know you haven't forgiven him for Hassock's fire . . . but he mustn't be made to feel he's to blame for Jean-Louis's accident. He mustn't, Zipporah. I know what that sort of guilt can do to an impressionable child. I suffered it myself."

"I don't think Dickon suffers from that. I don't think he gives it a thought."

"There are things you don't understand about Dickon. I know you think your mother and I spoil him . . ."

"I understand how you feel about him. He's your son."

"I'm so proud of him," said Sabrina. "He's beginning to look so like his father."

Dear Sabrina! Hers had been a tragic life, in a way. I went to her and kissed her.

"It's so fascinating to be here . . . in the old place I know so well."

"I don't think we should stay more than two weeks."

"Why, Zipporah, we have only just come. You don't want to go home already."

I thought: I do. I am going to be miserable here. . . . There is too much to remember.

"You hate leaving Lottie. Admit it."

"Yes," I said. "I want to be with her."

"It'll soon pass . . . and we shall be on the road again."

I nodded fervently, wishing that I had never come.

I spent a restless night, haunted by dreams. Once I woke up and thought there was a rattle on the window. I got out of bed foolishly expecting to see Gerard there. Oh, I should never have come. There were so many memories.

Although the atmosphere of the house had changed subtly

and it now had a more conventional aspect, there were one or two incidents to remind me of the past.

I had an opportunity to be alone with Uncle Carl and he smiled at me knowingly, making me feel that there was a secret between us.

"It's right," he said, "that you should come now and then . . . Zipporah. Come more often. You must keep an eye on things, mustn't you? Because one day you'll be mistress here. That was the will, you remember."

"I remember," I said.

"You and your heirs will live here one day. And gradually all the ancestors will be at rest. Oh, it's a very comfortable life here for me. You're a clever girl. You saw how it should be done, didn't you? Life is good here. . . . You said something to Jessie . . . did you?"

"I pointed out that her well-being depended on yours," I said.

He gave a deep laugh in his throat and went on laughing. For a moment I thought he was going to choke.

"That was it. Oh, I'm cosseted, Zipporah. Mustn't be upset . . . they've got to keep me alive, haven't they?"

"They are here to look after you. And you have not signed any more pieces of paper?"

He shook his head and looked crafty. "Nothing," he said. "I've not been asked to. You must have explained it all pretty clearly. Clever girl, Zipporah. You'll be a good mistress of Eversleigh. I feel very pleased with myself."

"You still have the same agent?"

"Oh yes, Amos Carew is still here . . . couldn't easily do without him."

"I see. Well, everything seems to have worked out satisfactorily."

"Clever Zipporah!" he said.

I was amazed that he could calmly contemplate keeping a housekeeper who might possibly want to get rid of him—but why couch the language in such terms? Why not say, who would be prepared to murder him if the stakes were high enough?

How could he tolerate such a woman! But it was of course that sexual magnetism. She had that, I was sure, and it would appeal very strongly to a certain type of man. It was her weapon, and heaven knew she used it to advantage.

Still, I no longer felt uneasy. Uncle Carl would be well looked after until the day he died, for it was very necessary for Jessie to keep him alive.

Dickon, true to his word, explored the house from top to bottom. Evalina showed him round. It was Jessie's suggestion that she should. He was completely entranced by the place and when he asked that he be permitted to accompany Amos Carew on his rounds of the estate, and he was allowed to do so, he came back, eyes shining.

"It's worth three of Clavering," he said.

He went out a great deal with Amos Carew and the two of them seemed to be getting really friendly. Amos told Sabrina that he was more than an interested observer. On one or two occasions he had given Amos a hand with the estate work. He really enjoyed it and had a flair for it. "He seems to grasp a problem in no time. He's got a gift for estate management, if you will forgive me saying so, madam," he told Sabrina.

She was very proud of her son. It was the first time Dickon had ever shown interest in work of any kind. We had heard from the curate that he was a reluctant scholar, quite different from Tom Sanders, the vicar's son with whom he shared his lessons.

Quite often Sabrina and I rode together. I think we both shared mixed feelings about these excursions — indeed about the entire visit. Sabrina's memories were not so recent as mine nor so poignant; they were melancholy, though. She hated to go past the lake near Enderby where once she had had an accident while skating and was saved by her mother, whose death, many said, had been hastened by the event. And yet... her horse always seemed to lead her to Enderby. There was an irresistible urge to go near the place where she had been unhappy. I understood perfectly because it was the same with me. I also found it hard to keep away. When we went out on foot I could never resist stepping over the broken palings and walking into the haunted patch. Perhaps I felt that Gerard would suddenly appear there as he had the first time I saw him.

"It's a gloomy spot," said Sabrina. "I don't know why we come here."

"There's something fascinating about it."

"Fascinating but repelling," agreed Sabrina.

"I'm tired," I said. "Let's sit."

"Here? Within sight of old Enderby and the ghost patch?"

"Why not? I've a feeling we are safe here today."

We sat down leaning against those palings where they were not broken.

"I wonder they don't clear up this place," said Sabrina. "This was a rose garden at one time."

"Perhaps no one wants to have anything to do with it."

Sabrina said: "Sitting here like this when it is so quiet all around I could go right back to my childhood."

I nodded. I was back on that evening at dusk when I had stepped over those palings and first met Gerard.

"You'll have Eversleigh one day, Zipporah," said Sabrina.

"That is if Uncle Carl doesn't change his mind."

"How can he?"

"Well, Jessie might persuade him to yet."

"She'd have to get over those solicitors of his. I reckon they'd soon be up in arms if she tried to do anything like that. His mind seems very lively."

I nodded, thinking of myself going into his room starry-eyed from my encounter with Gerard and Uncle Carl's looking at me and calling me Carlotta. Had that been deliberate or had he really thought for a moment that I was the girl he had once admired so much?

"Your mother and I have talked a lot about . . . Dickon."

I smiled and Sabrina went on: "I know you think we talk about little else."

"You are rather devoted to the boy."

"You understand, Zipporah."

"Yes, I understand."

"Well, we are a bit concerned about him . . . what he'll do when he grows up. You see . . . if you have Eversleigh . . . Jean-Louis will go there with you. He can't manage Clavering as well. Clavering belonged to your father and you are the heir to that. You see you are rather a fortunate young woman, Zipporah. Two estates falling into your lap."

"Clavering belongs to my mother," I said quickly, "and she is young yet."

"Oh, I know . . . but we talked of these things. They have to be arranged, you know, and it is unwise to put off talking of them because you're trying to delude yourself into thinking your loved ones are immortal."

"My mother discussed this, did she?"

"Yes. We thought that if and when Eversleigh is yours she might—if you were agreeable—make over Clavering to Dickon."

"I see," I said slowly.

"You see," went on Sabrina eagerly, "he will have no inheritance really except what I have had from my father. He was not rich and times have been hard. Money has lost much of its value. Houses . . . land . . . they are the only assets which don't seem to deteriorate. It would only happen of course if Eversleigh became yours. You can't be in two places at once."

"No. . . . What of Jean-Louis?"

"We thought you could talk it over with him."

"He has put a great deal into Clavering."

"I know."

"He loves the place. He was brought up there, you know, as I was . . . apart from the time I spent in London before, before . . ."

Sabrina had turned sharply away. She could not bear any reference to my father's death.

I went on quickly: "I am sure he would realize that if I were to inherit Eversleigh we should have to come here. That is the idea, isn't it? The family continuing through the generations. Then of course he couldn't be in Clavering. I will talk to him about it."

"Thank you, Zipporah. You see, if Dickon develops this love of estate managing, it would be just what he needed . . . and with an estate of his own . . ."

"I do see," I said. "I think it would be the only solution . . . if . . . and when. . . . But I don't count on it, Sabrina. I know you see my uncle as an old man looked after in a well-run household by a housekeeper who takes a few liberties to which we have to turn a blind eye because she really is doing a necessary job and Uncle Carl is satisfied with the way she does it. When I came before it didn't seem quite like that."

"Well, it is all right now. Jessie sees which side her bread is buttered and she'll keep on enjoying it for as long as she can, which means Uncle Carl lives on."

As we were getting up a woman walked by.

She was fresh-faced, middle-aged and gave us a pleasant smile.

"Good day," she said and hesitated.

We returned the greeting and she went on: "I have seen you around in the last few days. You're staying at the Court, aren't you?"

We told her we were and she said: "I live at Enderby."

I felt my heart begin to beat fast. Gerard's friends—the owners of Enderby who had lent him the house while they were away. Perhaps I could get news of him.

Sabrina was saying: "My parents lived at Enderby until they died."

"Oh, well, you would know the house well."

"We can't resist coming to have a look at it."

"Then you must come in and see what you think we have made of it."

Sabrina was as excited as I was.

"It's so kind of you," she said.

"Not at all. We're thinking of cutting down some of the trees to make the house lighter."

"That was done once," said Sabrina. "My mother did it when she went to live there."

"They seem to grow so quickly here. Sometimes I feel that

141

one morning I'll wake up to find us completely shut in by them."

She feels it, I thought. She feels the supernatural power of the house.

On the other hand she looked happy and proud as she opened the door and let us in.

Memories came rushing back. I fancied I could hear the sounds of the fair in the nearby fields. I felt sick with longing to be with Gerard again ... to go back in time, to mount that staircase with him to the bedroom with the white and gold brocade curtains that had ... for an instant looked red in the afternoon sunlight.

Sabrina was looking up at the minstrels' gallery.

Our hostess laughed. "Oh, that's the part that is said to be haunted. When we bought the house we were warned. I said I was not afraid of the ghost and would leave out a glass of wine for him ... or her ... if she would deign to visit me."

"And you still feel the same now you live here?" asked Sabrina.

"I've never *seen* anything. Perhaps I'm not the type they like to visit."

"I think a great deal depends on your attitude towards them," I said. "When I was here last time I met someone who was staying here...."

At that moment a man appeared on the staircase.

"We have visitors, Derek," said our hostess. "They know Enderby well. Isn't that interesting? Come down and meet these ladies. This is my husband, Derek Forster. I am Isabel."

He was as pleasantly welcoming at his wife.

"You'll have a glass of wine," she said. "I'll send for it. Just a moment. Derek, take them into the winter parlor."

He ushered us in and Sabrina said: "I'm Sabrina Frenshaw and this is my cousin's daughter, Zipporah Ransome."

"I'm delighted to meet you," he said.

His wife returned to us. "Refreshment is coming," she said. "Do sit down, mistress ... ?" She paused and looked at Sabrina, who said: "Frenshaw."

"Mistress Frenshaw spent her childhood in this house."

"Then you must be . . ."

"Sabrina Granthorn, that was. The daughter of Jeremy Granthorn, who once owned the house."

"Oh yes, we had heard. That's fascinating. So you spent your childhood here."

"Yes, and so did Zipporah's mother, for she was brought up by my mother."

"I daresay you know every nook and cranny."

I was longing to find out what she knew of Gerard and said: "When I came here to see my uncle I met a friend of yours who was staying here."

They looked at each other in a puzzled way.

"Gerard d'Aubigné," I said.

They looked blank.

"You had lent him the house while you were away," I went on.

"We've not been away. We've never lent anyone the house. . . ." Then Derek Forster smiled suddenly. "Well, we haven't been here two years yet. When did you come?"

I felt a great relief. I had begun to feel that I had had some uncanny adventure and that Gerard was indeed someone risen from the grave.

"It was three years ago."

"Well," said Derek, "that explains it. Gerard d'Aubigné, you say? That sounds like a Frenchman."

"Yes," I said, "he was."

"They were strange people, I believe. I never saw them. They left in rather a hurry. The sale was affected through some proxy. It was all rather mysterious. It was said that they had been working for the French and had to leave the country quickly. Your Frenchman seems to confirm the story."

"I didn't meet them myself," I said. "I gathered they had lent the house to him for a short period."

"Spies, I imagine. Well, there is nothing like that about us, is there, Derek?"

"No, I'm afraid we're rather dull."

"And you enjoy the house?" I asked

"It's an interesting house," said Derek.

"Now you mention it," said Isabel, "I sometimes feel it's not quite like other houses."

"We got it at a very reasonable price," said Derek. "Too good to miss, in fact. My brother said we should be fools not to take it. He was particularly anxious that we should because he's going to start a practice in the town. He's a doctor, you see."

"It feels different," said Sabrina. "I think the atmosphere is something to do with the people who live in a house."

"That would seem inevitable, I suppose."

The wine was excellent, so were the little wine cakes which went with it and we were both sorry when we had to rise to go.

"How long are you staying?" asked Isabel.

"Not long. A fortnight perhaps."

Sabrina said: "Lord Eversleigh is getting so old now. I think he likes to see his relations."

I wondered if there was any gossip in the village about the situation there and I was sure that if there was, a woman like Isabel Forster would hear of it.

"He has a housekeeper who seems to keep a tight hand on everything."

Yes, I thought there might be a certain amount of gossip.

We said good-bye and were asked to call again if we could spare the time. The Forsters would be delighted to see us at any time.

We went back to Eversleigh feeling we had had an interesting morning.

I decided that I must call on Jethro and seek a time when I might find him alone. I imagined if anyone was in Uncle Carl's confidence here, it would be Jethro. After all, he had used him once before.

At the midday meal Jessie had been more talkative. I was under the impression that she had felt her way carefully with Sabrina and was still a little in awe of her. She did not eat with us as she had on my previous visit but was always bustling round to make sure, she implied, that everything was to our taste. "You can't trust these maids nowadays," she was fond of saying.

We rose from the table. Sabrina was going to call on the Forsters that afternoon. I knew Sabrina well and I imagined she liked to think of the past even though it was unpleasant. I decided that I did not want to go to Enderby again. I knew I could find out nothing about Gerard and I felt no desire to go there and revive memories which caused me such longing.

Jessie was looking at me rather slyly as I brushed past her. "I reckon you're missing your little girl, Mistress Ransome," she said.

I nodded.

"Well, she'll be all of . . . what is it? two years. You see, I remember. She must have been born about nine momths after you left here. . . ." She gave me a little nudge.

I felt the color rush to my face. I looked at Sabrina. She had noticed nothing. I turned back to Jessie and said: "Well, I shall soon be back with her."

And went out. The remark had shaken me. What did Jessie mean by it? When I had turned to look at her her expression had been one of bland innocence. But the nudge . . . Well, nudging was a habit with her.

Was I oversensitive? I was a married woman. It was to be expected that I should have a child and if I did so after a visit, even though she had been careful enough to mention the time lapse, it was not so very significant.

I went out to find Jethro and I did. He was in his cottage.

"Ah," he said, "I thought maybe you'd be calling on me sometime, Mistress Zipporah."

"I had to talk to you, Jethro. Tell me, how is everything at the Court?"

"It's all as it should be, it seems. His lordship is happy. Jessie gives herself airs and still behaves as though she's the mistress of the house—which in a way she is, there being no mistress there . . . mistress of the staff, you might say—but she does take her rule on the other side of the screens, if you get my meaning."

"I thought she was a little more respectful."

"Oh yes, she is that. And she takes great care of his lordship."

"I have seen that and I don't think it is just for our benefit. She is really anxious to keep him alive."

"She changed after you went, Mistress Zipporah. I don't know what you did . . . but you did something."

"I just pointed out that the easy life was hers only as long as Lord Eversleigh was alive to provide it."

Jethro's brown old face wrinkled up into a grin.

"Well, it did the trick and everyone seems happy."

I wondered if Jessie was, for she had had grandiose schemes for getting her hands on Eversleigh.

I said: "And the afternoon visits to Amos Carew, do they still continue?"

"They do, Mistress Zipporah."

"Jethro," I said, "I shall have to go soon. Can you keep me informed?"

Jethro looked embarrassed and I realized I had been tactless. Of course, he couldn't read or write.

I went on: "Perhaps you could send a messenger to me. . . . Is there anyone . . . ?"

He looked dubious and I went on: "It would only be in an emergency of course."

"I'd do my best, Mistress Zipporah, but all is well now and has been since you came, before which is some time now."

I had to leave it at that.

I came away thoughtfully from Jethro's cottage and as I did not feel like returning to the house I started to walk in the opposite direction.

I was deep in thought. I was visualizing myself living here with Jean-Louis and meanwhile Dickon would be at Clavering. Life would be so different. I should have to get rid of Jessie quickly and I wondered what her reaction would be. I had not liked her remark about Lottie's birth nor the suggestive and significant nudge which had accompanied it.

So deep in thought was I that I had not noticed that the sky had darkened; I heard a rumble of thunder in the distance and thought I should have to hurry back if I was to reach the house before the storm broke.

I was near one of the farms which was a quarter of a mile from Eversleigh when the rain started to come down in torrents. There were patches of blue sky on the horizon so I guessed that it was only a passing storm. I was not far from a barn and I sprinted across, opened the door and went in. It would only be for five minutes or so, I was sure.

It was dark in the barn after coming from the light and my eyes took a few seconds to adjust.

Then I saw that I was not alone.

They were lying in the hay...two people. I tried not to look at them for they were in a state of disarray and were in such a close embrace that at first I had thought it was one person who lay there.

I felt my heart begin to beat as the realization came to me that the two people lying there were Dickon and Evalina.

I wanted to turn and run but I felt as though my feet had taken root.

I stammered: "Dickon...Evalina..."

Dickon was looking at me; he was still holding Evalina. She had turned her face toward me.

"Don't look at me like that," cried Evalina. "What about yourself, eh? Some people shouldn't condemn others for what they do themselves."

I felt sick. I turned and ran out into the blinding rain.

My boots were sodden; my clothes saturated and my hair hung damply round my face as I stepped into the hall.

Jessie was there talking to Sabrina.

"My goodness," cried Jessie. "You're wet through."

"Why...Zipporah," said Sabrina, "you shouldn't have come through that rain."

"You should have stood up...and waited," said Jessie.
"Get them wet things off. Rub yourself down with a towel.
Would you like a cup of hot soup?"

"Nothing," I said. "It was foolish of me."

I thought as I went upstairs: I want nothing but to get away
from this house.

I had discarded my wet things and put on dry ones. I went
along to Sabrina's room.

I said to her vehemently: "I want to go home...soon."

"Well," she said, "perhaps we should start making plans.
Dickon won't like it. He's happy here."

Dickon. I thought: Don't talk to me of Dickon! I could not
shut out the memory of his face as he lay there in the barn
looking at me...insolently.

She would tell him. He would know my secret. It must have
been Evalina who had listened outside my door.

What did she know? What had she told Dickon? Most as-
suredly she would have told him of her suspicions.

I began to feel afraid as I had not before.

I saw her a few hours later. She was in the hall with her
mother.

She looked at me defiantly, as though to say, *Tell on me
and I'll tell on you.*

It was blackmail. I remembered that other occasion when
she had bought my silence with the key of my door.

I wanted to get away from this house. It was evil, I knew
it.

She was smiling at me blandly.

"You got very wet, Mistress Ransome," she said. "Mother
told me that you came in really soaked. Did you change? You
ought to. You don't want to catch a cold, do you?"

"Thank you for your concern," I said.

She gave me an innocent smile.

Two days later we left Eversleigh. Sabrina, I think, was
happy to go, though Dickon was rather sullen.

"I believe you've really fallen in love with the place," said his mother fondly.

"I like it," answered Dickon. "I like it a lot."

And all the way home I was wondering what Evalina had said to him.

Harvest Home

*M*ore than a year had passed since our return from Eversleigh. It had been an eventful time as far as the country
was concerned for George the Second died and his grandson
ascended the throne. The third George was a youth of twenty-
two and very much under the influence of his mother and Lord
Bute, the man who was said to be her lover and that, most
people said, augured no good for England.

In the country I was too immersed in my own private affairs
to think much about which George ruled us — second or third,
it seemed unimportant to me.

During the year I had not visited Eversleigh. Sometimes I
felt I should go but I could never bring myself to it. The thought
of facing Jessie and Evalina repelled me so strongly that I made
excuse after excuse to myself not to go. There was no need, I
would say. Uncle Carl had written — there were about four
letters over the year — and he was well and happy and very
well cared for. These words he underlined. Life was as good
as it could be for an old man who could do little but sit in his

chair or lie in his bed and review the days of glory—or folly, whichever way one looked at it.

Time passed so quickly and I had given up hope of ever seeing Gerard again. I did not think of him so frequently as I had in the past and when I did it was to look back on that adventure as something not quite real. I could even believe that Lottie was Jean-Louis's daughter. She was four years old now and beautiful. I suppose all mothers think that their children are more beautiful and intelligent than others but I don't think I was exaggerating her charms. Those violet eyes, with their fringe of dark lashes, and dark curling hair alone would have made her a beauty. She was not plump as some children are; her face was oval, her chin a little pointed. There were times when she looked older than her years. She was spritelike, mischievous, not fractious but fun-loving. Needless to say she was adored.

My mother, who could only vaguely remember her own mother—the legendary Carlotta—said she was sure there was a resemblance between my daughter and her great-grandmother.

Dickon had never betrayed by a look or a word that he knew of what had happened to me at Eversleigh before Lottie's birth. He never referred to my surprising him in the barn with Evalina. Perhaps he had not asked her what she had meant when she had shouted at me. It might have been the sort of remark that could have been thrown at anyone. Perhaps he thought that his behavior with Evalina was commonplace—as it might well be with him—and that my stepping into the barn at such a moment was no more than opening someone's door before they were properly dressed.

His attitude toward me had never been of a friendly nature. He had always sensed my disapproval—or rather my refusal to adore him as his mother and my mother did.

Our visit to Eversleigh had changed him, though. He became thoughtful and serious; he was to go away to school but he persuaded his mother and mine that he should not go.

He wanted to learn about the estate.

"Darling," said Sabrina, "you have to be educated, you know."

"I am. I'll go on with old Faulkner. But I want to be here. I want to be with you, dear mother, and you, Aunt Clarissa."

It amazed me how he could get his way with them. He was not demonstrative by nature and to have him declaring that he wanted to be with them—as though for their own sakes—seemed to put them into such a delirium of joy that they were ready to grant him anything.

They exchanged glances, their eyes brim full of joy.

"Well, shall we leave it for a while?" said my mother. "Postpone school for another year, shall we say?"

He was now in his fifteenth year but he looked eighteen. He had shot up amazingly and was nearly six feet tall and there was more growing time left to him. He was very handsome, with light blond hair—thick and waving—and very piercing blue eyes; he had perfect teeth and his skin was flawless; moreover, his feature was so perfectly chiseled that he might have been a Greek god. In fact he reminded me of Michelangelo's *David*. There was one flaw and it was only apparent at times. It was most obvious when that calculating look came into his face and then it reminded me of a fox's mask. Cunning was there, ruthlessness, an absolute disregard for what stood in the way of his getting what he wanted. But I seemed to be the only one who saw this. I knew that he had tried to shift the blame for the fire onto the gardener's boy. I would remember that because it was the beginning of the decline in Jean-Louis's health. I knew too that for some time he had come to manhood physically. I had seen his watchful eyes on some of the prettier maids; he reminded me then of a fox waiting to spring on a chicken. I knew that he was growing up into a ruthlessly ambitious man whose sexual appetites would be voracious and that he would not care in what manner they were satisfied as long as they were. Perhaps these qualities were born in him—although I understood his father had been a kindly idealistic man, and Sabrina might have been rebellious in her youth but there was an inherent goodness in her. But the indulgence he had received from those two doting women had certainly not helped to eradicate his less attractive qualities.

But there was no doubt now that he was going to work hard. He was constantly with James Fenton and would ride with him round the estate listening intently to all that passed between the agent and the farmers. He was also often in the company of Jean-Louis, which meant that he came over from the Hall almost every day.

"That boy has a real flair for estate management," said Jean-Louis. "He reminds me of myself at his age. I always wanted to manage the place."

"He seems to have changed so suddenly," I said. "He did not seem to be interested in work before."

My mother and Sabrina were delighted. They thought he was more wonderful than ever—if that were possible.

I found James Fenton very interesting. He was fond of talking. He had been abroad for some time in France so that he felt he had a knowledge of that country. That was what had first aroused my interest in him. He was a very good agent, Jean-Louis said; and he was grateful to have someone on whom he could rely just now, for he tired very easily and he could not walk at all without the aid of his stick. I often wondered whether he was getting worse but he always shrugged aside my inquiries, and as I knew he hated talking of his disability I refrained from mentioning it.

They were peaceful days and there were long periods when I was lulled into a sense of security. My life with Jean-Louis was satisfactory. I knew my attitude toward him had changed since I had made that fateful visit to Eversleigh. I had been very solicitous towards him and he was immensely grateful and I believe he thought it was something to do with his disability. He loved me very tenderly and was always anxious to assure me of this. I knew I was lucky in my husband. I did sometimes wonder what life would have been like with Gerard—wild, passionate, stormy. There would have been jealousy perhaps, misunderstandings, quarrels and reconciliations. Life would have been lived on a different plane, but would our love have stood the stress? I wondered. Could such violent passion as that which we had shared go on? Surely its power must diminish. Sometimes I even thought it had been so overwhelming for me because it was illicit. I couldn't understand myself yet. I still longed for that ecstasy I had shared so briefly with Gerard. That comes once in a lifetime, I told myself. You achieved it; you have recovered from it; you have had a miraculous escape. Be contented.

And I had my Lottie—my delightful wayward sprite of a child, who was, my mother was fond of saying, so unlike what I had been at her age. "You were such a good little thing, Zipporah," she said often. "So easy to understand."

So life went on. Uncle Carl coddled and contented through our clever strategy with his Jessie; myself a happy wife and mother who had succeeded in forgetting her own now long ago lapse; and my mother and Sabrina looking on with admiration at their darling's preoccupation with work.

James Fenton said to me: "It is a good thing really that he is taking such an interest. It could be useful to have him working with us when he's older, for Jean-Louis gets more tired than he will admit, and young Dickon does make himself useful."

I knew what was in Dickon's mind. He believed that one day Jean-Louis and I would go to Eversleigh and that he would inherit Clavering. Anything that was his would loom very important in his mind. Thus it was with Clavering. He saw it through new eyes.

There were long summer evenings after Lottie was in bed when we sat and talked—Jean-Louis, James Fenton and I. There were occasions when Dickon would join us; and if he did the talk was all about the estate.

One day a cousin of James's called on him. He was a soldier and he had come from France and stayed a few days with James before going on to his family in the Midlands. James brought him to sup with us and we learned from him a great deal of what was happening on the Continent.

The war was still dragging on but, said James's cousin Albert, both sides were getting tired of it and as no subsidies were being sent fighting was desultory. Each side seemed to spend the time in retreating and advancing and no progress was made.

"It's a mess . . . as most wars are. It can't go on . . . and it's inconclusive anyway. They say there are negotiations beginning for peace."

I was thoughtful. If there were peace, I thought, would Gerard come again?

"The people here are indifferent," said James. "They see the war as something happening a long way off and therefore of no concern to them."

"The taxes to pay for it are their concern," his cousin reminded him.

"Well, there are always taxes for something."

His cousin was thoughtful for a moment. Then he said: "Something is happening in France."

"What?" I asked eagerly.

He turned to me, his brow puckering. "There's a certain mood among the people. They resent the king so much that he dare not appear in Paris. He has had a road built between Versailles and Compiègne to bypass the city so that he need not ride through it."

"You mean he is afraid of his people?"

"He is too indifferent to them to feel fear. He just despises them. He does not want to see them. Their problems are of no interest to him."

"But surely he depends on their approval to hold his throne!"

"The French monarchy is different from ours . . . just as the people are. They are more formal . . . and yet they could be more terrible. They are more excitable than we are . . . more impulsive. Though I suppose the people here would rise up if provoked too far."

"What happens there?" I asked. I was thinking of the Château d'Aubigné, the name of which was so engraved on my memory that I would never forget it.

"There is a subtle change. The king is so dissolute. He cares for nothing but his own pleasure. He leaves everything to the

Pompadour, who is consequently hated and shares the blame with the king. He seems concerned only with his own debaucheries and the infamous Parc aux Cerfs is discussed and reviled throughout the country. There is the dauphin, whom the king hates. They say he does not wish to see him because he will be his successor and he cannot bear to think of death. Even the nobility is changing and the wealthy are buying themselves into the aristocracy. It isn't the same. They haven't the same sense of responsibility. I don't like it. It makes me very uneasy."

"Is this feeling general throughout France?" asked Jean-Louis.

"So many seem intent on nothing but their own pleasure. The king for one. It has been said that he was heard to remark when warned of signs of unrest, 'Oh, it will last my time.' 'And after you, sire?' he was asked. 'After me,' he said, shrugging his shoulders, 'the deluge.'"

"How terrible!" I cried.

"Oh, these things happen in countries," said Jean-Louis. "Everything seems desperate and then there is a change . . . and prosperity comes and the dark days are forgotten."

"I trust it will be so," said James's cousin.

While they were talking a caller arrived.

It was Hetty Hassock who had come to ask if James would call on her father in the morning when he was making his rounds.

James rose, smiling at Hetty.

"Well, of course I'll come," he said. "What time would suit your father? Say eleven o'clock?"

"That would suit him very well, I'm sure," said Hetty. She was a very pretty girl about seventeen, I think, and rather different from the rest of the Hassock family. She had recently come to the farm, having been brought up by an aunt in London.

Hetty apologized for intruding and Jean-Louis assured her that she had done no such thing and he added: "Come and sit with us a moment, Hetty." Hetty flushed a little and returned to the table. James looked pleased.

"Would you like to try this malmsey?" asked Jean-Louis. "We're rather proud of it."

Hetty declined gratefully but she sat down.

"How are you liking it at the farm?" I asked. "You must find it very different from London."

"Oh yes, I miss the town . . . but everything is interesting here and I suppose I should be with my family."

There were four Hassock girls and three boys. Hetty was quite different from all the others. I believed Farmer Hassock was very proud of her. I had heard him say only the other day "Our Het's been brought up like a lady."

While she sat there making light conversation I was struck by James Fenton's expression. He was watching her with obvious pleasure. I thought, He's halfway to falling in love with her—perhaps he is already there, and I felt pleased.

That night I mentioned it to Jean-Louis. He agreed with me that he had noticed.

"It would be a good thing for James to marry," he said, "and I think Hetty would make him a good wife. She is intelligent as well as pretty and she is different from so many of the girls around here. More likes James himself. I'd be glad to see James marry. He'd feel more settled. Let's hope something comes of it."

The matter about which Farmer Hassock wanted to see James turned out to be the strip of land between his farm and that of Farmer Burrows. Long ago it appeared there had been some controversy about this particular spot because there was uncertainty as to which farm it had originally belonged. My father—who had been a lover of peace and who had really been more interested in gambling than the estate—had solved the problem by saying that neither should have it. Therefore it had been fenced off and lay idle for some years.

Now Farmer Hassock wanted a little more space for his wheat and he was sure that Farmer Burrows had forgotten all about the controversy which had been in the time of his father.

He wondered whether he might take down the fence and take in this strip of land.

James and Jean-Louis discussed it for a while and they both agreed that to allow the land to lie idle was rather foolish when Hassock, who was a better farmer than Burrows in any case, could make good use of it.

"Let Hassock have it," said James. "I'll tell him to go ahead and prepare the land. It will need a bit of work after all these years. He should get a start on it right away."

James rode over to the farm to tell Hassock the verdict and I had no doubt to have a word with Hetty while he was there.

It was a few days later when Dickon came over. We were at table still after the midday meal, for we liked to sit awhile and talk of the affairs of the estate and of the country as a whole.

Dickon appeared flushed and I was struck afresh by his handsome looks. He seemed to have grown a little every time I saw him.

He sat down unceremoniously and said: "Do you know what Hassock is doing? He's taken down the fence of that no-man's-land strip and is obviously intending to use it."

"That's right," said James. "He's going to extend his wheat field."

"But it's not his."

"He's been given permission," said James.

"Who gave him permission?"

"I did," answered James.

"But who said you might?" Dickon's voice was cold and haughty.

Jean-Louis said quickly: "I did. James and I discussed it and decided it was foolish to let the land lie idle and Hassock was the one to make the best use of it."

"I don't agree," said Dickon.

"*You* don't agree," cried James. He was less calm than Jean-Louis, and Dickon's behavior was certainly provoking.

"No," retorted Dickon, "I don't. Burrows has as much right to that land as Hassock. I've told him so."

"Dickon," said Jean-Louis, "I know how much you care about the estate, and you have been very helpful, but James and I must decide on these matters. It is our job to run the estate profitably."

"Hassock must be told to stop what he is doing immediately. James, you should tell him that before he goes too far."

"The matter has been decided," said James. "If Burrows is dissatisfied he had better come here to discuss it with Jean-Louis and me. There has been too much trouble in the past over that strip of land. It is very insignificant in any case."

"I have told Burrows that he shall have it since Hassock has taken it into his head to filch it."

"Filch it!" I could see that James's temper was rising. "This is absurd. You have been helping us on the estate for a few months and you think that you are fit to manage it . . . going over our heads. We have had years of experience in these matters."

Dickon stood up. "We shall see," he said.

When he had left we looked at each other in amazement.

I said: "He has gone to my mother."

"Lady Clavering will understand that we are managing the estate," said James.

"I hope so. But she is inclined to indulge Dickon."

James shook his head. "She will see the sense of this."

"Shall I go over to see her this afternoon?" I asked.

"I'll come with you," said Jean-Louis.

My mother was delighted to see us as always and asked questions about Lottie, whom she hadn't seen for two whole days, which seemed a long time to her.

"We've come to talk business," I told her. "James is rather put out."

"Oh yes . . . Dickon was saying that there had been a disagreement about that land. He's given it to Burrows."

"No," I put in. "Jean-Louis and James had decided that Hassock should have it."

"And he has already been given permission to use it," added Jean-Louis.

"Oh, dear," said my mother, "how tiresome these people are! Your father always said, Zipporah, that the land was almost useless."

"Well, Hassock can make good use of it," said Jean-Louis.

"And," I added, "he has already been given permission to have it."

"Oh, but Dickon has promised it to Burrows."

"Mother," I said, "Dickon has no right to promise anything. Just because he has been allowed to have a little insight into the way the estate is run he thinks it belongs to him. It's yours, and Jean-Louis and James manage it. How can they do that successfully if this . . . *boy* comes in and tells them what to do."

"Don't let him hear you call him a boy," said my mother.

"What else is he? Please be sensible. I know how you dote on him but . . ."

She looked as though she were going to burst into tears. I think she sensed some reproach in my words implying that she cared for this son of the man she had once loved more than for her own daughter.

I went to her quickly and put my arm about her. "Mother dear, you do see that Jean-Louis and James must have a free hand. I know the estate is yours . . . but you know little of it. You can't undermine the manager's standing with the tenants, otherwise there would be chaos. And just because this pampered boy suddenly takes an interest and thinks he can have his own way you cannot give in to him. I think we should probably lose James if you did."

"We can't afford to lose James," said Jean-Louis. "I need him now."

He looked sad and I felt fresh anger against Dickon for creating this absurd situation.

My mother looked apologetically at us both and said: "It was so wonderful to see him . . . enthusiastic . . . and caring about it all."

"It doesn't mean he can run it, mother," I said. "You can't seriously be thinking of letting him have his own way."

She hesitated and I cried out: "You are. Then I think you

had better hand over the management to Dickon. James will resign and so perhaps will Jean-Louis."

"Zipporah. How can you say that? You and Jean-Louis are my own . . . my daughter and my son. . . ."

"But you will still have Dickon, you know," I said angrily. For I realized now that I hated Dickon, and because my hatred was tinged with a certain emotion—not exactly fear but uneasiness—I was unusually vehement.

My mother was at heart a very sensible woman and it was only when her emotions were deeply involved that she would behave without good sense.

She saw in that moment the absurdity of the situation and must have realized that she was jeopardizing the love of her own daughter for the sake of Sabrina's son.

She said quietly: "Of course. . . . Jean-Louis and James know best. Poor Dickon, he will be very disappointed. It is such a pity that this should have happened just when he is getting so excited about the place."

We had won the battle. Hassock would continue preparing the land. Burrows would have to accept that and realize that Dickon was not in a position to make promises which he had no power to keep.

It was the next day that Dickon came over when we were at the table. I guessed that he had just heard of the decision, for I could imagine my mother's putting off telling him for as long as she could.

He came in glaring at us. His glance was cold but I could see the anger seething beneath it.

"So," he said looking at James, "you have been to Lady Clavering."

"James did not," I said. "Jean-Louis and I saw her."

"And you have persuaded her to go against me."

"It's not against you, Dickon," said Jean-Louis. "It's a matter of what we consider best for the estate."

"What! That strip of land! It's been idle for years and years! What effect does that have on the estate?"

"Hassock asked for it," said Jean-Louis, "and James and I decided he should have it. That could not be rescinded."

"Why not? Burrows has just as much right."

"We decided that Hassock should have it. He asked for it first, Burrows did not," said Jean-Louis.

"Hassock! Yes, of course!" Dickon was glaring at James. "You have a special fancy for Hassock . . . the girl. . . ."

James stood up and said: "What do you mean?"

"I mean that you can't refuse dear little Hetty anything, can you, and if she says papa wants that bit of land, papa has to have it."

"Hetty Hassock has nothing to do with this," said James. "Please do not bring her into it."

"It seems to me she is there . . . say what you will. I've eyes in my head, you know. I don't go around blind."

Jean-Louis said sternly: "You must behave properly in this house, Dickon, or I shall ask you to leave."

Dickon bowed ironically: "I do not exactly yearn to stay," he said. "But let me tell you this, James Fenton, I shall not forget this insult."

"Don't be ridiculous, Dickon," I burst out, "You haven't been insulted. You've probably been sympathetic to Burrows but he doesn't expect a boy like you to make important decisions on the estate."

His glance swept over me fleetingly. He looked for a few seconds at James and that look of cold implacable hatred in his eyes made me very uneasy.

He turned and went.

Jean-Louis shook his head. "That boy should be sent away to school," he said.

After the haymaking Lottie's nanny developed a bad cold which turned to bronchitis. We missed her very much because she was an extremely efficient young woman. I did not like to leave Lottie to the servants and took over the care of her myself.

It was James who suggested that I should have some temporary help. I soon understood why.

"Hetty Hassock would like to come over and give you a hand with Lottie," he said. "I think you would find her very useful."

I was amused because I knew now that James was interested in Hetty. Jean-Louis and I had discussed the matter often. We were both very fond of James; he was no ordinary agent for not only did he take a keen interest in the estate, the management of which he did extremely well, but he was an amusing companion; meal times were enlivened by his conversation; moreover, I had noticed that he took over, most unobtrusively, much of the work which he thought would tire Jean-Louis.

Hetty came and I did find her a delightful young woman and during the time she stayed with me I learned quite a lot about her. She was not one to give her confidences easily, being somewhat introspective, I imagined, but in due course we became good friends.

She told me it had not been easy to adjust to life at the farm, coming to it, as she had, when she was grown up.

"Of course," she explained, "I used to pay visits during the summer. I always enjoyed the haymaking and the Harvest Home, but I did find I had little in common with my brothers and sisters."

I understood why. Tom Hassock was quite a good farmer but he had a large family to feed. It was for this reason that his wife's sister had taken Hetty and brought her up, educating her and giving her a different life from that of her brothers and sisters.

"Aunt Emily had married well," Hetty told me, "a tradesman with a mercer's business in Cheapside, and they had lived over the shop." She and her husband had been childless and for this reason soon after Hetty was born they had asked if they could take the burden of a new child off the already pressed Hassocks and bring her up as their own. The farmer and his wife had seen this as a good opportunity for the daughter which must not be missed. So at the age of two Hetty had gone to London.

She had gone to a school in London and had been fed and

clothed in a manner which by the Hassock family was considered affluent.

"It became a little upsetting going home sometimes," she said. "I had so much more than they had. It didn't seem fair. They were always so proud of me, though. Particularly my father. He used to say: 'Hetty is the lady in the family.'"

"Well, that should have made you proud. You mustn't feel ashamed because you were the fortunate one and made use of your good fortune," I said.

"Oh, I don't. But sometimes I think they expect too much of me. When my aunt died I stayed on with my uncle; but after he died his nephew took over the business . . . and he had a wife and four children. There was no room for me so I came home."

"I see. So now you have to adjust to being a farmer's daughter."

"It's difficult. I'm really glad to get away from home for a while."

"Oh, you'll settle down," I said. "And you might marry."

She flushed slightly and lowered her gaze.

Of course she would, I thought. It was obvious that James felt very seriously about her.

The summer had almost gone and autumn was in the air. It was a good harvest that year and everyone was delighted. Preparations for harvest festival went on with great enthusiasm. The church was decorated with all the products of the earth from cabbages to dahlias and chrysanthemums. But the great occasion was in fact the Harvest Home, which would be celebrated on the Saturday before the church festival.

It had been the custom on the estate that the celebration should take place at Clavering Hall, so that all the farmers and the families who lived on the estate could celebrate together. There was a great deal of bustle at the Hall and Dickon threw himself wholeheartedly into the preparations and I think that my mother and Sabrina were especially interested because of Dickon's excitement.

The trouble over the strip of land had not done anything to

diminish his interest and he was still riding round with Jean-Louis or James Fenton and going to the estates office to learn about inside management.

James was very pleased about it and made it clear that he had not liked what had to be done one little bit. Dickon shrugged it aside and I thought that he had forgotten all about it.

He himself concocted the brew in the great punch bowl and the cooks were busy for a long time preparing the feast. No one talked of anything but Harvest Home; every farm had its corn dollies, which were hung up to decorate the hall and bring good luck beside the sheaves of wheat. The fruit, vegetables and great cob loafs would be distributed throughout the district when it was all over.

Fiddlers had been engaged and if the weather was bad there would be dancing in the great hall; if not it would be out of doors—which everyone was hoping for.

Great tables were set up and filled with refreshments. It was going to be one of the best Harvest Homes ever to have been known, said my mother to Sabrina; and they exchanged smiles. It was of course because Dickon had taken part in it.

Lottie's nanny had now recovered but I said she must take things easily for a while as she must be considerably weakened and Hetty should stay with us until she was really strong. As neither of them had any objection, this was arranged.

Two days before the Harvest Home, a message came for James. His cousin, the one who had visited us, wrote that his father was dangerously ill and he wanted to see James before he died.

"You must go, James," said Jean-Louis. "You'd never forgive yourself if you didn't. We'll manage the Harvest Home without you. We have enough helpers. Besides it's more or less settled, and with the harvest in this is the best time for you to take a break."

So James left the day before the Harvest Home.

It was a great occasion with much merry making. The weather was good enough for people to be out of doors so the young ones danced on the lawns and the older ones sat inside and did full justice to the punch and pies and good food which the kitchens had provided.

Dickon had more or less placed himself in charge. He was rather pleased, I think, that James had been called away. I saw my mother and Sabrina watching him admiringly. He looked incredibly handsome, being affable to everyone and dancing the folk dances with such gusto and grace that he was admired by all.

He made sure to dance with most of the farmers' wives, which was a duty James—since Jean-Louis could not—would have performed had he been there.

At ten o'clock Jean-Louis spoke to them and thanked them for the year's good work and then we all sang together Harvest hymn.

It was moving and particularly so perhaps because this year there was so much to be thankful for.

After that Jean-Louis and I went home.

"A most successful Home," he said. "One of the best I remember. A pity James couldn't have been there to see it—because so much is due to his good management."

"Dickon enjoyed it," I said.

"Yes, he seems to have got over that bit of trouble. Learnt his lesson, I daresay."

"I hope so," I said.

The days seemed to fly by. It was the end of October with the days drawing in and the threat of winter in the autumnal mists. James had been away for three weeks. His uncle had died and he had stayed for the funeral. Hetty was still with us, although nanny had recovered now. I had thought she might resent having another woman in the nursery but she liked Hetty; they got on well together and as they both adored Lottie they were happy.

I was pleased because I had grown more and more fond of Hetty and I did know that she was happier with us than she had been on her father's farm.

I noticed gradually that she was rather preoccupied and she

began to lose some of her healthy color. I had the idea that something was troubling her. I asked on one occasion whether there was anything wrong and was told emphatically—perhaps too emphatically—that all was well.

But there *was* something, I knew. Sometimes I would see a blank look in her eyes as though she were trying to make some plan. I thought I detected a certain desperation.

There was a dignity about Hetty which made it impossible to intrude and to ask for confidences which she was not prepared to give. I fancied that she tried to avoid me, and I became seriously worried and decided that I would keep a sharp eye on her.

I considered speaking about her to James, but I thought she might resent that very much. I wondered if something had gone wrong between them. I did mention it to Jean-Louis.

"Some lovers' tiff, I should imagine," he said. "It's always wise to keep out of that sort of thing."

"I suppose I must, but I am worried about her."

So I was watchful—and how thankful I was to be that this was so.

It was November . . . a warm damp day with the mist hanging in patches. I was looking from my window when I saw Hetty leave the house. Whether it was some premonition, perhaps the air of dejection and dogged determination that I seemed to sense, I did not know. But what I did know was that I had to follow her. I had to see where she was going.

I put on a cloak and ran out. I was just in time to see her disappearing round a bend in the lane.

I guessed now that she was going to the river.

To the river! On such a day! For what purpose? Perhaps for a walk. It could only be that.

I kept a good distance between us because I knew that she must not be aware of me. I had to find out where she was going. Perhaps she was meeting James. If so I would discreetly disappear and leave them together. But why should she walk so far to see James when she could see him in the house or near it.

Now I could smell the river and I heard the faint murmur of the water as it lapped the bank.

I watched her. And then suddenly I knew. She let her cloak drop from her shoulder and started to walk toward the water.

"Hetty!" I screamed. "Hetty!"

She stopped and looked round.

I ran to her. I seized her arm and looked into her face. It was white and her eyes were large pools of despair.

"What are you doing?" I demanded.

She stammered: "It's all right. I was only looking at the river."

"No, Hetty, not that. You were doing something. You must tell me. You must let me help."

"There is no way out," she said simply, "but this. Let me go."

"You mean . . . you were going to walk out into the river . . . and not come back!"

"I've thought a lot about it," she answered. "It is hard to do . . . but I can do it. . . ."

"What is it, Hetty? You can tell me. There must be a way out of your trouble. We'll find it. I promise you. You mustn't talk like this. It's wrong . . . it's foolish . . . nothing is so bad that something can't be done about it."

"Nothing can be done about this. I can't face them, Mistress Zipporah. This is the way. I've thought and thought and can see no other."

"Sit down. Tell me all about it."

"I'm wicked," she said. "You could never understand how wicked."

"I can understand. All of us do wrong at times. We fall into temptation. Please tell me, Hetty."

"I'm going to have a baby," she said.

"Oh. Well, James loves you. He'll understand. . . ."

She shook her head and stared blankly in front of her. "It's not James's," she said.

"Hetty."

"Yes, you see. It's shocking, it's awful. There is no way

out . . . but this. I can't face them, any of them. I don't know
how it happened . . . I can't understand. Yet I can't make excuses . . . it was my fault."

"I thought you loved James."

"I do."

"Then . . ."

"You wouldn't understand. How could you? Nobody could
who was not . . . depraved I suppose as I am."

"I'm not so good, Hetty, that I can't understand how these
things happen."

We sat down on the river bank and she turned to me. "It
was on the night of the Harvest Home. I had drunk too much
punch. . . . I know it now but I didn't at the time. Oh, I'm
making excuses."

"Please go on," I said. "Who . . . ?"

But she didn't have to tell me. Because I knew. I remembered that look of implacable hatred I had seen across the room.
Oh, he was a fiend. This was his revenge on James.

"Dickon?" I said.

She started to shiver and I knew I was right.

"It was the Harvest Home . . . the punch . . . the dancing.
. . . He danced with me . . . and we went out into the gardens
. . . into the shrubbery. I don't know how it happened. . . . But
I was there . . . lying on the grass . . . I can't tell you. It was too
depraved . . . I didn't seem to realize until it was too late. . . ."

I turned away. I could not bear her misery. So this was his
revenge.

She was desperate, poor girl. I had to comfort her. I was
going to take her back with me, talk over the matter with Jean-
Louis. He would understand and try to help.

I said: "There is a way out."

"There is no way," she said. "I cannot face anyone now. . . .
My father, my mother, my brothers and sisters . . . and James.
. . . No, I have thought and thought and this is the only way."

"You must not talk like that. It's nonsense. It's feeble. At
the worst you could go away and have the baby. My husband
and I would help you."

"You are the kindest people in the world."

"We shall understand. This is the sort of thing that can happen . . . to anybody . . . to *anybody*," I added vehemently. "I am going to help you, Hetty."

"There is no help. I could drown myself . . . and perhaps my body would never be found."

"I should have thought you would not want to take such a cowardly way out."

"Perhaps I am a coward, but I just cannot face my parents. They thought too much of me. They would be so horrified . . . so ashamed. . . ."

"My dear Hetty, this happened. . . . You had had too much punch . . . you did not know. . . ."

"There were other times," she said.

"Hetty. But why . . . ?"

"Because he said he would tell if I did not."

"Blackmail!" I said aghast. I could see him so well—that handsome, cruel face. What havoc he had wrought in our lives.

"When he knew that I was pregnant he let me alone. He seemed . . . satisfied."

"He is a monster, Hetty. He hates in a cold and calculating manner which is by far the worst sort of hatred. But we're going to outwit him. We're not going to let him win."

"How?" she asked.

"By not running away from this, by facing it, by looking at it and finding the way to act."

"I can't do it."

"You can because I'm going to help you. Will you let me?"

She threw herself against me and then she was sobbing bitterly. The tears I knew brought relief. She was no longer alone.

She trusted me. My own experience had perhaps helped me to understand hers. I had been able to choose the right words to give her the support she needed.

I took her back with me to the house, put her to bed and told the household that she was suffering from a chill and was sleeping. No one was to disturb her.

* * *

I went straight to Jean-Louis. He was resting as he often had to do now.

I said: "A terrible thing has happened. I have to talk to you about it. It's Hetty."

"She's been looking a bit strained lately. Is it something to do with James?"

"We've got to help her," I said. "That girl will find some way of harming herself if something isn't done. She's going to have a child."

"Well, she and James will marry, I suppose. They won't be the first who have forestalled their wedding."

"It's not as simple as that. James is not the father."

"Good God."

"You may well be surprised. She has just told me. Jean-Louis, she was going to drown herself in the river. By a miracle I saw her. I have been watching her lately. I knew something was terribly wrong. It happened on the night of the Harvest Home. She had had too much punch and he . . . this er . . ."

"Do you know who it was?"

I looked at him steadily. He would have to know. I realized how calm and practical he had always been, how kind, uncondemning.

I said: "It was Dickon."

"Good God," he said again, and there was an expression of horror on his face. "He's only a boy. . . ."

"I suppose someday people will stop saying 'He's only a boy.' He may be young in years but he is old in sin. There is something evil about Dickon. Jean-Louis, what are we going to do? Hetty is desperate."

"She couldn't marry Dickon."

"Marry Dickon! That would be quite impossible. Besides, she hates him."

"Then why . . .?"

"Oh, don't you see, it's a plot of revenge. Dickon knows James is in love with Hetty. Dickon was angry about the strip of land which was given to Hassock. That's how it is with Dickon. It's revenge."

"Oh, surely not . . ."

"I think I know that boy. It was due to him that you . . . that you are not as well as you were. . . . He's evil. I think it would have been better for Hetty to have walked into the river than marry Dickon."

"We could send her away somewhere where she could have the child."

"I thought of that. I don't know whether she would go. You see, her life seems to her to be in ruins. Her family boast so much about her . . . and then this to happen. And of course James . . . She just can't face it, poor girl."

"She will gradually come to it."

"Jean-Louis, what if James . . . ? James loved her. If he really loved her enough . . ."

"Yes, if he really loves her he will care for her no matter what she has done."

I looked steadily at him and said: "If . . . I had done something like that . . . you would always love me, Jean-Louis, always care for me . . . ?"

I could not look at him. I wondered if he would notice how my heart began to hammer against my bodice.

He took my hand and kissed it. "No matter what," he said. "I should always love you and protect you as far as was in my power."

"Not many love like that," I said. "Jean-Louis, I shall always be grateful for you."

"My life would be nothing without you," he answered and my thoughts were transported to that time when I had considered . . . going away with Gerard.

I said: "Thank you, my dear. I wonder if James's love for Hetty is as strong as yours for me." I rushed on because I felt too emotional to talk further of myself and had to get back to Hetty's problem. "Do you think we could speak to James?"

He was silent for a long time. Then he said: "Would Hetty wish that?"

"No. She could never bring herself to. I don't think he has asked her to marry him. I suspect that since the Harvest Home her attitude towards him would have changed. Jean-Louis, I think we have to speak to James. There is so much tragedy in the world because people don't look facts straight in the face. If she goes away James will have to know. He should have a chance to show his love for her."

"I think you're right," said Jean-Louis.

We deliberated for some time before we made our final decision and then Jean-Louis sent one of the men out to find James and bring him to us as soon as possible.

When he came Jean-Louis said: "We want to talk to you, James. Zipporah made a discovery today . . . about Hetty. . . ."

I said: "James, she was going to drown herself in the river."

He stared at me unbelievingly.

"It's true," I said. "I prevented her in time, and she told me why."

He still did not speak. His face was quite white and his hands were clenching and unclenching as he stood there.

"She is going to have a child," I said. "Poor, poor Hetty, this is a terrible thing that has happened to her."

James had turned away to the window. I guessed he did not want us to see his face. He said in a tight voice: "Are you telling me that she will marry . . .?"

"No, James."

"Who is it?" he demanded. He turned now and his eyes were blazing. "Who is this man?"

I dared not tell him then. I thought he would go out and kill Dickon in the heat of the moment. I looked at Jean-Louis, who nodded, understanding my reasoning.

I said: "It happened on the night of the Harvest Home. You were not there, James, you remember. She had had too much punch . . . and it was very potent. I can only say that some unscrupulous person took advantage of this."

"Who was this unscrupulous person . . . ? Tell me."

"James," I said, "Hetty is in a state of collapse. She needs so much care. Let's think of her, shall we? I have her here in bed now. I've given her something to make her sleep. She is frantic with worry. We love her—Jean-Louis and I—and no matter what happens we are going to help her."

"What does she say . . .?"

"Poor child, she is too stricken to say anything."

"Does she mention me?"

"Yes. She loves you. I think it is partly because of you that she cannot face up to this situation. Oh, James, what can we do for her? If you could have seen her when I found her by the river. . . ."

His face was working with emotion. He was thinking only of Hetty now; for a moment he had forgotten the author of her troubles—but that would come later. James was a man of strong emotions; he generally kept them in check but he would want to find the man who was responsible for Hetty's condition.

There was a long silence. I could not bear it and I said: "James, what are you going to do?"

He shook his head.

"James," I went on, "you can help her . . . only you. This happened . . . such things do happen. . . . You can't blame her. She is so young. . . . Please, James, try to understand. There's so much at stake. I don't know what she plans to do but I am afraid for her."

Still he did not answer.

Then he turned away and walked to the door. I ran to him and held his arm. I could see that he was beset by conflicting emotions—bewilderment, dismay, fury, frustration . . . but I think there was love there . . . love for Hetty.

He looked at me and said: "Thank you, Zipporah. . . . You are good. . . . Thank you . . . but I want to be alone. . . ."

I nodded and he went.

Jean-Louis and I were silent for a few moments after he had left. Then I said to Jean-Louis: "When he knows it was Dickon, what then?"

Jean-Louis shook his head.

"He mustn't be here," I said. "He must go away. . . . Heaven knows what James might do. . . . He mustn't know."

"It can't be kept from him. He'll discover."

"Not yet. He mustn't, Jean-Louis. Dickon will have to go away for a while."

"He never would. He would stay here and perhaps get some amusement out of the storm he has raised."

"I see you know Dickon as well as I do. I was beginning to think everyone saw him through his and my mother's eyes. He has to get away, Jean-Louis. I have to frighten my mother and Sabrina into helping us."

"Yes," said Jean-Louis slowly. "I see what you mean."

"And there is little time to lose. I'm going to see them now."

"Dearest Zipporah," he said, "are you being a little hasty?"

"I think this is a situation which needs prompt action. If James discovers Hetty's seducer he will be enraged. I fear there might be murder here. I am going to see them now."

"You may be right," said Jean-Louis.

"Come with me. Your voice will add weight to mine. They may think I am impulsive but they never will think that of you."

When we arrived at the Hall we were relieved to find both my mother and Sabrina at home. When I told them what had happened they were astounded.

"I don't believe it," said Sabrina.

"The girl is making it up," added my mother.

"Hetty is telling the truth," I said. "You must know what Dickon is like. I have seen him with the servant girls." I had a quick vision of him in the barn with Evalina and I went on: "Dickon could be in danger, that's what I have come to talk about."

That startled them.

"In danger . . . you mean . . . ?"

"Yes, I mean from James. James loves Hetty. I believe he was planning to marry her himself. It is not difficult to understand his emotions now. If he learns that the man in the case was Dickon . . . and he gets his hands on him . . ."

My mother had turned pale. "This is terrible," she said. "I don't believe for one moment . . ."

"There is no time to start protesting Dickon's innocence. And I don't want him to know that he is accused or he might refuse to go."

"That surely would show his innocence," said Sabrina quickly.

"No, it would show a mischievous desire to cause trouble."

"And risk to himself?"

"And risk to everything and everybody. Please don't let us have a tragedy here. I have come to ask you to take Dickon away . . . until James has calmed down. I don't want Dickon to be here when he discovers."

"She is falsely accusing Dickon."

"She is not. Why should she? I know Dickon if you don't. He wanted revenge for Hassock's getting that land. I understand exactly how his mind works."

In their hearts they knew, of course; and I could see that they were already coming to terms with what they called Dickon's manliness.

But I had succeeded in alarming them.

"Sabrina," I said, "you did mention that you might pay a visit to Bath to see the new springs they had discovered there."

"Yes."

"Please, Sabrina, go there and take Dickon with you. *Please*. He won't need any persuading. He loves to travel. Jean-Louis, I am right, aren't I?"

"Zipporah is right," said Jean-Louis. "She has Hetty now under her care. The poor girl was going to kill herself."

"Oh no!" murmured my mother.

"Does James know?" asked Sabrina.

"Yes, but he doesn't know who seduced her . . . raped might be a better word."

"No!"

"Oh, please, this is not a time to pick and choose our words to make them sound nicer. Jean-Louis knows what happened. He has seen James with me. Dickon is old for his years. He is capable of fathering a child; I think he's in danger. Do get him away!"

My mother was trembling. She said: "Yes, Sabrina, we must. I know it's not really true but if he is *suspected*."

They knew in their hearts that it was true. Perhaps they knew too that he had used Hetty to take his revenge on James.

Sabrina said: "I could leave in two days. I know he wants to come with me."

"Two days," I said. "But no longer, please. James mustn't know until you are out of the way."

Jean-Louis and I went home feeling exhausted. Hetty was still sleeping peacefully. I should be with her when she awoke; and I was going to keep my eyes on her for a while.

We did not see James. He was grappling with himself, I imagined. I was glad because I wanted Dickon out of the way before we met just in case we should let the truth escape.

Two days later I went over to Clavering Hall. Sabrina and Dickon had left for Bath. They planned to be away for two weeks.

I felt immensely relieved; and so did Jean-Louis.

Poor Hetty looked like a wraith. I told the servants that she had been very ill and I kept her alone in her room. I was with her a great deal. Sometimes she would not speak for a long time and when she did the confidences poured out. Dickon had terrified her. She had seen him assessing her even before the Harvest Home. She did not know how she could have let herself be taken into the shrubbery. She had been mildly enjoying the Harvest Home but regretting James's absence when he had come up with the punch and forced it on her. Then he brought more for her. She had refused it and he had said "Don't be a simple country girl," or something like that, and foolishly she had taken the punch. She had been dizzy and he had said the fresh air would do her good and had taken her out. Then they were in the shrubbery and she grew more and more dizzy and could not stand up. Then... it happened.

"Oh, I was such a fool," she cried. "I should have known. I thought I was wiser than the country girls... but I was not. And then he said that he would tell Lady Clavering that I had asked him to take me to the shrubbery.... She would have believed him. He said he would let everyone know what I was like. 'Anybody's for the asking,' he said. Those were his words. And so I must go with him again. It was only when I told him that I was with child that he left me alone...."

"There is evil in him," I said. "But it's over. Nothing can alter what is done. We have to go on from there."

"What can I do?"

"My husband and I will arrange something. We'll send you away from here. You can have the baby quietly...and then we'll think again."

"I don't know what I should do without you."

I said: "Something will be arranged. You have to think of the child. All this grieving is bad for it. You will love it when it comes. People always do."

"But a child conceived in such a way," she said. "*His* child."

"The child will be innocent enough. But, Hetty, you must stop all this wild fretting. I tell you we will take care of you."

She fell into weeping then and she said such things of me which made me ashamed. She would not believe that I was not a saint from heaven, and she brought home to me the extent of my own deceit and it was all fresh in my mind again.

James came over. I saw him arrive and ran to meet him.

"I can't stay forever," he said. "Where's Hetty?"

"She's here. Poor girl, she's in a sad way. I worry about her a good deal."

"Thank you for taking care of her...you and Jean-Louis."

"Of course we will take care of her."

"You know who it was, don't you?"

I nodded.

"Please tell me, Zipporah."

"James, I'm fond of you. We're both fond of you...and of Hetty. This is terrible. Please, please don't make it worse. Hetty needs care, tenderness...she's bruised and wounded. Don't you understand?"

"I do...and I want to take care of her."

"Oh, James...that makes me so happy."

"Bless you, Zipporah. I've grappled with myself. I was planning to marry Hetty."

"I know. You love each other."

"How could she . . . ?"

"She couldn't help it, James. She was half intoxicated . . . she couldn't hold him off. He overpowered her."

"Who . . . who . . . ?"

I said: "It was Dickon."

I saw his teeth clench and his face whiten. I was so thankful that Dickon was far away.

He turned as though to stride out of the house. "You won't find him," I said. "He and his mother have gone away. They'll be away some weeks."

"So he's run away because . . ."

"No. He didn't know that Hetty tried to kill herself."

He winced. "Why didn't she come to me?"

"How could she come to you? She thought you would never want to see her again."

He looked infinitely sad and I went on: "Oh, James, you do . . . don't you? You do."

He nodded without a word. Then I put my arms round him and held him tightly to me for a moment.

"Oh, James," I said, "please help me to heal this poor broken child."

"I love her, Zipporah," he said. "I love her."

"I know, James. And how deep is that love? Is it big enough, strong enough . . . do you think?"

"I know it is."

"James," I said, "will you go to her now? Will you speak to her? Will you tell her that you love her, that you will look after her . . . that you understand? That's the most important of all. To understand. It was no fault of hers. . . . If you had been there it could not have happened. Oh, James, please, *please*."

"Where is she?" he said.

"In her room upstairs."

"I'll go to her," he said, "and, Zipporah, bless you."

* * *

James was going to marry Hetty. Jean-Louis and I were delighted, but then came the blow.

It would be quite impossible for them to remain at Clavering. James could never trust himself near Dickon. Hetty never wanted to see him again. James's uncle had recently died—it was his reason for not being at the Harvest Home—and his cousin wanted him to go in with him on the farm.

How we should manage without James was a great problem. We could get another agent, it was true, but James had been especially good and in view of Jean-Louis's weakness we needed someone who was more than ordinarily good.

In time we found Tim Parker, who seemed to be efficient and keen, but we missed James in so many ways. Our consolation was that he and Hetty were settling down at the farm.

Three months after they left we heard that Hetty had had a miscarriage and three months after that that she was pregnant again.

I thought the child's death was not such a tragedy after all because it would have been a constant reminder to them all through their lives. Now they had the opportunity to start afresh and I believe James, being the sensible young man he was, took it wholeheartedly and Hetty was grateful for all he had done for her.

When Dickon and Sabrina returned from Bath, which Dickon had thoroughly enjoyed, he took extra care with his clothes and turned into a dandy.

I hated him and in my hatred there was an element of fear. He was an evil influence on our lives, I was sure. My mother and Sabrina seemed to dote on him more than ever. He still professed a great interest in the estate and became quite friendly with Tim Parker. He was pleased that he had driven James away. He knew why, of course, and was secretly amused when he heard that James and Hetty were married. I think he thought he had shown James that no one could displease him and not expect to pay for it.

We had just had the news that Hetty's son was born. We were settling down as well as could be hoped. Tim Parker was a good enough man so it had worked out not too unsatisfactorily. Then one day when I was in my stillroom one of the maids came to tell me that there was a young man below to see me.

I said he should be brought into the hall and I would come down.

He was not much more than a boy, and I thought I had seen him before.

Rather awkwardly he pulled his forelock and said: "Me grandad sent me. I've rid all the way from Eversleigh."

"Your grandad?"

"Jethro, mistress."

"Yes, yes."

"He wants me to tell you, mistress, that he thinks you should come. There's something going on up there that ought to be looked into."

The Conspiracy

I sent Jethro's grandson back with messages for Jethro and Uncle Carl. I should be coming to see him and setting out before the end of the week.

Jean-Louis wanted to come with me but that would not be easy. Tim Parker was understandably not yet so conversant with the management of the estate that he could be left alone; also we both knew that Jean-Louis would find the journey exhausting and that this would be an anxiety for me.

What of Sabrina or my mother? wondered Jean-Louis. But since Hetty's affair my relationship with them had undergone a change. They couldn't quite forget my animosity towards Dickon and took it as a sort of affront to themselves. Perhaps the real reason was that I was afraid of what Jessie or Evalina would hint. In any case I knew that I had to go and I wanted to go alone.

So after some argument with Jean-Louis, who was fearful of my traveling alone, it was agreed that I should take six grooms with me, as I had on the first occasion, with an extra one to look after the saddle horse.

It was spring again. The days were long and we made good progress and it was an early afternoon when we arrived at Eversleigh. Jessie was waiting for us. She greeted me with something like affection and relief, and she looked more discreetly dressed than I had ever seen her. Her gown was a pale gray, rather simple, and her complexion was only very lightly touched up.

"I am so glad that you have come. I have been so worried. I told him that we should let you know but when he was able to understand he was rather distressed. He didn't want to upset you. I did not know what to do but when you sent your letter saying that you was coming I was so pleased. He couldn't read it himself. He's not fit. You'll see. You must be tired after the journey. Would you like to rest first . . .?"

"No," I said. "First I want to hear about him and see him."

"I am not sure when you can see him. It will depend on the doctor."

"The doctor is here?"

"He wouldn't have the local man. He sent for his own doctor. It's lucky for us that Dr. Cabel, having retired from practice, was able to stay here. He's here now."

"What happened?"

"It was some sort of seizure. I thought it was the end. Fortunately Dr. Cabel was already here. You see, he'd been ailing before. I suppose he was working up for this and I had said we must call in the doctor. He wouldn't have it, and at last he agreed to my sending for his old friend Dr. Cabel. They had been friends for years and Dr. Cabel had looked after him before. Well, he came, and he stayed, expecting trouble, so he was here when Lordy had his seizure. He's been here ever since."

"I'd better go and see my uncle."

"He must not be disturbed while he's sleeping. Well, he's sleeping most of the time, but he mustn't be excited. Do you mind waiting until the doctor comes in? He's just taking a little exercise at the moment. As soon as he comes in I'll tell him you're here. Let me take you to your room so that you can wash and change if you want to. Then we can talk about it . . . and I daresay Dr. Cabel will allow you to go in for a few moments."

"My uncle sounds very ill."

"My dear." She gave me a little push, a reminder of the old days. "I thought it was the end. I did really. But let me take you to your room. It's the same one. That's all right, is it? And when you've washed the journey off you and had a bite to eat you'll feel rested."

It sounded reasonable enough but Jethro's message had been that something strange was going on. I decided to see him at the earliest possible moment.

I went to my room, washed and changed from my riding habit into a dark blue gown. Then I went down to the winter parlor, where some wine and cakes were on the table.

"I don't know how hungry you are," said Jessie, "but I thought you'd better have a stopgap between now and supper."

"I'm not hungry at all. What I want is to hear about Lord Eversleigh."

"You shall see him as soon as Dr. Cabel comes in. He can tell you more than I."

"How long has Lord Eversleigh been ill?"

"It's nigh on two months since the seizure."

"All that time! I wish I'd known."

"I wanted to tell you. . . ." She lowered her eyes and I wanted to shout at her: *Then why didn't you?* but I said nothing and waited.

Her eyes were on one of the cakes. She picked it up almost absentmindedly and started to eat it.

I said: "It is a big responsibility for you."

She stopped chewing and raised her eyes to the ceiling. "Lord bless you," she said, "you've said a mouthful. Still, I'm fond of him and want to give him my best. He's been good to me. It's the least I can do."

I felt nauseated and, as always in the company of this woman, a sense of something sinister which was all the more alarming because it was dressed up to look like normality.

I rose. I couldn't sit there any longer and I had no appetite for the wine and cakes to which she had referred as a stopgap.

"I'll walk round the garden," I said. "I feel the need to stretch my legs. I'll look forward to seeing Dr. Cabel as soon as he returns."

"He'll be wanting to see *you*."

I went straight out to the garden. I walked round awhile and then slipped through the shrubbery.

Jethro knew that I was coming and I guessed he would be on the lookout for me. I was right. He was.

"Oh, you've come, Mistress Zipporah," he said. "I'm right glad about that."

"Thanks for sending your grandson. What's going on at Eversleigh?"

"That's what I'd like to know. It's all a little odd . . . if you'll forgive me saying so."

"What do you mean by odd?"

"I haven't seen his lordship since it happened. That must be well nigh on two months ago."

"Couldn't you slip in during those afternoons?"

"Well, I couldn't be sure of them. Amos Carew, he's more often at the house now."

"What. You mean he's moved in?"

"Not . . . not exactly. He's still got his house . . . the agent's house, you know. Oh yes, he's still there, but more often at the Court."

"You mean he sleeps there."

"'Twould seem so, Mistress Zipporah. I've seen him coming out in the morning."

"And that is since Lord Eversleigh's seizure?"

"That's right. They never called in Dr. Forster."

"Dr. Forster?" I repeated. The name seemed vaguely familiar.

"He's the new doctor here," went on Jethro. "Been here a year or two now. People like him. He's good, they say. But he wasn't called in to the Court. His lordship sent for his own man."

"Dr. Cabel," I said. "Had he ever visited Lord Eversleigh before?"

"No. Seemingways—so I heard from some of the girls up at the Court—Dr. Cabel was an old friend of his lordship and he sent for him and he being retired from his doctoring like, he stays. They say his lordship won't trust anyone else."

"That is what Jessie Stirling told me. Well, Jethro, what is strange about all this? It seems Lord Eversleigh has had a stroke, as many people do at his age, and he has called in his own doctor."

"I don't know what it be, Mistress Zipporah, but there's something strange about it. I've never been allowed to see his lordship since."

"He has to be kept quiet, I'm told."

"Still, I'm not that noisy. I reckon he'd like to see me. He always did. He'd sleep in the afternoons sometimes and never minded being wakened. He used to say 'Come when you can, Jethro, and if I'm dozing wake me.' I tried to see him . . . I crept up there. I know Jessie was out . . . and where, and Dr. Cabel he was out too. . . . But I couldn't get in to see his lordship though I tried."

"You mean you went up to his room?"

Jethro nodded. "The door was locked. It was almost as though they were expecting someone to call. I thought it was odd, Mistress Zipporah. And one of the maids who's rather friendly with my grandson told him that Jessie cleans the room herself and none of them is allowed to go in."

"Well, mightn't that be that he is so ill she doesn't want him disturbed?"

"That's as might be but Jessie was one who never liked to sully her hands and I doubt they'd made contact with a broom for many a long day." Jethro frowned. "Now I talk of it to you, Mistress Zipporah, it sounds all natural like. It was when I was brooding on it to myself that there seemed something wrong. I hope I haven't upset you like . . . bringing you here. . . ."

"You did absolutely right, Jethro. It is as well that I'm here and can find out from Dr. Cabel how my uncle really is."

He looked relieved. I said to him: "What else has been happening here? It seems to be just the same at the Court, except that Lord Eversleigh is so ill they have had to call in a resident doctor, and Amos Carew visits the house more often."

"Oh, there's Evalina."

"What happened to her? Isn't she there now?"

"She married."

"Oh . . . and she's gone away?"

"Not far. You remember Grasslands."

"Yes, of course, it's the rather big house . . . close to Enderby."

"That's right. Well, she went as housekeeper to old Andrew Mather. In a few months she'd married him."

"Oh," I said, "so Evalina is mistress of Grasslands."

"A regular little madam she is now. Rides round in her carriage. They say that she fooled the old man good and proper; warmed his bed for him and wormed her way in till she'd got him where she wanted him. She's learned a trick or two from her mother."

"What about Enderby?"

"The Forsters are there."

"Oh yes, I remember. I did meet them when I was here once."

"Dr. Forster, whose got his practice in the town, is related to them. He's at Enderby quite a bit, though he has a house in the town."

"Things have really happened since I was last here. I shall keep in touch with you and if you discover anything that you think I should know do tell me. I'll call on you again. First I have to see Dr. Cabel. There's a lot I want to know about my uncle."

I left Jethro and went back to the house. I went to my room and had not been there very long when there was a knock on the door.

It was Jessie.

"Dr. Cabel is here now. He's so pleased you've come. Will you come down now and see him?"

"With pleasure."

Eagerly I followed her to one of the small sitting rooms, where Dr. Cabel was waiting for us. He rose and bowed as I entered. He was of tall and commanding appearance and looked every inch the medical man. He was by no means young but he gave the appearance of carrying his years lightly. I guessed he must be some five or ten years younger than my uncle.

"Mistress Ransome," he said taking my hand, "how glad I am that you have come. I have been saying for some time that you should be sent for."

"How is my uncle? Is he very seriously ill?"

Dr. Cabel lifted his hands and let them sway from one side to another. "He is," he said, "and he isn't. If you mean could he pass away at any moment, the answer is yes . . . but then so could we all. If you say will he live another six months, a year . . . two years . . . even three . . . well, that could be possible. He has, as I think you know, had a seizure. He is not a young man. But he has survived . . . and there are indications that he may go on surviving."

"There seems to be very little certainty."

Dr. Cabel shook his head. "Mind you," he said, "you will see a great change in him. I hope you are prepared for that, dear lady. He is paralyzed down one side . . . as often happens in seizures of this nature. His left hand is useless . . . he cannot walk even a few steps . . . his speech has been impaired . . . and you will find certain changes in his appearance. I'm afraid you will be a little shocked at the sight of him. Don't let him see it. It would upset him. At times he is lucid . . . at others naturally he wanders a bit. He needs very careful nursing. He is fortunate in having Mistress Stirling on the spot."

"I do my best," said Jessie casting down her eyes. "There's such a change. . . ." Her voice faltered. "He used to be so . . ."

"He has a great determination to hold on to life," said the doctor quickly. "The fact that he has come through as he has shows this. We must be careful not to overexcite him. If you will excuse me a moment I will go to his room and if all is well I should like you to come up."

He rose and left us.

"He's a good man," said Jessie. "Mind you, he likes to give the orders. Sometimes he'll keep me out of the room. But there you are, he's the doctor. I suppose we have to do as he says."

I was silent. Dr. Cabel had made me feel that my uncle was in good hands.

He returned shaking his head.

"He's sleeping," he said. "He usually does at this hour. I'll go up again in ten minutes. I want him to wake naturally."

Dusk had crept into the room. We were silent for a few moments. Then the doctor said: "Do you intend to stay long, Mistress Ransome?"

"I am not sure. My husband is not really well and we have recently had a change of managers. Then there is my young daughter. . . ."

"Of course . . . of course. I see you have your responsibilities. I would keep you informed of Lord Eversleigh's condition. He could go on like this for a very long time."

"And it seems as if I can be of little help here."

"Oh, I'm sure it do him good go see you," said Jessie smiling at me.

"If he knows you . . . yes," said Dr. Cabel.

"You think he might not . . .?"

The doctor lifted his hands and swayed them from side to side again. "Well, we know how he is, don't we, Mistress Stirling? There are times I think when he doesn't know even you."

"It's true," said Jessie, "and I'm silly enough to let that hurt a bit. . . . He was always . . ."

Dr. Cabel put his head on one side and looked at me quizzically.

He was a man of many gestures; immersed as I was in the state of my uncle's health I could not help noticing this. But he did exude an air of comfort and efficiency.

After a while he said he would look in again. It was dark now and he took a candle to light himself up the stairs.

"He keeps us all in order," said Jessie when he'd gone. "Sometimes you'd think he owned the place. But I turn a blind eye for I reckon he's done a lot for Lordy."

Dr. Cabel came down and nodded to me.

"Come now," he said.

I followed him up the stairs, Jessie keeping up the rear.

Outside my uncle's door Dr. Cabel turned to me. "You can't stay long. I'll give you a sign when I think he has had enough. Then I shall want you to slip away."

Quietly he opened the door and we tiptoed in. Two candles were burning on the shelf over the carved fireplace.

The curtains were half drawn about the four-poster bed, shutting out much of the little light there was.

Dr. Cabel gently drew back one of the curtains and beckoned to me. I approached the bed. He was lying there with his eyes closed. He wore a nightcap which was pulled forward over his forehead. I had been warned but I was deeply shocked. I thought of him as I had last seen him; I remembered particularly those lively dark eyes. Now they were shut and he seemed only half alive. The skin was the same parchment color as I remembered—dry and wrinkled.

His hand was lying on the counterpane and I recognized the heavy signet ring which he had always worn.

"Take his hand," whispered Dr. Cabel.

I did so. I felt the faintest pressure.

"Uncle," I whispered.

His lips moved and there was a whisper. I thought it was: "Carlotta."

"He's trying to speak to you," said Dr. Cabel.

"He thinks I'm my great-grandmother. He did sometimes."

"Tell him you've come to see him. Tell him you've been thinking of him."

"Uncle Carl," I said, "I have come to see you. I hope we shall be able to talk while I'm here."

I lifted the hand and kissed it. I noticed the smudge of brown near the thumb. He had once drawn my attention to it and called it one of the flowers of death. "Old people get them," he had said. "It means youth is over."

I felt overcome by emotion.

Dr. Cabel touched my arm lightly and nodded significantly. He meant I must go.

I turned and was led out of the room.

Outside the door Dr. Cabel lifted the candle so that the light fell on my face.

"It was a shock," he whispered. "I told you to be prepared."

Jessie patted my arm.

"He might be a bit better tomorrow," she said. "What do you think, doctor?"

"That's so. He's been told you're here. He might remember tomorrow . . . I think he was pleased to see you. You've done him good."

"He pressed my hand," I said.

"And he tried to speak. That's a good sign. Oh yes. Even though he mistook you for someone else. He was way back in the past. That was good . . . very good."

"I'm glad I've seen him," I said. "I think I'll go to my room. I'm rather tired."

"Yes, do," said Jessie. "I'll come along with you just to make sure everything's all right. Doctor, light us to a candle will you."

There were candles in various places about the house in case they were needed. I later realized that the servants placed them there an hour before dusk and collected them in the mornings.

We found two on a chest along the corridor and I said good night to Dr. Cabel, who went downstairs, and Jessie and I went to my room.

She lighted the four candles which had been put there for my use and looked round the room.

"You'll sleep well," she said. "You must be well nigh exhausted. Nothing for tiring you like traveling. What did you think of him? Did you expect to see him like that?"

"You had told me," I said.

"When I think of what he was . . . and now lying there . . . it's tragic."

She 'linked as though to hide a tear. I thought: Well, I suppose she is uneasy. If he died her comforts here would stop.

"If there's anything you should want," she said.

"Thank you."

"Well, then, I'll say good night."

She went out. I looked at the door. I saw the key was there.

I unpacked a few of my things. The room seemed full of shadows . . . eerie, menacing even. I remembered vividly arriving here on that night . . . before I had met Gerard . . . before Lottie was conceived.

I locked the door and undressed. I tried to sleep but I found that impossible. There were too many memories here for my peace of mind; and I could not get out of my mind that of that poor old man lying there . . . the gentle pressure of his fingers . . . the name Carlotta . . . slurred, barely audible.

The sun was streaming into my room when I awoke next morning. I had slept late.

Almost as soon as I opened my eyes a maid came in bringing hot water.

She said: "Mistress Stirling said to let you sleep on. She reckoned you was worn out."

"What time is it?"

"Eight of the clock, mistress."

And I usually rose at seven!

I dressed and went downstairs. Jessie was in the hall in conversation with Dr. Cabel.

"How is Lord Eversleigh this morning?" I asked.

"Not so well," said the doctor. "I think he was overexcited about your coming."

"I'm sorry."

"You mustn't be. He's delighted really . . . but of course any excitement is not good for him. We'll go a little carefully.

Leave him alone for today. He's sleeping now. I've given him something to steady him."

"I suppose I'd better not go in to dust round," said Jessie. And to me: "I do it myself. I don't want any of them girls banging around."

"Leave the dust for today," said the doctor.

"You'll be wanting breakfast," said Jessie to me, and I followed her into the winter parlor. There was oaten bread with ale and cold bacon. I noticed Jessie lick her lips as she surveyed it.

"You must be hungry. You must eat well while you're here. I know what it's like traveling. Never cared much for inn meals myself."

I ate a little of the bacon and the bread. It was good. Jessie's interest in food meant that she kept what we used to call a very good table.

"What will you do today?" I was asked.

"I'll go for a walk, I think. Perhaps I'll ride this afternoon. My horse needs some exercise. But I don't intend to go far. I want to be at hand in case my uncle wakes up and would like to see me."

"That's an excellent idea. He may remember last night . . . on the other hand he may not."

"Well, I'll walk this morning. Just visit a few of the old haunts."

I went to see Jethro. I told him that I had seen my uncle and he was very relieved about that.

"Why, Jethro," I said, "I believe you thought he'd been spirited away."

"Well, not having seen him, mistress . . ."

"He's very ill evidently. This Dr. Cabel seems a very efficient man. I was only allowed to see my uncle briefly. I hope, though, that I shall be able to be with him longer today . . . perhaps I can have a little talk with him. He tried to speak."

"Well, I'm that relieved, Mistress Zipporah, and I hopes I done the right thing in bringing you here."

"You did, Jethro, and I can tell you I have felt a little happier knowing that you were here."

He was very pleased and told me that things were much as usual on the estate. Amos Carew kept a sharp eye on everything—just as he always had—and everything was running smoothly. Lord Eversleigh never had much say in the way things were done.

I said good-bye to Jethro and returned to the Court.

I dined there with Jessie and the doctor. He seemed to have accepted Jessie's position and after the meal he strolled out to the stables with me.

"Lord Eversleigh will probably want to see you later on. He's still sleeping and I want to keep him like that . . . until he wakes naturally. We'll see. I am so glad you have come, Mistress Ransome. It is a relief to me to have someone of the family here."

He looked at me rather helplessly. "Mistress Stirling," he went on, "well, the position I gather is somewhat irregular . . . but I'm afraid Eversleigh was always like that. He enjoyed life in his own way and it was generally rather an unconventional way. Still . . . this, er . . . Jessie is here. I gather he was quite fond of her. . . . He seems more at peace if she's there about the place. He got used to her, I suppose, and she's a good manager. The great thing is that Carl shouldn't be worried. He needs rest. You know I feel that with the right treatment he could go on for a very long time."

"It is fortunate that you were able to be here."

"Well, he likes it . . . but you know any doctor could have done as much. There's a very good fellow in the town, I've heard. I can't do more than he would . . . but there is a point that I'm on the premises."

"Well, thank you, Dr. Cabel."

"Which is your horse?"

"The bay mare. We get on well together."

"You ride a good deal, Mistress Ransome?"

"Yes, I always have done."

"Good exercise."

195

One of my grooms came up. He was preparing to return to Clavering.

"Master won't be content till I'm back and tell him you've arrived safe," he said.

I smiled. "Will you saddle for me, Jim? I'm taking a ride. When will you be leaving?"

"In less than an hour."

"Well, tell them all it won't be long before I'm sending for you to escort me back."

"I'll tell master that. It'll please him."

The doctor looked on benignly and was still there when I mounted and rode out of the stables.

It was almost as though my horse led me there, for in a very short time I could see the towers of Enderby. I rode up to the haunted patch thinking of the day I had stepped over the palings and found Gerard. I wondered if the people whom I had met at Enderby were still there and decided it might be interesting to call. I dismounted and as I did so my heart started to beat fast, for a man was leaning over that part of the palings which was firm and upright and for a moment I thought he was Gerard. Then I saw that he most certainly was not.

He was tall as Gerard had been but much more loosely built and far from elegant. He wore a small wig, hair drawn back from the face and tied at the back with a black ribbon, as worn by almost every man; his coat was wide skirted and came to just above the knees to disclose the ends of knee breeches and legs in dark brown hose and buckled shoes—his white cravat was plain, so was his waistcoat and of the same brown as the material of his coat. He had a pleasant expression, perhaps a little austere. It was an air of seriousness about him which made me think how different he was from Gerard.

"Good day," he called.

I returned the greeting.

"Are you calling at the house?" he asked.

"Yes, I was going to."

"Oh, you are a friend of the Forsters?"

"A neighbor...temporarily. I am staying at Eversleigh Court."

"Oh?" he was clearly interested.

"Lord Eversleigh is a sort of uncle," I explained.

"He's very ill at the moment, I believe."

"Yes," I said.

"I too am calling at Enderby," he told me.

I tethered my horse to the palings and we walked together toward the house.

"I hope they will remember me," I said.

"I am sure they will. They have spoken of you."

"To you?"

"Yes," he said. "I'm there often. As a matter of fact I'm Derek Forster's brother."

"Oh...are you...?"

"The doctor," he said.

I smiled. "I have heard of you."

"Good reports, I hope."

"Nothing to your detriment."

"That is all a doctor can hope for."

"When I came here before, your name was mentioned. You were not here then."

"That must have been a little while ago. I have been here for about two years."

Enderby looked different. A great number of trees had been cut down and there was a new lawn. It made the place brighter, less eerie. It must have been something like this when my mother's aunt Damaris was the mistress of it. It no longer looked the dark, menacing house it once had.

The door opened and the woman I had previously met gave an exclamation of surprise.

"Charles!" she cried. "And..."

"I've brought a visitor," he said.

"You won't remember me," I put in hastily. "I'm Zipporah Ransome."

"But of course I remember you. You came before...oh, it was a long time ago. You're related to Lord Eversleigh.

Come in. Derek will be so pleased. And, Charles, how are you?"

She kissed his cheek lightly while she kept her eyes on me.

We went into the hall. Yes, it was considerably less gloomy.

"Derek!" she called.

Her husband came running down the stairs past the haunted minstrels' gallery and I immediately remembered him. They had both been so friendly.

"You remember each other," she said.

Derek Forster looked at me for a moment and I said: "Zipporah Ransome." Then his face creased into a smile and he held out his hand.

"What a pleasant surprise! Come in. I am sure you are thirsty."

"Not in the least," I said.

"Oh, you must give Isabel a chance to try her elderberry wine on you," said Derek. "She'll be heartbroken if you don't."

"Will you try it?" she asked. She had such a pleasant, kindly face that I warmed to her immediately, and I remembered how much I had liked her previously when I had called with Sabrina.

"It would be lovely," I said.

"Shall I tell them to bring it?" asked Dr. Forster.

"My dear Charles," cried Derek, "there's no need. It's the order of the day. Visitors are here: Bring out the elderberry. Mind you, it does change sometimes. The brew of the season might be dandelion or even sloe gin."

"He's exaggerating," said Isabel. "What do you think of the house, Mistress Ransome? Do you see any changes?"

"It's lighter . . . it's . . . happier."

She gave me a warm smile. "I know exactly what you mean."

Soon we were sitting in the little room I remembered well, sipping the wine and nibbling the wine cakes which were, I gathered, part of the ritual.

"And how are things at the Court?" asked Derek.

"I arrived only yesterday."

"We are flattered that you called so soon," said Isabel.

"I remembered how welcoming you were last time."

"We like to have visitors. It's not exactly a social neighborhood now, is it, Derek?"

"I agree with that," he said. "It would be so different if there were large families in the three houses...Eversleigh, Enderby and Grasslands....I suppose there were at one time. Not anymore, though. How is Lord Eversleigh?"

"I have seen him only briefly. Apparently he had a seizure."

Dr. Forster nodded. "He has a doctor in residence, I hear."

"Yes, Dr. Cabel. He was an old friend. My uncle must have felt ill because he asked him to come and almost immediately afterwards he had this seizure."

"I suppose he is fairly old," said Derek.

"Yes...he's old. He was confined to his room when I came some years ago. It's wonderful that he has gone on so long."

"We do occasionally see the housekeeper and I believe they have a very good man managing the estate."

"Yes," I said.

"It must be a comfort to know that he is well looked after." Isabel went on: "The housekeeper's daughter went to Grasslands and married Andrew Mather."

"They're quite a clever family," said Derek.

"Now, Derek," said Isabel.

"Well, they say that the housekeeper at the Court is mistress of the house, *maîtresse-en-titre* as it were, whereas her daughter is mistress *de facto*."

"Derek!" Isabel was shocked that he should be so frank in my presence. She turned to me: "You must forgive Derek. He just speaks without thinking."

"I understand," I said. "Uncle Carl was very fond of Jessie Stirling and she looks after him. He showed his gratitude. And I expect Evalina did the same for her master."

"He must be all of seventy," said Derek. "What is she? Sweet sixteen?"

"A little more, I imagine. I met her when I was here before."

"Andrew Mather is in good health and spirits," said Dr. Forster. "I can vouch for that."

"Then what are we tittle-tattling about?" demanded Isabel. "Let's talk of pleasant things. Isn't it nice that the king and queen have a son. I think it is so right that the first born of a monarch should be a son. They say the little Prince of Wales is strong and healthy and the apple of his mother's eye."

"Well," said Dr. Forster, "talking of pleasant things, we have our young king and queen, our little Prince of Wales and last November the Peace of Fontainebleau. We have come rather well out of the affair, I should say."

"Indeed," agreed Derek. "Canada from the French and Florida from Spain."

"Yes, but we have given up our gains in the East Indies."

"But we have kept Senegal and some of the West Indian islands."

"I'm sorry the people don't care so much for Mr. Pitt nowadays," said Isabel. "He used to be so loved. People relied on him, and just because he has accepted a pension . . . Poor man, he has to live. Why shouldn't he have a pension?"

They talked very knowledgeably about what was going on in the world. I gathered they all went to London from time to time, and I felt I had shut myself away too much in the country. I seemed to learn so much just by listening to them—even frivolous items like the cost of the king's coach, which was seven thousand five hundred and sixty-two pounds, four shillings and three pence. Isabel was aghast at the cost and thought the money might have been better spent. I learned that there had been riots at Drury Lane Theatre and Covent Garden because the manager refused to admit people at half price at the end of the third act; and that Lord Bute had resigned and Mr. Fox had become Lord Holland, and that John Wilkes had been committed to the Tower.

I liked the Forsters very much and perhaps what I particularly enjoyed so much was the normal lighthearted company.

"You must come to see us again," said Isabel when I rose to go.

I said nothing would please me better.

"Are you going too, Charles? I thought you would stay to supper."

"I'll take Mistress Ransome back to the Court and then I'll come back."

"That's kind of you," I said, "but there's no need."

"It's not a need . . . just a pleasure," said the doctor smiling at me.

His horse was in the stables, and he walked it out to where I had tethered mine.

"You will come over again and see us, won't you?" he said.

"You mean at Enderby. Yes, certainly. I did enjoy being there this afternoon. Your brother and his wife are charming."

"A perfect example of the pleasures of matrimony," he said lightly. I looked at him quickly for I thought I detected a cynical twist of his lips. I wondered about him as I realized I had been doing during the afternoon. Had he a wife? He was not young. He must have been in his early forties . . . a few years older than I was.

"Very pleasant to be with," I said.

"Yes, Derek was lucky. Isabel is a delightful person."

"I gathered so. It is amazing what they have done for the house. It was such a gloomy old place. Now it seems quite different."

"It had quite a reputation, I believe. They had great trouble in getting servants at first. It's different now. Isabel soon showed them that Enderby was a very happy place to work in."

"You're very fond of her."

"Who wouldn't be?"

"And you have a house in the town?"

"Yes, with the practice."

"Do you enjoy living here?"

He hesitated. "It's not the best spot for a doctor to flourish. It's too sparsely populated. One's patients are too scattered; but it does have the advantage of being near a hospital in which I am interested—and Derek and Isabel, of course."

"And I expect you are there a good deal."

"I practically live there. There is always a welcome and if I don't appear for a few days I am severely reprimanded."

"That must be very pleasant for you."

"It is," he said.

We had come to the Court. I said good-bye to Dr. Forster and he expressed hope that we should meet again, which I endorsed.

As I turned to ride towards the stable I saw Jessie. I guessed she was just returning from her visit to Amos Carew.

She was staring after Dr. Forster, who had turned his horse and was riding back to Enderby.

Jessie followed me into the stables; her face was very red, which may have been due to the exertion of walking.

"I saw you riding with . . . your friend. . . ."

"My friend? Oh, you mean Dr. Forster."

"I didn't know you knew him. . . ."

"I didn't till this afternoon."

I saw that her hand was trembling slightly. She seemed somewhat out of breath.

"Oh," she said. "You met him for the first time."

I suddenly realized that she was putting me through a cross-examination, which I resented. I dismounted and one of the grooms took my horse.

I smiled coolly at Jessie and walked so fast toward the house that she couldn't keep up with me.

As I entered the hall one of the maids came running down. "Oh, mistress," she said, "there's a visitor."

"Who is it?" I asked.

By that time Jessie came puffing up behind me, and the maid immediately addressed herself to her.

"He's come to stay for a while, mistress," she said.

"Who? Who?" cried Jessie. I had never before seen her so agitated.

At that moment Dickon appeared at the top of the staircase. He cried: "Hello . . ." and came running down.

I stared at him—no less aghast than Jessie.

He was smiling at me. "They insisted that I come," he said. "They seemed to think you needed looking after."

I was shocked and angry. My dislike of him was as great as it had ever been.

Jessie had recovered herself. "I must go and see about getting a room ready for you. And are you hungry?"

"Very," said Dickon showing his teeth in a grin.

He was aware of my feelings and was enjoying the situation.

At supper, which was taken at six, Dickon was very talkative. Dr. Cabel joined us, and Jessie, in view of her very special position in the household, as usual sat with us.

She had got over her dismay and was very affable to Dickon. The doctor seemed pleased to see him too.

Dickon said: "I was simply badgered to come. Zipporah's mother was so worried about her ewe lamb traveling alone."

"It was hardly alone . . . with seven grooms."

"Well, she considers it alone if you are not with a member of the family. 'I shan't have a moment's peace,' she said, 'until I know you are there to take care of my little girl.'"

"Really, Dickon, you're talking nonsense."

"Or words to that effect," he said. "So I simply could do nothing but gather together a little baggage and come along. I wanted to, you know. I wanted so much to see the place again. I'm longing to explore. What was the name of that wonderful manager?"

"Amos Carew," I said.

"Oh, old Amos. He's still here, I hope."

"Yes," said Jessie. "He's still here."

"He and I became very great friends," went on Dickon. "I shall go and see him tomorrow and get him to take me round the estate again."

"He'll be that pleased," said Jessie.

"And poor Eversleigh is not so well?"

"He's as well as can be expected," said Dr. Cabel, "after a seizure such as he has had."

"And he is so lucky to have you here, Dr. Cabel."

"I am glad to do all I can for an old friend."

"Old friends, yes. By the way, I miss one familiar face. Your daughter." He had turned his smile on Jessie.

She flushed—with pleasure I think. "Oh, Evalina did rather well for herself. She's a married lady now."

"Indeed!"

"Yes, indeed. She's Mistress Mather of Grasslands."

"Isn't that the other big house . . . ? There were three of them."

"Yes," I said. "Eversleigh, the manorial residence, then Enderby and Grasslands."

"The two rather less glorious luminaries," said Dickon, "but nevertheless quite bright when not put in the shade. So your charming daughter is mistress of Grasslands."

"Yes, she is. She's settled in very nicely."

"I wonder if she would like me to call."

"I'm sure she would."

I felt nauseated by the smile about his mouth; I was recalling that moment in the barn. He looked at me and knew it. He was becoming a very disturbing person now that he was reaching maturity.

We had left the table and dusk was falling when Dr. Cabel approached me.

He said: "Lord Eversleigh has had a restful day. He is conscious now. If you would like to see him for a few minutes?"

"Yes, I would."

It was the same time as it had been last night, I noticed, and remarked on this.

"Yes, there is bound to be a certain regularity," said Dr. Cabel. "That might persist for a day or so and then the pattern could change and the mornings could be the best time to see him. Are you ready now?"

He lighted a candle, for it was dark enough now for us to need one.

Dickon met us on the stairs.

"We are going to see Lord Eversleigh," said the doctor.

Dickon nodded and turned away as we went into the room.

The doctor put his candle down on the mantelpiece beside the other one which was burning there. Jessie was at the bedside.

She put her fingers to her lips.

"Is he sleeping?" whispered Dr. Cabel.

"No. But he's drowsy."

"It won't do any harm for you to say a word to him," said the doctor to me. "I fancy he remembered your visit last night and was looking forward to another."

I went to the bed. His face was turned away and, as last night, his nightcap was slightly askew; his hand with the signet ring lay outside the coverlet. I bent to take it and just at that moment there was a movement at the head of the bed.

Dickon stood there.

Both Jessie and the doctor turned sharply. Jessie let out an exclamation.

The doctor went swiftly to Dickon and whispered something.

Jessie turned to me: "He wants you to take his hand. He knows you're here." I took the hand and kissed it just below the ring. I was thinking of Dickon's impertinence in coming in when it had been made clear that he was not wanted.

I felt the fingers curl round mine, though he did not move his position and half his face was still buried in the pillow; but his lips moved and I thought I heard him say: "Zipporah."

I bent over him.

"I'm here, Uncle Carl. You must get better. There's so much to talk about."

His eyes were closed and his head moved slightly. The doctor came back to the bed; he had evidently prevailed on Dickon to depart.

He seemed a little agitated. He raised his eyebrows and nodded to me.

"Better go now." He mouthed the words.

I followed him out of the room. Jessie joined us.

"That was rather upsetting," said Dr. Cabel.

"You mean Dickon's coming in like that?"

"Yes, we have to be careful."

"But my uncle couldn't have been aware of it."

"He was aware of something. I sensed the change in him. We have to be so careful. That is why I want only you to see him even when he is well enough to stand the strain of visitors."

"It was all so quick . . . and quite silent . . . he couldn't have been aware . . ."

Dr. Cabel smiled at me as though he couldn't expect me to understand.

Then he said to Jessie: "I think I'll go in. It might be necessary to give him something to calm him down."

I said good night to them. I would go to my room. I wanted to read awhile.

I thought they were making a great fuss, although I deplored Dickon's irresponsibility in walking in to the sick room when it had been made so clear to him that he wasn't expected to do so. On the other hand I could not see that Uncle Carl, who seemed only just able to recognize me, could possibly have known about it.

I went to my room but I couldn't read. I was disturbed. First of all by Dickon's visit. What I wanted to think of was the pleasant afternoon I had had at Enderby but now these strange thoughts were persisting. It had all seemed so odd suddenly in that sick room that evening, although he had been lying in almost the same position with his face half buried in the bedclothes. His only response had been in the pressure of his fingers and his lips moving to say my name. I wished that I could see him alone. I supposed that would make no difference. But in the room tonight there had been something . . . I was not sure what . . . something strange . . . something that was worrying me.

I must go to bed. Perhaps tomorrow I might look in at Enderby again. Was that too soon? Perhaps not, as I should not be staying here long. They had said to come again.

I liked Isabel Forster very much. She was the sort of woman in whom I could confide. It was strange how my fate seemed wrapped up in Enderby. I half wanted to go and half wanted to stay away, for I couldn't enter the place without remembering that day when Gerard had said he would show me the house. I wondered whether the brocade curtains still enclosed the four-poster bed or whether Isabel Forster had changed the inside of the house as much as she had outside. I felt if I went to sleep I would dream of that house . . . lying in the bed there with my lover beside me . . . while the sounds of the nearby fair echoed in my ears. Then I would long to be back in time. I was never going to forget.

So I lay thinking of long-ago adventures, of my own sweet daughter in whom I fancied I sometimes saw something of Gerard. Oh, it was long ago. It must be forgotten as he surely would forget. I wanted to go home. There was very little I could do here. Uncle Carl was in his doctor's hands. If he grew very much worse they could let me know. He might go on for years in this state . . . and it was clear that Jessie—with the help of the doctor—would do everything in her power to keep him alive.

I dozed. Then I was awake. I wondered what Dickon was doing now. He was hardly likely to be in bed. Would he try to see Evalina? I could imagine what would happen if he did. But I didn't want to think of Dickon. I was just angry that he had dared to follow me here, pretending that it was his mother and mine who had insisted that he come. As if anything would ever get Dickon to do what he did not want to.

No, he was fascinated by Eversleigh. Perhaps he wanted to see Evalina again. I was sure the fact that she now had a husband would have little effect on his plans.

I had dozed again and awakened startled.

I had been dreaming and my dream had been vivid. I was in the room. It was the night which had just passed. Jessie was at the bedside and so was Dr. Cabel. I was looking down at my uncle and his hand was lying on the coverlet.

I was staring at his hand—at the signet ring with the un-mistakable Eversleigh crest on it. But it was his hand which held my attention. It was pale, unblemished. Where the flowers of death had been there was just plain white skin.

I sat up in bed.

No. I was imagining it. But I had it so clearly in the dream. Why should I dream that? I could really believe that the hand I saw in my dream was exactly as I had seen it that night. Had a faint surprise come to me then? It had been disturbed by the sudden realization that Dickon was in the room.

No. It was just imagination. I had just not noticed.

I lay down and tried to sleep, but it was a long time before I was able to.

When I got up next morning the imaginings of the night seemed not worth thinking of for a moment. My main concern was to avoid Dickon. I went for a walk almost to the sea and back. I was hoping I would meet someone from Enderby but I thought it was too soon to call yet—which I should have liked to do.

We met for the midday meal. Dickon was in high spirits. He told us he had explored the house and called on Amos. He had ridden out with Amos for about an hour and he was delighted to be back.

"Eversleigh!" he cried. "What a mine of treasure! Well, I suppose it has been collected through the centuries. I couldn't find one or two of my favorite pieces from last time I was here. I suspect *you*, Mistress Jessie!" He paused and wagged a finger at her. She blanched and I saw her fingers catch at the table. "Yes," he went on, "I suspect you of that female habit of changing things round."

She relaxed a little. "Well, I like a bit of change . . . now and then."

"Don't we all," said Dickon. "Variety adds flavor to the monotony of the day. When I was last here I was very taken with the jade collection. Uncle Carl traveled a great deal and picked up some pieces, as they say. I reckon his jade is worth a good deal."

"He acted a bit strange before his seizure," said Jessie.

"That's not unusual," put in the doctor. "You did tell me something about that. Didn't he have an obsession about being

208

short of money and talk of selling some of his possessions . . . pictures, I thought you said."

"I wasn't sure," said Jessie. "He'd have people to the house . . . and then perhaps you'd notice something wasn't there. . . . You'd just find it gone. But he used to hide things. Put them in different places."

"How very disconcerting," said Dickon. "Well, there is that piece of jade I missed. I'll go hunting. I expect he's put it somewhere. It'll be a pleasant exercise. I do hope he didn't *sell* the incense burner. That was a very special piece, I believe, and a great favorite of mine."

"It's very likely here somewhere," said Jessie. "You must describe it to me and I'll get the maids to look. It's very likely hidden away in some place you'd least think to find it."

"We'll have a new game . . . hunt the jade," said Dickon. "By the way, I hope he wasn't upset last night."

"Well, he was a little disturbed," said the doctor.

"Because I appeared, you mean. He didn't even look at me. He couldn't have seen me with that nightcap right down over his eyes."

"I don't think he was actually aware of you exactly," said the doctor, "but he might know something unusual was going on and be vaguely uneasy. Believe me, his condition is so precarious that I can't have that. I want him kept quiet, and I do think it is best that I supervise the visits."

"Not too many visitors at one time, eh?"

"I think that is understandable."

"It's very understandable," said Dickon flashing his smile on them. He changed the subject abruptly. "There was an old chest I was rather interested in. Not a very good one . . . but the brass fittings were fine. The wood was a bit rotten in places, though. The worm had got in. I noticed it. It was Tudor, I think. I was always interested in furniture, wasn't I, Zipporah . . . ? The trouble with me is that I'm interested in the wrong things. Never mind. I'm only a boy, as the family are fond of saying."

"What about this chest?" I asked.

"Oh, I just looked for it, that's all. I thought it was in that winter parlor . . . but I must have been mistaken because you've got that one of a much later period there now. Perhaps it was somewhere else I saw it. What do you propose to do this afternoon, Zipporah? I suppose you are not going to see Uncle Carl."

We were both looking at Dr. Cabel. "Unthinkable," he said. "I am not sure that you will be able to see him today at all. He's not had one of his good days."

"Too many strangers in the house," said Dickon.

"How would he know that?" I asked.

"You never know," said Dickon showing all his teeth. His eyes glittered so strangely that it could hardly be said that he was smiling.

I was glad when I could leave the table. I wanted to get away from the house, away from Dickon. My dream had disturbed me more than I would care to admit. I went for a long ride, not to the sea this time, and it was past four when I decided I should return. I came back by way of Grasslands— a very pleasant house this, about the same size and type as Enderby but very different, surrounded by grassy lawns from which I suppose it derived its name.

A horse was tethered near the mounting block. I recognized it as Dickon's.

He has lost no time, I thought. I hesitated. My impulse was to ride away as quickly as I could. I did not want to see Evalina and be reminded of the last time I had seen her and the words she had directed at me. Then I wondered whether I should speak to Dickon. After all he was of the family; he had come down here on my account; he was not really much more than a boy. It was very different frolicking with an unmarried girl but if that girl had a husband he might land into serious trouble.

Perhaps, I thought, turning my horse away, it is just a friendly call and I am misjudging him. Misjudge Dickon! It was hardly likely.

But no. I would call. I tied up my horse and walked boldly to the front door and pulled the bell rope.

It was opened by a maid who looked questioningly at me.
I said: "Is Mistress Mather at home?"

"Yes, mistress."

"Will you tell her Mistress Ransome has called."

"Please to come in," said the maid and I was taken into a
hall slightly smaller than that at Enderby and lacking the minstrels' gallery which was such a feature of that place.

"Mistress has a guest now," said the maid, "but I'll tell
her."

A short while after she came back. "Please to step this way,
mistress."

I followed her up the wide staircase to the landing. The
maid opened the door and I walked in.

Evalina came toward me, her hands outstretched. She was
somewhat elaborately dressed in a rose-colored gown, her face
delicately painted and her hair elegantly arranged. She was
beaming with satisfaction. She certainly enjoyed playing the
lady of the house. Seated in a chair was a man whom I guessed
to be Andrew Mather, and in another, his well-shaped legs
encased in finest hose spread out before him, was Dickon.

"What a pleasure," she said in a lightly affected voice. "Do
come in and meet my husband. I have told Andrew quite a lot
about you."

I thought I detected an undercurrent of meaning in her words
but pretended I did not. Andrew Mather had risen. He walked
toward me with the aid of a stick.

"I am so pleased to make your acquaintance," he said.

I was looking into a pair of mild blue eyes. His smile was
pleasant and really welcoming.

"My other guest, you know," went on Evalina.

Dickon stood up and gave me a mocking bow.

"Yes," I said, "I saw your horse."

"Such detection," murmured Dickon, raising his eyes to the
ceiling. "Do you know they sent me here to keep an eye on
her, but I fancy she is keeping an eye on me."

"It would be quite impossible to follow all your activities,"
I said.

Evalina gave a little giggle. "Sit down, dear Andrew love," she said. "You know how tiring you find it standing." She took his arm and led him tenderly back to his chair.

"She fusses over me far too much," he said to me.

"Not more than you deserve," Evalina had forced him into his chair and planted a kiss on his forehead.

He looked very happy.

"Now please sit down, Mistress Ransome," said Evalina. "I am longing to hear how you find it at the Court."

"I believe Lord Eversleigh is very ill indeed," said Andrew. "My mother takes good care of him."

"Excellent care," murmured Dickon. He exchanged a glance with Evalina.

"She always has . . . as I do of my own Andrew."

She smiled possessively at her husband, who returned the smile.

I thought: She overacts . . . and that makes one begin to feel there is something not quite right. It is the same with her mother.

"I bet you were surprised to find me married."

"I don't know why I should be."

"Well, married so well," she said with a fond look at her husband.

"I am pleased to see you are so happy and it must be pleasant to be so near your mother," I said.

"Well, there is that," she said. "Would you like some refreshment?"

"No, thank you. I merely called to congratulate you."

"It was kind of you," said Andrew Mather.

He looked to me to be a deeply contented man, and I reminded myself that Uncle Carl had been contented with Jessie. What was it these women had which could make their men contented even though they must be aware that they were paying a price for their comfort? But I was being unfair to Evalina. She seemed as though she really were devoted to her husband. Then I thought of Jessie, so kind and tender to Uncle Carl, so solicitous of his comforts and slipping off to spend the afternoon with Amos Carew.

Perhaps I was prejudiced against Evalina. Perhaps she had changed and was no longer the same girl who had blackmailed me over the key, frolicked with Dickon in the barn and then thrown that remark at me on the very last occasion we had met.

"This is a very pleasant house," I said.

"We like it, do we not, Evalina?" said Andrew. He had turned to Dickon. "You were quite complimentary about it."

"I said what I felt," said Dickon, "and that is that it had great charm. Your lady wife showed me everything. . . . It was a fascinating voyage of discovery."

He was looking at her slyly and I saw the glance which passed between them. I believed then that they were continuing with that relationship of which I had had a hint in the barn. I was sure it was a situation which would appeal to Dickon — aging, uxorious husband, wife who was much younger than he was and decidedly loose in her morals . . . and the gay philanderer looking where he could for easy gratification of his ever demanding senses.

"I was telling your cousin . . . is he your cousin?"

"The relationships in our family are very complicated to explain," I said. "Dickon's mother is my mother's cousin. I'm not sure what that makes us."

"Cousins is good enough for me, dear Zipporah," Dickon said.

"Well, I was telling your cousin that I want him to take a look at the chest in the second bedroom on the third floor of the west wing. I feel certain it is thirteenth century, very simple, decorated with chip-carved rondels. Really Gothic."

"I'm interested to see that," Dickon confirmed.

"Andrew is very taken with old things," Evalina explained, pouting a little. "I think he would like me better if I were old."

He smiled at her fondly.

Dickon sighed. "Alas, people do not grow more beautiful with age."

213

"They may grow more interesting," I suggested.

"Oh, Mistress Ransome," cried Evalina, "you are telling me that I am a foolish little thing. I think you are probably right, but that is the way Andrew likes me."

I felt it was all rather nauseating and said quickly: "Is it just antique furniture which interests you, Mr. Mather?"

"Mainly," he replied. "I'm also interested in art generally, pictures, statuary . . . objets d'art generally, I suppose."

"I understand you have a very fine collection," said Dickon.

"Well, not as extensive as I should like it to be. You are rather knowledgeable yourself, I see. Do go and have a look at that chest sometime."

Evalina leaped up. "I'll take him now," she said. "Then he can give you his opinion right away. You will excuse us," she went on. "It won't take long, will it?" She looked archly at Dickon.

"We'll be quick," he said.

I was left alone with Andrew Mather. I was picturing those two and wondering what they would be saying as they studied the chest. That Dickon would cynically make some assignation with her, I was sure, and that she would accept seemed equally certain.

"I am surprised," I said, "that Dickon is regarded as an expert on fine furniture. I can't think where he could have acquired his knowledge."

"He has a feeling for it. I sense that by the way he talks. He's very young, of course, and therefore lacking in experience but some people have instinct. I think he might have that and I'd like his opinion on the effect it has on him."

"It is a great interest for you, I'm sure."

"It is. When one is crippled it is good to have those interests which are not too demanding physically. I have always had this love of art. I lived in Italy for a time, years ago. In fact it was there that I first met Lord Eversleigh."

"Oh, I was not aware that you knew him."

"We lived there for some months. We were both interested in art treasures and Florence was the Mecca for people like us.

214

It was he who told me about the houses near Eversleigh when I was wanting to buy one. The other one, Enderby, was occupied at the time so I bought Grasslands."

"Was that very long ago?"

"Long before his illness."

"Have you seen him since?"

"No. That doctor of his frowns on visitors. I have not seen him since his seizure. I used to call occasionally but it wasn't easy for either of us. He was crippled and couldn't leave the house and I was plagued with my rheumatism. I walk around with a stick but I don't feel inclined to go far afield. The doctor says I should take a little exercise but not strain myself."

"Do you know Dr. Cabel? He was a friend of my uncle long ago. I wonder if. . ."

"No, I never met him. He is retired from his profession now, I believe, and that is why he can give so much attention to Lord Eversleigh. I have a very good man myself. Dr. Forster."

"Dr. Forster!" I cried. "I did meet him."

"A very good man, I think. As a matter of fact I should like him to take a look at Lord Eversleigh."

"Wouldn't that be somewhat unethical?"

"I suppose so, since he has his own doctor. On the other hand. . . Dr. Cabel is retired and Dr. Forster is a comparatively young man. He might have more up-to-date knowledge."

"I. . . should like that very much. . . but I don't see how it can be suggested."

"No, I suppose not. He has done me a lot of good. Special pills, you know, and he takes a real interest. He gives me confidence."

"Lord Eversleigh is hardly conscious. I think he recognizes me but so far he has said little except my name."

"Well, I suppose he is fortunate to be alive at all. So many people die after an affair like that. But I do have such confidence in Dr. Forster. He's a good man, you know. I only discovered a few weeks ago that he runs a home for unwanted children."

"Oh, does he? I didn't know that. I only met him briefly. I think he did mention a hospital. I happened to be wandering past Enderby, where his brother lives. I had met them on another occasion and they asked me in and then the other day I saw them again and that was when I met Dr. Forster."

"Yes, he puts a lot of work into this hospital of his. It's a fine thing. He has a special feeling, they say, for children."

"Has he any of his own?"

"I don't think so. I believe he was married . . . something happened. The wife died or something . . . and after that he started this place. He spends some time there I believe because it's not a large practice here."

"That's very interesting," I said. "I thought he was an unusual man, although as I said our meeting was brief."

Evalina had come back with Dickon. She looked flushed and I noticed that one of the buttons on her blouse was not done up. Dickon was as calm and self-possessed as ever. I guessed there had been some sort of amorous encounter, and as I felt a liking for Andrew Mather my disgust for the two of them was greater than ever.

"What did you think of the chest?" asked Andrew.

"Interesting," said Dickon. "Very interesting. Crudely made rather . . . I suppose that is because it is thirteenth century. I thought the chip-carved rondels were exciting. By the way that's a lovely piece you have inside the chest. I wonder why you shut it away and keep it wrapped up? Are you afraid of someone stealing it?"

"What piece is that?" asked Andrew.

Evalina said: "Oh, it's nothing really. It's just one of those things you have in the chest."

"I didn't know there was anything there."

"You'd know about this," said Dickon. "It's a treasure."

Andrew looked puzzled and Dickon said, "I'll go up and get it. I did want to ask you about it."

"Oh, another time," said Evalina. "I'm tired of all this talk about old things."

Dickon smiled at her and went out of the room.

Evalina was frowning. She said rather crossly. "Oh, I do wish we could do something sensible."

"What would you like to do?" asked Andrew fondly.

"Have a ball or banquet . . . something which I could *plan*."

"We'll have to see."

I said: "I think I should be going."

"It was good of you to call," said Andrew.

"Yes, it was nice seeing you again. I remember the last time . . ." Her eyes were malicious, daring me to mention it. "It seems quite a long time ago."

Dickon came back. He was holding a bronze statuette in his hands, which he held out to Andrew.

Andrew gasped. "Where did you find that?"

"It was in the chest."

Andrew took it and turned it over and over in his hands. He murmured: "I'll swear this is the one. I've seen it before. It was in Florence years ago. It's a beautiful thing. It was said to have been done by a pupil of Michelangelo."

"That," said Dickon, "would account for the purity of the lines."

"And it was in my chest! Impossible! How could it have got there? It belongs to Lord Eversleigh. . . . At least it did when I last saw it . . . if it's the one. We both wanted it. He could bid higher than I . . . and it was his. But how . . . ? I don't understand."

Evalina sat on a stool and laid her head against her husband's knee.

"I'd better confess," she said. "Although I swore to my mother I wouldn't tell. It's hers. I'm keeping it for her."

"Here?" said Andrew. "But this was one of the pieces Lord Eversleigh most prized."

"I know," said Evalina. "That was why he gave it to her. He wanted to give her something good . . . something valuable. I suppose he was thinking it was something she might sell after he died if she fell on hard times. I was holding it for her. She thought that if it was left at the Court and Lord Eversleigh died she wouldn't be allowed to have it. I'm sorry. Have I done wrong?"

Andrew touched her hair caressingly. "Of course not, and

I suppose there is something in that. She would have to prove that he'd given it to her."

"How could she do that? She can't very well say 'I want it written down that you've given me this'... or that.... He's given her one or two things... and she's asked me to mind them for her. I thought I'd wrap them up and keep them for her. There's no harm in that, is there?"

"Of course there's no harm. But this is a very valuable piece. I don't suppose your mother realizes the value."

"Oh, she said Lordy wouldn't give her any old rubbish. Some of the things he gives her she leaves there and hopes for the best. It was just the things she thought were special."

Andrew was turning the statue over and over in his hands.

"Exquisite," he said. "Well, I suppose I should be honored to have it in my house for a little while."

Evalina took it firmly from him.

"I think I'd better wrap it up and put it away," she said. "I promised my mother I would take care of it."

I sensed tension in the atmosphere. Evalina threw a glance at Dickon in which there was a certain dislike. She had not cared that he should find the hiding place of the bronze statue and then show it to her husband. Dickon's expression was inscrutable.

I said I really must go and I thanked them for their hospitality.

Dickon said he would stay awhile. He wanted to talk about the chest and have a closer look at the bronze statue.

I left the house and rode slowly back to Eversleigh.

At supper that evening Dickon was rather more quiet than usual. At dusk I was taken once more to Uncle Carl's room. It was the same ritual; the brief visit, the hovering Jessie and the doctor, the brief pressure of the hand, the murmuring of my name, and then all too soon the request to leave the room.

I wondered if I was ever going to speak to my uncle.

I retired early but not to sleep. I sat in the window for a long time looking out and thinking about the events of the day—the marriage of Evalina to Andrew Mather and Dickon's discovery of the valuable statue which had belonged to my uncle and which Evalina had said he had given to her mother.

Had he? I wondered. How easy it would be for Jessie to help herself to valuable objects and hide them away somewhere!

Of course it was perfectly plausible that he had given them to her, and she might have been denied them if Uncle Carl died. What would happen then? I suppose Rosen, Stead and Rosen had some instructions. Would they come in and assess his possessions? Would they know if anything was missing? How could they? He was perfectly entitled to give his valuables away if he so wished. But it would be difficult for someone like a housekeeper to say some valuable object had been given to her if it were still in the house. He might very well have given her the statue—and other things besides—and she felt she had to get them out of the house while she had a chance.

It was an unusual situation and very difficult to assess. Something should be done, I was sure, but I did not know what. Perhaps I should go and see Rosen, Stead and Rosen. I wished there was someone whose advice I could ask.

I could only think of the Forsters. But I hardly knew them well enough and could scarcely put such a private matter before them when I had met them only twice.

My mother always said: "When in difficulties always wait. Sleep on a big decision. It's often wisest." My father would have been different. He would have been more impulsive.

My sleep was once more fitful. I could never settle to regular sleep in this house. I suppose it was because my mind was so uneasy.

I was awakened from a light doze because I thought I had heard a noise below. I sat up in bed. It was two o'clock. I was sure someone was out on the lawn.

I got out of bed and went to the window and was just in time to see a figure go into the house.

Two o'clock! Who could it be? I immediately thought of Amos Carew coming to visit Jessie. Old Jethro had said that he came some nights. On the other hand it might have been

Dickon. I imagined that he could have been paying a late-night call on Evalina. It was the sort of situation which would amuse him. I could imagine his making love with Evalina in a room close by that in which her husband lay. It was a Boccaccio situation and one I was sure which Dickon—and perhaps Evalina—would find highly diverting. But she had not been very pleased with him when he had brought out the bronze figure, I was sure; and he knew it and metaphorically he snapped his fingers at her. The incident could have brought about a coolness between them.

There was so much that needed explaining. I went to my door and listened. Stealthy footsteps were coming up the stairs.

I waited pressed against the door. If it were Dickon and he were returning to his room, those steps would go on past my room, for he was at the end of this corridor.

I waited. There was silence. I heard the sound of a door opening and being quietly shut.

It seemed as though it was not Dickon.

I locked my door and returned to bed. It must have been Amos Carew visiting Jessie.

The next morning Jessie was hovering in the hall when I came down dressed for my morning walk.

"Hello," she said. "Off out?"

"Yes." I hesitated. "I wonder what good I'm doing here," I went on. "Lord Eversleigh doesn't know I'm here, I'm sure."

"He knows it, all right. It's just that he's lost the power to say so. But I know what you mean. . . . We're all so frustrated."

"It goes on," I said. "I suppose it has been like that for weeks."

She nodded.

"I was wondering," I said, "if there is anything that could be done."

"We're doing all we can."

"Yes, I know, but there have been so many new ideas in the medical profession recently. Some of them have worked wonders."

"That's why I'm so glad we've got Dr. Cabel living here."

"I've been thinking about that. He's retired and he was an old friend and I am sure Uncle Carl likes to have him here . . . but since his day there may have been advances in medicine. I was wondering whether we could call in a new opinion."

She was silent. She had turned slightly away from me. It seemed a long time before she spoke and when she did her voice was trembling a little.

"I'm sure I've thought of everything," she said. "You can imagine what he means to me. Oh no, you can't . . . nobody could. I know you think he is a meal ticket to me. He is, of course, but that's not all. I've loved the old fellow . . . I still do. I can't bear to think of him gone. . . . Oh, I know you'll say . . . yes, where will you be, Jess Stirling, without him. Out on your ear, that's where. Well, it's not quite like that. I've looked after the future."

Yes, I thought. Italian Renaissance statues tucked away for a rainy day!

"I'm fond of him. I've said to him: 'Ought we to get another doctor?' He doesn't like it. He said, 'Old Cabel is the best I've ever known.' Wouldn't trust himself with any of these modern quacks. That was what he said . . . quacks."

"When did he say this?" I asked quickly.

"Oh, it was before the seizure. When he was working up for it, you might say. I said then that we should get another doctor and he wouldn't hear of it. Got quite worked up at the thought."

"I see," I said. "But he would hardly be aware, would he now? He doesn't really know me. If we called in Dr. Forster . . ."

"Dr. Forster! You mean . . . the doctor here!"

"I was thinking of him. I met him at Enderby. They're very nice people. I don't see why we shouldn't call him in. Two opinions are better than one."

"I believe Dr. Cabel would go if we did. Doctors don't like that. They like you to trust them."

"I suppose it might be unethical."

"Well . . . I don't know. Don't do anything yet, though. Perhaps I could sound them . . . both Lordy and Dr. Cabel."

"You mean you would *ask* Lord Eversleigh? He would never understand."

"Oh, I think he might. You're worried, aren't you? You think he shouldn't go on like this. Dr. Cabel thinks it a bit of a miracle that he does."

I said: "I wish I could see him more often. Those brief visits by candlelight . . ."

"I know."

"At night," I said, "when he is probably tired."

"It was his wish that he sees people after dusk. He's changed such a lot. It's done something to his face. . . . It's draws his mouth down one side. It's made his hair come out. He'll never take off that nightcap and he wears it so as to hide half his face. He was a very vain man . . . very fond of his own appearance. . . . He can't bear the change in himself. I keep the mirror well out of his way."

"All the same I should like to see him in the light of day."

"You'd hardly recognize him. He's a pitiful sight."

"Dr. Forster seems to have a good reputation," I said.

"You're worried . . . just like me . . . I know. I pray God he'll recover." She crossed herself as she spoke and looked rather anxiously upward. It had never occurred to me that Jessie was a religious woman and I had thought the gold cross which she always wore about her neck was an ornament rather than a symbol.

I said: "I shall go for a walk now."

"You're a good walker," she said.

"Yes, I like the fresh air. It makes me think."

She nodded and I went out. At the door I turned to look back at her. She was watching me and as she did so was fingering the cross about her neck.

I walked briskly towards the town. It was a long walk. I remembered how Gerard had driven me in that post chaise he had borrowed when we were concerned with Uncle Carl's will. There was no time to go to the solicitor this morning. Moreover,

I was not sure whether it was the right thing to do. I imagined that Mr. Rosen might not be the most tactful of men, and if he were to upset Jessie or Dr. Cabel we might succeed in worrying Uncle Carl to such an extent that his condition grew worse.

I wished there was someone whose advice I could ask.

I wished I knew the Forsters better; I wished I could trust Dickon.

There seemed nothing to do but wait. I had always been able to see several sides to a question. It sometimes had the effect of making me hesitant because one was never sure which way to act for the best. People who had definite ideas need not hesitate. They were sure they were right even when they were wrong. But I could never be entirely sure.

As I saw it, Jessie was immoral; when she had been Uncle Carl's mistress she was also that of his agent. But at the same time she had provided comfort such as he longed for. The three of them had been happy. Whereas had she done the honorable thing and left Uncle Carl he would have been miserable. It was the same with Evalina. There was no doubt that she had made Andrew Mather very happy. If she was indulging in sexual adventure outside her marriage, as long as Andrew didn't know . . .

It seemed mixed morality in a way. After all, I had the example of my own lapse before me.

So I remained undecided. I went back to the house. At dinner Dr. Cabel was as affable as ever toward me so I presumed Jessie had not said anything about my suggesting calling in other advice. Dickon was vivacious and said he was going over to Grasslands in the afternoon.

"Andrew likes me to enjoy his treasures," he said looking at me mischievously.

I walked toward Enderby hoping that I should accidentally meet one of the Forsters. I was unlucky. I just stood by the palings looking at that incredibly gloomy piece of wasteland and hoping for a sign to tell me what to do.

After supper I went to visit Uncle Carl again.

"He is a little better today," said Dr. Cabel as we went up

223

to Uncle Carl's room. "I think your coming has done something for him. I think you could stay a little longer with him. Let's see how we go...shall we?"

He was lying there, blotched hands on the counterpane, his fingers twitching a little as I sat down. An indication, I thought, that he wanted me to take his hand.

I did so.

"Uncle Carl," I said, "it's Zipporah."

His eyes were half closed... I could see that his mouth was drawn up at one side. It made him look unlike the man I had known. His nose looked sharper... I thought his face looked a little fuller. But it was his eyes I had always noticed about Uncle Carl—those lively dark eyes—and now the lids were drawn down over them and he wasn't like Uncle Carl anymore.

"Zipporah..." he whispered.

"Dear Uncle Carl. I came when I heard you weren't well. You're better now.... Able to see me...able to tell me you know I'm here."

He pressed my hand and nodded.

"Good..." he said, "good people..."

"Yes," I said. "You are well looked after."

"Good doctor...friend..."

His hands fluttered. He groaned. "Don't go.... Good Ralph ...Mustn't..."

I presumed Ralph to be Dr. Cabel. It seemed that he had had some inkling that I had suggested another doctor be called.

I said: "No, no...everyone you want will be here.... It's all right."

I felt a great desire to soothe him for he had lifted his head slightly and it was swaying from side to side.

"Rest," I said.

Dr. Cabel was beside me.

"Now, old fellow," he said. "I'm here. Your old friend Ralph is with you all the time. I'm not going to leave you. All's well. There! You trust me, don't you?"

He nodded to me. And I got up.

"Take his hand," he whispered.

I took it and kissed it.

"Good night, dear uncle," I said. "I'll see you tomorrow."

He was lying back with his eyes closed.

I went to my room but before I had mounted the stairs to the next floor I heard the doctor and Jessie come out of the room.

Dr. Cabel was saying angrily. "What did you say to him? Did you tell him I was going? You should have had more sense."

Jessie spoke almost tearfully. "I just said that we might call in another doctor . . . as well . . . two heads are better than one. . . . I didn't think he understood."

"You know very well he takes in a lot. I would pack my bag tomorrow . . . if I thought I could safely leave him."

"Oh, Dr. Cabel . . . please . . . please . . . don't. I was just talking it over with Mistress Ransome. It just seemed like an idea."

"The great idea is to keep his mind at rest. I understand him. I've known him for years. I thought he was going to be so good tonight. I did want Mistress Ransome to be able to talk to him a little. For heaven's sake, Mistress Stirling, be careful what you say in his presence."

"I will . . . oh, I will."

I went into my room and shut the door.

I felt guilty but my uneasiness outweighed my guilt.

Next morning I walked into the town and called on Rosen, Stead and Rosen. I was immediately shown into the office of Mr. Rosen senior. He greeted me with as much warmth as I was sure he was capable of showing and begged me be seated.

"It is very pleasant to see you here again, Mistress Ransome," he said. "Tell me, how is Lord Eversleigh?"

"I see very little of him. He is very ill, you know."

"I do know that, but there is a doctor in residence, which is very comforting."

"Yes, he was an old friend of Lord Eversleigh . . . now retired and so it is possible for him to give up all his time to look after my uncle."

"Splendid! Of course, I doubt very much whether this state of affairs will last. A man in Lord Eversleigh's condition . . . Ah well, he is not a young man."

"I wondered about one or two things. Have you visited Eversleigh?"

"My nephew went some time ago . . . soon after Lord Eversleigh had his seizure. He saw the doctor. Lord Eversleigh was scarcely in a state to see anyone, and it was agreed that we go on as we had been doing for some time. Lord Eversleigh had given us power of attorney, so the bills came to us and we pay the salaries of the staff . . . as we had been doing for some time."

"I see. I did wonder about certain things."

"For the time being everything seems to be in order."

"You are satisfied with the way in which the house is being run? I mean . . . expenses are not excessive."

"Indeed no. The . . . er . . . housekeeper seems to be a woman of good sense who manages the household quite skillfully. The doctor takes no remuneration at all. I gather he is a man of means. He told my nephew that he had known Lord Eversleigh for many years."

"Yes, that is so. I just wanted to make sure that you were satisfied that there was nothing . . . unusual about what. was happening."

"It is not an ideal situation, but I think in the circumstances the arrangements couldn't be improved on. The accounts are more or less what they have always been. I have no reason to believe that the housekeeper is not running the house in just the same manner as when Lord Eversleigh was . . . er . . . *compos mentis*, in a manner of speaking."

"I see."

"I am relieved that you have come to see Lord Eversleigh. There is no secret of the fact that you are his heiress and I am delighted to have your assurance that you are satisfied with the manner in which the affairs of Eversleigh are being conducted."

"It is a little bewildering. I have not been able to exchange a word with Lord Eversleigh."

"The seizure, I gather, has taken the form of paralysis and partially robbed him of speech. That's not uncommon."

"I wanted to assure myself that you were satisfied with the manner in which Lord Eversleigh's affairs were conducted at the Court."

"I should be more satisfied if some member of the family were in control. But this doctor inspired great confidence in my nephew and we feel that as long as he is there he will see that everything is in order. The . . . er . . . housekeeper does seem to be a woman of good sense and she appears to honor her obligations. If you could reside at the Court until everything resolves itself that would be ideal, but I understand you have your other family commitments which make that impossible."

I agreed that this was so and we talked awhile and then I rose to go.

He took my hand and held it firmly.

"Rest assured, my dear lady, that should anything happen you will be notified without delay."

I thanked him and left feeling considerably relieved.

I was rather late for the midday meal. Jessie sat with us as she sometimes did and there was the doctor, Dickon and myself.

I explained that I had walked a little farther than I had meant to and didn't realize it until I began to make my return journey.

"It's such a lovely day," I finished lamely.

"Roast pork should be eaten hot," said Jessie, a little severely, I thought. She was so devoted to food that she considered a lack of enthusiasm to get to it a kind of lese majesty.

Dickon was in a talkative mood. He was very affable to everyone and seemed almost in a state of excitement. I wondered whether this had anything to do with his reunion with Evalina, or perhaps he had found a new light o' love. In any case he seemed to be suppressing excitement.

His eyes sparkled. He was incredibly good-looking—handsome with that hyacinthine type of fair hair which curled about his head and those startling blue eyes which were alert and filled with lurking laughter. A mixture of the handsome dignity of Apollo and the mischief of Pan.

I asked how Lord Eversleigh was and the doctor replied that he had had a little setback last night.

"I am so sorry, Mistress Ransome. It was just at the time when I thought he was really showing some improvement."

He looked rather angrily at Jessie, who lowered her eyes and gave even more attention to the food on her plate than usual.

"Well," went on the doctor, "we have these upsets. They pass. He seemed more at rest during the morning."

Dickon said: "I had a wonderful morning. I rode quite a way . . . to country I hadn't seen before. I found the most wonderful old inn. Forgotten the name of it. It was very traditional . . . just what an old inn should be. I took a snack there."

"What did they give you?" asked Jessie, always interested in food.

"Ripe stilton with hot bread—rye, I think it was, . . . dark and crusty."

"You want plenty of butter on it," said Jessie. "Let it sink in and then a good hunk of cheese on top."

She was tasting it, I knew, in spite of the pork on her plate.

"That's how it was—with the inn's special brand of cider. Delicious."

"And you came straight back here to your good dinner. I haven't noticed any lack of appetite, Master Frenshaw!"

"You know how you admire my strength at the table. You and I are a pair, Mistress Jessie."

"Go on with you! I never could abide people who pick at their food."

"It was a typical gathering. The old blacksmith came into the inn parlor. There were several of us there. He was a gloomy man. He'd evidently got a reputation for it. The others teased him a bit. 'We have a wager every year on Blacksmith Harry,' they told me. 'If anyone can get him to smile between Christmas Day and Twelfth Night we give 'un a shilling . . . and that's six of us. You can reckin we work hard to make blacksmith smile.

No one's had any luck yet.' He was obviously a favorite of them all and I discovered why. He'd got a real gift for telling a story."

"Did he tell you some?" I asked.

"One," said Dickon.

"Was it interesting?"

"It was the way he told it. Now that's the test of a story-teller. If an old tale which must have been heard many times suddenly holds your attention then that's the mark of a good story-teller. Blacksmith Harry had us all ears, I can tell you."

"Tell us the story as well as he did."

"Oh, I'd spoil it. I'm a man of action. I'm no story-teller."

I said: "It's most extraordinary, Dickon, to hear you admit you can't do something."

"You are really whetting our appetites," added Dr. Cabel.

"Well, I'll have a try. But you really need the blacksmith. There was a man in the village whose daughter kept house for him. He was an old miser and an objectionable character in many ways and gave the daughter a bad time. He'd sent off the man who wanted to marry her so that she could go on keeping house for him. He'd already worried his poor wife into the grave."

"In fact," I said, "a most undesirable character."

"Exactly," said Dickon. "Well, one day the man wasn't there anymore. He had gone off, said his daughter, to see his brother up in Scotland. The daughter changed the house . . . made it merry . . . put up fresh curtains. Her lover came back. There was nothing to stop them getting married now. They could do it while the man was away and when he got back it would be too late to stop it. So preparations were made for a wedding feast . . . and everyone said what a good thing it was that the old man had gone to visit his brother in Scotland.

"It was all very happy and showed what misery some people could make for others . . . for the daughter was very pleased with herself these days. Then all changed . . . and in a way you might not believe."

"The old man came back," I said.

"Yes . . . in a way."

"Oh, come on, Dickon," I cried. "No need to hold back the suspense."

"He came back . . . but not in human form."

"A ghost," cried Jessie turning pale.

Dickon lowered his voice: "The old man was seen hovering near the well. Several people thought they saw a man there. But he disappeared before they could make sure. Nobody believed them at first . . . but then the daughter saw him. She let out a shriek and fainted dead away (the blacksmith's words). She was in a fine state. They couldn't calm her. Well, to cut a long story short, since I haven't the blacksmith's gift, it seemed that the old man had not gone to Scotland at all. He had fallen down the well, with a little help from his daughter. She told the whole story. He'd slipped when drawing water. That was her story. He'd called out and she did nothing about it. She just left him there screaming."

Jessie had turned pale and was clasping the cross about her neck.

"Well," said Dickon, "they found his body in the well. They reckoned his daughter had had great provocation and it was never proved that she'd actually pushed him down. She just hadn't done anything to save him. They gave him a decent burial and he never appeared at the well again. That was all he was asking for . . . a proper grave. The blacksmith reckoned he knew he'd made his daughter's life a hell. He didn't want revenge on her, all he wanted was a decent burial. So the body was put in a coffin and the burial service was said over it. And from that day to this his ghost has never again been seen." Dickon leaned back in his seat. "You ought to have heard the blacksmith tell it."

Jessie was staring down at the uneaten food on her plate.

Two days passed uneventfully. I paid only one visit to Uncle Carl. Dr. Cabel said he was not well enough on the first of those days; the second I saw him and he held my hand and said a few words.

"Improving," said Dr. Cabel, his eyes shining. "I can't tell you how happy I am when he shows a little glimpse of his old self."

I walked over to Enderby and was disappointed when I heard that Derek and Isabel had gone to London for a few days.

It was on the second day when I came upon Jessie sitting in the winter parlor with the cook, Daisy Button, a plump woman, waistless so that she looked rather like a barrel, good-natured, easily offended, dedicated to her cooking, determined to protect her dignity. I knew that Jessie had had a few tussles with her but there was a certain friendship between them and whatever airs, the cook complained, Jessie gave herself, anyone who was so appreciative of Daisy Button's culinary master-pieces could be forgiven.

Daisy Button, I had heard, could tell whether a girl was pregnant almost before the girl knew it herself; she had even been known to prophesy correctly the sex of the child; her grandmother had been a witch and she had powers.

When I approached, Daisy Button got up and bobbed a rather reluctant curtsy and said she was discussing the day's supper with Mistress Stirling, and she hoped she was giving satisfaction. A large part of her beautiful tansy pudding had been sent back to the kitchen from the dinner table.

I said the tansy pudding was absolutely delicious and if those at the table had not eaten of it as voraciously as it deserved it was because they had gorged themselves on the very excellent roast beef which had preceded it.

I saw the cards in Daisy Button's apron pocket and guessed she had been giving Jessie what she would call "a reading."

I said: "I see you have the cards. Have you been telling fortunes?"

"Oh, well," said Daisy, "Mistress Stirling did ask me to have a peep for her."

"Has she good fortune in store?"

"Couldn't be better," said Daisy. "A rosy future . . . with love and money. She's going for a journey."

"Oh?" I said. "Are you going to leave us, Jessie?"

"Not while I'm needed," said Jessie sententiously.

"No, it's for the future," put in Daisy. "She's going to meet a rich stranger and she's going to find peace and happiness in this new friendship."

"It sounds very interesting," I said turning away.

Jessie surprised me. When I had first met her I thought her a hard-headed, scheming woman. She was probably all this, but in addition she was religious and very superstitious as well. She had been really shaken when Dickon had told his story of the man in the well. And now Daisy's promised good fortune had made her very happy.

How unwise it was to make snap judgments about people's characters. The only thing one could be certain of was that there were many more facets to their natures than to a well-cut diamond and because one understood their reactions to one situation it was no use thinking one really knew them.

It was dusk. I was about to go for my visit to Lord Eversleigh when I paused. There was a terrible commotion in the kitchens.

Dr. Cabel looked at Jessie, who was standing still, listening. Then one of the maids came running up.

"It's May," she said. "She's seen something."

"Seen what?" asked Jessie.

"We can't get a word of sense out of her. She's having hysterics at the kitchen table."

Jessie looked at the doctor and he said: "I'd better see her."

We went down through the screens to the kitchen. May, one of the housemaids, was sitting back in a chair staring ahead of her. The cook had a glass of brandy in her hand and was trying to force May to drink it.

"Now what is this?" said Dr. Cabel taking the brandy, which he put on the table.

"I see a ghost, sir," said May, her teeth chattering.

"What is this nonsense?" The doctor spoke sharply.

"I see it, sir. Clear as I see you. He was standing there at the top of the stairs. I looked at him and he faded into nothing."

"Now, now, May, tell us exactly what happened. It must have been one of the other servants you saw."

"In his lordship's hat and cloak."

"His lordship's!"

"Oh yes, they was his all right. I've seen him before . . . you know . . . before he was took so ill."

"And he disappeared?"

"Well, that's what ghosts do, sir."

"It's a bad sign," said Daisy Button. "It's death in the house. I felt it a long time. I reckon it's his lordship. His spirit is already gone . . . and in its early form as yet . . . outside looking on. That's how it goes. Mark my words, we shan't have the dear gentleman with us much longer."

"Stop that nonsense," said Dr. Cabel. "What May saw was one of the servants . . . or she imagined she saw something. You're all right, May. Now I'm going to give you something to drink and you're to go to bed."

"I'd be frightened, sir. I don't want to see that again."

"You saw nothing. It was a figment of your imagination." He bent over. "Good heavens, have you been drinking?"

"I give her a glass of my sloe gin," said Daisy Button. "But then we all had some."

"It may well be that your sloe gin is more potent than you think, Mistress Button."

"Well, you might have something there."

The doctor smiled. "Distribute it in smaller portions in future, will you?"

"Well, my sloe's always been took in the same quantities before, sir."

"Each year's brew won't be exactly the same, will it?"

"That could be true, sir. You know what sloes is."

"Shall we get May to her room and let the doctor give her something to make her sleep," I said.

"Come along, May," said Jessie.

They went up to the maid's room.

I noticed how subdued Jessie was. She was really frightened and behaving rather unlike the Jessie I had come to expect.

* * *

Dickon was very interested when he heard of May's experience. He was on some sort of acquaintanceship with several of the maids. I had seen his eyes rest speculatively on several of them. I imagined that he waylaid them in dark places and indulged in certain familiarities. I had seen the manner in which some of them looked at him. Dickon was the sort of person who only had to be in a place to change the nature of it.

He held forth a long time at dinner over May's adventure.

"These girls are very superstitious," he said. "I've no doubt May imagined the whole thing."

"Yes," said Jessie, "that's all. She just saw a shadow or something . . . and thought up the rest."

"She was very shaken," I pointed out.

"Of course she would be," said Dickon. "What did the poor girl see? I beg your pardon . . . what did she *think* she saw?"

"Some garbled story about a man in a cloak," said Dr. Cabel. "And a hat."

"Evidently a visitor since he was hatted," said Dickon.

"She said he was like Lord Eversleigh," I said.

"Probably she saw him in a hat and cloak once," put in the doctor.

"The cook adds fuel to the flames," I remarked. "She says that the apparition was a sort of angel of death."

"Interesting," said Dickon. "Come to announce some disaster?"

"Daisy Button is full of tales—always has been," said Jessie. "Thinks she's rather clever, she does. If she wasn't such a good cook . . ."

"Good cooks should be allowed their little foibles," remarked Dickon. "Do tell me more of this angel of death."

"She seems to imply," I explained, "that it's the spirit of someone who has departed taking on the guise of his earthly body."

"It's very complicated," sighed Dickon. "I didn't know that cook added supernatural knowledge to her culinary skills."

The doctor said rather impatiently: "It's all a lot of women's nonsense. I think we'd do well to forget it."

"You are certainly right, doctor," agreed Dickon. "But is it not strange how interested we all are in unnatural phenomena, even those of us who should know better."

"The girl has come to her senses. I gave her a draught and a good night's sleep will do the rest. Now I hope we shall have no more of this nonsense."

His hope was not fulfilled for that very night the ghost made another appearance.

This time it was to Jessie herself.

There was a wild scream and we all ran to see what had happened. Jessie was half fainting when I arrived on the scene. I had been outside for a breath of fresh air before retiring, for I had just had one of my brief visits to Uncle Carl.

Jessie was lying on the floor. She had fainted. With all the blood drained from her face so that the carmine stood out unnaturally she looked like a painted doll.

Dr. Cabel was kneeling beside her. "Give her air," he was crying, for several of the servants were crowding round.

"What has happened?" I asked.

"Mistress Stirling has fainted," the doctor announced. "She'll be all right. It's nothing much. The heat, I expect."

It was not really very hot. It never was in the house behind those thick stone walls even at the height of summer.

Jessie was already opening her eyes. She screamed: "Where is he? I saw him."

"All is well," said Dr. Cabel. "You're all right. You were overcome by the heat."

"I saw . . . he was on the stairs. . . . Just as he used to look . . . before . . . before . . ."

"I think," said Dr. Cabel, "we'll get her to her bed. She needs to lie down." He signed to one of the men servants and the man with the doctor got Jessie to her feet.

"Now," said Dr. Cabel soothingly, "we'll get you to bed. I will give you something to drink . . . it will help you to sleep."

"It was terrible," murmured Jessie.

"Never mind now," said the doctor.

Dickon had appeared at the top of the stairs. He ran down, "What's wrong?"

"Jessie has fainted."

"Good heavens. Is she ill or something . . . ?"

Dr. Cabel silenced him with a look. Dickon's eyes were round with wonder.

Then Dickon gently pushed the man servant to one side and himself took Jessie's arm.

"Yes, to bed," he said, "that's the best place."

"I saw him. . . ." Jessie was murmuring. "With my own eyes I saw him. . . . It was him . . . I could swear it."

"You've been working too hard," said the doctor.

"I never fainted before," said Jessie.

"Come along . . . to your room."

I followed the procession. In her room I noticed the crucifix hanging on the wall. A further sign of her religion. She lay on the bed. Her eyes were wide and frightened, though some color had returned to her face. It was clear that Jessie had had a very bad shock.

"Now," said Dr. Cabel, "there's nothing to do but rest, and when you've drunk what I shall bring you, you will sleep."

"I don't want to be alone."

"I'll stay with you," I said, "till the doctor comes back."

Dickon remained in the room too. He had seated himself by Jessie's bed and watched her intently.

"I saw it so clear," she said. "It was him, all right. . . . Him like he used to be."

"I can't think what you saw," I said, "but the light does play funny tricks."

"There was hardly any light in the hall."

"That's why you thought you saw this . . . apparition. In daylight you would have seen there was nothing there."

"I saw him. . . . What's he doing? Why? Why?"

Dickon leaned toward the bed. He said: "Cook believes that somebody's going to die and he's come to warn us."

"It's him. . . . It's Lordy," she cried.

I said: "He's very ill. I think Dr. Cabel is expecting him to die at any time."

"The blacksmith said that it was someone who wanted a burial," Jessie started to shiver.

"I wish the doctor would hurry with the sleeping draught or whatever it is," I said.

Dickon took Jessie's hand and held it firmly. "You mustn't get so agitated. You won't be able to look after everything there is to do, you know. Why you might be ill. You've got to take care of yourself, Jessie."

"Yes," she said smiling at him.

"Where would all this be . . . without you, Jessie?"

She nodded.

"So here is the doctor with his sleeping potion. Take it, Jessie, and rest. You'll feel better in the morning. You'll know how to cope with all this."

She was silent. It seemed that Dickon had chosen the right words to comfort her.

She gulped down the liquid. She didn't want me to leave her until she was asleep.

She had been very shaken and I realized that she was afraid to be alone in case the apparition returned.

Jessie quickly recovered from her fright and was her old self in a day or so. I was now wanting to go home. I found the house oppressive, and my visits to Uncle Carl seemed to me unnecessary. I made no progress with him and I could not believe my presence was very important to him.

I missed Lottie and Jean-Louis and was longing for the peace and normality of Clavering.

I had passed Enderby once or twice hoping for a glimpse of the Forsters, but I assumed they were still away and felt I could not call. Dr. Forster would, I supposed, not come there since his brother and sister-in-law were away; yet I continued to walk that way, drawn by memories.

Once I walked past Grasslands and saw Dickon's horse tethered there. I hoped he was not going to cause any trouble to that very nice Andrew Mather. I should have liked to visit him again, but that of course would entail meeting Evalina and I had no great desire for that.

Often I would find Dickon's eyes on me—maliciously, I thought. It occurred to me that he was involved in some plan and that it concerned me. If I caught his eyes he would smile at me in a rather amused, mischievous way but sometimes I thought I caught a glimpse of something there which was by no means lighthearted and gave me a twinge of alarm.

I had never liked him; I had never trusted him; and I knew he was quite unscrupulous.

I wondered what he was planning; what he talked of with Evalina. I was sure they discussed me together.

I thought of speaking to Dr. Cabel and telling him that I was thinking of returning home. Why not? I had been to Rosen, Stead and Rosen; they seemed perfectly satisfied with the state of affairs. There was the matter of the valuable statue. Could it be that Jessie was taking goods from the house as a sort of bulwark against the time when she would have to leave? I thought that was a possibility. But of course it was true that Uncle Carl had been very generous to her. The first time I had seen her she had been wearing quite a large amount of jewelry—presumably gifts from him, as she had worn them in his presence.

Perhaps, I thought, we should make an inventory of what was in the house. I might have asked Rosen that. But that would be tantamount to accusing Jessie. She might be affronted and leave; and if my uncle really was aware of what was going on that could upset him very much.

I must think clearly. But I was determined to make up my mind to go soon.

My steps had again led me to Enderby. I was still hoping that one of the Forsters would appear. The house looked silent. I turned away to the haunted patch. It looked quite normal in the light of day. I wondered someone didn't mend the palings or have them taken away.

Absentmindedly I stepped over and walked on the grass.

My mind went back to that evening at dusk when I stood on this spot and suddenly Gerard had arisen from the ground, as it were . . . as though he had stepped out of . . . a grave.

I shook myself. I had given up that nonsense of pretending that he was some long-dead gallant and that I had assumed a personality not my own. No . . . I had been revealed to myself I had loved Gerard. Everything that had happened had been my desire. He had shown me my real self.

I could hear his voice saying: "I was looking for my fob. . . ."

And then suddenly I saw the glitter as the sunlight caught something lying there.

I immediately thought: It's Gerard's fob. And I ran forward.

But it was not a fob. What I was looking at was a crucifix which had been stuck into the earth.

I knelt down and touched it. It was firmly entrenched and it looked as though it had been put there not so very long ago because the grass had not grown round it.

How strange. I wondered who had put it there.

I stood there puzzled. Had it been there when Gerard and I had met here? It could hardly have been. Of course the grass could have hidden it. But there was very little grass growing just at that spot.

It was almost as though it marked a grave.

I stood up. I was beginning to feel very uneasy, and I had a great desire to get away. I felt I was walking rather blindly into something of which I was beginning to get a glimmer of understanding. I had a great desire to get away from this place.

I walked across the stretch of grass and stepped over the palings. I listened. I fancied that I heard a movement somewhere. It was just that uncanny feeling that I was being watched.

I started to run. It was not very far to Eversleigh, about fifteen minutes walk perhaps, but I always took the shortcut through the wood. It was scarcely a wood. Just a little stretch where the trees grew close together.

I made for it and as I entered wondered if I should have gone round by the road. It was foolish. The sight of that crucifix had unnerved me. I knew there was some meaning behind it.

Suddenly the realization came to me. I had been observed. I was now being followed. For what reason? I felt the goose-pimples rising on my skin. This was real fear. I heard a footstep behind me and started to run.

I was thankful that the trees were thinning and I would soon be in the open. I ran as fast as I could and when I had put some distance between myself and the last of the trees, I turned.

A man was emerging from the wood. This was my pursuer. Dickon!

He sauntered up to me.

"Hello, Zipporah," he said.

I said breathlessly: "You've just come through the wood."

He nodded, smiling at me, and I fancied there was an odd flicker in his eyes.

"Did you see anyone in there?"

He raised his eyebrows in surprise.

I stammered: "I wondered. . . . People don't often use that stretch of wood."

"There might have been someone," he said. "Are you going back to the house?"

I said I was.

"I'll walk with you." He fell in by my side. I was very much aware of him and I was still trembling a little from my scare. I refrained from mentioning my feelings to him. I thought: He was my pursuer. Why was he frightening me? Was it just his mischief?

Then I noticed there was something different about the swing of his coat. Dickon was fast becoming a man of fashion and perhaps this was why I noticed that his coat bulged a little. He was carrying something in an inner pocket.

A sudden gust of wind made his coat swing open, and because I was really wondering what he carried I happened to glance down at that moment.

It was a pistol.

I was really shaken. What was he doing with a pistol? And why did he not call to me in the wood? He must have been aware that I was running away. Yet he had emerged casually sauntering as though there was nothing unusual about chasing people in woods. I had noticed lately a change in him. There was a hard glitter in his eyes which might have indicated a certain pleasure, as though he were engaged in some activity which intrigued him. I had put this down to his renewed acquaintance with Evalina and perhaps involvements with some of the Eversleigh serving girls who might seem more attractive than those at Clavering. They would be different and I imagined Dickon would like variety in his seductions.

But I was unsure of him now. Amorous encounters were second nature to him. I had a fancy that he was involved in something other than those.

Why should he be carrying a pistol? To shoot ... what? Rabbits? Birds? For what purpose except the lust to kill? He had no need of food. That was plentifully supplied by Jessie, and he was a man whose sports would be conducted indoors rather than out.

Where did he get the pistol? There was a gun room at Eversleigh, of course.

So disturbed was I that I went to find it. I was not quite sure where it was. Nobody had pointed it out to me but I had some idea.

I found it. It was a small room but there were guns of all sorts there. It was impossible for me to see if any were missing. But of course it was from this room that he would have taken the pistol. Or he might have brought it with him in case he needed it on the journey.

Perhaps then there was nothing unusual about his having a pistol in his possession. Perhaps I was trying to make something out of nothing. Quite clearly I was getting a little overwrought and should go back to Clavering.

When I was in my room there was a knock on the door and when I called "Come in" Jessie entered.

"I hope I'm not disturbing you, Mistress Ransome," she said, "but I have a message for you from Amos Carew. He says he'd be obliged if you would call on him tomorrow afternoon. He'll be at the house between three and four and if that's not convenient to you would you please name another time."

"I can certainly see him tomorrow," I said.

"That's settled then," she smiled.

I said: "I hope you're feeling better now, and have got over that little scare."

"I don't know what got into me. It must have been a trick of the light . . . and that kitchen girl having said she saw something put it into my head. Well, I'm downright ashamed. I am that. It's not like me, I can tell you."

"We're all surprised in ourselves sometimes," I said.

She nodded. "I'll get a message over to Amos," she told me.

That night I was disturbed again. There was someone in the house who made nocturnal visits. I was wakened again and saw that it was two o'clock—the same time as before.

First the awareness that someone was below and then the creak of a door and the sound of stealthy footsteps.

It was either Dickon or Amos, I told myself. Their amorous adventures were really no concern of mine. I turned over and went to sleep.

The following afternoon I walked to Amos Carew's house. It was the first time I had called there but I knew exactly where it was as Jethro had pointed it out to me very shortly after I had arrived on my first visit.

It was a pleasant house with a lawn in front and a porch in which pots of flowers were growing.

Before I had time to knock Amos Carew opened the door.

He took me into a sitting room which was comfortably furnished, though not large, and bade me be seated.

He said: "It was good of you to come, Mistress Ransome."

"Not at all. I have been wondering what it is you want to see me about."

He looked at me in rather an embarrassed fashion and said: "It's not easy to explain."

"I am sure that you will, though," I said.

"It's . . . er . . . things at the Court."

"Oh yes?"

"They can't go on the way they are. I mean his lordship is growing weaker . . . in spite of what the doctor says."

"He seems to me to be in a very weak condition."

"Well, what bothers me . . . is what is to happen if he was to go. I'm sorry to seem . . . hard like . . . but I was thinking of my position here. It bothers me a bit. A man has to think of his future."

"I understand that."

"Well, when his lordship goes this passes to you."

"How can you be sure of that?"

"Oh, his lordship has explained it to Jessie. There was not much he kept from her . . . when he was well enough, that was. . . . I daresay she wonders too. It could be hard on her . . . and on me."

"I understand. But I really think it is a matter which will have to be decided later. You see, it may be that my uncle has changed his mind. I don't think we can make arrangements about something which has not come to pass."

"Jessie says that he has left it all to you, and she would know. It was just that I had it in mind that if I could put a word in for myself to you "

"If it happens as you say I am sure my husband and I would not want to turn good people away. I can't make promises about something which is not mine. One never knows what will happen."

He nodded gravely.

"I want to show you how well I keep the place . . . inside and out. I've done wonders with my bit of garden at the back. I even supply vegetables to the Court. . . . I was hoping you'd take a look at it."

"I am absolutely sure that everything is in perfect order."

"But you will look at it, won't you?"

I said I would.

"Then I'll show you the garden."

We went through a passage to the garden and he led me

out toward some fruit trees. I was struck by the quietness of all about me.

I said: "You appear to be very isolated here in spite of the fact that you are not far from the Court."

He didn't answer. There was a strange look in his eyes. The thought suddenly struck me that he had brought me here for a purpose other than to speak of his future, and an unaccountable cold fear took possession of me. This was the man who was Jessie's lover, who had calculatedly brought her here to become Uncle Carl's mistress, to fleece him of what she could. They must have planned it together. They were unscrupulous people. I had a great desire to say a hasty good-bye to him and go back to the Court as fast as I could and when I was there pack my bags and go home to Jean-Louis, to Lottie, to my mother and Sabrina.

He said: "Come and look at the trees. I'm going to get some good fruit there this year."

His voice sounded different . . . strained in some way.

I hesitated. Something told me to get away.

And then suddenly I heard a noise. Someone was knocking on the door. Then I heard a familiar voice. Dickon's! And he was coming towards us.

"I did knock. But the door was open. Oh . . . hello, Zipporah. Amos, I came over to talk to you."

"I'm busy," said Amos.

"Oh, all right. I'll wait. Looking at the garden, are you? He's very proud of his garden, Zipporah."

I noticed the bulge in his coat. So he was still carrying the pistol.

"I wanted to ask Amos a few questions about the tenants," he said.

"Then I will leave you two to talk," I answered.

Dickon almost leered at me. "I'm not driving you away, I hope."

"No, no," I assured him. "I was on the point of leaving."

Amos looked resigned and I wasn't sure whether he was

angry or relieved. I could imagine that Dickon might be becoming a nuisance to him.

As I walked back to the Court I thought how often Dickon seemed to be where I was. I could almost believe he was following me. However, on this occasion I had been quite pleased to see him. I was really quite alarmed in that garden alone with Amos Carew. There seemed to be no logical reason why I should have been. I think the fact was that the situation here was beginning to upset me more than I had believed possible.

I really wanted to get away . . . back to normality. There was nothing else I could do here.

When I came into the hall Jessie was there. She started when she saw me and turned a shade paler.

"Are you all right?" I asked.

"Yes. . . . Did you see Amos?"

"Yes, I saw him."

"And . . . was everything all right?"

I raised my eyebrows. It was not the first time I had resented her interrogations and felt an irresistible urge to remind her of her position.

"We had our talk," I said and walked past her.

I could feel her staring after me.

I went to my room thinking about Amos Carew. It was natural that he should be worried about his position, for it was quite clear that Uncle Carl could not live much longer in the state he was in. I think I had allowed myself to grow too fanciful. I was as bad as Jessie with her ghost.

I had one or two sewing jobs to do. I could have given them to one of the maids but preferred to do them myself. There was a tear in my skirt where I had caught it on a bramble — not much but it should be done at once — and a button was half off my dressing gown and the stitches in a petticoat had come undone. I would do them this afternoon. I had no sewing material and I knew that the maids went to Jessie's room to get them.

I knocked at the door. There was no answer so I went in. My eyes went at once to the blank space on the wall. That was where the crucifix had hung. It was no longer there. Of course it wasn't. It was in the haunted patch and Jessie was the one who had put it there.

I forgot all about the sewing materials and went back to my room.

What did this mean? I asked myself. Why should she have taken the crucifix from her wall to put in the wasteland?

It meant that there was a grave there in the wasteland. Whose? Wild thoughts chased each other through my brain. A possibility had occurred to me.

I had to find the answer.

One thing was becoming certain: I was in the midst of intrigue and what was shown to me was not the true state of affairs.

I wished there was someone whose help I could ask. I wished the Forsters were there, or that calm practical-looking doctor. Could I go to him? No! The people to whom I should go were Rosen, Stead and Rosen. Mr. Rosen already knew of the rather unconventional ménage at Eversleigh Court.

What could I say? The housekeeper has put her crucifix in the wasteland . . . ?

I would have to have more tangible evidence than that.

I must think about this clearly, reason it out. I must know the best thing to do. I went over everything that had happened. The strangeness of the atmosphere in this house. But I had felt that on my very first visit.

It would soon be suppertime and I must face them all; after that there would be my visit to the sick room. I must be watchful. I must not be so easily gullible. I must realize that I was here with scheming, unscrupulous people. And what part was Dickon playing in all this? He was devious and I was an enemy. I really must discover all I could and then go to Mr. Rosen.

I suppose I had been right about the crucifix. That might be some sort of clue. We would go the wasteland and we would dig up and discover why Jessie behaved as though a grave was there.

I had been right about the crucifix, hadn't I? I hadn't imagined it.

That was absurd. I had seen clearly that space on the wall with the nail protruding where the crucifix had hung, but I had to make sure. I had to look again. I was going to creep along to Jessie's room when she was not there, open the door and take a quick look.

Opportunity came about half an hour before supper. It was safe then because Jessie was always in the kitchen at that time supervising the meal. That was something which was too important to be left entirely to others.

I was ready. I heard her go downstairs and slipped up to her room. Quickly, silently I opened the door.

I stared. The crucifix was in its place on the wall.

I could not believe it. I was sure earlier that day it had not been there.

Could I trust myself? Was my imagination betraying me?

I felt very alarmed.

Tomorrow, I promised myself, I will go to the wasteland. If the crucifix is there then it was not Jessie's and I must have imagined I saw that blank wall. How could I? I was a practical woman of common sense, or so I had always believed.

What was happening to me in this strange place? Why did I fear I was being followed in the woods? Why did I see something sinister in Dickon because he happened to be where I was a great deal lately? Why should I feel this increasing menace just because he carried a pistol with him?

It was night—restless, uneasy night. I had got through the evening tolerably well. Although Dr. Cabel did say at supper: "You are very thoughtful this evening, Mistress Ransome."

I said I was feeling a little tired and would retire early.

I had not seen Uncle Carl that evening. Dr. Cabel had said he was no worse but just very very tired and he was sleeping deeply so it was not wise to waken him even to see me.

"It must be something in the air," he said. "You are both tired today. It's the weather. It can have that effect."

I had made my excuse to retire early and I did so.

But not to sleep. I had made up my mind that the next day I was going to see Mr. Rosen. There was one thing I wanted to do first and that was ascertain that the crucifix was no longer on the wasteland. Whether it was or not I should go straightaway to Mr. Rosen.

I would ask what I should do before going home, for I was determined to go home soon.

I was still wide awake at half past one when I heard movements similar to those which I had heard before. I got out of bed and went to the window and waited. It was not long before a figure emerged from the house. It was a man in a long cloak who was certainly not Amos or Dickon. Then who?

I watched him walk across the lawn. Then an idea came to me. I put on my dressing gown and opening my door stood for a second or so listening. Then I went down the short staircase to the corridor in which was Uncle Carl's room.

I sped along to it. I turned the handle and went in. There was enough moonlight to show me the furniture, the fourposter bed . . . with the curtains half drawn as they always had been.

I went to the bed. I think I had half expected what I saw. The bed was empty.

Events suddenly slipped into place like a jigsaw puzzle.

My earlier suspicions were proved to be founded in truth. The man in the bed had not been my uncle.

I looked round the room. I opened one of the cupboards. Clothes were hanging there. There was a shelf on which were various pots and pads and brushes . . . such as I imagined were used by actors.

Actors! They had been playing a drama . . . comedy . . . a farce . . . whatever, it was for my benefit.

They were actors . . . all of them . . . the doctor, the man in the bed . . . and Jessie knew it. She was one of them.

I had the proof I needed now. I could go along to Mr. Rosen tomorrow with the evidence I had gathered.

In another cupboard were playing cards. I smiled grimly. That was how they whiled away the time when they were not coaching this man for the part of Lord Eversleigh, while they were waiting for the moment when they would play their little scene for me.

They were ingenious people and they would be desperate. They must not know that I had uncovered their little plot before I had seen Mr. Rosen.

Shortly the bogus Lord Eversleigh would be returning. I imagined he took exercise at night for clearly he could not go out during the day.

I was aware that if anyone found me here I should be in acute danger. If they were bold enough to work out such a devious plan how far would they carry it?

In sudden panic I went swiftly to the door. I looked out into the corridor. All was quiet.

I crossed the corridor to the window and because of the heavy curtains I believed I could conceal myself there.

I went over and tried it. Yes. I could satisfy myself that no part of me was visible. I would now await the return of the actor who had played Uncle Carl in the piece.

I was cold and cramped through having to conceal myself, but I was rewarded.

Soon after two o'clock there was the familiar creak of the door followed by the sound of soft footsteps on the stairs.

I peeped out and saw him open the door of the room and disappear within.

I crept back to my room.

This is a gigantic fraud, I thought. And what happened to Uncle Carl? I was certain now that he was dead and buried in the haunted patch.

I knew the spot. It was where the crucifix had been.

My mind was working so fast that I almost played with the idea of getting a spade and digging up that grave.

That would be unwise. I could not do it on my own. I must get help.

How I wished there was someone who could advise me.

I played with the idea of calling in Dr. Forster. Could I bring him in? I did not know why I thought so much about him. It must be his connection with Enderby and the fact that I had first seen him in that spot where I had found Gerard.

No. Mr. Rosen was the one, although I could not imagine what his reaction would be to the bizarre story I should have to tell him.

It was foolish to expect to sleep. I lay in bed impatiently waiting for the morning to come.

I was out of bed at dawn and as I reached for my dressing gown I saw that the button which I had meant to sew on yesterday had come off.

A horrible thought struck me. Suppose I had dropped it in what was ironically called the "sick room"? They would know I had been there. Then I should certainly be in danger.

Everything must appear as normal. I went down to breakfast. Dickon was there. He smiled at me almost patronizingly, I thought, and it occurred to me that had he been different, if I could have trusted him, I might have confided in him.

I would not dream of doing that. Sometimes the thought came to me that he was involved with it all, but I did not see for what purpose, and Dickon would always have to have a purpose, one which worked to his advantage.

"You're in a hurry this morning," he said.

"No."

"And you seem preoccupied."

I shrugged my shoulders.

"Thinking of the adventures of the day to come, I'll swear." It was almost as though he knew.

"I don't suppose they will be as exciting as yours."

He laughed. "Zipporah," he said, "I wish sometimes that you liked me a little. It worries your mother and mine that you're not more fond of me."

"If esteem is wanted it has to be earned."

"I know," he said mockingly. "Alas."

I stood up.

"So soon," he said. "You've eaten scarcely anything."

"I've had enough."

"I'll see you later."

I did not answer and went out.

I should need my horse because I was going into the town to see Mr. Rosen. First, though, I was going to ride out to the haunted patch to see if the cross was there.

I felt better now that I was taking action. I began to piece everything together. My uncle had died. . . . Would someone have helped him to die? I wondered what advantage that would have brought, for Jessie had seen that he was more use to her alive than dead. That was why she had brought in her fellow actors. . . . They knew how to play their parts. . . . What was their motive? To enjoy a comfortable life at Eversleigh and take what they could. I thought of the statue at Grasslands.

Mr. Rosen would take charge and deal with everything.

I had reached the haunted patch. I slipped off my horse and tethered him to a bush. This was necessary as I couldn't see from the path whether the cross was there or not. I stepped over the palings and walked forward. I stared down at the disturbed earth. The cross had been taken away.

Now I was certain. Jessie had placed it there because she had been truly scared by the ghost. Afterward she must have felt she had been foolish to do so and had taken it away.

I must get to Mr. Rosen at once.

I mounted my horse. How silent it was. It was really rather lonely country between Enderby and Eversleigh. There was the short stretch where the trees grew close together and I slowed down to walk my horse through them.

I heard a sudden movement. I wasn't sure what it was . . . perhaps the displacement of a stone . . . but it startled me and I felt myself shiver with apprehension for I was certain that I was not alone among the trees. A sensation of horror seemed to crawl over me then. Instinctively I knew that I was in danger. I hesitated whether to ride on or dash back toward Enderby. I had no time to do either for a man was coming towards me. He carried a gun which was pointing at me. I could

251

see eyes glittering through the highwayman's mask, and his cocked hat was drawn down over his face.

I was staring into the muzzle of a gun.

I stammered: "I have very little money with me."

He did not speak; he raised the gun and I knew I was looking into the face of death. He did not want my money; he wanted my life.

This was the end.

I heard the report. I was slipping from my horse. There was a buzzing in my ears and I saw blood spattered on the trees.

The dizziness was passing. I was not dead then.

A body was lying on the grass. Someone else had appeared. This can't be real, I thought. Because it was Dickon standing there with the pistol in his hand.

He was calling to me. "You're all right. I got him . . . just in time. I've shot my first man. It was you . . . or him, Zipporah."

"You . . ." I began.

He knelt down beside the figure on the grass. "Dead," he said. "Right through the heart. Good shot. And in the nick of time."

"Who . . . ? What . . . ?"

He said: "Didn't you see what was going on? No . . . not till what might have been too late. It was so clear to me. . . . But let's go. There's a lot of talking to be done."

So Dickon had saved my life.

The first thing we did was ride into the town to Rosen, Stead and Rosen. Mr. Rosen senior sat very still as he listened to the story Dickon had to unfold.

"I shot Amos Carew," he said. "He was dressed as a highwayman . . . and it was either him or Zipporah."

Mr. Rosen raised his eyebrows and they went higher and higher as he listened. "It was self-defense," he said. "Quite understandable. No charges can be brought."

"I knew something was wrong from the moment I arrived," said Dickon. "All that elaborate preparation to see the old man!

252

When I went in they were in a state of wild apprehension. So I started to look about me. I guessed that the housekeeper was on to too good a thing to want it to end and therefore she had pretended Lord Eversleigh was not dead and brought in her own man to play the part."

"Very devious," said Mr. Rosen.

"All rather obvious. The housekeeper was no ordinary one. She was a special friend of Lord Eversleigh."

"I had heard of it," said Mr. Rosen.

"Then I discovered that valuable pieces were being taken from the house. I think that was the main business. They wanted the housekeeper to stay there until they had successfully disposed of certain objects, which they could only do gradually, and make a fortune for themselves."

"You say *they* . . ."

"Jessie, the manager of the estate who was her lover and the two men who took the part of doctor and invalid."

"Quite a little party of them."

"All necessary to the plot. I knew that Zipporah was gradually stumbling on the truth—though it took her a long time—and they knew it. She was close. I think Carew was the main mover in the affair. He was the desperate one. I daresay the housekeeper just wanted to go on living in comfort for a while. But she was his mistress and did what he said. Well, they were realizing that Zipporah was hot on their trail, but they didn't think of me. I had a reputation for being . . . not very serious and I lived up to it. It helped me. I discovered certain things from the housekeeper's daughter. She was not as discreet as they would have liked her to be. There's quite a bit of stuff from Eversleigh in Amos Carew's house. I discovered it when I called on him. I think they may have had difficulty in disposing of it. I don't know what their future plans are . . . but they must have realized they couldn't go on like that forever. I daresay when they realized the value of some of the stuff they had stolen they wanted to carry on and get more. Zipporah was getting too close so they were taking the play into its final act. They were going to get rid of her. I realized this. My mother and hers had sent me here to look after her. I was determined to do that."

"It would seem," said Mr. Rosen, "that she owes her life to you."

Dickon smiled at me maliciously. "I rather think she does. I saved it twice. Carew was going to kill her when she called at his house. I don't know where. I suppose he was hoping to make us believe that a highwayman had shot her. He would have staged something, I don't doubt. They were very good with their plots . . . as long as people didn't look too deeply into them. Well, I was there and saved her . . . just as I did in the wood. I was ready . . . waiting. I heard them talking this morning. They knew she had been into the room and that there could be no delay. They said something about a button."

"Yes," I said. "I went into the sick room last night. There was no one there. The invalid was taking a stroll in the gardens. The button came off my dressing gown."

Mr. Rosen cleared his throat. "It is an extraordinary story you have told me. What we shall have to do is to find Lord Eversleigh's body. If it was murder . . ." He lifted his shoulders.

"I don't think Jessie would have allowed that," I said. "No . . . it was just deceit . . . not murder, I'm sure."

"This woman is quite unscrupulous as well as immoral," said Mr. Rosen. "You did right to come straight here. Now . . . we must see what can be done."

They found Uncle Carl's body buried in the spot where Jessie had placed the cross. It was in the chest which Dickon had noticed was missing from the winter parlor. It was a simple plot they had conceived and they might have carried on with it until they had disposed of most of the valuables at Eversleigh but for the fact that Jethro had sent me that message that all was not well.

The doctors were satisfied that Uncle Carl had died from natural causes and so this was not a case of murder. It was true it might have been if Amos Carew had succeeded with his plan to be rid of me, and it was fortunate for me that Dickon had foiled that. Amos Carew had been avid for wealth and was determined to have some of Uncle Carl's. That was why he had brought Jessie to Eversleigh to enslave poor Uncle Carl, which she had done expertly. She might be a harpy but she was no murderess and I gathered she had become increasingly frightened when she saw that she was getting drawn into an intrigue such as Amos Carew had built up when she had believed that all she had to do was cajole an old man into pampering her.

Jessie had been used to getting what she could from her admirers; it was her profession; but she had never before been engaged in criminal intrigue.

She had been frightened by the ghost and I discovered who the ghost had been. Dickon, of course, who had found some of Uncle Carl's clothes and dressed up in them. He had thought it might be useful, he said modestly; and indeed it had for it had sent Jessie to mark the grave with her crucifix.

Amos was dead. Jessie had decamped with her two actor friends—the bogus Dr. Cabel and Lord Eversleigh. We recovered many of the valuables which were in Carew's house and some which Evalina gave up, protesting that she had been under the impression that they had been given to her mother.

Rosen, Stead and Rosen took over the management of everything; Uncle Carl was given decent burial in the Eversleigh mausoleum and I became the new owner of Eversleigh.

Dickon and I returned to Clavering. Dickon was very pleased with himself. It was agreed unanimously that he was a hero. True, he had killed a man but the slaying of highwaymen was regarded as a service to humanity. Moreover, he had been very astute—more so than I had been—and his prompt action had foiled the criminals as well as saved my life.

When we arrived home my mother and Sabrina were in a state of great jubilation. They had to hear that story of our adventures over and over and over again.

"It is an extraordinary story," said my mother.

"What would have happened but for Dickon!" cried Sabrina.

"We are so proud of you, Dickon my dear," they said in unison.

Dickon basked in their admiration, watching me with that quizzical look in his eye.

"You'll have to like me now, Zipporah," he said. "You must never forget I saved your life."

"I sometimes wonder why you went to such lengths to do so."

"Shall I tell you," he said, coming near to me and whispering. "If you had died, heaven knew who would have got Eversleigh. He wouldn't have left it to Sabrina because then it would come to me . . . son of a damned Jacobite. Your mother, no . . . because she might have left it to me, too. Who then? Some remote connection of the family perhaps. You had to have Eversleigh to keep it in this branch of the family . . . and when you have it I shall have Clavering. You see, that makes it all so neat. There was another reason."

"What was that?"

"You won't believe me but I do rather like you, Zipporah. You're not quite what you seem . . . are you? I like it . . . yes, I do."

I looked at him steadily: his lips turned up at the corners mockingly.

I knew he was telling me that he knew about my love affair with Gerard.

I ought to have been grateful to him — but I couldn't be. I disliked him as much as ever.

Mistress of Eversleigh

*I*t was early in the New Year when we went to Eversleigh.
I knew that Jean-Louis did not really want to go. He had
been brought up at Clavering and it was home to him; he loved
every acre of the place, but he realized that we must go and
that Eversleigh, the home of my ancestors, was a property of
far greater value. Moreover, he knew that my mother and
Sabrina were delighted because Clavering could now reasonably
go to Dickon.

"It's the sensible thing to do," said my mother, "and I am
sure that Zipporah agrees with us."

I did. One of the reasons why I was pleased to leave Clavering was because I should not have to see Dickon.

I was a considerable heiress for Eversleigh was a wealthy
estate, and although Amos Carew and Jessie had stolen a few
valuables there was so much left that their loss was scarcely
missed. Then a great many articles were brought back from
Amos Carew's house. They had been stored in his attic as he
had had to go very carefully in the task of disposing of them.

The prime villain in the scheme was dead; his accomplices had disappeared and eventually efforts to trace them were dropped.

Lottie was excited by the move. She was now eight years old—a lovely creature, impulsive, affectionate, volatile, in the highest spirits one moment and the depth of depression the next. She had violet-colored eyes with thick dark lashes and abundant hair—almost black, a rare combination and invariably beautiful.

My mother said of her: "I think she must be the image of her great-grandmother. She's not like you or Jean-Louis. You were always such calm, sensible little things even when you were babies. It's like Carlotta born again. Strange that she should have been called Charlotte. You'll have to keep a watch on her, Zipporah."

I said I intended to.

"I often wonder how you feel about going to Eversleigh ... after all that happened there," she said.

"Well," I replied, "it seems that everyone thinks we should go."

I looked at her a little wistfully. She was ashamed that her love for Dickon was greater than that which she bore me. She had been obsessed by that adventure of her youth when she had loved Dickon's father and the fact that his child was Sabrina's made no difference to her love for the boy.

Sometimes I wondered whether people who were predictable like myself—apart from that one lapse—did not inspire the same affection as the wayward ones. Carlotta had evidently made a great impression on everyone and yet her life had been far from orthodox. Dickon inspired love such as I never could, although he acted in a manner which even those who loved him must admit was by no means admirable.

"What Lottie wants is a brother or sister," said my mother. "It's a pity ..."

"At least," I said, "we have a child."

That was a phrase I often used to myself. Whatever wrong I had done, it had given us Lottie.

So we prepared to leave. Dickon was to live in the house

which we had occupied. There had been protests about that from my mother and Sabrina. Why did he want his own house? Why couldn't he go on living at the hall?

"It's the manager's house," said Dickon. "I am the manager now."

"My dear boy," said Sabrina, "how can we be sure that you will be properly looked after?"

I remember the way Dickon grinned at me. "I think I've proved that I can look after myself," he said.

Of course they couldn't go against him. He wanted to live in the house so he did.

I tried not to mind that he would be in that house where I had been happy with Jean-Louis. Jean-Louis understood. He said: "It will no longer be ours. We'll forget it."

As we journeyed to Eversleigh—Lottie seated between us in the carriage—I thought how tired Jean-Louis looked, and a little sad; and I was filled with tenderness toward him. I had wronged him in the most cruel way a woman could deceive a man in making him believe he was the father of a child who was not his. I must make up for what I had done. I think I had in a way. Looking back, my affection had been at least more demonstrative since Lottie had been born.

She was calling out excitedly and jumping up and down to call our attention to landmarks. Jean-Louis smiled at her. Poor Jean-Louis, he looked rather exhausted. It was a good thing that we had made the journey by carriage. He would never have been able to do it on horseback.

The house looked different. I suppose that was because it was mine and I couldn't help feeling a glow of pride to think of all my ancestors who had lived here before me, and now here I was taking possession.

We alighted from the carriage and I stood for a moment looking up. It was some two hundred years old, having been built in the days of Elizabeth, so it was in the familiar E style with the main hall and the wings on either side.

It was comforting to see old Jethro come hurrying out from the stables.

259

"I heard the wheels of the carriage," he said. "So I knew you was here."

"This is Jethro," I said to Jean-Louis. "The old faithful retainer."

Jethro touched his forelock to Jean-Louis and Lottie regarded him curiously.

"You'll find everything in order inside, Mistress Zipporah," said Jethro. "The servants has done well."

"The same ones?" I asked.

"Most on 'em scuttled off. That must have been friends of Jessie Stirling. I took the liberty of sending Mrs. Jethro over to take a hand and she got some girls from the village to come until you see what you want."

"Thank you, Jethro."

We went into the house. I stood in the hall with its rough stone walls on which hung the armory of past Eversleighs. Most of it would have seen action, for we had been a military family in the past.

"What's that?" cried Lottie and she ran to the fireplace.

I joined her. "It's the family tree. It was painted over the fireplace more than a hundred years ago . . . and it is constantly added to."

"I shall be on it," cried Lottie ecstatically. "Shan't I?" she added anxiously.

"Of course."

"And," said Lottie, "my husband. I wonder who he'll be? There's something you put on your pillow, or under it . . . on Christmas Eve . . . or is it Hallowe'en? And when you wake up the first thing you see is your future husband's face. Oh, dear mama, dear papa, we must find out what it is and when. I can't wait to see my husband."

"Why, Lottie," I said reproachfully, "here you are in your new home and all you can think of is husbands."

"It was the family tree that put me in mind of it," said Lottie. "What's down those steps?"

"I tell you what," I said. "We'll let Mrs. Jethro take us to our rooms . . . and then later on you can explore the house."

"I want to explore *now*!"

"We'll explore together," I said, "and your father is a little tired."

She was all contrition. "Dear papa, is it your old leg again? I'm sorry. You ought to have had another cushion in the carriage."

"I'm all right, my dear," he said, "but as your mama says, let us go to our rooms first and then we'll explore the house together later."

"It is exciting," said Lottie. "And mama, it is all yours." She spread out her arms as though to embrace the house. "It must be wonderful to have a house like this . . . all to yourself."

"It's ours," I said firmly. "Come on. Here's Mrs. Jethro."

The largest bedroom in the house had been prepared for us. Here Eversleigh wives and husbands had slept through the ages. It was the room in which the actor calling himself Lord Eversleigh had lived.

Jean-Louis sat down on the brocade-covered bed. I went to him and put my arm about him. I was wondering afresh whether we should have come back to the scene of my infidelity. It was into a room in this house that Gerard had climbed to be with me. The memories which I had sought to suppress for so many years had come flooding back more vividly.

I put my arm tighter round Jean-Louis and held him close to me.

"I do love you so much, Jean-Louis," I said. "I am going to take such care of you."

He turned to look at me. I could have believed in that moment that he understood exactly why I felt this emotion.

It was pleasant to renew my acquaintance with the Forsters. Isabel came over the day we arrived at Eversleigh. She was delighted that we were going to be neighbors and she wanted to know if there was anything she could do.

I told her that we were all rather bewildered at the moment.

It had been such an upheaval. She must meet Jean-Louis and my daughter.

This she was delighted to do. Jean-Louis had already seen a little of the estate and he was of the opinion that we should need a manager. Derek said he would do all he could to help. The few farms in his possession were easily manageable and until we had settled in he might be of use to us.

The visit of the Forsters seemed to cheer Jean-Louis. I think before they came he was seeing the management of Eversleigh as a task too formidable for his strength. The journey had, of course, exhausted him. I knew it; but I never liked to refer to his weakness, which usually depressed him a little.

Lottie could not be found. She was in the paddock, they thought, exercising her pony—a favorite pastime of hers. She loved horses and in particular her own pony, which would soon have to be replaced by a small horse, I supposed.

Naturally the Forsters talked of the activities which had been going on at Eversleigh and which had shocked the neighborhood. It would, I knew, be talked of for years to come.

"We always guessed that something extraordinary was going on," said Isabel. "That housekeeper . . ."

"Well," I said, "that was not such an extraordinary situation. She was my uncle's mistress in the first place and that was how her ambitions started."

"Yes, but it was that manager," said Derek. "He was the real organizer of the plot. He was a good manager, too. I've often said how lucky Lord Eversleigh was to have got hold of such a man."

"Well, I suppose it began in a simple way. Jessie was to get what she could . . . and then she had hopes of the house. . . . That must have been Amos Carew's idea. It was too ambitious and it was really what made Uncle Carl decide he must make his will . . . and then after the will was signed they decided to get what they could. Unfortunately for them my uncle died too soon for their schemes to be as rewarding as they had hoped."

"If it wasn't for the fact that his living was so advantageous to them they might be suspected of murder."

"I'm glad it wasn't that," I said. "Although it might have been. It was what was intended for me."

"That young relation of yours—he's a bright young man."

"Yes...yes..."

"I wish we'd met him. He sounds so interesting."

"You probably will one day," said Jean-Louis.

"Oh..." I began almost protestingly.

"You can't believe Dickon won't be paying us a visit, can you?" said Jean-Louis. "He talked of nothing but Eversleigh for weeks after he came home from here."

"He has Clavering now to claim his attention."

"Ah yes," Jean-Louis agreed wistfully.

I said to Isabel and Derek: "We're boring you with our family affairs."

"Not at all. It's all so interesting and it is so wonderful that you have come back."

"You still enjoy living at Enderby?"

"Oh, I think we've routed the ghosts."

"It must be pleasant not to have them around."

"I think I miss them a little," said Derek. "We've cut down so much of the foliage which darkened the place. My brother said it was positively unhealthy to have so many things growing close to the house and shutting out the sun."

"Your brother?" I said. "Is that...the doctor?"

"Yes, Charles. He's settling in very well now. He's happy, I think, living here. It's very convenient for his hospital."

"Where is that, then?"

"It's near the coast, about a mile or so from here. He's able to get to it every other day. His practice doesn't occupy him all that much. The hospital is his great delight."

"It must mean a lot of hard work for him."

"He thrives on it."

"What is it...for the elderly?" asked Jean-Louis.

"Quite the contrary...for the very young. Mothers...and babies. It's really a maternity hospital."

"Such matters are his speciality," said Isabel. "He's a very good man."

"Don't let him hear you say that, Isabel," said Derek.

"Well, I say it when he can't hear it," she said. She turned to us. "He has done a great deal of good work. He has saved many a life... mothers and children."

"It seems very noble," I said.

"He says it is his work. He could of course live quite comfortably... without working."

Derek smiled apologetically to us. "Isabel is a firm supporter of my brother," he said. "He... Charles... inherited a great deal of money. It gave him an opportunity to set up his hospital."

Just at that moment Lottie came running in. She was flushed and excited and stopped short when she saw that we had visitors.

"This is our daughter," I said. "Lottie, come and meet our guests."

I was proud of her for I could see they were deeply impressed by her beauty. She smiled, and when Lottie smiled she was completely enchanting. I thought I could see Gerard in that smile. It could not fail to charm everyone as he had charmed me.

She was bubbling over with excitement and when she had curtsied and the introduction was over she could not wait to burst out: "I've been exploring."

"And what did you find?" asked Jean-Louis.

"There are two houses... not very far away... close to each other... or fairly close."

"I'll warrant one of those was Enderby," said Derek, and he described it.

Lottie nodded. "But it was in the other one that I found the baby. Oh, mama, it was the dearest little baby. It was lying in a sort of cradle in the garden... and I couldn't help going through the gate to look at it!"

"Oh, Lottie, have you been trespassing?"

"Yes, but it didn't matter. There was a nurse and a lady."

"It must have been Grasslands," said Isabel.

"There were two big lawns in front of the house."

"Grasslands, certainly."

"Well, I played with the baby. It liked me. It's a little boy . . . named Richard."

"That is the Mather's baby," said Isabel. "It must be about six months old . . . perhaps not so much."

I couldn't stop myself saying: "Evalina . . . !"

"Yes," said Isabel. "Evalina Stirling. She married Andrew Mather, you know. They say the new baby is the apple of his eye."

"She was a very kind lady," said Lottie. "She says that I'm to call whenever I want to. She said she was ever so pleased that we'd come to Eversleigh. She said she knew you, mama."

"Yes," I said slowly. "I did meet her."

I felt rather uneasy. I kept remembering that occasion when I had seen her with Dickon in the barn; and I could recall exactly the steely look in her eyes and the words which had implied that she knew what had happened between myself and Gerard.

I was very occupied during the next few days and was glad of the help I received from Mrs. Jethro and Isabel. I was relieved that Jethro had dismissed those servants who had been brought in by Jessie Stirling, for, he said, you never knew how mixed up in it all they were. He thought that some of them were not sorry to go after what had happened. He knew one or two girls in the village who would be suitable and if I approved they could have a trial. Isabel's servants were helpful. They had friends whom they could recommend and in a very short time we had the place staffed and I was able to feel that it was becoming my own.

There were problems, of course. Lottie would have to have a governess. At Clavering she had taken lessons at the vicarage, but both Jean-Louis and I agreed that she should have her own governess now that she was growing up. Getting the house in order was a trifling matter compared with running the estate.

Criminal though he was, Amos Carew had been an excellent manager and although he was dishonest, he had got the best out of the estate.

"What we need," I said to Jean-Louis, "is a first-class manager. Someone like James Fenton."

"We shall be extremely lucky if we get anyone as good as James," said Jean-Louis.

"I wonder how he likes farming with his cousin?" I mused.

"Well, he was the sort of man who would strike out on his own one day, I daresay," said Jean-Louis.

"We must look round for someone to manage the estate," I insisted.

"I'll be all right for a while," Jean-Louis replied.

It was sad. Before his accident he would have been equal to the task of looking after an estate the size of Eversleigh. I knew now though that we could not wait too long before finding the right man. After the experience of Amos Carew we should have to be careful. I think I should always be suspicious of everyone after having known him. Sometimes I woke up out of a nightmare when I was looking into a masked face which I believed to be Dickon's. I would always awake with a terrible start and have to convince myself that it was all a dream; and in any case my would-be murderer had not been Dickon. He had been my savior.

I was in discussion with Mrs. Jethro one afternoon when one of the servants came to tell me that I had a visitor.

I was so certain that it was Isabel that I did not ask who it was.

"She's in the winter parlor, madam," said the servant.

I hurried down and opened the door, smiling. I stood absolutely still. The woman who rose from the chair was not Isabel. I felt a tingle of fear run through me. It was Evalina.

She came forward smiling.

"I thought I'd better be neighborly," she said.

I stammered: "It was good of you to call."

"Well, we live close now, don't we? You mistress of Eversleigh Court and me of Grasslands."

I nodded. "Would you care for some refreshment?"

"Oh no. I'm getting so fat. I'm a little too fond of the good things of life. Aren't we all?"

"I suppose so. Do sit down."

She did so. I sat too. I felt my heart beating uncomfortably.

"It seems a long time," she said. "But it's not all that time, is it?"

"I hear you have a little boy."

"My Richard." She looked straight at me smiling. "What a blessing! Nothing like little ones, is there? My poor Andrew...he's overcome with joy. You can imagine. He never thought for a moment there'd be a child. Well, life's full of surprises, isn't it?"

"I am sure he is delighted."

"Just as your dear husband was when you told him you were expecting, I daresay. These men...they do like little ones, don't they?...particularly when they've given up all hope."

"I am sure the little boy has brought great happiness to you both."

"Yes...just like your little girl. I say, what a little beauty, eh? Wait till she's a bit older! She'll have them all buzzing round her, won't she? Little bit of honey, that's what she is...and you can't keep bees off honey. I told Andrew what a little pet she was. Nice laughing ways...Frenchified, I said to Andrew."

She was baiting me. Why had she come here like this? I was beginning to wish I was back at Clavering.

But I was not going to let her intimidate me with her innuendos.

I said: "How is your mother?"

"Oh...I never hear a word from her now....She'll be off somewhere. Shouldn't be surprised if she's gone abroad. It wasn't her fault, you know. It was Amos. He always made her do what he wanted. There's some men like that. You and me...we're lucky. We've got our two dear little children. It was funny the way they took to each other. My little Richard just laughed up at her and wouldn't stop looking. He don't do that to everyone, I can tell you. It was as though they knew they were two of a kind."

"Two of a kind?"

"Yes, my little Richard and your little Lottie. A sort of fellow feeling. Funny how these children are."

She was looking at me insolently. I was thinking: Dickon was here. They were together.... Was she telling me something? Did she mean that she and I were of a kind?

Her eyes were sparkling.

She said slowly: "I shall never forget the first time we met. You came to Eversleigh... and there was that man over at Enderby, that French gentleman. He was a charmer, wasn't he?" She laughed. "Well, he went off, didn't he? Very different they are at Enderby now. The Forsters... not the sort you'd expect to find in a house like that. The doctor's a fine gentleman. Have you met him? You'd like him." She laughed. "Different from the French gentleman.... A bit on the gloomy side... but a change is nice, isn't it?"

"What are you talking about?" I asked suddenly.

"Oh, nothing. Just rambling on. I do, Andrew tells me. He likes it... he laughs at me. He's a very grateful man. Well, who wouldn't be, presented with a son at his time of life? Just what he'd always wanted and never thought he could get."

She started to laugh.

I stood up. I said: "I know you'll forgive me. As we have only just come there is so much to do."

She rose drawing on her gloves. She was very properly dressed for the call.

"Well, we're neighbors now," she said. "There'll be plenty of opportunities for little chats."

She took my hand and smiled into my face.

I thought she looked sly, menacing.

I conducted her to the door and watched her walk away.

I felt more than a twinge of alarm.

The idea of giving a housewarming party came to me when I was with Isabel one morning. We were becoming good friends and I found her presence very comforting. She knew so much about the customs of the neighborhood and was on good terms with most of the people.

She was saying that I should meet some of the families round about; there might only be three big houses but the farms were occupied by some very pleasant people and although there were a few of these on the Grasslands and Enderby estates most of them belonged to Eversleigh.

Then I said: "There must be a gathering . . . a party."

Isabel was delighted with the idea. "I believe in the old days," she said, "there was one given every year at the big house."

"That would be in Carleton's day, I should imagine. Perhaps my great-uncle General Eversleigh continued the tradition."

"Well, it lapsed when the last Lord Eversleigh was there."

"He was too ill, and I daresay Jessie didn't relish having half the neighborhood there."

"I wonder she didn't invite them in her role of mistress of the house."

"There must have been some lengths to which even Jessie wouldn't go. But now I think, it's a good idea to get back to the old ways."

"I am sure everyone will be delighted."

"You must help me draw up a list of the guests."

We spent a pleasant hour doing this.

"I hope you won't forget my brother-in-law."

"The doctor. No, of course not. If he wishes to come. Perhaps he will be too involved with his work. Will you ask him?"

"I will indeed. And what about some of the people in the town? The solicitors, for one thing?"

"Oh yes, Mr. Rosen . . . both senior and junior."

"There, you see. It is quite a formidable list. Oh . . . I don't think it will be necessary for me to ask my brother-in-law. I can hear voices. Yes, it is he. You can ask him yourself."

So that was how I met Charles Forster again.

I had forgotten how tall he was. Also that air of melancholy.

It was not my custom to find unhappy people interesting. I was attracted by lively characters—people like Gerard and my dear Lottie. But Charles Forster fascinated me from the first. I wanted to know more about him; why he wore that air of almost desperation. His face was thin with high cheekbones and very deepset gray eyes; the gray wig drawn from his face and tied at the back with a black ribbon was perhaps a little out of date but he was the sort of man who would make no concessions to fashion—in fact I believed he would be entirely unaware of it. His dark blue coat was full and came to the knees, hiding his plain cloth breeches; his long muscular legs were encased in light brown stockings and as he came in he carried a three-cornered hat unadorned by feathers.

"Charles!" cried Isabel, her face lighting up with pleasure. "How nice to see you. Here is Mistress Zipporah Ransome. You have already met . . . some time ago."

He took my hand and we looked steadily at each other.

"You've forgotten me," I said.

"Indeed I have not. You were staying at Eversleigh."

"Yes . . . and now I live there."

"That unfortunate business is settled, I hope."

"Oh yes . . . as near as it can be."

Isabel was already pouring out a glass of wine.

"Now, Charles," she said, "you must take refreshment. He doesn't look after himself, you know."

"Isabel clucks over me as though she's a mother hen and I'm one of her wayward chicks," he said.

"I should never have thought of calling you a chick," said Isabel. "What news is there?"

He gave me his melancholy smile. "My news is always the same and therefore it doesn't deserve the name news. Several fresh cases at the hopsital, and I expect the population will be increased by five before the end of the day."

"I have heard about your hospital," I said. "It must be rewarding work."

He frowned a little and said: "Not always. There are times when it is. . . . But then that's life, isn't it?"

"I suppose so. It can't be good all the time. We can only rejoice when it is and hope it will get better when it isn't."

"I can see you have the right idea."

"Are you busy with the patients?" asked Isabel. "I hear there is a lot of sickness about."

"No more than usual. I've just come from Grasslands. And as I was close I thought I'd look in."

"I should have been most put out if you hadn't. Is it Andrew Mather?"

"Yes. He's not strong, you know. It's his heart. It will give out one day. He's got a great will to live, though. I think that's due to his young wife and the baby. He's a very happy man. Not the sort that will give up. He'll cling to life as long as he can."

"And that will help?" I asked.

"Indeed yes. Many people die because they lack the will to live. Andrew Mather will never lack that."

"It's strange," said Isabel, "that a girl like that could bring so much to a man like Andrew Mather."

"Yes," mused the doctor. "I remember him before his marriage. He was ready to give up then . . . and slip gracefully into the role of invalid and then that girl comes along . . . fascinates him . . . and although her motives might not have been entirely altruistic she has given him a new lease of life."

"It reminds me of the old saying which goes something like this: 'There is a little good in the worst of us and a little bad in the best of us and it ill behoves any of us to criticize the rest of us.'"

"Neat," said the doctor, "and true. In any case I'm delighted with Andrew since his marriage, and now that he has a son . . . why, he could live to be a hundred."

"By the way," I said, "we are going to have a housewarming. I do hope you will come."

"I will with pleasure," he said.

"I am delighted."

"You'd better put him on the list," said Isabel.

"I shall remember," I said. I rose. I had a great deal to do back at the house, I explained, and I should be seeing Isabel again soon.

"Did you come on horseback?" asked the doctor.

I said I had.

"Then let us ride back together. I pass Eversleigh on my way to the town."

So we rode out together. We talked of many things on the way back, of the countryside, the hospital and his practice, of our return to Eversleigh.

As we walked our horses along the winding path that led to the house a rider came toward us. To my dismay I saw that it was Evalina.

She halted as she came up to us.

"Good day to you both," she said. Her eyes were sly as they ranged over us. "A lovely day to take a ride."

"Good day," I said and urged my horse on.

Dr. Forster bowed to Evalina and walked his horse behind mine. I felt the color rising in my neck. That look in Evalina's eyes disturbed me. What was she suggesting? That I was another such as I was sure she was? That I could pass from one man to another with the ease of a harlot?

There was so much in that look. Every time it said: *We are two of a kind.*

Of one thing I was certain: I would not put her on my list of guests. I could not have her at Eversleigh. I should be reminded of her mother . . . and perhaps at the back of my mind was the fear of the hints she might drop . . . perhaps to Jean-Louis.

The doctor had brought his horse to walk beside mine.

"You look annoyed," he said.

"It must be that woman. She reminds me . . ."

"I suppose she is not to blame for her mother's misdeeds. But I know how you feel."

"I shall not ask her to Eversleigh."

"Oh . . . the housewarming, you mean. I don't think for a moment that her husband would be able to come. I was saying how much better he was but he is still an old man. Such festivities are not for him and he would be the first to admit it."

"Then he wouldn't expect an invitation."

"I'm sure he wouldn't."

"That makes it easier."

We had stopped. He was giving me another of those steady glances.

"I hope," he said, "that someday you will come and see my hospital."

"I should like that."

He bowed his head and turned away.

I rode into the stables. It had been a most enjoyable morning apart from the meeting with Evalina in the lane.

Preparations were going ahead. Jean-Louis thought it was an excellent way of bringing everyone together and showing them that life at Eversleigh was going to be as it had been in the days of Carleton, Leigh and General Carl. The manor house should be the center of the community. The farmers were pleased. It was different taking one's grievances to a landowner rather than merely to his manager. They had all been shocked to learn that they had a criminal in their midst; and although the affair had provided a great flutter of excitement while it had lasted, there was nothing like normality to bring prosperity to an estate—and when that was present everyone could benefit from it.

I heard through Charles that Andrew Mather was confined to his bed with rheumatism, so I felt that I was justified in not sending an invitation to Grasslands.

The new cook, Mrs. Baines, was in her element: the servants were in a state of perpetual excitement decorating the place with the help of the gardeners; the house was filled with the smells of cooking, and the main topic of conversation was the party.

Lottie seemed to be everywhere; she tried on her dress ten times a day, danced round the ball room with imaginary partners, was in the kitchen tasting the various cakes and sweetmeats; prevailing on Mrs. Baines to cook her what she called little tasters.

"I wish," said Lottie, "that we had a party every day."

"That would be far too much," I assured her.

"Well, one a week," she temporized.

Lessons, which she had taken with me since we came to Eversleigh, we passed over for a few days. I had warned her that as soon as we were settled we must look for a governess. Lottie grimaced but she could not think beyond the party.

It was about three days before the party when having walked over to Enderby for a chat with Isabel to tell her of the final plans for the great day, I encountered Evalina.

I believed that she had lain in wait for me.

"Oh . . . good day to you," she cried. "You must be very busy getting ready for your party."

"Good day," I replied. "Yes, I am." I prepared to pass on. But she was barring my way with that sly look in her eyes.

"All the neighborhood will be there," she said. "So I hear . . . but there are exceptions."

"It is impossible to ask everyone, I suppose," I said.

"Impossible? Oh, no, not that. Unneighborly, I'd say."

I replied: "I didn't send you an invitation. I know that your husband is not fit to come."

"But I am," she said.

"I had not thought you would wish to . . . without him."

"Andrew is a kind husband. He wouldn't want to spoil my fun."

She was leering at me in a way I found most unpleasant. I thought, somewhat irrelevantly, that I preferred Jessie to her daughter.

"Well," I said lamely, "the invitations have all gone out now. I naturally thought . . ."

"There's time to send out one more."

This was blatant. She was asking for an invitation. Asking? She was demanding it.

"I reckon," she said, "it would look funny if I wasn't there. People would say: 'Why weren't you there?' I'd have to think up something to tell them, wouldn't I? I wouldn't want to but I couldn't let that pass . . . somehow . . . could I?"

This is blackmail, I thought.

She was smiling at me sweetly, helplessly, as though I were forcing her into a situation which had no charm for her.

Standing there in that lane I was suddenly afraid. I wished I was back at Clavering. I thought of her whispering something into Jean-Louis's ear and a vision of his kind, patient face rose before me

I loved him; I would do anything rather than hurt him. I know I had forgotten him when I had been caught in the fascination of passionate love with another man. If I could go back I would be different. I would never let it happen. But that was not true. It would be exactly the same, I knew it. I yearned for Gerard. I longed for Gerard. I loved Jean-Louis, yes . . . but what I had felt for Gerard was something different . . . beyond love, perhaps.

There was one thought hammering in my brain. Jean-Louis must never know.

I looked at this girl with her hateful sly face, with her veiled threats, and I loathed myself as I said: "Well, it is not too late, as you say. If you really want to come."

She smiled at me, looking young and innocent

"Oh, thank you. So I shall get my invitation? I don't suppose Andrew will be able to come but he wouldn't want to stop me enjoying myself."

I couldn't look at her. I turned away hating her, hating myself.

The party was in full swing. It had been a glorious spring day—as hot as summer—and everyone was saying that it was like old times. Eversleigh was coming into its own again. The farmers with their wives and families were delighted to have what they called the "Family" in command. I suppose poor Uncle Carl had been an invalid almost from the moment he had arrived and he had taken little interest in the estate. It was different with Jean-Louis; he had managed an estate before he came and all those who had talked with him recognized a man who knew his job.

Many of them remembered my mother and one or two of the really aged remembered the great Carleton Eversleigh, who, a hundred years before, when he had been a young man, had saved the mansion and estate from Cromwell's rule.

They liked to feel that the family was in command again and things were not being left to the rogue Amos Carew had turned out to be. And as for that Jessie . . . they had all deplored her presence.

So it was a happy occasion until Evalina came.

It was asking too much to expect these people to forget who she was. She was the daughter of the infamous Jessie, who had been the mistress of the old lord at the same time as she was carrying on (as they said) with Amos Carew.

Some of the older people were aloof with Evalina but the younger men found her irresistible. I couldn't help watching her. I was afraid that she might talk to Jean-Louis. But he was busy with the farmers, who seemed as if they were not going to let him escape. He wouldn't want to join the dancers on the grass outside. So I felt comparatively safe.

In the great hall on the dais was one of the new pianos and there were violinists, too, to provide the music. The tables were laden with food of all descriptions and people were invited to help themselves whenever they felt the inclination to do so. Needless to say, many constantly felt the inclination and Mrs. Baines and her kitchen staff were in a twitter of excitement and gratification at the fast disappearances from dishes, which needed constant replenishing.

The music floated out to the grounds and in the light of the torches flaring on the walls people wandered through the grounds while others sat and talked and some of the younger ones danced.

I found Charles Forster at my elbow.

I said: "Are you enjoying this? No. It's an unfair question. It isn't much to your taste, is it?"

"I'm a bit of a sobersides, I'm afraid."

"Well, you are occupied with more serious matters. Though this is a serious matter. I think all the tenants are rather pleased that we are here and this is a way of telling them that we are not making great changes but are going on in the way the family have run things for years and years."

"That's true," he said. "It's a worthy occasion. I'm just not a good socializer. Let's walk a little, shall we? The night air is refreshing after the heat of the day."

"It's certainly wonderful weather. I was terrified that it would rain, which would have meant having it in the hall. I suppose we could have managed but not quite so pleasant, I think."

"This is ideal. I am pleased you have come here."

I felt absurdly delighted by that remark.

But he went on: "You are good company for Isabel. She needs a friend."

"Isabel is the sort who makes friends easily, I am sure. It is I who am grateful for her friendship."

"Isabel is a fine woman. I often tell Derek how lucky he is. She is calm, good-natured and sound in judgment."

"I see you are as fond of her as she is of you."

"They are my family . . . my brother and his wife. They came here, you know, to be near me."

"Well, that seems a reasonable thing to do. Families should be together when they can."

"The hospital was here. . . . It's an ideal place for it. It's facing the sea . . . an old house which was more or less derelict when I took it. But it had everything I needed. The isolation was important."

"Why did you have to be so isolated?"

"It was comforting for my patients."

"They are young mothers, aren't they?"

"Yes," he said, "unfortunate young mothers."

"Unfortunate?"

"Yes, that is the reason why they are there. It is for people whose circumstances are rather distressing. That is why they want to get right away from people. It's a helpful start."

"So your hospital is for those who are . . . friendless."

"They are often friendless."

"And unmarried?"

"Some of them."

"I believe you are doing a wonderful job. Isabel says . . ."

"Oh. you mustn't listen too much to Isabel. She will give you an entirely false picture of me."

"Surely anyone who works as you do for such a cause is worthy of praise?"

"Well, I suppose most of us earn a little praise now and then. It's a matter of setting the good deeds against the evil . . and seeing which weigh more."

"What do you mean?"

"I see I'm talking in riddles, which is foolish and incredibly boring. I am sure."

I leaned toward him and touched his hand lightly.

"Not boring in the least."

At that moment I saw Evalina stroll by. She was arm in arm with one of the young sons of a farmer. She turned her head and smiled at me.

"Having a wonderful time . . ." she said. "Aren't we?"

She had spoiled the moment for me. I knew what it was I hated: that inclusive smile . . . or word. That implication: *We are at the same game, you and me.*

I said: "I think we should go in."

Immediately we turned to the house. I felt frustrated. I wanted to go on talking to the doctor.

Jean-Louis was sitting down in deep conversation. I went over to him. He smiled at me and took my hand.

"All going well," he said. "It's a very satisfactory evening. An excellent idea to meet our friends thus."

Yes, a satisfactory evening . . . an excellent idea . . . until Evalina had appeared like the serpent in paradise.

One of the maids was making her way towards me.

"Yes, Rose?" I said.

"It's one of the men from Grasslands. madam." she said.

"They want to know if the doctor is here so he can go over. Mr. Mather is taken worse."

Andrew Mather died that night of a heart attack. Charles Forster told me about it the following day when he called to thank me for the party and to ask me if I would go back with him to see Isabel.

As we walked over to Enderby he told me what had happened.

"By the time I arrived at Grasslands he was unconscious. I knew there was only an hour or so left to him. His wife was distraught. She seems really heartbroken. She looked scared too, I thought. I suppose she relied on him to take care of her."

"I think Evalina would be able to take good care of herself."

"Yes . . . that woman's daughter . . . you would think so. But somehow she seemed pathetic . . . vulnerable."

I smiled at him, wondering if he too had fallen under the spell of Evalina's fascination.

I had to admit that there was something appealing about her; it was a certain helplessness which I supposed could be called femininity; whatever it was it aroused the interest of men of all ages . . . even Charles Forster, who was the last man I should have thought would be affected, was taken in by it.

"At least," he went on, "it was expected. I had warned him . . . and her . . . of the state of his heart."

Isabel greeted me warmly and we talked of the success of the party until the doctor had been called away and had left with Evalina.

"Poor Andrew," said Isabel. "At least he had some happiness at the end. To see him with that child was heartwarming."

"I wonder what will happen now?" I said. "Of course Grasslands is not a large estate. How many farms are there? . . . only two, I think."

"Yes, I think so. Andrew had a good man in Jack Trent. I daresay he will go on . . . if Evalina stays here."

"What else would she do?"

"She might sell up and go."

I thought that was an outcome which would be very desirable as far as I was concerned.

During the next days members of Andrew's family began to arrive at Grasslands. I saw one of them—a man who looked to be in his forties. I thought he looked rather grim and disagreeable. Isabel, who had called on Evalina to offer her condolences and to ask if there was anything she could do, told me that the man was a nephew of Andrew's and that she did not seem to be very pleased that he had come.

The funeral took place about a week after Andrew's death. I attended the service in the church with Jean-Louis, and Evalina spoke to me as we came out of the church, asking me to come back to the house with the mourners. She looked fragile in deep black with a flowing veil hiding her face.

"Please come," she said. It was almost like a command; but perhaps that was my imagination as I had begun to feel that she thought she had a right to make demands on me.

This seemed a small thing to ask and I went back.

It was very somber in the hall where refreshments were served. The nephew seemed to be taking charge of the proceedings, which I suppose was natural, as he would be the nearest relative apart from Evalina and the baby.

I was glad when we left. I supposed the reading of the will would take place and that was no concern of ours.

Jean-Louis and I walked back to Eversleigh very slowly. I always slackened my pace when walking with my husband because I knew that he found it painful to walk quickly and that he would not admit this, so I pretended that his pace was mine.

"Poor child," he said. "She seems so young."

"Everyone is sorry for Evalina," I said, a little impatiently. "I am sure as her mother's daughter she will know how to take care of herself."

"*She* did no wrong as far as we know," said Jean-Louis. "Poor child, it was not her fault she had such a mother."

"She must have known that her mother was stealing things from Eversleigh. She was hiding them for her at Grasslands."

"That's understandable. Her mother told her they were gifts."

I was silent. The men found excuses for her. First Charles Forster and now Jean-Louis.

"Well," I said, "I don't think we need worry too much about her for I am sure she will be able to take care of herself."

She was perhaps not so self-sufficient as I had thought, for the next day she sent one of her servants to Eversleigh with a message for me. She wanted me to meet her... "You know the old haunted patch," she wrote, "where they buried Lord Eversleigh. It's quiet there. No one ever goes there. It's near Enderby but sheltered from it. Meet me there at two o'clock this afternoon."

It was a little peremptory, I thought, and for a moment felt inclined to ignore it; but on second thought I changed my mind. Secretly I had to admit that I was both unsure and afraid of her.

She was waiting for me, looking distraught, walking up and down impatiently.

She said: "It's quiet here. Nobody comes here. They never did, and since Lordy was buried here it's even more spooky."

"You had something to say to me?"

She nodded and I saw the look of fear in her face.

She said: "It's him. It's John Mather . . the nephew. Andrew would never want it. He'd turn in his grave. Andrew was all for me . . . he was . . . and the boy."

"What about the nephew?"

"Andrew's left everything . . . just everything to me . . . in trust for Richard. Richard's to have all this and I'm to share it with him . . . Grasslands . . . and Andrew's money . . . everything. But the nephew is going to contest the will."

"He can't do that, can he?"

"He says he can. He says Andrew was duped . . . by me. He says I forced him to marry me. He says Andrew was incapable of having children . . . and Richard can't be his."

"I think he's just trying to frighten you."

"He says it would be better for me to give up Grasslands

to him . . . and take a small income which he would be prepared to give me to save a lot of unpleasantness."

There was a short silence while she looked at me appealingly.

"What . . . what do you expect *me* to do?" I asked.

"I want you to tell me what to do . . . how I can stop him?"

"How should I know? You are Andrew's widow. You have his child. It seems to me his nephew is talking nonsense."

She looked at me steadily. "But if he can prove . . ."

"What do you mean?"

"Suppose Richard . . ." She looked at me steadily. "*You* know how these things can happen . . . even to people who seem to be so respectable. You've got to help me. You've got to tell me what to do."

"Are you telling me that Richard is not Andrew's son?"

She was silent. I had a sudden inspiration and the words came out before I had time to consider them: "Richard is Dickon's child."

She covered her face with her hands.

"They'll take it all away from me . . . from him. It was the way Andrew wanted it. He loved Richard . . . it made a new man of him, he used to say . . . no matter who Richard's father was, he did that for Andrew."

"He was certainly very happy," I said.

"He was. I made him happy. I liked making him happy. He was good to me, he was. He took me in . . . he made a pet of me . . . and when it all happened . . . when they found out what my mother was . . . and all that . . . he never threw it up at me. All he said was 'My poor little girl.' He understood I never wanted to be like that. I wanted to be good and respectable like you were"—she paused and looked at me with the old sly look in her eyes—"until you came here."

I felt my hatred of her welling up in me and at the same time I was sorry for her. I knew she was very frightened. I thought: She is another of Dickon's victims. He is a devil. He creates mischief wherever he goes. But could I blame him?

Evalina was the sort of girl who would frolic in barns with whatever lusty young man beckoned her.

She was looking at me almost defiantly. She had some absurd and childish faith in me; she was begging my help; no, demanding it. I had to make her problem mine or she would make it uncomfortable for me.

Oddly enough I wanted to help her . . . apart from the fact that I was afraid not to.

I said: "Andrew accepted Richard as his, didn't he?"

"Yes, he did. He thought it was a miracle. He'd been told he could never have children . . . nor could he. Well, I wanted a little one of my own. You can't blame me. So it happened and he thought it was his and there was no harm in it. It made a new man of him. He kept saying that. He was almost crazy with joy when Richard was born. 'A boy,' he kept saying, 'my own son.' I felt pretty good, I did, lying in that bed . . . giving him a son. He just couldn't do enough for me. Proved his manhood and all that, he said. What was wrong with it, eh? You tell me that."

"There was some good in it, obviously," I said. "But why are you so worried?"

"Because of this nephew. He's threatening all sorts of things . . . talking of lawyers. . . ."

"How can he? The will is there. No one can go against a will."

"Yes, the will's there. Andrew was very careful about that. He made it when Richard was born. He said to me: 'That's taken care of. Everything is for you and the boy. So if anything should happen to me suddenly I know you're safe.'"

"I am sure the nephew can do nothing."

"But you see, if he can prove Andrew couldn't have children . . ."

"Surely no one could be absolutely sure of that?"

"Couldn't he be?"

"No."

"Then no one must know that Richard's not . . ."

"No one must know."

"*You* know."

We looked at each other steadily. It was like that moment in the bedroom when she had bought my silence with the key of my bedroom.

We understood each other. I felt a tremendous relief because I was free of her. She had played into my hands.

But I wanted to help her now. I was beginning to see her as a sad little creature, born into a world where it was necessary to fight for all the comforts her body craved; she had to fight against a sensuous nature which betrayed her at every turn. Who was I to blame her for that?

I said to her: "He cannot do anything. Andrew made the will. He cannot prove that Richard is not Andrew's. Who should know this? Perhaps it was his."

She was smiling at me shyly, almost gratefully.

"The nephew is trying to browbeat you. Obviously, he guesses the child is not his uncle's and by showing your fear of him you are playing into his hands. You must insist that the child is Andrew's. I don't see what good can come in denying it. And you should go to a solicitor. Go to Mr. Rosen. I am sure the nephew won't have a leg to stand on."   —

"Would you come with me to Mr. Rosen? You can talk so much better than I can."

I wanted to laugh out loud. When I thought of how she had disturbed me, the anxious thoughts I had suffered because of her, I felt it had turned out almost comically.

We were blackmailing each other. We had a pact. No word of my misdemeanors and no word of yours.

I said: "We will go to Rosen, Stead and Rosen tomorrow. I will explain the case to Mr. Rosen senior, and I am sure then that you will have nothing to worry about."

A Visit to London

*I*t was as I had said it would be. *Mr. Rosen senior took over
the matter with calm efficiency; the will was perfectly in
order and there could be no doubt of Mr. Mather's intention.
Everything with the exception of one or two legacies—including something for the nephew—was left to Evalina in trust for
Richard. "Perfectly straightforward," declared Mr. Rosen. "I
will see the gentleman who is raising objections."

This he did and that gentleman was soon departing—slink-
ing away might be a more apt description. "He is thoroughly
ashamed of himself," Mr. Rosen commented to me. "It is my
belief that he thought he could delude an ignorant female."

His parting words to Evalina were: "You did right to come
to me. If you are ever in any difficulties I shall be pleased to
help you."

Evalina was grateful to me. She looked upon me as a very
clever woman. But in everything she said I felt there was a
reference to my love affair with Gerard. Even now the implication was: How clever you are. Look how well you managed

your own affairs. Jean-Louis has not a suspicion. She had done very well herself in deluding Andrew but she had to admit she had gone to pieces when that sly old nephew had arisen.

However, all was well. He was sent packing by that wily Mr. Rosen and now we were safe . . . both of us.

So although I felt relieved I was still a little uneasy, and I often wondered how far I could trust Evalina.

She settled down without Andrew and quite clearly loved her baby. There were rumors of a somewhat torrid relationship between her and Jack Trent, who looked after the Grasslands farms, but I think everyone felt that something of the sort was to be expected. She was a young woman without a husband and clearly she had a fancy for men and they for her.

I saw her frequently, which was inevitable, our being such close neighbors. She would be at church gatherings; it was quite clear that she wished to be an accepted member of the community and wanted me to help her. I did so—half because I was sorry for her, half because I felt it would be expedient to do so, and we began to succeed. People could not go on remembering that she was her mother's daughter forever.

Letters came from Clavering. They were well and they were thinking it was a long time since they had seen us. They missed us very much. The estate was being perfectly run. Dickon had a flair for the work. He was so enthusiastic, and it was such fun to see him thinking up new schemes which would be so very advantageous to everyone.

I said to Jean-Louis: "They behave towards him one moment as though he is some blessed infant and the next some towering genius."

"He'll be in his element," said Jean-Louis. "He was always longing to get his hands onto everything."

"Yes," I agreed. "He's a very acquisitive young man."

"We must meet at Christmas," my mother continued. "Dear Zipporah, we can't be separated much longer, can we? I long to see darling Lottie. Perhaps we will come to you for Christmas or you must come to us. We must be together then. . . . By the way, a letter came for you and Jean-Louis. I am enclosing it herewith...."

I looked at the letter and recognized the handwriting. We had once been very familiar with it.

"It's James..." I cried. "James Fenton."

We opened it at once and read it together. James would be staying at the Black Swan in London for a week. He wondered if we could come up and see him. He had given us good warning because he would so much like to see us. He would make the journey to Clavering but we would understand that he had no great wish to come there for fear of unpleasant encounters.

I looked at Jean-Louis. "We must go," I said. "Look, there is time. His week doesn't end until next Thursday."

Jean-Louis looked dismayed. He did not see how he could get away on so little notice. If he had a manager it would be so different, but as it was so much depended on him. I looked at him sadly. It was not only that, I knew. The journey to London would be exhausting for him.

"I will write to him and tell him we are here. There could be no reason why he shouldn't come to Eversleigh."

I said nothing but I was going to do my best to go to London and see James Fenton.

I went to Enderby later that day because my friendship with Isabel Forster had grown even more firmly and I made a habit of talking over my problems with her.

She said: "To catch him you would have to go by the end of the week. It need only take two days to get to London. You could make reservations at the Black Swan."

"Yes," I said, "but I can't very well go alone."

Isabel said: "I don't see why Derek and I shouldn't come. We were going to London later on. As a matter of fact we have stayed at the Black Swan. We could bring forward our visit and make the arrangements now."

"Oh, Isabel," I cried, "that would be wonderful. Jean-Louis would have no fears if I traveled with you."

As soon as Derek came in she put the plan to him.

I said earnestly: "I have an idea that it is rather important for me to see James. I think he might be able to recommend someone who can help Jean-Louis. After Amos Carew he is reluctant to engage anyone."

"Who wouldn't be? I daresay Amos had some good recommendations."

"It just occurred to me that James might know someone . . . well, let me tell you what is exactly in my mind. I was wondering whether I could persuade him to come to Eversleigh."

Jean-Louis was delighted when he heard that the Forsters were going to London for he hated to disappoint me and he knew how much I wanted to go. This seemed an admirable solution.

The day before we were to set out I went over to Enderby to discuss last-minute preparations and found that Charles Forster was there.

"Here's news," said Isabel. "You tell her, Charles."

"It's about London," he said.

My heart sank. I thought there must be some last-minute hitch and so strongly had I convinced myself that I should see James Fenton that I found the momentary anxiety intense.

"I wondered if you would mind my being a member of the party," he went on.

Floods of relief swept over me and with it pleasure. I said: "I am sure we should all like that very much."

"There you are, Charles," said Derek. "I told you Zipporah would be pleased."

So we made our arrangements and when I went back to Eversleigh and told Jean-Louis he was delighted. "Another man in the party is all to the good," he said.

It was in high spirits that we set out on that June morning. There was a decided chill in the air which made us appreciate the sunshine as the morning wore on.

"It's the best weather for traveling," said Charles. "I made this journey in August and it was intolerable."

"Do you often come to London?" I asked.

"Occasionally. It's necessary to get supplies of medicines and so on. . . . Not more often than I need, I do assure you."

"You are not fond of London?"

"Oh . . . it's a great city . . . full of vitality and interest but . . ." I waited, for I had the idea that he was on the verge of a confidence and I was beginning to realize that this man interested me considerably and I wanted to know more about him. He said: "Shall we say associations . . . ?"

"Something you would rather forget . . . ?"

I was aware that I had gone too far. He nodded and it was as though a mask had come down over his face. His expression warned me that it was not polite to pursue a subject which was not agreeable to one's companion. I was ashamed of myself and asked at once if he had a preference for any of the inns, as a means of changing the topic of conversation.

He occupied my thoughts a good deal during that journey. In fact he had from the moment we had met. I felt there had been a tragedy in his life and that it had set that melancholy look on his features. I wondered why Isabel, who was a rather garrulous woman not given to harboring secrets, had said very little about her brother-in-law apart from the fact that he was a good man whom she very much admired.

The journey was uneventful, the weather being perfect for it, and as Derek had made careful reservations and was a frequent traveler on the route we were very comfortable at the inn where we stayed the night.

To my great delight James Fenton was already at the Black Swan and his pleasure at seeing me was great. He looked well, I thought, and when I inquired after Hetty and the children he assured me that they were in good health too. I introduced him to the Forsters and I was delighted that they seemed immediately to like each other.

During the morning of the day after our arrival all the Forsters went out discreetly leaving me with James. Charles said he had to see about ordering supplies for the hospital; Derek had business and he took Isabel with him. James told me that he was glad we could be alone. He wanted to know how things were with us.

He was surprised to hear that we were at Eversleigh. I explained that that was why we had been unable to let him know I would be here. The letter had had to be sent on and then it was too late to let him know.

"Hetty will be so interested to hear that I've seen you," he said. "She would have liked to come with me but there are the children, you know."

We discussed the children for a while and he asked after Lottie.

I explained that we had not been so very long at Eversleigh.

"And Jean-Louis?"

I shook my head sadly. "He never really recovered from that accident at the fire all those years ago. He never complains so it is difficult to know how he is, but sometimes he looks so tired. I think Eversleigh is too much for him."

"It is bigger than Clavering, isn't it?"

"Much bigger. We do want a man to act as manager."

I saw a rather wistful look in his eyes which made my heart beat faster.

Then he said: "Shouldn't be difficult to find someone."

I told him we were being rather wary and gave him a brief résumé of what had happened.

He was astounded and found my story difficult to believe. He listened avidly.

"My goodness, Mistress Zipporah, you had a lucky escape."

"It was strange that the one who saved me should be ... Dickon."

I saw his fists clench and unclench.

"Well," he said at length, "it turned out all right then, and you're here. If I hear of a good man ... someone I can recommend ..."

I was sinking into deeper gloom every minute. I realized now that my conviction that I must come and see James was because I had had some wild hope that I might persuade him to come back.

"Well, how are you getting on at the farm?" I asked.

He was silent for a few moments and that silence was significant.

"Oh . . . all right," he said. "I'd like to be on my own, of course. Two people don't always see eye to eye."

"You mean it's not working out?" Hope was springing up again. I hoped he didn't hear the lilt in my voice.

"Oh, it's working all right. It's just that . . . well, there are things I miss."

"Eversleigh is a fine estate," I said. "You should see it. Jean-Louis often talks of you. He says you were the best man they'd ever had or were ever likely to." I decided to plunge: "Could you come back to us, James . . . ? There's a pleasant house . . . everything you could want."

He shook his head. "I won't beat about the bush," he said. "I'd be glad to. I often think of the good times we used to have. Jean-Louis and I always saw eye to eye. Something I don't do with my cousin . . . but even at Eversleigh I might see him . . . Dickon."

"He hasn't been over yet. It would be very rarely. We're quite a way from each other."

"I wouldn't trust myself. He could come over anytime. No . . . I'll stay where I am. I'm safe there. It's not ideal. I'll make no bones about it. If it weren't for him I'd be there like a shot. Well, come to think about it if it weren't for him I'd never have gone."

"James," I said, "you don't know how badly we want you."

"I want to come . . . but no. Not with him likely to turn up at any time. It wouldn't do, Mistress Zipporah, and that's flat."

"I wish I could persuade you."

"Wouldn't be any need for persuasion but for that one thing. Hetty couldn't bear to see him either."

"She's got over all that."

"Never will completely. But we manage. He's right out of sight and that helps put him out of mind."

"Jean-Louis was so sorry he couldn't see you. We did wonder if you knew anybody."

"Well, that's something I might do. I could hear of someone. I'll keep my ears to the ground and if I find a suitable man . . . I'll have him down there in no time."

I saw that it was the best I could do.

"I wish you could see Jean-Louis. He'd be so pleased. Why don't you come and stay with us for a few days? I assure you that there would be no possibility of your meeting Dickon. They are considering coming for Christmas but that's way ahead."

He hesitated and said he would think about it.

"The journey only takes two days. . . . Not a lot of time really. Do think very seriously about it, James."

He did and at length decided that he would accompany us.

I was delighted, although my scheme had failed. I don't know why I had felt that I had to come to London to see James. I had been convinced that something good would come out of it, and the good must be that he would come back to us.

The Forsters, who had taken a liking to James—and he to them—were very pleased to hear that he was going to travel back with us. "First, though," said Isabel, "we must remember that we were having a jaunt to London and we must take advantage of the opportunity to do those things which we could not do at home.

"Charles," she said, "you know how you always liked the theater. What if we all went to Drury Lane?"

Everyone agreed that that would be an excellent idea and accordingly I found myself seated in the stalls with Charles next to me, enjoying every moment, for it was a privilege to see the great Garrick perform. Charles, who had evidently been an ardent theatergoer at some time, was very knowledgeable about the stage. He told me that the best performance he had ever seen was that of Peg Woffington playing with Garrick in the *Beaux' Stratagem*.

"Alas," he said, "she is no more, though only a few years ago she was striding across the boards full of vitality. A great actress, and she and Garrick, you know, were lovers. It was believed they would marry. It was a surprise to us all when he left Peg for that foreign dancer . . . Eva Maria Violetti."

Much of his melancholy had lifted. I had noticed that when we had driven through London. He pointed out certain landmarks to me almost with pride. I thought: *This was once his home and he loved it*.

I was carried away by the play and the players and I sensed that my enthusiasm pleased him. He said: "I once knew actors . . . I was a great theatergoer in my young days. Mind you, it's a hard life. They look so pleased with themselves when they can win the approval of the audience that you'd think they hadn't a care in the world beyond that. The reality is somewhat different."

I said: "Surely you were never on the stage?"

He gave a sudden laugh. "Me? Good heavens, no." Then the mask seemed to slip over his face and his mood changed. I longed to know what had happened to him to make him so withdrawn, for I was sure something had. I was intrigued because I had at times been aware of a different man peeping out from behind the mask. I wanted to bring out that man. I was burning with curiosity to know more about Charles Forster.

We walked back through the streets to the inn.

"Safe," said Derek, "because there are so many of us. There are plenty of pickpockets about after dark."

Charles took my arm as we walked along the narrow street, not only to assure me of his protection but to keep me free of the mud which was splashed up as the coaches rattled by.

I felt very happy that night; even though my mission in getting James to come and act as manager had failed, I could not despair and I was delighted that he had agreed to come back with us.

We supped on cold venison and pigeon pie with muscatel wine and it all tasted delicious. I was excited by the London life and I remembered the days of my childhood when my parents had had a house in Albemarle Street and we had spent much of our time there. My father had preferred the town life; he had spent a great deal of time at his clubs and the houses of gambling friends but he too had imbued in me a love for the metropolis. I did not realize until this moment how much I had missed it although I had paid other visits to London before.

We discussed the play. Charles seemed to have thrown off his melancholy once more and spoke of it, criticizing certain points, praising others.

"You are so knowledgeable," I said.

"Oh yes," said Isabel, smiling at her brother-in-law. "I always enjoy going to the theater when Charles is a member of the party."

"I hope that is no reflection on me," said Derek.

"Of course not, idiot," said Isabel. "I like the way in which Charles brings out certain things, making it more of an experience."

"I always thought that the best part of an evening at the theater was the aftermath—when the play and players are on trial, as it were."

"The inquest," said Derek.

"Just imagine," pointed out Charles, "Cromwell shut down the theater. He might have known the people would never accept that."

"It was his first step to destruction," put in James. "Thank goodness we're at peace at last."

"There is every sign that we are not taking advantage of the peace," said Charles. "We need Pitt. But he goes into retirement worn out by a war which could be said to have been won by his wise policies . . . and we've had years of unwise government . . . not helped by the king."

"Charles gets very fierce on the subject of the colonies," said Isabel to me.

I listened. I liked hearing Charles talk. He was a different man again, his eyes glowing with enthusiasm. He was passionate in his defense of Pitt; scornful in his denunciation of the policies of the government supported by the king.

"What about the colonies, Charles?" asked Derek.

"They're getting restive. We shall have America up in arms

against us if we don't show a little restraint . . . a little common sense. But you'll never get that from the government."

"I like the royal family," said Isabel. "The king and the queen are so . . . homely."

Everybody laughed and then we were discussing our plans for departure.

"We do have one day left to us . . . only one, did you realize it?" said Derek.

"I have certain business which I must do tomorrow," said James.

"We have to visit the Chensons, remember?" said Isabel to Derek.

"Oh yes . . . we promised we would. They don't know you're here, Charles, but they'll be pleased to see you and you must come along with us, Zipporah."

Charles said: "I don't think they're expecting me and they're certainly not expecting Zipporah. She was saying she has never been to Ranelagh. I was wondering whether I might suggest to her that we take a look at it . . . together."

I felt the color rising to my cheeks. They were all watching me, and I tried not to sound too ecstatic as I said that I had always wanted to see Ranelagh.

That was the happiest day I had spent since that period when I had abandoned myself to the joy of being with Gerard. In a way this was similar. I was able to forget everything that had disturbed my peace of mind for years. I suppose always at the back of my mind was the fear that one day my sin would be discovered; and although I almost forgot it for long periods it was always there as a vague shadow, an apprehension. I would sometimes remember with a jolt, and my peace of mind would be in ruins.

Charles Forster could make me forget. That was significant in some ways. For my part I was so anxious to make him lighthearted, to make him forget whatever it was that oppressed him. I understood what it meant to be oppressed in such a way.

We were in a mood to enjoy the day, both of us. Charles was such an interesting companion when he cast aside his gloom. I found his conversation lively and he made me realize how much I had been tucked away from affairs. Vaguely I remembered the excitement of being with my father, who used to talk to me sometimes. He had never been serious like Charles, but he had talked of worldly matters; I realized that I had been rather shut in between my mother, Sabrina and yes . . . Jean-Louis.

However, I was determined to enjoy the day and as I was sure Charles felt the same, it was inevitable that we did.

Charles knew London so well that he could explain so much to me. First he took me riding through the streets, for he said that Ranelagh should not be seen in broad daylight. It was meant to enchant like a veiled beauty who might not be able to face up to the harsh reality of a too bright sun.

I said: "That throws a new light on your character. I should have thought you stood for the bare stark truth."

"There are times when it is better to veil it," he said.

"So you are a romantic after all?" I asked lightly.

"I see that you have put me into a niche — unromantic, dour, looking on the grim side of life. . . . Had you?"

I hesitated. "I thought there was a certain sadness about you. But beneath it . . . well, I just think if you could throw that aside you might be very merry."

He put his head on one side, smiling at me.

"For today," he said, "this very special day, I am going to do that."

"Can you?" I asked.

"With your help," he replied. "You will see."

"Tell me your plans."

"We ride through the streets to an inn I know of where it is possible to get the very best steak pies in London. Do you like steak pies? Ah, I see you hesitate. Withhold your verdict until you have tried the Rainbow variety. The Rainbow is an inn in Fleet Street. They have excellent roast beef and pork, if you prefer that. It is the place to eat for those who like good food. Will you trust me?"

"I am in your hands," I said.

296

So we rode out. We rode slowly through those crowded streets. I was fascinated by all I saw. He showed me where the great fire had started and where it had been stopped; he pointed out the magnificent churches which Sir Christopher Wren had built to replace those which had been burned down.

"A moral," he said. "Out of the ashes rises the phoenix."

He talked of the streets as though they were old friends. Cheapside, the center of the mercers and the haberdashers. Paternoster Row, where the makers of rosaries and those who earned their livings by writing text had resided; Cowcross Street with its cook shops and tripe and pork; Billingsgate, which smelled obnoxiously of fish; Fleet Street, the home of the lawyers. . . .

He was amusing, even witty. I saw another person emerging and I thought: *This is how he was meant to be;* and I knew that it had something to do with me and that made me very happy.

We skirted one area—the Whitefriars quarter, which he called Alsatia. "It stretches from Salisbury Court to the Temple," he told me. "It's a sanctuary of debtors. They dare not emerge and debt collectors dare not enter. They'd risk their lives if they did."

"Could we not take a look?"

He shook his head. "I might not be able to protect you, and you wouldn't like what you saw. It's getting late. It's time we made tracks for the Rainbow."

At the Rainbow Inn we left our horses in the stable yard and went into the dining room.

The innkeeper's wife appeared; she was very obsequious and I realized that she knew Charles well.

"I've brought a friend to try some of your steak pie," he said.

"And you'll take William's home-brewed cider with it, I'll be bound."

He said we would and we sat down opposite each other.

He regarded me steadily. "I think," he said, "you are liking your jaunt in the big city."

"I never realized it was quite so exciting before, though I do remember long ago . . . when we lived here. My father used to take me out with him sometimes."

"You look sad now," he said. "You were very fond of your father, weren't you?"

"He was wonderful . . . or so he seemed to me. He was a gambler. My mother was the steady one. He was killed in a duel—senselessly."

"Don't think of sad things . . . today," he begged.

"If I don't, you won't. Is that a promise?"

"It is."

The pie was brought and with it flagons of cider.

I agreed I had never tasted such food. But I knew in my heart that everything would be good today.

He talked more about London, about the contrasts one could see during a short walk through the city. Such luxury, such extravagance, and such poverty.

"Like that place we passed."

"Whitefriars, oh yes."

"Have you ever ventured there?"

"I did once . . . for a patient." He shuddered.

"Were you alarmed?"

"I was going to see a sick person. I didn't think beyond that. It became like a nightmare. A young girl ran up to me when I was passing and cried out that her mother was dying. I said: 'I'm a doctor. Take me to her.' And she took me. As soon as I stepped into that maze of streets there was the sound of horns blowing. I couldn't understand what it meant. Then I learned that the whole community was being warned that a stranger was in their midst. The young girl screamed out that I was a doctor and she was taking me to her mother. I realized then what a fool I had been to come. I could have been murdered just for my watch. But I was going to a patient . . . and at such times one doesn't think much beyond that."

I said: "I think you must be a very good doctor."

"A very ordinary one," he said.

"Tell me about Whitefriars."

"The woman I was being taken to was in labor. I delivered a child. That was my profession. . . . It was fortunate that the girl had run into a doctor. I think she thought it was a sort of miracle. Afterwards I escaped in possession of my watch and coins in my pocket. Looking back I think *that* was the real miracle."

"So you really did have a glimpse inside."

He was thoughtful. "For some time I felt I wanted to do something for those people. I wanted to take them out of White-friars I had the usual dreams and ideals which beset the young until they realize that all they can do is what they're qualified for. I was meant to care for the sick. It was for the politicians and such like to change the living standards of the people."

"You have always been devoted to your work?"

He looked at me steadily. "It is like a crutch," he said. "It helps me through life. When I am weary and melancholy and I feel no great enthusiasm for living . . . I work . . . and that soothes me. I limp along on my crutch and get by."

There were so many questions I wanted to ask him. I was certain that there was some tragedy, some shadow hanging over him, something which had happened in the past and which he could not forget. But this was a day for forgetting, a day for enjoying.

I said: "How shall we get to Ranelagh? Shall we ride?"

"Good heavens no. We shall go in the traditional manner. We shall wait till dusk and then we shall take a wherry along the river. We shall alight at Ranelagh; we shall walk through the enchanted glades and at the Rotunda there is a treat in store. There is a young genius who has come to this country for a short tour. I was determined to hear him. He is but eight years old and a composer already."

"Is that possible? A boy?"

"Possible with this boy. Apparently he was astonishing people when he was but six years old. It will be interesting to hear if he is really as good as we have been led to believe. He has come to England from Salzburg with his father and sister,

Marianne, I think. A musical family, it seems. He will play some of his own compositions on the harpsichord."

"I so look forward to hearing him."

"As well as Master Wolfgang Amadeus Mozart we may also hear the chorus from *Acis and Galatea* and "Oh, Happy Pair" from *Alexander's Feast*. I think that Tenducci is singing the solo."

"I can see it is going to be most entertaining. I wonder you live in the country when you could obviously find so much to enjoy here." I waved my arms as though to embrace the town.

He said quietly: "I had my reasons. . . ." And there was that in his voice which told me I should ask no further questions on that matter.

We sat for a long time in the Rainbow Inn and when we came out we left the horses there and walked down to the river. There we took a boat and were rowed along the river past Westminster and right out to Hampton.

The red-brick manor house, which had been transformed into the palace of Hampton Court, looked magnificent.

"A palace of great importance in the country's history," commented Charles. "I have heard it is an interesting place. The Tudors enjoyed it and King William and Mary were fond of it. The alterations they made have transformed it into a most magnificent palace."

"I should love to explore it," I said.

"It's full of ghosts and shadows, they say. Memories leaping out from every corner. I have heard that the ghost of Catherine Howard appears in the gallery along which she is reputed to have run seeking the king when she knew she was accused. Poor girl, remembering the sad fate of her cousin Anne Boleyn, she must have known what hers would be."

"There must be pleasant memories, too."

"It's strange how the unpleasant ones are those to be remembered. I heard that our present George won't go there because it is said his father once boxed his ears in the state apartments. As there were others present he felt so humiliated that whenever he sees the place he remembers the incident."

"Poor George. People seem to enjoy humiliating him."

"It must be something in his nature which provokes the teasing spirit."

"And being a king that must be doubly hard to bear."

"Don't let's waste sympathy on him. It's not going to help him in any case. I should like to go along the river to Windsor but if we are going to get to Ranelagh to hear our child genius there would not be the time."

Oh, what a happy day that was, sailing along the river, among hundreds of others who had had the same idea as we had. I thought the company added to my pleasure. It was good to see so many people laughing, calling to each other; there were some who had music on board, and the sound of it was very sweet to me.

We took the wherry just as it was beginning to get dark and we went along to Ranelagh.

The pleasure garden was like a fairyland. Thousands of golden lamps illuminated the scene and as we stepped ashore we heard the strains of music coming from a band hidden somewhere among the trees.

Charles took my arm as we started to walk through those laid-out paths paved with gravel and bounded on each side by hedges and trees.

Beautifully dressed women with male companions strolled by. Pleasure was in the air; one knew that everyone here was bent on enjoying the evening.

"There are more and more attractions every year," said Charles. "Every time I come I notice something new. It can't be much more than twenty years since the grounds were purchased from Lord Ranelagh and what has been done with them is amazing. We will eat before the concert begins. I believe it is possible to get an excellent cold collation and that is by far the best."

I allowed myself to be led into that enchanted garden. We walked past grottoes, lawns, temples, waterfalls, delightful colonnades and rotundas with their decorated pillars and statues. The lamps were beautifully arranged to look like constellations. Because it was a warm, fine night tables had been set under the trees and here we sat and enjoyed the cold collation Charles had mentioned and watched the passersby until we left for the concert in the Rotunda.

I was enchanted by the music. Everything was of the newest fashion. For the first time I heard the cello, that instrument which was only just being introduced into the country, and to hear the great Pasqualino perform was wonderful. The band played the overture from Doctor Arne's *Thomas and Sally*, which was wildly applauded. But the great event of the evening was the appearance of the child prodigy. I admitted afterward to Charles that I was prepared to be skeptical. It did not seem possible that a boy so young could play to compare with the experienced, but that he should compose was surely just too much to believe. Stories about the boy had been circulated to arouse people's interest and bring them to the Rotunda to see him. There they would be entertained by superb artists and forget that they had been brought there under false pretenses.

Just talk, was what I thought, an unusual story to arouse people's curiosity enough to bring them to the child.

How different was the truth! He came onto the stage—a small figure, dressed like a man in a blue coat and embroidered waistcoat, white cravat and frilled lace cuffs. His breeches, knee-length, showed beneath the waistcoat as his coat was unbuttoned and he wore silken hose and black shoes with silver buckles. I heard that his clothes were copied in a larger size from his gala suit, which had been presented to him by Maria Theresa of Austria on the occasion of his playing before her two years before when he was six years old. On his head was a crimped wig tied back with a black ribbon. Dressed thus in an adult style seemed to have the effect of making him seem more of a child than he actually was.

There was an air of self-assurance about him as he sat down at the harpsichord; and a silence reigned which I can only describe as indulgent. The audience had settled to hear a clever child perform for them.

But how mistaken we were! As the boy sat there and played

302

we were transported from this fashionable rotunda. I don't know whether others felt as I did, but it seemed to me that I was flying through space and the music so delicately played, so inspiring and yet so mysterious, was carrying me along.

I glanced sideways at Charles. He was sitting very still, completely entranced.

I think a good many of us that night realized that we were in the presence of genius.

When the boy stopped playing there was silence for a few seconds before the applause rang out.

The boy bowed calmly and then walked off the stage with dignity. I could see a man waiting for him in the wings and I presumed this was his father.

We did not want to hear any more music that night. To hear that child play his own composition was something I wanted to carry away with me, to remember forever, as I was sure I would.

Charles whispered: "I can see you were as impressed as I was."

"It was wonderful. I couldn't believe it was that little boy who was playing as he did."

"Let's get out into the fresh air. We can take a little walk if you wish before we get the wherry back."

I said I should like that.

Silent, still under the spell of the music, we were leaving the rotunda when I heard a voice cry: "Charles."

A woman was coming up to us. She was exquisitely dressed in a gown of blue silk cut away in the front to reveal an embroidered petticoat in white satin. On her head was a most elaborate hat of white straw on which was perched yards and yards of blue ribbon the same color as her dress, ruched in the front and culminating in an enormous bow at the back where it was tilted forward over her elaborate coiffure.

The woman went on to call her companion. "Ralph! Here, Ralph. Who do you think I've found? Charles . . . Charles Forster."

A man appeared, fashionably dressed in velvet frogged coat

with large turned back cuffs, long waistcoat, fine silk hose and buckled shoes; under his arm he carried a cocked hat.

"Charles!" he cried. "My dear fellow, what a delightful surprise. Haven't seen you for years... since... er..."

Charles said: "I am escorting a friend of my sister's. Mistress Ransome.... Dr. and Mrs. Lang."

We bowed.

"Have you just come from the Rotunda?" asked the woman. "Did you see the child prodigy? Quite interesting, wasn't he? Wonderful for his age. What about supper...?"

"We ate before the performance and I really think I should be taking Mistress Ransome back to her friends."

"Oh, come, Charles," said the woman. "There's no need to rush, surely? We were talking about you the other day, weren't we, Ralph? We said it's such nonsense of you to bury yourself in the country. You ought to come back. All that trouble is forgotten now. People soon forget. Nine days' wonder and all that. I doubt whether anyone would remember if you came back now."

Charles had turned rather pale. I felt the magic of the evening slipping away.

Ralph said: "Sybil's right, Charles. Anyhow let's talk of pleasant things. You and your friend must sup with us. We have a table near the colonnades. It's very pleasant there and you can hear the band in the background."

"No," said Charles. "Thanks, but we must go. Goodbye."

"Are you in town for long?" asked the man.

"No. I'm leaving tomorrow."

"Pity. I should have liked to talk. I wish you'd bring Mistress... er... Ransome? along to see us before you go."

"Thanks but there's no time. Good-bye."

"Au revoir," said the woman.

Charles took my arm. I could feel the tension in him.

He was silent on the way back and I knew that that chance encounter outside the Rotunda had spoiled the day for him.

* * *

He was different now. The mask of melancholy which I had flattered myself I was helping to remove was now in place firmer than ever. I wished I could have asked him about the nine days' wonder, whatever it was, which people would have forgotten by now.

One thing I had learned. It was that—whatever had happened—which was responsible for his melancholy. There was some tragedy in Charles Forster's life and he could not forget it.

The wonderful companionship which we had shared during that magic day had gone; he was aloof, absentminded; and most of the time seemed hardly aware of me.

The journey back to Eversleigh seemed tedious. I rode between Isabel and James most of the time. I was of course pleased that James was coming back with us for a brief visit because I was sure Jean-Louis would be delighted to see him. At the back of my mind the thought persisted that I might even yet be able to persuade him to come to us.

As I was saying good-bye to the Forsters, who were about to ride on to Enderby, Jethro came hurrying up. He looked very solemn and I knew at once that all was not well.

He looked at me with unhappiness in his eyes and I said quickly: "What's happened, Jethro?"

"It's the master," he said.

I felt myself go cold with fear.

"It was an accident. He fell from his horse."

"He's..."

"Oh, he's all right, mistress. I mean he's not..."

"How bad, Jethro?"

"Well, it happened two days back. They got him to his bed. He's not moved from it since. The doctor's been with him...the one who came in Dr. Forster's place."

I nodded impatiently. "I will go to him...at once."

"You may be shocked, mistress. The horse threw him, you see. 'Tweren't her fault. Master's leg troubling him made him an unsure rider sometimes."

Charles was beside me. "I'll wait," he said, "in case you want me to see him. Derek, you and Isabel go on to Enderby. I'll be with you soon."

"I'm going straight to him now," I said.

I ran up to our bedroom. Jean-Louis was lying in bed. He looked different—his face was white and drawn. But his eyes lit up at the sight of me.

I went to him, kissed him and then knelt beside the bed.

"Oh, my dearest . . . what happened?"

"It was my fault," he said. "I was careless. This old leg . . . and the pain in my back . . . Well, I was off my guard and old Tessa threw me."

"And the doctor . . . ?"

"He wants Dr. Forster to look at me. I can see he's a little grim, although he won't commit himself."

"Grim?" I asked.

"Well, I believe he thinks I won't walk again."

"Oh, Jean-Louis! And while I've been away . . ."

I thought of that day . . . the meal in the Rainbow, the trip down the river and most of all the enchanted evening. And while I was enjoying all that Jean-Louis was lying in great pain.

I vowed to myself that I would look after him for as long as he should need me. I must do that . . . to make up for the way in which I had wronged him.

"You mustn't be upset, dearest Zipporah," he said. "It might not be so bad. The doctor seems to think a chair on wheels . . . You see, I don't seem to be able to use my legs."

He looked up suddenly. Charles had come into the room.

"I've come to see you," he said. "What happened?"

Jean-Louis told him what he had told me.

"May I examine you now?"

"Oh, do please," I said.

Charles turned to me and said: "Perhaps you would leave us."

I went out. Poor Jean-Louis. Why did this have to happen to him! He was such a good man. I thought if Dickon had never started that fire in Hassock's barn this wouldn't have happened. Jean-Louis, who had been an excellent horseman before his accident, had become a clumsy one afterward. I felt waves of hatred against Dickon.

It was stupid. It was unfair. Dickon had acted as any mischievous boy might in making a fire in the barn.

I had forgotten we had a guest. I hurried down wondering what James would think of me. He was all sympathy. I was not to worry about him. Someone would tell him where his room was and then he would hope to see Jean-Louis when he was well enough.

As Jean-Louis was in our bedroom with the doctor I had water sent up to another and there I washed the grime of the journey from my face.

I went down to the hall to wait for Charles.

"He's been badly hurt," he said when he came. "I don't know whether he will ever walk again. He appears to have lost the use of his legs." He looked at me sorrowingly. "There is another thing: he may suffer a good deal of pain."

"Oh no . . ."

"I fear this is inevitable in view of the seat of the damage. But don't worry. We will alleviate it all we can. I will get you some laudanum and morphia perhaps. You will have to be careful how you administer them. They can be easily fatal. But I shall give you full instructions."

"Oh, thank you," I said. "Thank you."

He smiled rather sadly and laid his hand on my shoulder. "A sad homecoming," he said. "A pity . . ." He turned to the door and there he paused. "These things happen," he went on. "Don't fret. He will be my patient and you may be sure that I shall do everything I can . . . for you both."

I ran to him and he took both my hands in his. Then he bent forward suddenly and kissed my forehead.

I felt a great desire to throw myself into his arms. I wanted him to hold me . . . to shut out the cruelty of the world . . . I wanted us to cling together and I to forget my guilt for what

307

I had done to Jean-Louis and for him to cast out forever that shadow which was haunting his life.

It was over in a few seconds.

"Don't fret," he said again. "Everything will be all right." Then he was gone.

I went along to see Jean-Louis. He smiled and held out his hand.

"What did the doctor say?"

"He doesn't seem to know what damage has been done yet. But he'll be there to look after you, and I have great faith in him."

"Yes," he said, "so have I."

"He said you might have some pain but he can give you something. And, Jean-Louis, I shall be there to look after you."

"My Zipporah," he said. "My little love."

I was holding his hand tightly and he said: "You mustn't cry."

I did not realize I was but he had felt the dampness on his hand.

"Zipporah," he said, "look at me." I did. His eyes met mine steadily. "Whatever happens," he said, "I've had a good life. I owe so much to your mother, who took me in . . . but to you most of all. I'll never forget what I owe to you. . . . Whatever happens . . . it will always be so. Nothing . . . nothing could change that."

For a moment I thought: *He knows. He is telling me he knows.*

But no. He did not know that his beloved Lottie was not his. It was one of the greatest joys of his life to think that he had fathered her.

He was talking of her. She had been so good, he told me. She had been with him in his room, looking after him. "I made her go out, otherwise she would have been in the sick room all the time. She'll be back soon and the first thing she will do is come and see me. Oh, I am indeed blessed in my family."

"It'll be all right," I said. "I will look after you always."

He smiled. I looked into his good patient face and prayed that he would not have to suffer pain.

It turned out that good sometimes comes out of evil.

Jean-Louis was very pleased to see James. They talked a good deal together and Lottie, who took a fancy to James, took him out to show him the estate.

It was three days after we had returned home when James came to me.

There was a purposeful look in his face.

He said: "Zipporah, I've been thinking. . . . With Jean-Louis incapacitated . . . what are you going to do?"

"The first thing is to get a man to manage the estate, I suppose."

"I've been thinking . . . but this is subject to Hetty, of course . . . I'd have to see her. . . ."

"Oh, James!" I cried.

"Yes," he said. "He'll need someone he can trust . . . someone who speaks his language."

"There's only one who could give him the relief he needs."

"I'll come, Zipporah. Yes, I'll come. That's if Hester's not too set against it. But I can persuade her, and when she knows how things are I don't think she'll put obstacles in the way."

"Oh, James . . . James . . . this is wonderful."

"All right then," he said, "and if there's trouble later . . . well, we'll face that when it comes along."

The Secret Drawer

*C*hristmas was almost upon us. The months after that trip to London had been sad ones for me. The forecast had been right. Jean-Louis did have a great deal of pain, and there is nothing more heartrending than to see a loved one suffer. I was grateful for the laudanum with which Charles supplied me; no doctor could have been more assiduous in his care for a patient than he was toward Jean-Louis. He would come immediately I sent for him; he comforted me, too; and Jean-Louis had such faith in him that his very presence seemed to soothe him.

Jean-Louis was stoical by nature; and it was so touching to see his attempts to hide his pain from me because he knew how it upset me to see him in that state. Charles had warned me that in the extremity of agony he might try to increase his dose of laudanum and this must never go beyond that prescribed. He had said that only I should administer it and therefore I should be able to keep a strict watch on how much he took. "Keep the bottles locked away," he said, "and only you should have the key."

"Jean-Louis would never take his own life whatever the provocation," I said.

"My dear Zipporah, you don't know the extent of the provocation."

All this would have been unendurable if there had not been reasonably long periods when Jean-Louis was free from the pain. It could be absent for as much as a week at a time and that seemed to give us breathing space to recover and prepare ourselves for the next onslaught—and to get on with our lives.

I had engaged a governess for Lottie—rather to her displeasure. She liked her lessons with me, which were apt to be a little irregular. Now with the coming of Madeleine Carter, Lottie must be in the schoolroom precisely at the same hour every morning. She was not academically inclined and had what Miss Carter called a butterfly mind. It flitted from one subject to another. "If only it would settle," said Miss Carter, "something might be achieved."

Madeleine Carter was a spinster in her early thirties. She was the sister of a vicar and had kept house for him until his unfortunate and early demise which had left her stranded and forced to take on the only kind of occupation available for one in her position. She was prim, strict, very efficient; and I thought an excellent choice. It was quite clear that Lottie needed someone to curb her for she was growing decidedly self-willed, and although she was possessed of great charm she could be wayward.

The greatest piece of luck was that James Fenton was looking after the estate. He had gone home directly after our return from London to break the news to Hetty, and in view of Jean-Louis's condition he came back to us soon afterward, leaving Hetty, as he said, to pack up.

A few weeks later Hetty came with her two children and it was good to see her again. She was happy to be back but dreaded meeting Dickon, and as he would be coming for Christmas we arranged that she and James, with their children, should spend the holiday with James's cousin on the farm and stay there until my mother with Sabrina and Dickon had returned to Clavering. It seemed a reasonable and satisfactory arrangement.

Thus the months passed. James had been a great asset and spent a lot of time with Jean-Louis discussing estate matters and working out policy; and Jean-Louis was delighted to have someone who would carry out his wishes—and, more than that, give his wholehearted support towards what was being done. James did a great deal to raise his spirits.

My friendship with the Forsters had grown and we were often in and out of each other's houses. Charles Forster was frequently at Enderby, and as he visited Jean-Louis at least twice a week and more often of course when I called him in during one of Jean-Louis's bad bouts, the family had become an important part of my life.

Then there was Evalina. She had been very friendly towards me since the matter of the will. She reminded me of a contented kitten who has found a good home and intends to keep it. She was assured the comfort and comparative opulence of Grasslands; she had her baby, whom she undoubtedly loved dearly, and a good manager—and perhaps more—in Jack Trent.

It was the day before Christmas Eve when our guests arrived. Lottie and I had done everything we could to bring a festive atmosphere into the house and by great good fortune Jean-Louis was better than he had been for some time. He was able to walk a little about the room with the aid of a stick and I arranged that on Christmas day two of the men servants might carry him down to the great hall. I prayed that we could keep the pain at bay for a little while.

Lottie was devoted to him. I saw his eyes light up whenever she came into the room. She invariably brought something for him which she had picked up during her walks or rides in the fields and woods. She came in with a sprig of holly, the berries as red as her cheeks.

"This has the most berries of all we picked, papa," she told him, "so I saved it for you."

It was a great comfort to me to see the joy she brought him. But for what I did there could be no Lottie to brighten his days. Good out of evil. Indeed it was so.

I listened to her chatter. "This is wild clematis, papa. Miss Carter makes me learn the names. Miss Carter knows *everything*, but alas your daughter is an ignoramus, dear papa. Did you know that?"

He took her hand and his eyes filled with tears. He was very emotional nowadays. "My daughter is the best and dearest girl in the world," he said.

She regarded him with her head on one side. "As Miss Carter would say, it depends on what you mean by best. Best at jumping, yes . . . Best at climbing, yes. Best at sums . . . no, no, no! And rather wicked sometimes, I fear, and that's not best."

Her chatter amused him and she knew it. She might be rebellious at times, wayward often, but she had a good, kind and loving heart.

Together we watched the men bring in the yule log. She and I pored over the lists of food we should need for our guests. There would be games. Lottie's eyes sparkled at the prospect. We needed a lot of people. The Forsters would come, and what about Evalina Mather?

I said we would have open house at Christmas.

"We'll have dancing and fiddlers. Do you think the fiddlers will come on Christmas night, mama?"

"We'll promise them punch and Christmas cakes as well as money. In fact we'll make it irresistible for them."

She clapped her hands. She was so excited. Suddenly she clapped her hands to her mouth.

"What is it?" I said.

"I should love to see Miss Carter dance," she said.

"She might do so very well. People are full of surprises."

"That would be the most unlikely Christmas surprise."

"Wait and see," I said, and we went on with our lists.

I was happy to see my mother again. She hugged me and said we had been separated far too long. I saw the compassion and dismay in her eyes when they rested on Jean-Louis and I realized how he must have changed since we left Clavering.

And there was Sabrina looking as beautiful as ever, and with her Dickon.

He was a man now. . . . He must be nineteen. He stood smiling at me with that rather enigmatic look which was half affectionate, half teasing.

"Well, it is good to see you, Zipporah," he cried. "And this is Lottie. By Gad, you've grown." He had picked her up and held her above his head looking up at her.

She was laughing. "Put me down," she commanded.

"Not until you give me a kiss."

"Oh, so it's blackmail is it? All right then." She gave him a peck on the forehead.

"Not good enough," he said. "I don't call that a nice cousinly kiss."

"Put me down. Put me down!" shrieked Lottie.

I did not like to see her there held up in his arms and I was irritated by the indulgent manner in which his mother and mine were regarding him.

As I started to lead them into the house I saw Lottie kissing him again.

"Now," she said when she was on the ground, "you must meet Miss Carter."

"Always delighted to meet the ladies," said Dickon.

"Miss Carter is my governess."

"That does not preclude her from being a lady."

"Oh, she's that all right," said Lottie. "In fact, she's always so anxious that I shan't forget that I'm one she's forever reminding me. She's very good at her lessons."

"I thought it was for you to be good at yours."

"What I mean is she's a good teacher."

"With the naughtiest little pupil in the world, I don't doubt."

I was trying not to listen to their banter as I asked my mother about affairs at Clavering.

I took them to their rooms and heard from both my mother

315

and Sabrina how absolutely wonderful everything was on the estate since Dickon had taken over.

"I was sorry he didn't continue with his education," said Sabrina. "But he would have his own way."

"I think he'd always have that," I commented wryly.

My mother said: "He thinks a lot of you, Zipporah. He'll be in his element talking to Jean-Louis and your manager."

"Our manager is not here at the moment. He is with his wife. It is a good thing that he is not here."

"A good thing!" said my mother. "I thought that Jean-Louis looks so frail."

"Our manager, mother, is James Fenton. I don't think either he or his wife would want to meet Dickon."

My mother looked embarrassed and Sabrina said: "Oh, that. That all happened a long time ago."

I said: "And since it was due to Dickon it must become a sort of amusing joke."

My mother was shocked. "I never thought it was a joke. But it is all over now. These things are natural happenings."

I could see it was no use expecting them to understand. Dickon was perfect in their eyes and it was no use upsetting everything right at the start of the Christmas holiday.

Madeleine Carter was introduced to the visitors and my mother heartily approved of her. "She seems a good sensible young woman," she said.

Sabrina added: "Just the sort to keep Lottie in check."

Dickon irreverently called her the Holy Virgin Madeleine, and told Lottie that he couldn't quite detect the halo but he wondered whether her young eyes had seen it.

Lottie laughed and said: "You are not to make fun, Cousin Dickon. She's very *good*."

"And you like the good?"

"Of course I do."

"Oh . . . I'm desolate. That means you don't like me."

Lottie pursed her lips and nodded, which sent Dickon into fits of laughter.

I could see he was charming Lottie; in fact he set out to charm everybody, even Madeleine Carter.

He certainly gave out an air of absolute *joie de vivre*. He was enormously interested in Eversleigh . . . as he had always been, but now that he was older and I suppose was able to compare the estate with that of Clavering, his interest was even greater. I was glad that he talked so enthusiastically to Jean-Louis, which seemed to do my husband good. I was grateful to him for that, but all the time I was watching Jean-Louis for some sign that the pain might be returning.

Christmas morning was bright and sparkling with frost on the roads and the rooftops, but by midday the wintry sun had melted it and as the wind had dropped it seemed quite mild. Lottie and Miss Carter went out riding in the morning and Dickon accompanied them. I heard their laughter and looked out of the window to see them ride by.

I was glad that Miss Carter was with them. I was sure she would keep even Dickon in check. Last evening he had called at Grasslands. I had expected he might stay late into the night but to my surprise he returned to Eversleigh after about an hour of his leaving. I wondered whether Evalina had not been at home.

I shrugged my shoulders. If he were going to resume that liaison it would keep him out of the house perhaps.

The carol singers came to pay us their usual visit. The riders were back by then. I knew they would be. Lottie would never allow them to miss the carols.

We all joined in and it was Lottie who helped to pass round the punch and the cake.

Jean-Louis was well enough to be brought down to the hall. I watched him closely for the first sign of the pain, in which case I decided I would give him a dose of laudanum and have him taken back to his bed. But he sat there smiling and his eyes scarcely left Lottie unless it was to look at me.

I sat beside him for most part of the time, watching him anxiously.

He knew it. He said: "Don't worry, Zipporah. If I need a dose I'll ask. Now forget it."

So I tried to and I joined in the carols and took the punch which Lottie brought to me.

"You must have some, papa," she said. "It will do you good."

She brought the goblet to him, drank from it, smiling at him, and then handed it to him.

I heard him murmur: "Bless you, dear child."

We had eaten and the festivities had begun. The great hall was crowded. The farmers on the estate, with their families, had come according to tradition and they would all join in the dancing when the fiddlers started to play. I had been right in my prophecy that they would come if the rewards were sufficient and they were pausing between dances to drink their punch.

The Forsters came with Charles and the farmers on their estate, as did the one or two from Grasslands; for Eversleigh was the manor house and the custom for years had been that everyone came to dance at least one measure at the Court on Christmas Day.

Evalina arrived looking happy in a rather secretive way. I saw Dickon watching her but she seemed to be unaware of him. Jack Trent was with her.

I danced with Charles Forster. He was no great dancer— very different, I thought, from Dickon, who won the admiration not only of my doting mother and his own but that of the whole company by his cavorting. He took no one partner for the evening but danced with a different one every time, which was what would be expected of the host. I realized with vague annoyance that he had taken on that role. I was touchy. Of course he did. He was one of the family and Jean-Louis was unable to perform the duty.

Charles talked of Jean-Louis and said how pleased he was to see him in the hall.

"Do you think I was right to have him carried down?"

"Indeed I do. The more normal the life he leads the better."

318

"I couldn't have borne it if he had been ill tonight."

"He's in one of his quiet periods. I can see."

"I do wish they would continue."

"They might, and the longer time between each attack the better. When he is free of pain he has a chance to regain a little strength."

"It is such a comfort that you are near."

He pressed my hand. "It's a comfort to me to be of use."

We were smiling at each other and I was only half aware of Dickon's flashing past with Evalina.

Charles returned me to Jean-Louis and stayed to chat with us. Jean-Louis told him how much better he felt. "The laudanum seems to give me strength," he said.

"What it does," said Charles, "is give you a respite from pain and that helps to build up some resistance to it."

"Then it's good for me."

"In small prescribed doses, yes. I am sure Zipporah has told you you must never exceed the dose."

"She guards the bottle like a dragon breathing fire."

"That's as it should be," said Charles.

Evalina came up and said: "I want to ask you something."

Charles slipped away and she went on: "I know it's something I ought to do in my own home. But everyone's here tonight and I want them all to know. I know there's some who will say it's too soon . . . but well, what's the sense in waiting?"

"You don't mean . . ." I began.

She gave me a wide smile. "Yes; I do. It's Jack and me . . . well, we don't see why not. It's just right, isn't it? He manages the estate. It's my estate. He doesn't mind that. We'll share it. But I think it's best to make it all regular. So would you mind?"

I looked at Jean-Louis and he smiled.

At that moment Dickon went dancing by. His partner was Miss Carter. She seemed to be dancing very gracefully. She looked quite unlike herself. One lock of hair had broken free.

Lottie came running over.

She gripped my arm; she was laughing so much that she was quite incoherent. "Did . . . you see Miss Carter?"

I laughed back. "I told you so. But listen, Evalina is going to make an announcement."

Lottie clapped her hands. "Oh . . . what fun. Is it . . . that she's going to marry Jack Trent?"

I was surprised. I hadn't thought she would know of such matters.

I realized that I had to face the fact that Lottie was growing up.

I stood up and clapped my hands. There was a silence throughout the hall.

I said: "Mistress Mather wants to tell you all something."

Evalina went forward dragging Jack Trent by the hand.

"I know there's been a bit of gossip about us," she said. "Well, now you'll know there's going to be an end to all that. Jack and I are going to be married."

There was a short silence and then someone started to clap.

Dickon cried out: "This calls for a celebration. We must all drink their health."

There was a bustle while glasses were filled all around.

Dickon was standing close to Evalina. He held his glass high and looked at her. I saw the expression in her face as she returned his glance. I thought it was one of triumphant defiance. I saw too the glitter of amusement in Dickon's eyes.

The musicians started to play "Heart of Oak," which seemed somewhat inappropriate.

Dickon duly departed with my mother and Sabrina. Lottie clung to them all and tried to urge them to stay longer.

Dickon said: "My dear cousin, I have an estate to run. I can't stay away too long."

My mother held her tightly and said: "We must see each other more often. I will not endure these long separations."

I felt relieved when they had gone and we settled down to the normal routine. A few days after their departure James and

Hetty returned and Lottie ceased to miss them but turned to Hetty's children, to whom she had taken a great fancy.

The winter was a hard one and Jean-Louis's pain seemed to come more frequently. Charles was often at the house and our friendship deepened. Sometimes I felt it was deeper than friendship. I began to experience great pleasure in his presence. It was ironic that when he came it was because Jean-Louis was suffering. Sometimes I went into the town to collect the medicines. Charles didn't want to hand them to anyone but me. I became familiar with the house where he had his surgery. I thought it rather cheerless. He had a housekeeper—an elderly woman who I knew was most careful of his comforts. That was good, for he was the kind of man who would neglect himself.

Evalina married Jack Trent at Easter. There was a touch of spring in the air. Oddly enough it did not cheer me. A terrible depression settled on me as I saw Jean-Louis's condition deteriorating. I slept in the dressing room now. Often in the night I would get up and give him a painkilling dose. That cupboard with the key which I kept in a secret drawer in a small desk by the window haunted my dreams. I would dream that I had lost the key and was searching frantically for it. Sometimes I was riding through the night to Charles. I would cry out: "I've lost the key." The sound of my own voice often woke me and so vivid would the dream be that I would get out of bed, light my candle and open the secret drawer. The key was always there. "It's only a dream," I would say—and how many times did I say it during that long winter!

"He'll be better when the spring comes," I used to say; but in my heart I knew that his condition had nothing to do with the weather.

Later I was to blame the strain for what happened. I remembered how on another occasion I was ready to blame something other than the needs of my own nature. Then I had tried to convince myself that a long-dead ancestor had taken possession of me. What nonsense! It was I who had lain in that bed with Gerard and listened to the strains of music coming from the fair as I made passionate love with a man not my husband.

Now I said: "It is the tension . . . the strain . . . the fact that I have to watch Jean-Louis—whom I love—deteriorating.

One night I heard him move. I was like a woman with her baby. If he stirred I was usually awakened out of my sleep.

He was sitting out of bed in his chair . . . I was amazed. His hands covered his face and his shoulders were shaking.

"Jean-Louis," I cried running to him, "what are you doing?"

"Oh . . . I have awakened you. I tried to be so quiet."

"I hear every movement."

"It is selfish of me."

"I want to hear," I cried. "I want to be with you if you need me. What is it? Is it the pain?"

He shook his head.

"It's . . . the uselessness," he said.

"What do you mean?"

"It's obvious, isn't it? I lie in bed . . . or sit in this chair and think: What use am I? They'd be better off without me."

"Don't dare say such a thing," I cried.

"Isn't it true? I am a constant anxiety to you. You admit you cannot sleep deeply. You are with me all the time . . . I am useless in every way."

"Jean-Louis," I said, "it hurts me when you talk like that."

I knelt beside him and buried my face in his dressing gown. I couldn't stop thinking of how I had deceived him.

I cried out: "I *want* to look after you. Don't you understand? That is my life. It's what I want."

"Oh, Zipporah, Zipporah," he murmured.

"Please understand, Jean-Louis."

"I would always understand," he said. "No matter what . . . I would always understand."

What did he mean? Had he some second sight? Did he know of that passionate love between me and Gerard? Could he possibly suspect that Lottie was not his child? I felt a sudden urge to open my heart to him, to tell him what had happened.

I stopped myself just in time. Suppose he had no suspicion? What would the discovery do to him in his condition?

He said: "I have seen the pain in your eyes . . . when I have an attack. It hurts me, Zipporah . . . more than the pain of my body."

"Oh, dearest, of course I suffer. I wish that I could take over some of the pain I wish that we could share that together."

"Bless you, my darling," he said. "You have given me everything . . . you and your mother. In the past I often thought of what might have happened to me if she had not kept me. My own mother did not want me. I wanted to stay."

"Yes, I remember hearing how you refused to get up in the morning and would not let your nanny out of your sight."

"I came to look on you as my charge . . . and it's been like that every since. It's been a happy time together, hasn't it, Zipporah?"

"Yes," I said. "Oh yes."

"Thank you. Thank you. I want you to have happy memories. That's why I am afraid."

"What are you afraid of?"

"That there might be unhappy ones if this goes on. I have sometimes thought . . . suppose I doubled the dose . . . trebled it. . . . What would it be like? Sleep! Blessed sleep! When I have one dose you can't imagine the relief. It makes me sleep, doesn't it? Sometimes I feel that I would like to sleep and sleep . . . and never wake up to pain."

"Oh, Jean-Louis, you must not talk like that. It's as though you want to leave us."

He stroked my hair very tenderly. "Only because I cannot bear to see you suffer, my dearest one."

"And do you think I should not if you . . . went into that deep, deep sleep?"

"For a while. Then you could be happy again."

I shook my head.

"Oh yes," he said. "Oh yes."

"I will not listen to such talk."

"You make me feel . . . wanted," he said.

"How could you ever feel otherwise?"

"Because I am ungrateful. I am surrounded by loving care... and why should that be given to *me*? I am useless... whichever way you look. Zipporah... I am useless."

"Please stop such talk immediately. I will not have it. If you can get the better of this wretched pain you can enjoy so much... all the worthwhile things. And the longer we can keep the pain at bay the more chance you have of strengthening yourself. Isn't that what Dr. Forster says?"

"You're right. Zipporah. But if it should ever be that it is hopeless... and there is nothing left to me but pain... well, who would blame me...? Zipporah. would you help me. if the pain gets too bad?"

"Oh. please don't talk of such things."

"I think of them. Escape is in that bottle.... If it became unbearable... a little help..."

"Let me help you to bed. Let me lie beside you and hold your hand. Let me try to make you understand all you mean to me."

I stayed with him for the rest of the night lying beside him. holding his hand until he fell into a peaceful sleep.

There was a letter from my mother. We corresponded regularly for she was eager to hear of Jean-Louis's condition.

"I know that you cannot come to us and leave Jean-Louis." she wrote. "and if we come to you that disturbs the household. but why should not Lottie visit us? That nice sensible Miss Carter could come with her. We do so long to see her."

When Lottie heard she was eager to go. Dear child. I think she was beginning to be affected by Jean-Louis's illness. I thought it would be a good idea for her to get away for a while.

So she left at the end of June.

I watched her leave in the company of Miss Carter and six grooms and I gave them instructions that they were to send the grooms back the day after they arrived so that I should know they had reached their destination safely.

Then I went back to Jean-Louis.

He was lying in bed. He smiled when he saw me.

"I'm glad she's gone," he said.

"Oh, come," I answered, "you hate to lose her."

"I miss her," he said. "But it's good for her not to have to see me."

"Don't talk like that, Jean-Louis," I begged.

"It's true," he said, a little harshly. There was a faint irritation in his voice—so unlike him, but I knew that it was the herald of pain.

"We must face the truth," he said. "I'm a depressing object."

"Nonsense. Do you feel like a game of chess?"

"And you . . ." he went on, "you should be going with them."

"I prefer Eversleigh. I have no desire to go to Clavering. You know how I dislike Dickon. And as for my mother and his, they talk Dickon all the time."

"I hope Lottie won't get tired of the subject."

"She has her lessons. Madeleine Carter will never allow her to evade them . . . much as she might like to."

"Madeleine Carter is a stern taskmaster—or, I should say, mistress."

"I hope not too stern. I think she does preach a little hell fire to poor Lottie now and then. I don't want the child thinking her immortal soul's in peril because she commits some little peccadillo."

"Is Madeleine so upright then?"

"Completely so. She lives by a set of rules all laid down in her interpretation of the Bible. It makes life easy."

"Perhaps she has never had the temptation to be other than good?"

"Well, let's accept her for the good woman she is. I don't suppose Lottie will be any the worse for her discipline. I'll get the chessboard."

It was when we were in the middle of the game that the attack began. I hastened in to the dressing room and took out the bottle and gave him a dose with a shaking hand. His talk had unnerved me. I put the bottle on a table and made him lie down. The effect was miraculous. He opened his eyes and smiled on me and then I saw his gaze rest on the bottle.

"Try to sleep," I said. "I shall sit here until you do."

He was soon sleeping peacefully under the influence of the laudanum.

I picked up the bottle, and seeing that there was very little left, I decided that I would go straight over to Charles and get more.

We must not be without it.

I locked the bottle in the cupboard, put the key in the secret drawer and, putting on my riding habit, I went to the stable, saddled my horse and rode into town.

I was relieved to find Charles at home. He took me into his sitting room and I told him why I had come.

"I gave him a dose before I came out," I explained. "He is sleeping peacefully now."

"He will do so until morning."

He was looking at me intently. "You look worn out," he said.

I raised my eyes to his. The compassion and tenderness I saw there unnerved me. I turned away but he was beside me, gripping my shoulders, turning me round to face him.

"Oh, Zipporah . . ." he said; and I was lying against him and his arms were round me. He was kissing my hair.

"I can't bear it," I said. "It gets worse."

"It's inevitable."

"Is there nothing . . . nothing . . ."

"Only what we are doing. There is nothing wrong with him organically. Constitutionally he is strong."

"I don't think he can bear these violent attacks of pain."

"It's tragic. I would do anything . . . anything . . ."

"I know," I said. "I know."

"You know I love you."

I was silent. I did know it. I had known it for some time. Did he know that I loved him, too?

I stammered: "You have been so good."

"If there were only something I could do."

"You have sustained me with your care of him ... and for me. Oh, Charles, how long can it go on?"

He was silent.

Then he said: "I've told you at last. If only ... you were free ... If only ...

"Come and sit down. We are alone here, Zipporah. Mrs. Ellis is out."

I felt my heart beating fast. I was elated in a way and at the same time horribly depressed. To be loved by such a man, whom I admired above all others, could not help but bring me joy; and on the other hand Jean-Louis was uppermost in my mind, his dependence on me, his abiding devotion.

I said I should go. "Give me the medicine and I will leave."

"I want to talk to you first," he replied. "It is no use shutting our eyes to what is and cannot be denied. I love you and you love me. I believe that to be so."

"And if it is ... we must forget it."

"Forget it? You cannot push aside the truth and forget it."

"There is nothing we can do about it."

His hand closed over mine and gripped it tightly.

"We can be together," he said.

"And we shall know that the other is there, caring."

"Waiting," he said.

"Waiting."

"One day you and I will be together, Zipporah. It must be so."

I was silent. I couldn't bear it. It was talking of the time when Jean-Louis would no longer be there. It was like waiting for him to die ... hoping he would.

I said: "I could never be happy. If Jean-Louis ... died I would remember him forever and that I had not been true to him."

"These things pass," he said.

"Do they? Does one ever forget?"

"No, you're right. We can forget for periods at a time and then our guilty secrets raise their heads when we least expect

327

them and we are caught unawares to discover how vulnerable we are."

"I must go," I said. "Give me the laudanum and I will leave. It is better so."

He shook his head. "What harm is done by your staying awhile? Jean-Louis is sleeping. He would not know if you returned. Stay awhile with me, Zipporah."

He came toward me but I held him off. I was afraid of my emotions. I felt again that familiar desire which I had known with Gerard. It was there, I knew, ready to flare up and consume my resolutions. I knew that if I were not on guard all the time I should be swept away into the overwhelming need to slake my passion as I had done before.

There could not have been two men more unlike than Gerard and Charles and yet they both had this effect on me, this demanding, seering passion which I had never felt with Jean-Louis. Gerard had been so lighthearted, so ready to laugh, treating life as a joke. Charles was somber, weighed down by secrets, a man of deep passions when they were aroused, I was sure. Gerard's I fancied could be easily aroused but Charles would give long consideration to such matters and would not lightly fall in love.

I must be careful. I could not believe that I would be caught up in a whirlwind of passion while Jean-Louis lay ill — and yet thinking about it over the years I could feel the same irresistible impulses.

I was in love with Charles. I had been in love with Gerard. I loved Jean-Louis, too; I was weak, I realized that. So I must tread very carefully.

He said: "I want to talk to you. I have never felt for anyone before what I do for you. I had a wife once. You knew that, did you?"

I shook my head.

"I thought perhaps Isabel had told you."

"Isabel has talked of you a good deal . . . but she never really told me anything about you which I did not know."

"Zipporah, I want you to know about this part of my life.

328

Come and sit down. I've wanted to talk to you so often. I've wanted to tell you . . . to explain why these moods come upon me at times. I can never, never escape from my guilt. Whatever I do . . . it is there. I want you to know everything about me, Zipporah . . . I want to take you into those secret hiding places because I want you to know me for what I am. There must be no secrets between us."

I sat down beside him.

He went on: "It happened a long time ago . . . ten years to be exact. I was young and ambitious then . . . rather different from what I am now. Events change us more than time, perhaps. I was a doctor in fashionable London. My patients were among the rich; my reputation was growing, and then I met Dorinda. It was at the theater. She was a passionate theatergoer, and so was I. I was constantly at the Haymarket Theater and Drury Lane or Covent Garden. It was during a performance of *King Lear*, with Garrick magnificent in the leading role, that I was introduced to Dorinda.

"She was very beautiful—fair-haired, blue-eyed like an animated doll. She was high-spirited, full of vitality. I was completely enchanted. She enjoyed the company of actors and as I discovered later helped many of them financially. She had inherited a large fortune from her father, who had doted on her during his lifetime. Her mother had died soon after her birth.

"You can imagine what happened. I must have seemed something of an oddity to her. I was serious, the ambitious doctor; her life had been spent among stage people or those who never worked but were intent on the pursuit of pleasure.

"I could not understand why she accepted me, but she did. I think it was a sort of novelty. It was only after our marriage that I discovered my wife was one of the greatest heiresses in the country and her upbringing had made her highly unsuitable to be the wife of a doctor. She could not understand my desire to work. There was no need to work, she declared. She had never thought of money. It was something which was just there. As for work . . . My patients, she said, were all malingerers.

They fancied being ill for a while and thought it made them rather interesting. She found my absorption rather a bore.

"I realized within a month or so that I had made a great mistake. I used to go for long walks in the evenings into the poorer districts. That was when I went into Whitefriars. I told you about that. I had the feeling then that I wanted to get away from my work in fashionable London. I wanted to do something worthwhile.

"I tried to explain to Dorinda. She was skeptical. I had been noticing for some time strange things about her. And there came one night... I had been out looking after a poor woman... one of the servants of a wealthy family who had called me in. The woman was suffering from an incurable disease and I had been with her some time so that I was too late for the theater performance to which we had arranged to go.

"When Dorinda came back that evening she was in a bad mood and it was then that I had the first real glimpse of the violence in her nature. She abused me in a loud and hectoring manner. Then she threw a statuette at me. It missed and went into a mirror. I can still hear the sound of cracking glass as the splinters fell over the carpet. Then she picked up a paper knife and came at me. It was not a sharp weapon but there was murder in her eyes. She could have killed me. I was stronger than she was and managed to get the weapon away. She collapsed suddenly and I gave her a sedative.

"I was so disturbed that I went to a cousin of hers—her nearest relation—and he told me that I would have to take care. Her mother had had to be, as he said, 'put away.' There was madness in the family. Her grandmother had committed murder. There was a long tradition of insanity which seemed to be passed down through the women. They had hoped Dorinda had escaped because the violence had not begun to show in her until she came into her teens and then the attacks were not frequent. They had thought marriage would cure her.

"I said: 'Why did no one warn me?'

"The cousin was silent. I think they had wanted someone

to take the responsibility from them. Dorinda had a large fortune and I think they believed that that would be the compensation.

"You can imagine my feelings. I had already begun to know that my marriage was a great mistake. What I had felt for Dorinda was infatuation and I was not experienced enough to recognize it for what it was. And now to learn that I was married to a mad woman was the greatest blow imaginable.

"'You are a doctor,' the cousin had said. 'We had thought that marriage with you was the very best thing that could happen to Dorinda. We thought you would be able to treat her and she would be under your constant supervision.'

"I cannot tell you the terrible depression I suffered at that time. I saw myself as a prisoner bound to this woman . . . this mad woman . . . for the rest of my life. Then I was presented with the most fearful dilemma. Dorinda was going to have a child. I pondered this; I spent sleepless nights asking myself what I should do. If Dorinda bore a girl that baby would be tainted . . . doomed to madness if the pattern persisted as it had for generations.

"I was a doctor. I had it in my power to terminate Dorinda's pregnancy. I wrestled with myself. It was in a way taking a life, but surely that was better than allowing some maimed creature to come into the world. What was I to do? I had means at my disposal. I knew how. . . . The right dose of a certain medicine and the chances were that I could bring about a miscarriage.

"Well, I made the choice. I terminated the pregnancy . . . but I must have made a mistake for, at the same time, I terminated Dorinda's life.

"That's my story, Zipporah. I can never forget it. I could not let that child live. And yet . . . has anyone the right to take a life? I thought at the time I was doing what was best . . . what was right. I did not know that there would be complications . . . that Dorinda was not fit to bear children. . . . I tell myself that had the child been allowed to be born in the normal way its birth would very likely have killed Dorinda. I don't know. All I do know is that the child died, that Dorinda died and that there was a scandal concerning her death."

"Oh, Charles, how you must have suffered! But you did right. I am sure you did right."

"You see, she had this large fortune... and it came to me. It was well known that Dorinda and I were not on good terms. Everyone understood that. So many of them knew of Dorinda's strange behavior. There was sympathy for me ... oh yes, I had that ... but the smear was there. Dorinda was dead. I was a widower... a very rich widower whose worldly possessions were far greater than that of the needy bachelor who had married Dorinda."

We were silent for a while. I was seeing so clearly the people who would whisper about him; the horrible suspicion that surrounded him and most terrible of all the fact that he had brought about Dorinda's death.

"My close friends knew that I had never been greatly interested in money, that the fact of Dorinda's wealth had been a surprise to me. But that did not stop the whispers. There might have been an inquiry but her cousin did not want that. He was naturally anxious that the fact that there was madness in the family should not be brought into the open. He managed as much as anyone to hush up the matter. But you can imagine how it was with me. There were times when I would rather they had investigated. I would have been ready to admit that I had attempted to kill the unborn child rather than condemn it to its inevitable inheritance. I did not know that Dorinda was not fit to bear a child. I was ready to stake my defense on that and the almost certainty that had the child grown to its full size she would have died in giving normal birth to it. So I left London.... And the money came to me and with it, as you know, I built and maintained my hospital."

"I understand and I am glad you told me. I think you blame yourself too much. What you did may well have been right. You had to make a decision and you took that one."

"I took a life," he said, "two lives."

"But if it is better that a child should never be born..."

"Who is to be the judge of that?"

"Surely there are times when we have to make these decisions."

"I am sorry for anyone who does. Life is sacred. It is not for us to decide whether or not to destroy it."

"But we destroy flies, rats . . . vermin that carry disease. That is life surely."

"I am thinking of human life."

I said: "I am unsure. *I* think you did right. You acted out of no desire for personal gain. You did not know Dorinda would die. Your thought was to prevent a baby being born who was almost certainly doomed to madness. You were right."

"It is murder."

"The law commits murder . . . on people whom it says are a menace to the community. Yours was the same sort of killing. You must see that."

"I never shall. All I can do is try to expiate my sin and . . . forget."

"How many lives have you saved in your hospital?"

He smiled tenderly at me. "You are trying to comfort me. I knew I should find comfort with you. You are in my thoughts all the time. I believe that one day . . ."

I shook my head. "Don't talk of it," I said. "I cannot betray Jean-Louis . . . twice."

Then I told him of that period when I was Gerard's mistress and how ever after I had been unable to forget.

It was his turn to comfort me. He was not shocked as I feared he might be. He said: "It was natural. You are a warm-blooded woman. Do you think I don't know that? You need fulfillment of your emotions. . . . For a time you achieved that."

"I deceived my husband."

"And you loved him all the more because of it. You were more tender, patient. Nobody could have been a better nurse to Jean-Louis. He knows it and is grateful."

I said: "You are trying to comfort me. You do not know that Lottie is not Jean-Louis's child."

"Are you sure?"

"As sure as a woman can be. Jean-Louis is incapable of begetting children. As soon as Gerard and I were together . . . it happened. I could never bear Jean-Louis to know. . . . He adores Lottie. He is so proud of her. He wanted children always."

Charles took my hands and kissed them.

"We are a pair of sinners weighed down with guilt. Is that what makes us attractive to each other? What you did has in fact brought happiness to Jean-Louis."

"I am sure your action was right. But I know mine was wrong. 'Thou shalt not commit adultery.' How many times did I write that out in the schoolroom? The Ten Commandments. I had no idea what it meant. To me it was just number seven in those days."

"And thou shalt do no murder."

"It wasn't murder, Charles. You must stop saying that."

"How wonderful it would be if we could put the past behind us."

"Do you think we shall ever do that?"

"Yes," he said. "I will teach you how to . . . and you will teach me. We need each other, Zipporah, and one day we are going to be together."

Then he held me fast in his arms and I clung to him.

We heard a step in the hall. The housekeeper had returned.

I suppose it was inevitable. I think we both knew it. I fought against it until our resistance crumbled. Our need was too great and we both desperately wanted to be happy even for a brief moment. We wanted to escape together to that bliss which we knew we could give each other.

It was a matter of waiting for the opportunity and I knew it would come.

The housekeeper had gone to visit her sister and was to be away the entire day. He did not tell me this. The fact was that she paid these regualr visits about once every two weeks so it was certain to happen that on one of her days of absence I should call to have my bottle replenished.

The house was silent. I knew as soon as I entered that we were alone.

There was an air of excitement about him—almost gaiety. It seemed as though he had cast away his cares. I found that I was doing the same.

In the world beyond this house I had my duties, my unsatisfactory life to lead, my fears, my sadness, my terrible pity when I sat beside my husband's bed . . . but here in this small house, in those rooms over those in which he saw his patients, I could be happy.

He said: "Zipporah . . . we can't go on holding back what must be."

I shook my head: "I must go home," I said.

But he took off my cape and held me against him.

He said: "Surely we can have this."

I said again: "I must go." But there was no conviction in my voice.

I allowed myself to be led upstairs. I allowed myself to be disrobed not only of my clothes but of my honor. I shared with my lover that burning desire; again I knew the feeling that everything else must be forgotten, shut away to satisfy this need.

I was a deeply passionate woman; Charles was a deeply passionate man. We loved each other. I tell myself that what happened was inevitable.

And for the second time I became an adulteress.

Afterward we lay side by side on his bed and my thoughts went back over the years so that I could almost hear the sounds of the fair.

Gerard had been lighthearted, reaching out for pleasure. Charles was different. He was so serious. He would never have come to this if he had not cared deeply for me. He was serious-minded. This was not a lighthearted moment of joy. Was that what it had been with Gerard? This was solemn, binding. Charles and I were, apart from according to law, man and wife.

I felt that and so did he, I know.

"One day," he said, "all will be well. Won't it, Zipporah?"

It was in a way a promise...a bond. We did not want to mention Jean-Louis for only his death could make our marriage possible. But as we lay together we were as one and we knew that what had passed between us had bound us together for as long as we should live.

Now that we had become lovers our passionate need for each other had been sparked into a mighty conflagration. We no longer waited for opportunities: we made them. There were the days when the housekeeper visited her sister. But there were other occasions besides. We met sometimes in woods not too near the houses and we would lie together in secluded spots and talk endlessly and sometimes make love.

Charles had changed. There was a hopefulness about him which I felt must be noticeable. The gloom had lifted. He was like another man. I wondered if I had changed also.

Sometimes I noticed Isabel watching me covertly.

She said: "You're looking better, Zipporah. I'm so glad. You began to look quite seedy."

"I'm getting used to things," I answered. I hope there wasn't a lilt in my voice. I couldn't help it. I knew I was wrong, but I was so happy at times. At others I would sit by Jean-Louis's bed and then a terrible sense of guilt would weigh me down. Once he opened his eyes and I found him regarding me steadily.

"You're so good to me, Zipporah," he said. "You're so patient always. I'm afraid I get irritable. I'm always waiting for the pain. It's like a monster waiting to leap on me. Then I see you...and I feel I'm so lucky to have you."

"Oh, don't...don't," I cried. And I was near to breaking down. "What I do for you I want to do. I want to be with you...to make you happy."

Then he closed his eyes, smiling, and I thought: Insincere woman, wicked Zipporah, adulteress!

Once when Charles and I were returning from the woods we met Evalina. She came upon us suddenly as we were brushing the leaves from our clothes. I trembled to think that she might have come a little sooner. She looked plump and contented.

She hailed us. "There'll be lots of blackberries later on," she said. "Look at these bushes."

We looked.

"Taking a stroll in the woods?" she said. "So was I. Beautiful this time of the year, aren't they?"

Was her gaze a little malicious? I told myself she had changed but she was still Evalina.

"And how is your husband?" she asked.

Was there a certain emphasis in her words?

I said he was as well as we could hope. If he had four days free from pain that was very good.

She nodded; then she smiled suddenly. "Nice for you to be able to get out a bit. We all need it. I'm expecting again. Well, not for some time . . . but it's so."

"Congratulations," I said.

"Well, good day to you . . . doctor . . . Mistress Ransome."

"What's wrong?" said Charles when she had gone.

"I think she was spying on us."

"No, she was just walking."

"I remember her when she was at Eversleigh with her mother."

"She's changed now. She's become the lady of the house. She is a good mother to her little boy and she and Trent seem made for each other."

"But she saw us together."

"Why shouldn't we walk in the woods?"

"I suppose I feel guilty."

"Dearest Zipporah, please don't. You've made me so happy."

"I'm glad," I said. "I'm being foolish. I'm trying hard to forget what I've done. I want to be happy. Do you know, I think that the only way I can live through all this is by being happy for a time. It's like the laudanum . . . it gives me respite and then I can go on and fight."

He gripped my hand. He understood.

Lottie had come back from Clavering in high spirits. She

had had a wonderful holiday and chattered to Jean-Louis about Sabrina, Clarissa and Dickon. He liked to hear her and I was sure he was better for her presence.

I tried to prevent her—and so did he—seeing the pain. I felt she was too young to be disturbed, as she undoubtedly would have been.

It was a great joy to have her back. She was running about making sure that her dog and horse were all right. She must go over to see Hetty Fenton and the children. She had brought jars of my mother's jams and preserves for Hetty and little gifts for the children—a chocolate mouse and ball and skittles.

She played with them, and was always welcome, I knew, at Hetty's house.

Miss Carter seemed primmer than usual.

"Miss Carter is so good because she believes that if she's not she'll burn forever," Lottie told me.

"Poor Miss Carter," I said.

"Why poor Miss Carter? She'll go straight to heaven. It's the rest of us who she thinks are going to burn in hell."

"My dear Lottie," I said. "I am sure none of us is going to burn in hell."

"Not even the wicked ones? Miss Carter says that's God's words."

"I'm sure it's her way of interpreting it. If you repent you'll be forgiven. That's in the Bible, too."

"Sometimes I think Miss Carter would be disappointed if people didn't burn."

"Look here," I said, "you stop worrying about it. You be good and kind and thoughtful . . . which you are most of the time . . . and you'll be safe from the fires of hell."

She laughed with me, but I did wonder whether Miss Carter was too fanatical to have the care of a young girl.

I should have liked to talk to Jean-Louis about it but of course I could not worry him with such matters. I had to confess that when I was with Charles there were so many other matters with which to occupy ourselves. I did discuss it with Isabel, who thought that it was probably good for Lottie to think about the way she was acting.

Hester came over often to help me. I became very fond of her; she was a gentle person and I think that perhaps because of her experiences I felt at ease with her.

One day I was preparing to go to see Charles on the pretext of getting more laudanum and when I went to the cupboard I found that there was a new bottle there.

"I thought I'd save you the trouble of going into town," said Hetty. "I knew where you kept the key and I noticed last time you used it that you would soon be wanting more."

I felt deflated. I wondered what Charles had thought when expecting me he had seen Hetty. I could not go in after that. I was very disappointed and felt angry with Hetty. Poor girl, it wasn't her fault.

She was with me on one occasion when I had to give Jean-Louis a dose of laudanum. She saw my anguish and I knew she was very touched.

We sat in the dressing room talking in whispers after he had fallen into that deep unnatural sleep which was his only way to get relief.

"Life is so sad sometimes," she said. "To think that this could have happened. I remember Jean-Louis when I came back to my family. He was so different then. Everything was different then."

I said: "But you're happy now."

She hesitated. "I never forget," she said.

"But you must. It's all behind you."

"Everything that happens is there forever . . . in your memory. Everything makes its mark on your life. Things happen because something else has happened. I shall never forget."

"But it turned out well for you. You have James and the children."

"Yes . . . but the memory is there. It still haunts me. Sometimes . . . I wonder . . ."

I did not prompt her and she went on with a rush: "I wonder whether . . . I really wanted that to happen."

"What do you mean?" I said.

She said, and there was a faraway look in her eyes so that I knew she was there at Clavering on the night of the party: "I went into the garden with him . . . I think of him sometimes."

"Dickon!" I said. "He is evil. He causes disaster wherever he goes . . . and yet he saved my life. I must not forget that."

"Yes . . . you see. Nothing is all black or all white. Nothing is entirely good or evil. . . . I sometimes wonder if I was not under some spell. . . . Whether he didn't fascinate me in some way. I hated him. Yes, I hated him. I nearly died of shame and yet . . . and yet . . ."

I said briskly: "I should dismiss him from your mind."

"I do . . . for long periods . . . and then sometimes I dream . . . and I ask myself how much of what one believes happened really did . . . and whether one interprets it the way one wants it."

"You're getting too introspective, Hetty. It's much better to live life simply."

Live life simply! What a hypocrite I was! I wondered what Hetty would say if she knew that I was having a love affair with the doctor.

What if she did know? What if we failed to disguise it? I knew the way in which Charles sometimes looked at me . . . even in company. I saw it in his eyes. Did others? Had her trip to his house to get the laudanum been to prevent my going?

When one is as guilty as I was one suspects everything. First Evalina because we met her in the woods . . . and now Hetty.

The weeks slipped by . . . one very like the last. Nothing changed. Jean-Louis's pain was perhaps a little more frequent—the periods of respite fewer and less far between. And Charles and I deeper and deeper in our torrid love, with each passing week demanding more of each other, unable to keep apart, contriving meetings, loving, loving madly, hopelessly.

The summer passed and it was autumn.

There were letters from Clavering.

They longed to see me but they would not make the journey

to Eversleigh because they knew how ill Jean-Louis was. But let Lottie come again with that nice governess of hers. It wasn't good for the child to spend Christmas in a house where there was sickness.

So Lottie and Miss Carter left for Clavering and Christmas passed for us at Eversleigh quietly. Hetty and James came with Isabel, Derek and Charles and we were all together on Christmas day. Jean-Louis was not well enough to be brought down but we spent a lot of time in his room and I was thankful that he felt no pain on that day.

Evalina sent messages. She was near her time and unable to come herself; but Jack Trent came over and brought little Richard with him. He was a bright boy and amused us with his chatter.

It seemed to me that he had a look of Dickon already and the thought depressed me.

So we passed into a new year.

The weather turned cold and it was hard to keep the rooms warm. Old houses were notoriously draughty and Eversleigh was no exception. Beautiful as the high-vaulted ceilings were they meant that the rooms needed great fires and even then much of the heat they provided was lost.

The cold was not good for Jean-Louis. One afternoon in February I sat with him. He had had a bad night and I had slightly increased his dose because the normal one seemed ineffective.

He talked to me in a low voice. He was so exhausted.

"Sleep," he said. "It came at last. What a relief sleep is. 'Nature's soft nurse,' Shakespeare called it. What an apt phrase."

"Rest," I said, "don't talk."

"I feel at peace now," he said. "You sitting there with the firelight playing on your face. I'd like to stay like this forever, Zipporah beside me . . . and no pain . . . just nothing . . . Sometimes I wonder . . ."

I did not speak and he closed his eyes. Then he said suddenly:

"You keep the key in that secret drawer of yours, don't you?"

I was startled and did not answer immediately.

I heard him laugh softly. "You do. . . . You always liked that little desk and you liked it because of the secret drawer."

"Who told you that was where I kept the key?"

"Dearest Zipporah . . . am I a child not to be told these things? Even a child can reason. It's the obvious place."

"The doctor said: 'Put the key in a safe place which you know and no one else does. . . . You must be the only one who gives him the doses.'"

"Doctors think of their patients as children, don't they? The key is in the secret drawer. Sometimes I think it would be better if I drank enough of the stuff to let me slip quietly away."

"Please don't talk like that, Jean-Louis."

"Just this once and then I'll say no more of it. Wouldn't it be better . . . Zipporah? Be honest, wouldn't it?"

"No . . . no!"

"All right. I won't talk of it. Zipporah, you ought to be happy. Not sitting here with an invalid."

"I am happy. You are my husband, Jean-Louis. We . . . belong together. I want to be with you. Don't you understand that?"

"Oh, my dearest . . . you are so good to me."

"You excite yourself. You should rest."

He closed his eyes. There was a peaceful smile on his lips.

I prayed that he might rest peacefully that night. That the demons of pain might be kept at bay.

I could not sleep. I lay in my single bed in the dressing room and listened. He was quiet. He must be sleeping peacefully.

I thought of all he had said to me, of his tenderness and his trust; and I saw myself as a worthless woman, an adulteress who should be branded as they used to brand them, I believe, in the old days, with an A on their foreheads. He loved me absolutely and I was unworthy of his love. At times I wanted to give up everything to look after him; I did look after him, none could have nursed him better. But at the same time I was creeping off, when I could, to the bed of another man.

Life was so complicated. People were complicated. Nothing was plain black, plain white. I was kind to him; I was tender; I was never irritable. I smiled all the time; I soothed him. I had to because that was some balm to my conscience.

And as I lay there I heard movement in the room. Slowly, laboriously, Jean-Louis was getting out of bed. Had the pain started? No. It could not be. He could not get up and walk if it were so.

There was silence and then I heard the movement again. I heard the faint tapping of a stick.

Jean-Louis was coming toward the dressing room.

I lay very still. Something urged me to. Something kept saying to me: "It's for the best . . . for him . . . for you . . . for Charles . . . for everybody."

Before Jean-Louis entered the dressing room, I knew.

I lay still. He was there now . . . walking cautiously, feeling his way in the light from the stars which came through the dressing room's small window.

He was at the desk now. He had found the secret drawer. He had the key. He opened the cupboard door.

I knew what he had taken.

I must get up. Take it from him. Tell him he must not do this thing.

I thought of his poor face distorted with pain and the years ahead when there was nothing for him but more pain. How could he endure that? Wasn't this better?

I heard him go back to his room. I lay still with a thudding heart which shook the bed.

I lay . . . waiting. . . .

No sound. Only the faint starlight in the room to show me the unshut door of the cupboard which told me it had really happened.

I listened. I could hear his stertorous breathing.

I rose from my bed and went into the next room.

There was no sound now.

I lighted two candles with an unsteady hand and carried one to the bed.

He seemed to be smiling at me. A happy smile ... the lines of pain were no longer visible. He looked as young as he had when I had married him.

Dear Jean-Louis, he had made the supreme sacrifice.

Blackmail

*I don't know how long I stood there looking down at him. I
felt numb and a terrible sorrow swept over me.*

Tenderness welled up in me for his kindness, his sweetness
and all his goodness to me. And how had I repaid him?

I sank to my knees and buried my face against the bedclothes. Pictures kept coming and going in my mind. I saw
him as a boy when he had let me go with him, when we played
our games; and later when we had loved and married and
everything had seemed right — until I met Gerard and realized
that I had never known passion and erotic love and that I was
of a nature to find them irresistible.

I don't know how long I stayed there but when I arose from
my knees, stiff and cold, I saw that it was nearly four o'clock.

I took his hand. It was very cold; and the peaceful smile
was still on his lips.

I must call Charles. Though there was nothing he could do
for Jean-Louis now.

Somehow I could not take any action. I felt that I wanted

to be alone with Jean-Louis for the last time. I wished there was some way of letting him know how much I had appreciated him. I fervently hoped that he had never had an inkling of my infidelity. Then a terrible fear came to me that he might have known. Had I changed when I came back after that visit to Eversleigh and I did have a child . . . the child which he could not give me? Did he suspect that Charles and I were more than friends?

Dear Jean-Louis! One thing I did know was that if some instinct had told him the truth he would understand.

I kept my vigil by his bedside until six o'clock. Then I went to the bell rope and pulled it. The clanging rang through the house. They would guess that I needed help with Jean-Louis.

The first person to arrive was Miss Carter. She looked pale and different from usual with two plaits hanging over her shoulders tied at the ends with a piece of pink wool.

I said: "My husband died in the night. . . ."

She looked at Jean-Louis and turned pale. She closed her eyes and her lips moved as though she was praying.

She said: "I will go and get help."

"I think," I said, "that someone should go at once for the doctor."

She ran away and I noticed then the laudanum bottle which Jean-Louis had left on the table. I took it and locked it in the dressing room cupboard.

It was a great relief to see Charles.

He came hurrying into the room, and taking one look at Jean-Louis, went swiftly to the bed. He stood looking down at him. Then he took his hand and touched his eyelids, drawing them down over his eyes.

"He's been dead for some time," he said.

"Yes," I answered.

Charles bent over and put his face close to the dead one.

"Charles," I said, "he did it. He took the bottle from the cupboard."

"I thought . . ."

"Yes. I had the key in the secret drawer . . . but he knew it was there. It was the obvious place to put it . . . and he knew about the drawer in that desk. He came and got the key and the bottle. . . . He had talked to me about it just before. He had said it was the best way. I told him not to talk like that . . . but he must have had it in his mind to do it."

"Where is the bottle?"

"I put it back in the cupboard."

"Go and get it."

I did so. He looked at it. "When did you get this? Two days ago? My God, he's had enough to kill three people."

"It was what he wanted. He couldn't endure the pain anymore."

"Zipporah," he said quietly, "there mustn't be talk about this. In view of everything . . . we can't have it said that he died of an overdose of laudanum. . . . People might say . . ."

"That I gave it to him?"

"People will say anything."

"Charles . . . you don't think . . . ?"

"Of course not. I understand how it happened."

"In a way I did kill him," I said. "I knew he was going to do it . . . and I let him. That's as bad as killing, isn't it? I'm a murderess . . . as well as an adulteress."

"Hush. Don't say such things." He looked round him. "For God's sake be careful. It may be that . . . never mind. The thing is now that Jean-Louis is dead. Life was intolerable for him. He suffered a great deal of pain and naturally it weakened his heart. He died of heart failure. It was to be expected. I expected it."

I wanted him to put his arms about me, to reassure me.

He looked at me sadly and said quietly: "We shall have to be very careful . . . for a while."

Jean-Louis was buried in the Eversleigh mausoleum. There were many to mourn him for he had been very much liked.

"Poor gentleman," said the tenants, "he suffered enough, God knows. It can only be a happy release."

A happy release. That was the way to look at it.

I saw little of Charles. There was no excuse now for me to go to the house to collect the medicine. I did see him at Enderby and we had snatched conversations. There had been no love-making. It seemed that we had lost our taste for it.

We met in the woods a little distance from the houses.

Then he was as tender as ever. "We'll be married," he said. "It's what I've always longed for. But we shall have to wait a year . . . and just at present it should not be known that we are meeting."

I was concerned about Lottie. She mourned Jean-Louis deeply. It was strange to see her subdued. Hetty said that she hardly ever went to see the children now. I spoke to Isabel about her and she said: "She needs a new interest. Why don't you let her give a hand in the hospital? I am sure they could do with auxiliary helpers. Charles says they are always short of staff. It's nothing much they can do . . . but they can make beds and take the food round and things like that. If you'd like me to speak to Charles . . ."

I said I would and as a result both Lottie and Miss Carter went off every other day to work in the hospital.

I think it did Lottie good because she seemed to take interest in the work and was now talking a great deal about the mothers and their babies.

Letters came from Clavering. As soon as the weather al-lowed it they would come over and now that poor Jean-Louis was gone there was nothing to keep me from coming to them . . . often. I must pay a visit with Lottie. They longed to see me. But first they would come over to us.

There were always letters for Lottie which she would seize on with delight. She would take them to her room and emerge starry-eyed.

She was still young enough, I thought, to enjoy getting letters but she was growing up fast. She was mature for her age and it was touching to see her breaking out into woman-hood.

I felt as though I were in limbo. The days seemed long. I

filled them with trivial tasks and I kept telling myself: *This must pass*.

In a year's time I was to marry Charles. He had said that we had to try to forget everything that had gone before . . . and that applied to both of us. We had to start a new life. Once we were together we must never look back.

It was the end of March, a stormy day with rain clouds being harried across the sky by a blustering southwest wind.

I was in the hall when Lottie came in with Madeleine Carter. They had ridden home from the hospital and were soaked to the skin.

"Now you must get those wet things off right away," I said.

"All right," said Lottie. "Don't fuss, mama. All in good time."

"Good time is now," I said. "Come on."

I went with her into her room and while she was peeling off her riding skirt I got out fresh things from the drawers of her cupboard.

She stood before me without her bodice and hanging round her neck was a gold chain. I knew the chain well. I had given it to her myself but attached to it was a ring.

I looked at it in amazement.

A ring! And such a ring! It was a square-cut sapphire surrounded by diamonds.

I took it in my hand and looked at it.

She flushed a little. Then she said: "I'm betrothed. That's my betrothal ring."

"Betrothed! At your age!"

"I get older every day. I'm going to be married on the day I'm sixteen."

"Lottie! What do you mean? Who . . . ?"

"It's beautiful, isn't it?" she said. "We went to London and chose it together."

"Who?" I said. "Who . . . ?"

She looked at me roguishly. "You're going to be surprised."

"Tell me," I said.

"Dickon."

"Dickon!" I felt as though the room was spinning round me. You don't mean . . . ?"

"I knew you'd be surprised. He said not to tell you . . . yet. So I wore the ring round my neck instead of on my finger."

"Dickon!" I said again. "But it's nonsense . . . it's absurd."

"Why?" she asked sharply.

"He's old . . ."

"He's not old. I don't like young boys in any case. Dickon is forever young . . . and he's not old really. He's about eleven years older than I am. That's nothing."

I said: "You must send that ring back."

"I shall not."

"You must stop this nonsense."

"Why are other people's love affairs nonsense . . . ?"

"You don't understand."

"I do. You think I'm a baby. You want me to stay a little girl forever because it makes you feel young. Mothers are like that."

"Oh no . . . no, Lottie," I said. "Anyone else . . . but not Dickon."

"Why don't you like him? Everybody else does. Grandmother and Aunt Sabrina thought it was wonderful. They said I was the luckiest girl. We had a party to celebrate . . . just among ourselves . . . for now. Dear mama, don't quarrel. It has to be, you know. People have to marry. It won't make any difference to us . . . you and me . . . we'll always be the same."

I couldn't speak. I was so horrified.

She changed into her dry clothes and, taking the ring from the chain, put it on her finger.

"There's no need for it to be a secret now," she said.

I couldn't talk to her anymore. I put my arms round her and held her against me. She thought that was acceptance of her engagement.

Then I left her and went to my room.

I wrote to Dickon.

"This has to stop. I shall never give my consent to a marriage between you and Lottie. I know how unhappy you will make her. I realize your motives. You wanted Eversleigh and see this as a way of getting it. I will never consent to this marriage and if Lottie married without my consent she should never inherit Eversleigh. I want you to stop this nonsense immediately. Zipporah."

I sent a messenger off at once and tried hard to grapple with this new problem.

A week had scarcely passed when he came to Eversleigh. I was glad that I saw him first. I was in the hall when he burst in, having left his horse in the stables.

"You look surprised," he said smiling blandly. "I thought I detected a certain urgency in your note."

"You have come to see me?"

"You and my adorable Lottie, of course. But you first. I have something to say to you. I don't think either of us want delay. Shall we go somewhere where we can be alone?"

"Come to my sitting room," I said. "Come quietly. I don't want anyone to know you are here yet."

"You mean . . . Lottie?"

"I mean anyone."

He seemed to dominate my sitting room as he did every room. He sat down on a chair, crossed his well-shaped legs, flicked a speck of dust from his fine hose and regarded me with a kind of tolerant amusement.

I said I was shocked to discover what had been going on.

"You are too easily shocked, Zipporah . . . for a woman of the world."

I hated the veiled suggestion in the words.

I said: "Understand. There is no betrothal between you and Lottie."

"Oh, but there is! We have plighted our troth, as they say, and we have sworn that nothing . . . just nothing . . . shall stand in the way of our marriage."

"*I* shall stand in the way."

"I don't think you will, Zipporah. You are a very sensible woman. I have always thought that. I have admired you, you know. At first you gave the impression of being a little dull . . . but we know different from that. You are a woman who has lived dangerously. Oh yes, I have always had a great admiration for you, Zipporah."

"Spare the praises. I can't reciprocate."

"You are rather ungrateful, aren't you? Have you forgotten how once I saved your life?"

"You seem unable to forget it. And I am sure you had a reason for doing it other than saving me."

"Well, I was fond of you . . . and there was Eversleigh. You had to inherit it. Who knew who that crazy old Uncle Carl might have left it to, failing you!"

"You are quite cynical."

"I'm truthful. In your upright moments you surely believe in truth."

"Dickon," I said, "stop bantering. I want you to tell Lottie that you couldn't possibly be serious because she is only a child. Tell her gently. Imply it was only a game. I don't want her hurt."

"It's not a game. True, she is young yet. I have five . . . possibly six years' courting to do. That's all to the good. Look at you and Jean-Louis. I wonder if you would have married him if you had not been brought up with the idea that it was expected. That's how I intend it to be with Lottie. I shall charm her more and more with the years and when she is sixteen she will realize that she cannot do without me."

"It's Eversleigh you want. You believe she will inherit it."

"Of course."

"If Lottie married you she would not have Eversleigh."

"I think she would. Oh, you mean you will marry your doctor and you're not too old to produce a child. You could manage it . . . a forceful woman like you. Is that the idea?"

"No," I said. "It is not."

"Listen, Zipporah, you are going to give your blessing to our courtship. You have no alternative. In the first place there is your reputation to think of. Then, perhaps even more important . . . there is the doctor's."

"Will you stop talking nonsense and talk sense."

"This is sense, plain, hard, unvarnished common sense. Let me recapitulate a little. In the first place I know of your little flutter with the Frenchman. What is Lottie going to say when she knows that her father was not Jean-Louis but an unknown... gentleman. Very charming... very attractive, I grant you. But our dear little Lottie was begotten in sin, was she not? Owing to the adultery of her mother..."

"Be silent."

"All right," he said. "You wouldn't want it known, I know. You managed it all very well. I admired you for that, Zipporah. But I knew all about it. I have always been observant and made use of that. I have my spies posted in convenient places."

I thought: *Evalina, of course!* She must have seen him climbing into my room... perhaps she saw his leaving. But she knew and she passed the information on to where it could do me most harm.

"Nor is that all. You are deep, dear Zipporah. Why, you are a sinner such as I am. My heart goes out to you. You are not the sort of woman to accept meekly what fate deals out. You make life your own way. Now that is something I greatly admire. But we have to pay for our little adventures, don't we? I know about you and the doctor, Zipporah. You would like that to be nice and respectable now. It is best with the medical profession... particularly when there have been unpleasant rumors in the past. Oh yes, I made it my business to learn about your doctor and his mad wife.... He was lucky to get through that. But he is another like us. He does not let life take charge of him. He's a very worthy fellow... running a hospital for fallen women and the like... a philanthropist, no less. And then he falls in love. Poor Jean-Louis is in the way, but Jean-Louis is very sick. He needs the doctor's ministrations, and one day he dies. Poor Jean-Louis! He died of heart failure, says the doctor. Now I have a strong suspicion that he died of an overdose of laudanum."

I had turned very pale. He looked so evil standing there smiling at me.

"This is a ridiculous conjecture," I stammered.

"Well, I daresay it could be proved, could it not? I think they can tell these things. They're very clever, you know."

"Do you mean to say you . . . you . . . would . . . ?"

"I am a very determined man, Zipporah. I want to marry Lottie and I want Eversleigh. It's true that you could stand in my way. All I am doing is point out to you the foolhardiness of doing so."

"It's blackmail," I said.

"It's getting what I want. I intend always to do that, Zipporah."

I turned away, too sick at heart, too frightened to speak.

Jean-Louis had killed himself—but I had not stood in his way. It was what he had wanted. Should I have stopped him? And if I had then would he not have tried again? I could have put the key somewhere else.

No, I thought, a person in Jean-Louis's position should have the right to decide. Months, perhaps years of pain stretched out ahead of him and he had decided to end his life.

Because that meant giving me a glimpse of future happiness had I been to blame?

There were times when I called myself murderess as well as adulteress.

And there was Dickon smiling that cold insolent smile . . . putting all his cards on the table . . . his aces, which he would play with relish and ruin us . . . most of all Charles.

Charles could not afford to be involved in further scandal. It would finish his career as a doctor.

And I . . . how could I prove that Jean-Louis had taken the extra dose himself?

Dickon stood up and put his hand on my arm.

"Think about it, Zipporah," he said. "I'd be a good son-in-law. You'd be surprised how good. I've always been fond of you. . . . You mustn't stand in our way, though . . . and now I shall go and break the good news to Lottie that I am here."

* * *

I did not know how to act. I could not bear to tell Charles what had happened. I did not know what action he would take. I felt he might say, "Let him do his worst. Let us tell Lottie everything and let her decide what sort of man this is she plans to marry."

Lottie was a child. I could not believe that her feelings were very deeply involved as yet. But what could I do?

An idea came to me. Suppose she went right away . . . suppose she saw an entirely new world? Would such a prospect be attractive enough to take her away from Dickon?

It was a chance. It was something I had wanted to do for a long time.

In fact ever since I had thought of marrying Charles I had wanted to do this.

I went to the little ebony box which I always kept locked. I opened it and took out a small piece of paper.

Written on it were the words Gerard d'Aubigné, Chateau d'Aubigné, Eure, France.

I held it in my hands for a long time and I seemed to see his face smiling at me.

Would he remember? I was sure he would. He had sworn he would never forget but perhaps such vows came easily to men like him.

This was a flimsy straw. It was all I had. I clung to it. I picked up a pen and started to write, and as I did so . . . it all came back . . . the first meeting on the haunted patch, the head-long rush to passion.

"There was a child," I wrote. "A daughter . . . a delightful girl. She is in some danger now. . . . If you would invite her to your château, I would perhaps get her to come to see you. I am sure she would wish to see her father. . . ."

I sealed the letter.

Old Jethro's grandson was a good boy, an adventurous boy. I could trust him, I was sure.

I sent for him and told him that I wanted him to leave as soon as he could for France. It was a secret mission so he was not to tell anyone where he was going.

He was to hand this letter to a certain Gerard d'Aubigné and to no one else. If he could not find him or learned that he was out of France or dead, he was to come straight back to me with the letter.

Jethro's grandson's eyes sparkled at the prospect of carrying out the mission. As I said, he was a boy who dreamed of great adventures.

He was here in the house. Dickon the destroyer.

I hated him, because I could see that he held our destinies in his hands. Whichever way I turned I knew that we could not stand out against him.

I could for myself. I would defy him. But what of Charles? Suppose they discovered that Jean-Louis had died from an excess of the drug? Charles had said he had died of heart failure. He would be ruined. Old scandals would be revived. It would be remembered that he had prescribed that which killed his wife and child.

As for myself . . . I would stand exposed, adulteress and perhaps murderess. I would face all that to save Lottie . . . but should I save her? I could not do this to Charles.

I had to see him.

I rode into town and was relieved to find him there.

He listened in shocked silence to what I had to tell him.

"That fiend knows everything," he said.

"He admits to having his spies. Someone must have seen us together . . . and told him. Evalina! You remember that day in the woods. It might even have been Hetty. She was under his spell in a way, I believe. . . . One can never be sure with Dickon. He has a sort of evil power. Lottie's life will be ruined if she marries him. All he wants is Eversleigh. She would never understand his ways. He would break her heart. Charles, what can we do?"

He said: "We can stand up and face everything."

"They will say we killed Jean-Louis. We shall never be able to explain. Your career will be at an end. You will never be allowed to practice again."

"It would be the end . . . for both of us, Zipporah," he said. "Murder . . . yes, they would say it was murder."

"I could have stopped him," I said. "I will take the blame. It is mine. I should have stopped him."

"You knew how he suffered."

"But I let him do that. I knew what he was doing . . . and I let him."

"Because you knew it was his wish."

"Oh, Charles, what are we to do?"

"I don't know. We have to think. We must not act rashly."

"I have done something, Charles. I have written to Lottie's father. I have asked him to invite her there to see him. When I hear from him I shall send her to him. That will take her away . . . for a while. New impressions . . . I was thinking . . ."

"It might help. Who can say? In the meantime . . ."

"Yes," I said, "in the meantime . . ."

"We can only wait."

He kissed me tenderly.

"Perhaps it will come right in the end. Do you think it will, Zipporah?"

"Yes," I said, "if we let it . . . perhaps it will. We shall have to forget so much."

I saw his tortured face, then he said: "I don't think I ever could be at peace remembering. You see, Dorinda so much wanted to live. Jean-Louis wanted to die."

Then he held me against him. We clung together. We were both afraid to look too far ahead.

I rode slowly back to the house. It was deserted. There seemed to be an unnatural quiet everywhere. I went to my room and as I glanced out of the window I saw that there was a strange glow in the sky.

I ran toward it.

Fire. In the distance. I saw the billowing smoke and the flames shooting up.

I wondered where it could be.

I went downstairs. I saw one of the older women servants in the hall.

I said: "There's a fire somewhere."

"Yes," she said. "It's the hospital. They'm all gone over to lend a hand."

I ran out into the stables.

Within a short while I was riding hard for the hospital.

The Decision

I could not believe that this dreadful thing had happened. It had come so suddenly, so unexpectedly, shattering our lives.

Charles had died a hero's death. He had died rescuing women and children from his hospital. He had saved several lives and that would be the greatest compensation to him. I could only hope that he was happy now.

The Forsters took me back to Enderby. We mourned together. Everything forgotten but our loss. I think they had known how it was with Charles and me and they were pleased because I had brought some happiness into his life.

The mothers and children who had been rescued that night were taken to another hospital some miles away, for Charles's building was a complete wreck.

Life was ironical, for the hero of the hour was Dickon. He had mustered a fire-fighting force and had several times plunged into the inferno and rescued women and children. His heroic deeds were talked of everywhere.

I was unable to think of anything during the days that followed except that I had lost Charles. There would never be that life together which we had planned. Perhaps it would never have been idyllic because there would have been too many memories to overcome.

I went back to Eversleigh and thought: *What shall I do now?*

I had lost my lover but my problem remained. I must stand and face it alone.

I need not worry about Charles now. Nothing could harm him. But Dickon was still in a position to blackmail me, to have me accused of murder.

I felt numb . . . sometimes not caring what he did. . . . Only wishing to save Lottie.

But how could I save Lottie? If I stood convicted as a murderess would that make her turn even more to Dickon?

There was another tragedy. We discovered on the morning after the fire that Miss Carter was missing. Several people had seen her in the hospital and no one had seen her afterward; it could only be assumed that she must have been one of the victims. Lottie was very upset. She had been fond of Miss Carter for all that she had poked gentle fun at her.

Life had to go on. I was alone now.

I thought: *And Dickon is here . . . in this house.* And what will happen when he comes face to face with James Fenton, as he decidedly must?

Will James want to leave?

Trivial problems, perhaps, compared with the great one which stared me in the face.

Lottie's future . . . with Dickon. I could not bear to think of that.

He sought me out, as he said, for a little chat. . . . He was as suave and nonchalant as ever.

"A great tragedy this fire. All the doctor's good work gone up in smoke."

"His career, which you were planning to ruin . . . over."

"I was only planning to ruin it if you would not be sensible. I did give you the chance, didn't I?"

"Oh, Dickon . . . life is so tragic . . . can't you just try to let us be at peace for a while."

"My dearest cousin, it is what I wish more than anything. We will all be happy here at Eversleigh."

"Do you want it as much as all that, Dickon?"

"I want it completely and absolutely. I always made up my mind it would be mine. And it should be, Zipporah. I'm one of the family. I am the *man* of the family. It was crazy of Uncle Carl to leave it to you when I was there. I know my father was a damned Jacobite . . . but so was your grandfather . . . the most damned and mighty of them all. It's madness. It belongs to me and I intend to have it."

"Using Lottie as the means to get it."

"And at the same time making a very good husband to Lottie."

"I know what you're like. You'd never be faithful to her."

He cocked an eyebrow and looked at me quizzically. "Infidelity . . . what does it matter if the wronged doesn't know, eh? And it happens where you'd least expect it."

He had silenced me, as he knew he would.

"But to marry like this . . . so calculatedly."

"One should always calculate on important matters. Lottie wants it. I couldn't achieve it otherwise, could I?"

"You have taken advantage of her youth to present yourself as some sort of hero."

"I'm a buccaneer by nature. Lottie was a challenge. . . . I could never resist them. I'm sorry you've lost your doctor."

"His death makes your blackmailing less effective. I have only myself to think of now. I do not care very much what happens to me. I am going to tell Lottie everything. I am going to tell her that you are blackmailing me . . . that you want to marry her solely because she is the heiress to Eversleigh. I could cut her out of my will."

"To whom would you leave Eversleigh then? You couldn't leave it outside the family, could you? Uncle Carl couldn't, although he wanted it for his housekeeper-mistress. No . . . I'm the rightful heir. All the Eversleighs would rise up in their graves and tell you so. A bit of a rogue...but then most of us are. We are all sinners, even those who seem most virtuous. I'll tell you something. It was your Miss Carter who started the fire at the hospital."

"I don't believe it."

"It's true. I could have saved her...but she wouldn't be saved. She was a challenge, wasn't she? The prim virtuous spinster. It was wrong, I know...but I couldn't resist."

"You mean that you...?"

"Yes...you've guessed it. The lady lost her virginity at Clavering. I have a good line in seduction for earnest spinsters."

"You are a fiend."

"Yes, I am indeed. I was rather sorry afterwards, but you see, she was so pious. I just had to see if it worked. Of course she believed she was destined for hell fire afterwards. She was a little mad, you know....Once when the gardeners at Clavering were burning leaves...she tried to leap into the fire. I saved her then...I talked to her...but she was bent on self-destruction. She need not have taken so many with her, but you see, in her eyes they were all wicked too, fallen women the lot of them...and the doctor...well, he had fallen from grace too, hadn't he? I set her to spy on you. She knew that you and the doctor were lovers. She knew that there was something odd about the laudanum because when he was dead she saw the bottle on the table. All this she told me....She was very loquacious on the subject of sin. Everybody around us was a sinner. I think she reveled in the sins of others because she believed herself to have sinned heinously and that she was lost to glory forever. She was a fanatic. I saw her standing on a ledge with a piece of burning wood, like a flaming torch, in her hand. She was waving it about and calling on God to witness her repentance. 'Give me your hand,' I said. 'I can take you to safety' and she answered: 'Leave me alone. I may be saving my soul. I am expiating my sin by dying in this fire and taking other sinners with me.'"

"What a dreadful story."

"It's true. As for your Charles, I might have saved him too.

But he was like the captain who won't leave the sinking ship. Very noble, he was. . . . But then he was a sinner like the rest of us, wasn't he? And like poor Madeleine he had some notion that he was expiating his sins. Dear Zipporah. We're all sinners. Don't condemn one because his sins are a little different from yours."

"Oh, Dickon," I said, "I'm so tired of you and your talk and your ways. All I want is for you to leave me in peace . . . with my daughter."

"Be reasonable, dear Zipporah. Be sensible . . . and we shall all live happily ever after."

It is hard to remember those days now. They seem so long ago. Each morning I awoke I thought: *Charles is dead. I am alone now.*

Dickon went back to Clavering. He held my hands almost tenderly as he said good-bye.

"Don't forget," he said, "you hold your doctor's good name in these hands. Your own too. Don't throw it away. And don't forget I want to please you."

"You can do that by going away and never coming back."

"You will feel differently one day. Now I must go and find my sweet Lottie. I will say au revoir to her and assure her of my undying devotion."

How I hated him — handsome, debonair, so devastatingly attractive, the hero now to whom so many owed their lives. He had been so modest about his achievements — shrugging them aside as though saving life and playing the hero was commonplace with him.

With what relief I watched him ride away.

Now the days were long and meaningless. I felt that my visits to Isabel and Derek only saddened them because I reminded them of Charles.

Evalina came to see me to show me her bonny baby, of which she was very proud.

"The image of his dad," she said. She regarded me with sympathetic eyes. "I was sorry about the doctor," she said.

"He was such a good man...a lovely man...but I always thought he was too serious for you. You want someone to make you laugh because you can be a bit too serious yourself. You want someone like that Frenchman...you remember?"

I wanted to shout to her to get out; but I knew she was only trying to cheer me up.

James Fenton was a very sad man. He had been genuinely fond of Jean-Louis. Sometimes he looked a little wistful and I wondered why.

I sounded Hetty and she told me that he had always wanted a farm of his own. Farming was his first love really. He just hadn't wanted to share with anyone.

"Of course," she said, "he has the money now."

I said: "Does he want to go?"

Hetty answered firmly: "We'd never go as long as you needed us."

I felt I should tell them to go and find their farm. I was sure it was what they wanted. Yet how could I manage without James?

Everything had changed now. I was alone.

I felt desolate. I had lost Jean-Louis and Charles, and even Lottie preferred to be with Dickon and was indeed planning the day when she would marry him—although so far in the future, and even she accepted that in view of her extreme youth.

My mother had been close to me in my childhood but when I married Jean-Louis and her lover Dickon came back—although he married Sabrina instead of her—I seemed to move into the background of her life. And on the birth of Sabrina's son it was Dickon who claimed first place in her attentions.

I had been so loved...so wanted...and now I was a lonely woman.

I tried to look into the future. What was I going to do? Was I going to stand by and see Lottie marry Dickon? Or was I going to refuse my consent to the marriage, cut Lottie out of my will...and lose her forever. Although, of course, without Eversleigh she would not be so attractive to Dickon.

Whichever way I looked I was faced by a mighty dilemma. And there was no one to advise me.

Then one day when I sat in my bedroom there was a knock at my door and one of the maids entered to tell me that there was a visitor below to see me.

When I saw him standing in the hall my heart leaped with an excitement which I had not known for a long time.

He had changed a little. He was obviously older. He wore a neat wig, very white and wavy, which made his bright eyes seem darker than I remembered them. He held his feathered hat in his hand; his sword showed beneath his loose coat which had a more elegant cut than those I was accustomed to seeing.

I came down the stairs and he hurried toward me. He took both my hands in his and kissed first one then the other.

I had forgotten how he could excite me. I felt young again . . . young and foolish and reckless.

"You sent for me," he said, "at last."

"Gerard," I said quietly. "And you came."

"Certainly I came. Did you think I would not? And we have a daughter."

"Gerard," I said, "we must talk . . . together . . . undisturbed. First I must explain. . . . Have you anyone with you?"

"Two servants."

"Where are they?"

"I left them with the horses."

"I will send word for them to be looked after, but first come in here." I took him into the winter parlor and shut the door.

"There was a child," he said. "Why didn't you tell me . . . ?"

"How could I? My husband thought she was his. She was a great comfort to him."

"Where is she?"

"She is here."

"I long to see her."

"You shall. I want you to help me."

"What danger is she in?"

"I have to explain everything. Please, Gerard, listen to me." I told him as briefly as I could what had happened. Of how

Jean-Louis had suffered, of how the doctor and I had become lovers; I told of the wickedness of Dickon, of his ambitions through our daughter.

That was the most difficult part for him to understand. I could see that he did not understand why Dickon was such a villain in my eyes. But he listened intently and he would help me.

I said: "I am going to tell Lottie that you are her father. But first I want her to meet you . . . to like you . . . as I know she will. Do you understand?"

"Perfectly," he said.

"Then I want you to take her back with you. You can say you wish her to see your country . . . to show her your home . . . and then I want you to see that she is fascinated by all she sees . . . so that she does not believe the height of bliss is to settle down and marry Dickon. I want her to see something of the world . . . meet other people. . . . I want to get her away for a while."

"It shall be as you say."

"Now," I said, "I am going to have a room made ready for you. I shall tell her that we have a visitor from France. I want you to get to know each other. How does that seem?"

He was looking at me intently as I remember he used to look at me all those years ago.

"It seems to me perfect," he said.

Of course he fascinated Lottie. His elegance, his charm, all that had fascinated me and swept me off my feet when I was young. It was all there. It hadn't changed very much except perhaps to become more subtle, more mature.

I felt as I never thought I would again and before a week was out I found that I could explain to Lottie.

When I told her she stared at me incredulously. Her father! This exciting, fascinating man. He had talked to her of his château, of his life at the French court, of Paris, of the French countryside . . . and so vividly, as he had one purpose and that to make her wish to see them, and he succeeded admirably.

I saw the look of wonder on her face which she immediately suppressed because she felt it was disloyal to Jean-Louis. She kept looking at me as though she were seeing me in a new light.

Life had been revealed to her. It was not good and bad, neatly divided into black and white. People were not always what they seemed.

She was very thoughtful. But I could see that she was excited at the thought of having such a father.

He would take her back with him for a visit. How did she feel about that?

It was just what she needed. Her horizon would be widened; she would see another world apart from the small one in which she had lived. She would meet people — perhaps as fascinating as Dickon had been. She was already very conscious of the worldly charm of her father.

She was delighted.

"But to leave you, mama," she said. "Now that you are so sad."

I said: "You will come back to me."

"Yes," she said, "I have to come back . . . and marry Dickon."

It was almost as though she remembered him for the first time in several days.

I watched them go.

"I will write to you, dear mama," said Lottie. "I will tell you all the exciting things that are happening to me."

"I will write to you," said Gerard, "and tell you how much we miss you."

So they went. And how desolate I was watching them leave. His visit had brought back so vividly memories of the past. I would never forget him. Nothing would ever have effaced the memory of him. Not even Charles. I had loved Charles. I had loved Jean-Louis. But I realized that the feeling Gerard had roused in me was different from what I felt for either of them.

There was mystery about him. What did I know of him? That he lived excitingly. That he was deeply immersed in the affairs of his nation. That he had been in England on some secret mission.

He had come into my life and changed it; and if I knew little about him I had learned something about myself.

For the rest of my days I would think of him; I would relive my youth through him. I felt young when he was near. I wondered if I should ever see him again.

How long the days seemed. I missed Lottie very much.

Almost two weeks passed before I heard from them.

Lottie was ecstatic. She had been to Versailles. She had been presented to the aging king, who had spoken very kindly to her; she had met the young dauphin. I should see the gown her father had bought for her to go to court. There had never been such a gown.

I scanned the letter. There was no mention of Dickon. There was a letter from Gerard. It was not long but it was of such significance that I did not believe what I read and read three times before I really accepted those words.

He had seen me again. He had thought of me over the years. So often he had wanted to come to see me. It was not easy. When we met he had been married. He was married when he was very young, after the custom of families such as his. It was no love match; and he had made no secret of his amours. Yes, there had been others. But it was different with us. His wife had died five years ago. He was free. He was enchanted with his daughter. He could never let her go and it occurred to him that the parents of such a daughter should be together. We knew each other well. We knew we were ideally suited. Would I consider uprooting myself . . . giving up my home in England and becoming Madame la Comtesse d'Aubigné?

"Dear Zipporah," he wrote, "It is not because of Lottie. Though I like her very much. It is because of you . . . and of what we were to each other . . . which I have learned through the years is something that comes rarely and when it does is to be cherished. It never died with me. Did it with you? If it did not . . . then we should be together. I await your answer."

* * *

I was in a daze of delight.

I don't think I hesitated for a moment. I was young again. I was the girl who ran out to meet her lover so eagerly all those years ago.

Then I thought of Eversleigh. Of my responsibilities.

Well, the estate could go on. James Fenton . . . But James wanted a farm of his own.

Then I knew what I would do.

I wrote to Dickon. I asked him to come and see me immediately as I had come to a decision. I knew that would bring him.

Then I went to see James and Hetty.

I said: "James, I know you want a farm of your own."

"We would never leave you," said Hetty quickly.

"Suppose it was possible for you to do so?"

"Do you mean you have got someone else?"

I said: "Just suppose it were possible. Would you go?"

They looked at me in amazement.

"But James knows the estate."

"There might be changes. Please, I don't want to say anything yet. I just want you to answer a simple question. If it were easy . . . if I were suited . . . would you prefer to get your own farm? You could do that easily now, James. You know you could."

"Well," said James, "if you put it like that . . . naturally, most men like to be their own masters."

"That's what I wanted to know."

I went to them and kissed them. "You have been good friends to me," I said.

"What has happened?" asked Hetty. "You look as if you've seen some miracle."

"Yes," I said. "Perhaps I have. Be patient with me. If it works . . . you'll know soon enough."

Dickon arrived confident and certain of himself, sure, I knew, that I would have by now, what he would call, come to my senses.

I said to him: "Dickon. What would you say if I told you I was passing Eversleigh over to you?"

I had rarely seen him taken off his guard, but he was then. He looked at me suspiciously.

"I mean it," I said. "After all, it is Eversleigh you want. You'd be ready to forego Lottie for Eversleigh, wouldn't you?"

"Dear Zipporah, you talk most amusingly but somewhat obscurely. This is one of the few matters about which I do not care to joke."

I said: "Lottie is in France with her father."

His face clouded. "What is your game, Zipporah?"

"Very simple. You wanted to marry Lottie for Eversleigh. Eversleigh is what you want. You would manage it perfectly, I know. The ancestors would rise up and sing Hallelujah, I am sure. They never liked the idea of its being in the hands of a woman . . . although I had a husband to help me. Could you forget Lottie if you already had Eversleigh?"

"Do you mean could I be persuaded to forego my courtship?"

"I mean would you stop writing to her, talking to her of marriage . . . for Eversleigh?"

"Please, please explain."

I said: "James Fenton will buy a farm. He wouldn't stay here with you around. There will be many things to be worked out. I have had an offer of marriage from Lottie's father. I have decided to accept. I shall live in France after I'm married . . . and so will Lottie. Dickon, I am going to make over Eversleigh to you now. You are, after all, the male heir."

He stared at me. Then a slow smile spread across his face.

"Eversleigh!" he murmured and I had never seen him look so tender. I saw then that he loved the place as he could never love anything else.

I said: "You will have to put a manager in at Clavering. You will have to come to Eversleigh with Clarissa and Sabrina . . . your courtiers, as it were, and you will reign supreme . . . as you schemed so basely to do." I laughed suddenly. "It's virtue rewarded . . . in reverse."

Dickon looked at me admiringly.

"I do love you, Zipporah," he said.